I0685985

ENDLESS VACATION

BRAD WHITTINGTON

WUNDERFOOL

W P

PRESS

Also by Brad Whittington

Novels

Welcome to Fred

Living with Fred

Postcards from Fred

Escape from Fred

Muffin Man

Strange Vacation

Open Season

Endless Vacation

The Reluctant Saint

Essays

Build Your Own Relgion
And other bad ideas from The Door

Non-fiction

What Would Jesus Drink?
What the Bible Really Says About Alcohol

BRAD WHITTINGTON

ENDLESS VACATION

{ A NOVEL }

Copyright 2013 by Brad Whittington
All rights reserved

ISBN: 978-1-937274-17-7
Published by Wunderfool Press
Austin ,Texas

Dewey Decimal Classification: F
Subject Heading: Fliction / Mystery & Detective / General

All characters appearing in this work are fictitious. Any resemblance
to real persons, living or dead, is purely coincidental.

Contents

What they're saying about Whittington

Whittington spins an enjoyable literary story and is definitely a novelist to watch.
–Publisher's Weekly

Brad Whittington is an artist with a pen.
–Ethan C. McDonald, DancingWord.com

It is always a joy to find a new writer who knows what he's doing.
–Rick Lewis, Logos Bookstore

Whittington is a welcome new voice in the world of fiction.
–Cindy Crosby, author of By Willoway Brook

Who can resist a story of someone else's alienated youth if that someone else is as talented as Brad Whittington?
–JT Conroe, author of The Blue Hotel

The pacing, humor, honesty, and believable characters made me turn page after page in rapid succession until there were none.
–T Leigh

Brad Whittington paints some of the best word pictures I've seen.
–Cammi Ellis

What they're saying about Muffin Man

Brad Whittington is not only back, he's at his best. I haven't been this excited about a new fictional detective since Martin Walker's Bruno, Chief of Police. Have no doubt: Muffin Man delivers!
–J. Mark Bertrand, author of Back on Murder and Pattern of Wounds

I love the way Brad Whittington writes. Smooth and snappy as jazz. Whittington has baked up a winner in Muffin Man. With dry wit, poignant humanity, and a setting as rich as Texas earth, Whittington proves his flair for storytelling once again.

A great book.
–Tosca Lee, NY Times bestselling author of Demon: A Memoir, Havah: The Story of Eve, and The Books of Mortals series

For Andy

Who probably won't read it,
even though he was the first of many to carry the torch

His Stillness

by Sharon Olds

The doctor said to my father, "You asked me
to tell you when nothing more could be done.
That's what I'm telling you now." My father
sat quite still, as he always did,
especially not moving his eyes. I had thought
he would rave if he understood he would die,
wave his arms and cry out. He sat up,
thin, and clean, in his clean gown,
like a holy man. The doctor said,
"There are things we can do which might give you time,
but we cannot cure you." My father said,
"Thank you." And he sat, motionless, alone,
with the dignity of a foreign leader.
I sat beside him. This was my father.
He had known he was mortal. I had feared they would have to
tie him down. I had not remembered
he had always held still and kept quiet to bear things,
the liquor a way to keep still. I had not
known him. My father had dignity. At the
end of his life his life began
to wake in me.

"His Stillness" from STRIKE SPARKS:SELECTED POEMS, 1980-
2002 by Sharon Olds, copyright © 2004 by Sharon Olds. Used by
permission of Alfred A. Knopf, a division of Random House, Inc.

Day 1: Tuesday

Chapter One: Dave

In three days, life as Dave Fletcher knew it would end, and his biggest regret was that he had failed to equip the chair across from his desk with an ejection seat.

He would miss many things about life as a special agent for the Secret Service. Vanek was not one of those things.

Vanek sat in that chair, that lamentably underpowered chair, regarding Dave with the stare of a hyena standing just out of reach of a wounded lion, waiting for the moment it staggered to its knees. Waiting for the moment he could snatch the corner office from Dave, and the title of lead agent of the Austin regional headquarters.

A smile that was more like the baring of teeth flickered across Vanek's doughy face. "I envy you."

Dave stared back, declining to comment.

Vanek was barely fifty but looked well past the mandatory retirement age of fifty-seven. He worked hard, partied harder, and smoked like a beater with a broken head gasket.

"This time next week, you'll be chilling on your deck with a Mexican martini. I'll be stuck here, chasing leads like a rabid pit bull in a day-care center."

Dave almost smiled. The only way Vanek would chase anything was if it had a kolache tied to it. "Speaking of which, how about you just cut to the chase?" He glanced around the room. "Come to measure for curtains, maybe?"

Vanek's pained smile fractured into a grimace. "About the Rivera investigation." He rolled his chair closer to the desk. "Looks like we maybe caught a break."

Dave was annoyed to hear that Vanek had been working the one case he had held onto, but he remained impassive, refusing to give the satisfaction of a reaction. "How so?"

"Word has it Rivera's got a guy on the inside."

The suggestion was too absurd to deserve a response. Dave had scrubbed the case down to the bare metal. There was no agent in regular communication with Rivera—not Secret Service, not DEA, not FBI. In fact, the only agent to come in contact with Rivera was Dave himself, back when he bought the Jenny from him. Back before the counterfeit money surfaced.

"Every time we get close, the mole tips him off, and Rivera fades."

"A convenient theory." Especially convenient for one who preferred speculation to investigation. "Any evidence to back it up?"

"We have a bead on a guy with a past connection. Pretty solid."

Despite himself, Dave leaned forward, his elbows on the desk. "Who?"

Vanek leaned back in his chair, suddenly casual. "No need to worry. It'll take a few days to round him up. You'll be gone by then."

Dave leaned back in his own chair, echoing Vanek's posture. Best not to give the hyena even a hint of interest. Despite his incompetence as an agent, Vanek excelled at politics. Every conversation with him had to be treated with the care of a biological weapon.

The grin returned to Vanek's face. "But you might be surprised."

Me, Dave thought. He's saying I'm the inside guy. He suppressed the urge to punch Vanek out of daylight saving time and clear into the next time zone. Instead he leaned across the desk and planted his hands with a sudden intensity that threatened to topple the smug scavenger out of his chair.

"What?" Vanek barked in an unnaturally high octave.

"Careful. Don't do anything you'll regret."

Vanek returned Dave's glare with a calm stare. "Just giving you an update."

"It had better be a joke."

"Who's joking?"

Dave suddenly realized he no longer had to play this game. "Whatever it is you're doing, keep me out of it." He left Vanek sitting in the corner office he had lusted after for more than a decade.

"Hey, where you going?"

All Dave gave him was a wave of his hand over his shoulder as he strode past the cubicles and through the front door to the hallway.

The closing of the door mercifully cut off Vanek's reply. Too impatient to wait for the elevator, Dave took the stairs eight floors down in a controlled fall. In the parking garage, he put the top down on his Z-51 Corvette and escaped downtown as fast as traffic would allow.

Not content with finally taking the corner office, Vanek had evidently concocted some harebrained scheme to implicate Dave in a corruption charge. That wouldn't last long. Anybody with a brain would see through it.

Now that he had escaped Vanek's nauseating company, Dave looked for a destination and settled on an hour of aerial therapy in his restored WWI biplane, the Jenny.

As he wove through the pre-rush-hour traffic, his mind wandered to Stephanie. He wondered what she would say about his pending retirement. Probably something like, "It's not Friday, yet. We'll see."

If he'd left the service fifteen years ago, he wouldn't have lost her, wouldn't have taken the promotion to lead agent in the Austin field office to escape her memory. Unsuccessfully, as he would have known if he'd been thinking instead of reacting. He was still thinking about her fifteen years later.

He turned west onto Southwest Parkway and changed the subject—the security company he planned to open. As usual, the main hurdle was financial. Borrowing against his retirement account and pulling the equity from his house would get him, at most, three to six months of operating capital, not the three years Uncle Rex had suggested he accumulate before retiring.

Dave pushed that thought aside as well. He was taking the Jenny out to decompress, not to increase his stress. He'd resume worrying when he was back on the ground.

The last vestiges of Austin fell behind him and the road split a hill. As he topped the rise and the road curved left, the limestone walls dropped away, and Dave got a glimpse of the Hill Country. It was his favorite spot on the drive.

Layers of ridges coated with scrubby juniper and a few live oaks drew him toward the horizon, Spanish oak lining the watercourses in the ravines. Condos poked up between the trees like prairie dog mounds.

He caught a red light, and the stagnant air settled around him like a cocoon. A cloud drifted across the sun, cutting him a break of a few degrees. It was a mild day for the end of May, barely in the nineties.

At Lakeway Airpark, he drove past the Ercoupe perched on a pole by the entrance, idled up to the last T-hangar in the row, and saw something that spiked his pulse higher than a visit from Vanek. A candy-apple blue Lamborghini.

He had the car door open before the engine stopped. He strode to the access door, threw it open, and scanned the dim interior for Rivera, but something else commanded his attention. A Glock 26 pointed at his forehead.

Chapter Two: Dave

Dave stared down the barrel of the gun at Rivera.

"Oh, it's you." Rivera squinted at him and lowered the gun to his side.

"Who were you expecting?" Dave tended to resent it when someone pointed a gun at him. He set his foot on a toolbox, bent forward, and came up with his own Glock pointed at Rivera. "Now, how about you set that gun down on the floor and back away?"

Rivera's eyes narrowed and his body tensed, but his voice was as casual as a pair of flip-flops. "Dave, my friend, you wound me."

Dave nodded at Rivera's gun, keeping his aim steady. He wasn't in the mood for banter.

Rivera bent over, not easy given his size, and placed the gun on the concrete.

"Good. Now kick it here."

Rivera gave it a nudge.

"Back away."

Rivera took three steps back.

Dave stepped forward and kicked the gun into the corner by the door. "Now, let's talk about why you're here."

Rivera's gaze drifted from the gun in the corner to the gun in Dave's hand to the expression on Dave's face. "You have not been returning my calls. It is not polite."

"No point. We both know it's not going to happen."

Rivera glanced at the Jenny. "Sell it back to me. Name your price." He stroked the fabric on the upper wing.

"It's not for sale."

"Of all people, my friend, you know that everything is for sale. It's just the finding of the right price. Fifty thousand."

Dave shook his head.

"A hundred. I can fix it so it's tax-free."

One hundred thousand dollars. Plenty to set up that office downtown. He shook his head again. Even if he wanted to sell, he couldn't do business with a suspect. "Go home, Rivera."

"Two hundred." When he didn't get an answer, Rivera's gaze wandered around the hangar. "I always felt free in the Jenny."

Dave watched him, ready for a sudden move, but Rivera seemed focused on nothing, or maybe something only he could see.

"Sometimes a man just needs to go." Rivera grabbed a polished wooden wing strut. "To turn his face forward and not look to what is behind." He turned a resentful gaze on Dave. "Selling the Jenny to you, that I regret the most."

Dave's phone vibrated. Without taking his eyes off Rivera, he dug it out of his pocket and held it so he could see both Rivera and the caller ID. The name surprised him. "Uncle Rex. Can I call you back? I'm in a meeting."

"How about joining me for dinner?"

"Give Mr. Stone my regards," Rivera said.

Dave took a step forward, gesturing with the gun for Rivera to move back. "Sure. How's next week sound?"

"I'm thinking seven o'clock."

Dave frowned, both at the phone and at Rivera, who hadn't moved. "I can't get to Philly by seven."

"Probably not, but you can make it to Bee Cave."

"You're in town?"

"The Emerald, seven o'clock."

The call disconnected before Dave could respond. Uncle Rex was not an impulsive man. If he made the trip down from Philadelphia, it had to be for something that couldn't be done on the phone. Most likely bad news.

Dave pocketed the phone and returned his attention to Rivera, his pale face easily visible in the gloom of the hangar. Here was another man whose sudden presence was disturbing and whose reason for coming was equally unclear. Not likely it had anything to do with the Jenny. After all, Dave himself didn't know he was coming here until thirty minutes ago.

"Why are you here? How did you get in?"

"Even trade, the Lamb for the Jenny. You can keep the Z-51. And the cash."

Did it have something to do with Vanek's absurd claims? "Why were you waiting here for me? With a gun?"

"I just wanted to see the Jenny again, make sure it was in good condition."

Dave shook his head. "That's not it. Try again."

"I want to fly it, once more. I will pay for the fuel." Rivera reached for his billfold.

Dave jerked his gun, gesturing Rivera's hand away from his pocket. "Are you wired? Is that it?"

Rivera responded with a scowl.

"Your shirt. Take it off."

Rivera studied Dave for a minute, then shook his head and unbuttoned his shirt.

"Set it on the wing and step away." Dave waited until Rivera was ten feet from the wing and then inspected the shirt. Nothing. "Drop your pants."

"My friend," Rivera said, shaking his head. "You go too far."

"Just do it."

Rivera reluctantly complied until he was standing in his boxers and cowboy boots.

"Kick them here."

Dave checked the pants for a bug of some kind, especially the oversized belt buckle, but found nothing. He stepped back toward the door and gestured with the gun for Rivera to get dressed.

He debated what to do with the pathetic figure. Arrest him for breaking and entering? That would waste everyone's time, and he'd miss his dinner date with Uncle Rex.

Instead, Dave cleared the path to the door. "Get out of here."

Rivera buttoned his shirt as he left, but stopped at the doorway. "Maybe one short flight, my friend?"

Dave raised the gun. "I'm not your friend. I'm just the guy who made the mistake of buying a plane from you."

Rivera shrugged and bent toward his gun.

"Leave it."

Bent halfway over, Rivera frowned at Dave. "I have a CHL."

"You can pick it up at the office tomorrow." When Rivera hesitated, Dave said, "It's a lot cheaper than bail for burglary and assault with a deadly weapon."

Based on the glare Rivera focused on Dave as he straightened up, Dave doubted he would get a Christmas card from the man this year. As he watched Rivera's bulk fill the doorframe on the way out, he reflected that instead of *Güero*, Rivera's nickname should have been *Gordo*. Or maybe *Oso*.

Dave kept his gun trained on the doorway until he heard the Lamborghini drive away. Then he checked his watch and turned to the fully restored 1917 Curtiss JN-4D biplane.

He'd flown a lot of planes, but nothing gave him the open-cockpit experience of the Jenny. Even the cargo plane in Angola that had infected him with the flying bug as a kid couldn't compare. Buzzing low and slow to feel the rush of the terrain as it whipped past. Teasing the bottom of the clouds as you hit the inversion layer with a ride like a bucking bronco in the sky. Hovering above the earth close to stall speed, barely moving, like a hawk searching for dinner. Falling through the air and pulling out into powered flight, nothing between you and the sky but your clothes and a dose of adrenaline. Try that in a Learjet.

Dave still had enough time for a short flight before dinner, but the conversation with Vanek and the visit from Rivera seemed too much for coincidence. He scanned the hangar to see if anything was missing or disturbed, but all seemed as it should be.

Rivera didn't take anything away. Did he leave something behind? Perhaps Dave had been right about being bugged, but the room, not the body. He made a more thorough search with equally unsatisfying results. When he checked his watch again, he realized he was going to be late for dinner.

Figuring out the mystery of Vanek and Rivera would have to wait until tomorrow. Right now he had to figure out the mystery of Uncle Rex.

Chapter Three: Dave

Dave pulled off Highway 71 into the gravel parking lot of The Emerald, a small outpost of Irish culture established by the Kinsella family in 1984. In the intervening decades, civilization in the form of country clubs, subdivisions, and upscale shopping malls had gradually encroached on the little cottage nestled among the oaks, but it had stood its ground.

Near the door, Dave spotted the Mercedes that Rex kept at his Tarrytown house. He parked next to an SUV big enough to have its own ZIP code. As he entered through the vestibule of the rock cottage, a young woman with long, dark hair approached.

"Rex Stone," Dave said.

She directed him to the back room, where he found Uncle Rex, martini in hand. Rex set the glass down and stood, his arms outstretched.

Dave grabbed a hand to shake it, but Uncle Rex pulled it free and embraced him in a hug, one with plenty of bone and muscle behind it. Dave hesitated, then hugged him back.

Something was definitely up. He couldn't recall a single hug from Uncle Rex, not even the day Rex came to the boarding school to tell Dave his father was dead. The East Coast side of the family went for the polite handshake or the air kiss to the cheek. Mom had been the only exception, but Dave assumed she had picked it up from the Texas relatives, Dad's side.

Before Dave was fully seated, the woman placed a matching martini on the table and disappeared. Dave held his martini aloft. "You're not over the hill until the hill is over you."

Uncle Rex lifted his glass. "To life without regret."

Regret? Uncle Rex?

"Dave, good of you to meet me for dinner."

"Nonsense." Dave wouldn't miss a dinner with Uncle Rex if he had to break out of jail to attend. "But what brings you here in May?"

The Kinsella woman returned with flambéed onion soup.

Rex sampled it. "Bridget would have loved this."

Dave nodded. "Mom knew how to enjoy the finer things, even on a nurse's salary."

"You remember this?" Rex pulled a slender silver chain from the breast pocket of his jacket, a familiar pendant hanging from it.

Dave reached for it. A chip from the Rock of Gibraltar, fashioned from the mountain itself, the limestone edges smooth after four decades of service. He flipped it and read the inscription.

I SHALL NOT BE MOVED

The Stone family motto, a weapon that Bridget Stone had turned against the family itself.

Rex returned his attention to the soup. "We could all take a lesson from your mother in living without regret."

Twice was two times too many to ignore. "What's all this about regret? Think of all you've accomplished."

"Exactly! I've done quite well." Rex leaned over his bowl. "For myself."

"And others."

"But think of what I could have done."

The familiar intensity of Rex's gaze was mixed with a new element, something Dave couldn't quite place. Something that wasn't Uncle Rex.

"If it weren't for you, I would be living in a shack in Angola and giving inoculations to squirming babies." The life Dad and Mom had planned for Dave, the life had he escaped when they sent him to the States for his schooling.

Rex took the necklace from Dave's hand and rubbed the worn ridges with his thumb. Dave waited for an explanation. Rex resumed in a more relaxed tone.

"When Bridget turned twenty-five, took control of her trust fund, and ran off to Africa with Reggie, the family was outraged. Married to a nobody? Yes, he was a doctor, but no connections, no money, and worst of all, an idealist. Oh, the shame!"

Dave never tired of this story, but Rex didn't finish it. Instead, he returned the necklace to his pocket and finished his soup.

"I won't deny that your father had his faults—perhaps overzealous at times, completely inept at managing investments, prone to rash decisions and extremes. Especially at the end. But he recognized what was really important. And Bridget believed in him. Few people achieved that honor." His voice dropped to a whisper. "I sometimes wonder if she didn't make the better choice."

All this second guessing didn't sit well with Dave. As his early retirement approached, he'd done enough of it for both of them. "Uncle Rex, it's not like your life is over. And even if it were, you have nothing to regret. Or apologize for."

With his own disappointing financial situation, Dave felt like he had more reason to complain of wasted time than Uncle Rex, who had a long list of accomplishments.

The next course arrived before Rex responded. Dave sampled the Dublin Lawyer Special: lobster tail in a flaky puff pastry, simmered in heavy cream and Irish whiskey. Dave wondered why anyone ever prepared lobster another way.

Rex savored a bite with his eyes closed, and then went for another. "When was the last time you saw Hensley?" he asked without looking up.

"Same time you did. Mom's funeral."

"Do you know where he is?"

"I know as much about Hensley's whereabouts as he cares to tell me. Which, as you know, is nothing."

"Track him down."

"He knows how to find me."

Rex started to reply, but stopped himself.

Dave speared a bit of lobster and considered this new line of conversation. Did this mystery have something to do with Hensley?

They were nearly through with dinner, and Dave still had no more idea of why Rex was here than he did of why Rivera was in his hangar or why Vanek was playing games.

They were silent as the dishes were cleared away and the dessert delivered: fresh oranges and orange marmalade in a chocolate-covered pastry puff accompanied by Irish coffee.

Uncle Rex took a slow, appreciative sip. "Angola wasn't easy on Hensley."

Dave snorted. "I made it through okay."

Rex studied him. "After a fashion." He took a bite of the dessert. "It's not a one-size-fits-all world, Davison. Some of us are more broken than others."

"Hensley's world is every man for himself and the devil take the hindmost."

As much as Rex had done for Dave, for the family, he wasn't there when Hensley handed Dave his coin collection like a consolation prize and disappeared forever. When he made a token appearance at Dad's funeral and disappeared immediately after. And the same at Mom's funeral.

The dance had gone on long enough. Since Rex had already breached the line of reticence behind which the two of them typically kept personal matters, Dave decided on a little plain speaking. "Uncle Rex, pardon me for saying, but you don't seem to be yourself. What's going on?"

Rex cleared his throat. Dave watched him, but Rex focused on his coffee cup.

"Davison, I did my best as I saw it at the time, but . . . I thought Reggie was misguided. Sincere, but naïve. I . . ." He finally met Dave's stare, eyes misting. "I hope you know how much I treasure the years we've had, but I didn't do right by you. I'm sorry."

Dave's confusion prevented him from speaking. This was the reason for the evening? An apology for doing the right thing? He studied Rex, really saw him for the first time tonight. Rex was changed from the dynamo of industry Dave had always known. He seemed frail, diminished, defeated. Dave wanted to avert his eyes from the unwonted apologies. The making of excuses for Hensley, who had betrayed the family.

"You did more for me than my own parents did, or could do." Dave struggled to keep his voice steady, not sure that he had succeeded.

Rex held his gaze, his eyes moist. He seemed on the verge of speaking, but instead retreated behind his coffee.

Dave waited, both desiring and dreading an explanation. There had to be something else, but if it was more comments in the vein of apologies and suggestions that he hunt down his prodigal brother, Dave wasn't sure he wanted to hear it.

But Rex seemed to be done. He stirred his coffee and stared at the Irish crème swirling around the vortex.

What had happened to the Uncle Rex who had built a commercial empire with business interests on practically every continent?

Where was the man who preferred results to excuses, who didn't take no for an answer, who had eliminated the word "failure" from his vocabulary?

Neither side of Dave's family, the Stones or the Fletchers, talked much about feelings. But in the past five minutes, Uncle Rex had exposed more emotion than in the past thirty-six years combined. It left Dave unsure of how to respond. He felt like he should offer something to restore Rex to some kind of balance. The words were out before he realized he had said them.

"Maybe I'll hunt down Hensley."

Rex's expression as he glanced up from his coffee was an improbable mixture of doubt and hope.

Chapter Four: Dave

Dave and Uncle Rex parted in The Emerald parking lot with another uncharacteristic hug, and Dave pointed the Z-51 toward downtown. He was in need of serious decompression. Twenty minutes of cathartic driving later, he valeted the 'vette in front of Amicus Curiae, a bar on Colorado Street near the capitol. Inside, he took a seat at the end of the bar facing the door. The place was packed with judges, attorneys, clerks, and other nefarious types associated with the law.

He decided to start at the top and work his way down. He ordered the Talisker 25-year-old. As the bartender slid the stool over to reach the bottle, Dave texted Angela Martini, an assistant district attorney, inviting her to join him for drinks and possibilities. She lived ten blocks away in the 360 Condominiums.

The bartender set the scotch in front of Dave without a word. Dave used a straw as a pipette to transfer a few drops of water to the tumbler, inhaled the peaty aroma, and took his first taste. A memory rushed in with the vapors, a vision of the night Uncle Rex introduced him to scotch. The old Uncle Rex, the one who had never second-guessed anything in his life.

The stories Mom had told him around a fire in Angola of the family that she had left behind had seemed more like fairy tales than history. Stories of her younger brother, Rex, who was only ten when she married Dad, and how thirteen years later he took on the management of the Stone estate and reversed its decades-old decline.

Or her own story, the trust-fund baby who met an idealistic medical student working his way through school, who hid their marriage from her parents until she had control of her trust fund, who refused Stone charity when the clinic and poor investments drained their capital.

Even after Dad died, when Rex tried to rescue them, Mom had refused both the cash and the trust fund he had proposed as a compromise. She relaxed her stance of independence only once, to allow

Rex to sponsor Dave at Warfield Hall, the family prep school alma mater.

In the following years, she must have regretted that concession. It had placed Dave in the heart of Stone territory at an impressionable age. The transition from uncle to mentor was as gradual and inevitable as a glacier transforming the landscape. Dave never returned to Angola.

He thought back through the conversation at dinner. Rex had greeted him as Dave but at the end had called him Davison. Rex hadn't called him that since Dad died thirty years ago. What did it mean? Again, he wondered what Rex had left unsaid in those long silences.

The promise to track down Hensley loomed before Dave like a panhandler with a "Will Work for Food" sign. He didn't know where to start or even want to start, for that matter, but he'd made the promise. Surely it could wait until he got his business started.

A hand on Dave's shoulder interrupted his thoughts. Angela slipped onto the stool next to him and caught the bartender's eye, but Dave spun her stool away from the bar and kissed her. It had been a long, frustrating day, and the one person in his life who could change that had arrived.

Angela laughed and pulled away. "Hey, I was ordering."

"We need to do something about your priorities."

She ordered a glass of pinot noir. "Speaking of priorities, have you found office space yet?"

After the scene with Rivera and the dinner with Rex, he'd forgotten about his financial inadequacies. He took another sip of whiskey and turned to the woman next to him.

Like his ex-wife, Angela was tall, almost as tall as his six feet, but with red hair styled to look all business in the courtroom and all woman after hours. Unlike Stephanie, Angela preferred older men. She'd had a few bad experiences with men her age. Well, maybe that was something else she had in common with Stephanie.

"Time to start looking for change under the cushions."

She ran her fingernails through the short hair above his ear and around to his neck. "What are your options?"

Dave interlaced his fingers with hers and brought them back down to the bar. "Aside from the previously mentioned cushions? Recycling copper."

"What about your uncle? You want me to ask him for you? I can be very persuasive."

"I have no doubt, but that's not an option." The possibility hadn't even occurred to him. Obviously Rex would give him the cash in a nanosecond, and just as obviously, Dave wouldn't take it. Wouldn't even ask. Fletchers made it on their own, or they didn't make it.

Angela pulled her hand from his and turned back to her wine.

They had an on-and-off relationship. On when they first met, off when he discovered she was married. Yes, her husband was a philandering Neanderthal, but Dave would not stoop to poaching, regardless of how despicable her husband might be. Things had become somewhat serious, and it had cost Dave a few months of recovery when he called it off.

"I had a gun pointed at me today," Dave said.

"Dave!" She squeezed his arm. "How can you be so calm about it?"

Dave shrugged.

"Okay, be cavalier if you want, but I'm glad you only have a few more days." She sipped her wine, and then teased him with a sideways glance. "Did you cuff and book him?"

Dave shook his head. "I let him go. But I kept his gun."

"So you still have the handcuffs." She raised an eyebrow.

A smile slipped past his stoic nonchalance. A few years ago, Angela had appeared next to him at some fund-raiser, holding her drink in her left hand, her bare ring finger pointed at him like a sniper's scope. He had always appreciated her direct, no-games approach.

Soon they were on again, and it didn't take long to regain the lost ground. They were as steady as Dave was comfortable with, the arrangement he preferred after Stephanie left. In his estimation, law enforcement and marriage made a volatile potion that could explode at the most inopportune moment.

Angela broke the silence. "There's a long weekend coming up. My friend offered her house on St. Croix."

Dave studied her profile in the mirror behind the bar. They'd never done more than an occasional overnight trip. A weekend trip was an escalation of the rules of engagement. Dave's threat-level advisory climbed two notches from green to orange.

Angela leaned toward him. "With a private beach," she whispered. "And a hot tub."

As Dave considered the offer, he realized the old rules no longer applied. He had more than just a long weekend coming up; he had the rest of his life. And he could do worse than make Angela a part of it. In fact, it occurred to him that maybe that was what he wanted. He'd created a buffer to avoid repeating the past, but now that he was retiring, perhaps that was no longer necessary. The relief that seeped into his muscles surprised him.

But without a second career, it would be a life of eking it out on his retirement check. He wasn't willing to make the transition on those terms, to trade career tension for financial tension. "Can't," he said. "I have to find some capital to open the agency."

She met his eyes in the mirror. "Do it next week."

With considerable effort he shook his head. He didn't have the luxury of time. "The office space might not be available next week."

"This town is full of empty office space."

"Not like this one. All glass and steel and granite and fountains. Two blocks from the capitol, owner desperate for a tenant. He's going to cut somebody a deal, and I want it to be me."

A cold front crept across the bar. "Finding office space is more appealing to you than a weekend in the tropics with me?"

"Of course not. It's just a matter of timing." Dave mirrored her earlier gesture, brushing her hair behind her ear with his fingertips.

She picked up her wine glass. "You realize this is a one-time offer."

Dave took a deep breath. There would be other long weekends, like Independence Day or Labor Day. And after he got the agency running, they could take any weekend they wanted. Right now he had a lot on his plate. Getting financing, closing on the office space, setting up phones, computers, and networks, advertising, building a client roster.

But Dave knew better than to get into all that. "It's only Tuesday. Maybe I can get something going before the weekend."

Angela responded with a doubtful expression.

Dave nudged her. "Maybe we should go somewhere private and you can try to talk me into it."

She smiled.

"Plus, I've never been to the Virgin Islands. What should I pack?"

"Nothing," she whispered.

Dave took Angela's glass from her hand and finished off the wine. Then he leaned in toward her. "You want to come help me pack?"

Chapter Five: Dave

The gate opened as Dave approached his house in Lakeway. He whipped the 'vette into the two-car garage, leaving space for Angela to pull in her Lexus. She met him at the utility room door with a small overnight case.

Dave crossed the utility room, turned on the kitchen light, and held the door open. Angela entered and stopped, staring into the kitchen and blocking his path.

"Dave?" She stepped aside and he saw the room.

The kitchen was reduced to chaos, as if a sorcerer's apprentice had been called away suddenly in the midst of a particularly troublesome spell that had gone awry. He pushed past her and scanned the wreckage.

Dave held his finger to his lips and pulled Angela back into the utility room. Why hadn't the alarm system already brought the authorities? He glanced at the keypad by the door. No flashing lights.

As Dave attempted to decipher this new conundrum, a crashing noise came from beyond the kitchen.

"Stay here," he whispered.

Dave pulled the Glock 27 from his ankle holster, crept through the kitchen to the hallway, and peered to the left into the dining room. Nothing. He slipped noiselessly across the threshold and looked to the right into the den. Nothing.

He stepped to the left, intending to cross through the dining room toward the front entrance, when his feet tripped on something. He went down, sprawling on the floor. The gun clattered across the dining room, pinballing through chair legs.

He sat up and identified the cause of his fall, an olive-drab duffel bag. Dave got to his feet and inched his head around the corner. From behind the couch, backlit by the light above the wet bar, a head popped up. A large head with shaggy hair jutting out from under a tight-fitting cloth cap. Dave's pulse quickened. He scanned the room for something he could use as a weapon.

Then the head spoke. "Buckaroo! The hour produces the man!"

Only one person called Dave "buckaroo." From a long time ago. But it couldn't possibly be him.

The figure stood. It wore a long, white woolen shirt partially covered by a robe made of vertical strips of coarse brown-and-ochre cloth. The robe was secured with a long sash that trailed from the hip.

The figure held an ice bucket in one hand and a cocktail shaker in the other. "Fancy a martini?"

Dave approached cautiously, squinting. "Hensley?"

"In the flesh, as usual!"

A wave of relief and confusion coursed through Dave's limbic system. "What are you doing here?"

Hensley nodded. "Right, then, I'll just fetch some fresh ice." He skirted the couch, kicking aside stray ice cubes.

Seeing Hensley here, in his home, nonchalantly reducing it to a federal disaster area, affected Dave like the arrival of a dozen Vaneks. His right hand twitched into a fist. He longed to squeeze the ice bucket onto Hensley's head like a catcher's mask, but through the fading adrenaline rush he remembered Angela was present. "How did you get in?"

"Come on, Davison. Since when has a lock kept me out of anything?"

"The security system?"

Hensley snorted as he disappeared into the kitchen, then popped his head back out. "By the way, dinner's on you. Edamame salad, filet mignon, chicken Diane, lobster, butter sauce, grilled vegetable medley, bananas foster." He popped back into the kitchen. The sounds of ice rattling into the bucket flowed from ground zero.

The pan-European accent Dave remembered from Mom's funeral had intensified. Mainly British with flourishes of other accents tossed in to make it difficult to pinpoint a specific region. And what was with the gourmet chef impersonation? Dave retrieved his gun from under the dining room table and did a quick reconnaissance of the den. Hensley had set up camp. Clothes, dishes, blankets, pillows, TV on mute showing a *Knight Rider* rerun. He appeared to be here for the duration. But why?

What were the odds that he would agree to track down Hensley and a few hours later find his prodigal brother in his own house?

Evidently, Rex had left out a great many things during his cryptic conversation.

Hensley's voice boomed from the kitchen. "Hullo! Fancy a martini, love?"

Angela's voice answered. "Only if you're having one."

Hensley returned with an overflowing ice bucket, sloughing cubes like bread crumbs on the trail to the wicked witch's house. Angela followed him and stopped at the doorway.

As Hensley passed, Dave studied his outfit. The shirt hung past his waist, the robe down to his knees. Underneath he wore loose-fitting woolen pants tucked into high woolen boots decorated in a maroon, red, and green pattern and secured with blue lashings.

"Don't mind the mess," Hensley said. "I'll attend to it directly." He set the bucket on the bar and began pouring ingredients into the cocktail shaker.

Dave converged on Hensley and whispered, "What are you doing here?"

Hensley answered in his usual stentorian voice. "Do I need an excuse to visit my kid brother?" He dropped ice cubes into the shaker.

Dave studied him. Hensley had a face of the high-mileage variety, craggy and weather-beaten. Not quite to Keith Richards levels but a respectable effort. "When was the last time you visited?"

Hensley shook the martini vigorously, his jowls waggling from the effort. He had no trouble talking over the noise. "Mother's funeral."

"Fifteen years ago. And before then?"

"Father's funeral."

"Thirty years ago. And this time?"

Hensley didn't respond. Dave glanced at Angela. She took in Hensley in Sherpa drag whipping the cocktail shaker around and raised an eyebrow.

Hensley set down the shaker, which was rimed with a frosty coating, and rubbed his hands on his robe to warm them. He dumped the ice water from two martini glasses into the sink, dropped a spear of olives into each, and decanted the liquid. It swirled in the glasses, cloudy with air bubbles and ice particles.

"I found myself between engagements and at liberty to explore other pursuits," he said while setting the shaker aside. He sampled the concoction.

"So, what you're saying is, you're broke."

Hensley breathed out a sigh of satisfaction and lowered the martini. "As always, Buckaroo, you apprehend my circumstance precisely." He held the other martini to Angela. "For you, my dear. May you wear it in good health."

He inclined his head toward Dave. "You're off the clock. Dial it down a few notches and join the party. We're well stocked. I can mix another."

Angela grasped the handle of her overnight case with both hands in front of her like a schoolgirl, an image that would stick in Dave's mind for a long time. Especially since he was powerless to stop the inevitable.

She regarded the martini Hensley held out and shook her head. "I should be going. You guys have a lot of catching up to do."

"You have cut me to the quick," Hensley said, "and laid waste my foundations." He bowed deeply without spilling a drop of either drink. Then he held out the martini to Dave. "It's all yours, Buckaroo."

Dave ignored him and followed Angela to the utility room. "Can I come with you?"

Angela laid a hand on his chest. "That's your brother in there."

"But I like you better."

"You haven't seen him for how long?"

"Not long enough."

"He's family. If that doesn't matter to you, it should."

She kissed him, a kiss that held all the things that could have been but now were not to be. From the darkness of the garage, she spoke.

"Don't forget about St. Croix."

Dave turned back to the devastation of the kitchen. He would have that martini to build up his strength. Then he would have Hensley's gizzard on a spit. Then he'd have another martini to celebrate.

Chapter Six: Dave

Dave returned to the den, claimed the martini, and drank half of it in a gulp.

Hensley pushed buttons on the remote. "Can you get Japanese TV on this?"

Dave turned to the wannabe Sherpa embedded in the recliner like a multicultural meteorite. He yelled over random snippets of surround sound as Hensley bounced through the channels. "Why now?"

Hensley continued to channel-surf. Dave took another healthy sip and snagged an olive. Then he stepped to the entertainment console, grabbed the plug of the power strip, and pulled it free. The entire system died without protest.

Hensley looked up. "Did you say something?"

"Who died?" Dave could think of no other reason for Hensley's presence.

"Two million people die every year. Are you thinking of a particular person?"

Dave regarded Hensley. He did, in fact, have a candidate in mind. He checked his watch. "When are you leaving?"

"No definite plans. I am a creature of whimsy."

"With incredibly bad timing."

Hensley chewed on this.

Dave killed the martini. Perhaps one more before he escalated to fratricide. A pile of foreign coins of various sizes, metals, and countries lay on the granite counter next to the sink. He raked them aside in a burst of anger. They skittered across the hardwood floor like pucks on ice.

Dave had the ingredients in the shaker before Hensley connected the dots.

"Was that an overnight case in that fetching creature's impeccably manicured hands?"

Dave poured the contents of the shaker over the olives and tested the result. Almost as good as The Emerald.

Hensley sprang from the recliner with surprising grace for his build. "I shall take a room in an hotel for the evening. Could I trouble you for cab fare?" He glanced about distractedly and spotted his duffel bag by the kitchen doorway. "And the price of the room, if it's not too inconvenient."

"Too late for that."

Hensley settled back into the recliner. "This is most unfortunate. We must find some way to rectify the situation." He picked up the remote and pressed the power button, stared at it blankly, and set it back down. "Perhaps she would welcome you at her place for the assignation. Don't trouble yourself about me. I can get along on my own for the evening." He picked up the remote again, looked at it, and set it down.

Dave dropped onto the couch, slouched against an overstuffed armrest, and drank his martini. He waved the glass in Hensley's direction. "What's with the costume?"

"I was most recently in Nepal. I proceeded here post haste."

"Because?"

"I felt it was . . . opportune."

He didn't remember Hensley being so evasive, but Dave was only nine when they had their last real conversation. At the clinic in the jungles of Angola. Hensley was sixteen.

—

Davison plays soccer in the clearing with the locals. Or tries to. More like he runs back and forth, trailing the gang or getting run over when they suddenly reverse field. Then the supply plane arrives and everyone rushes to the dirt airstrip to help unload.

A rock bounces off the crate he's stacking. He looks up, puzzled. From the gloom of the jungle bordering the settlement, Hensley flashes their secret sign, the distress signal they alone know.

Davison runs to the edge of the underbrush. "Hensley, what—"

Hensley shushes him and pulls him farther in, out of sight of the plane. Davison peers back in the direction of the unloading and then at Hensley, confused.

Hensley holds up a finger, drops to one knee, unzips a backpack, and removes a stack of slender red and green albums. His coin collection. He holds them out. Davison hesitates and then slowly reaches for them.

"These are yours now, Buckaroo," Hensley says. "There are still some gaps that need filling."

"But don't you want to—"

"No," Hensley says brusquely. "I travel light."

"But . . ."

Hensley zips the backpack, stands, and slings it on, shrugging his shoulders to settle it. Davison watches, squinting at him at first, head cocked to one side. Then his eyes open wide.

"You're—" No. He couldn't.

"Shh." Hensley puts a hand on his shoulder. "I have to, Davison. But you can't tell anyone."

"But Dad—"

"No one," Hensley whispers fiercely, squeezing Davison's shoulder. "Now you take care of those coins, and one day I'll be back to check on you. But only if you keep this a secret. Otherwise, I'll never come back."

Davison's eyes teem. "Okay."

Hensley tousles Davison's hair and backs away, maintaining eye contact until he turns away with a jerk and runs.

Davison watches Hensley disappear into the brush, his only ally in this foreign land. Then he runs the opposite direction, back to the house, clutching the albums to his chest. He careens through the empty house into their bedroom and stashes the coin albums under Hensley's mattress.

And he keeps the secret, keeps to the code. Every morning he scans the edge of the clearing, hoping to see Hensley emerge from the jungle with a smile on his face. Every evening he watches the sun creep below the trees, wondering if Hensley will sneak in during the night and surprise him.

But Hensley doesn't come back.

Hensley smiled at Dave from the recliner. "You still with the CIA?"

Dave didn't bother to correct him.

Hensley studied his surroundings, taking in the flat-screen, the well-stocked bar. "Gone rogue? Soldier of fortune?"

"How did you find me? When you came to Mom's funeral, I was living in Virginia."

"You're not the only one with a vast network of informants."

Uncle Rex. Had to be. But why hadn't Rex mentioned it during dinner instead of telling him to track Hensley down? Dave suddenly felt tired. It had been a strange day. First Rivera pulled a gun on him, then Uncle Rex talked about regret and failure, and now Hensley appears, dressed like a clown and acting the fool. Dave didn't have the strength for this game. Not now.

He took a healthy gulp of the martini and leaned forward with his elbows on his knees. "Tell me you didn't come all the way from Tibet to play twenty questions."

"Actually, it was Nepal—"

"You haven't contacted me once in thirty-two years. Just tell me how much it is you need, I'll tell you no, and you can go back to whatever it is you've been doing."

Hensley's expression was eerily familiar. If Dave hadn't just been thinking of the day Hensley left, he might not have recognized it. Hensley avoided his eye. Dave was suddenly furious. He jumped to his feet, sloshing gin onto the carpet.

"You can go to hell. Who are you to pity me?" He drained the martini and threw the glass at the bar. It bounced off the granite countertop and shattered against the backsplash. He pulled out his wallet, grabbed a handful of bills, and threw them at Hensley. "Take your duffel bag and get out."

Hensley didn't move. He didn't speak.

Dave walked past him, through the demolished kitchen, and out to the 'vette. He paid no mind to his route until he was out of Lakeway. He cast about for a destination and turned toward downtown. He parked on the street, went to the intercom by the front door, and punched in Angela's condo number.

"Dave? What happened to your brother?"

"Jet lag. Right after you left, he dropped like a hog hit with a hammer. But I'm still trying to make up my mind about that St. Croix thing."

The lock buzzed and clicked open. "You've come to the right place. But as I warned you, I can be very persuasive."

Sometime around midnight, Dave and Angela sat curled up together in an oversized deck chair on the balcony, watching the night action in the warehouse district, such as it was. A show at the Austin Music Hall had just finished and the crowd streamed out to bars and cars and whatever trouble they could scare up on a Tuesday night.

Angela ran a fingernail up Dave's arm. "Persuaded?"

"I might need a little more convincing."

She laughed. "You're pretty ambitious for an old man."

Dave smiled. He wasn't even ten years older, but she liked to tease him about robbing the cradle. He recalled his thoughts earlier in the evening and realized she was right. He was ambitious thinking a beautiful career woman like her would want to settle down with a guy looking at retirement in three days, even if it was early retirement. "Not ambitious, just lucky."

"Better to be lucky than good."

"I like to think I'm both."

She laughed louder this time. "And humble, too."

For a while they listened to the sound of shouts and car doors slamming, engines cranking and horns honking as the crowd below dispersed.

"You know, I'm kind of looking forward to this St. Croix trip," Dave said. In the dark, he could almost hear her smile of triumph. "And to spending more time together now that I'm retiring."

"Typical man. Thinks just because his schedule is suddenly open, his woman will drop everything and come running."

"You mean you won't?"

"I didn't say you were wrong, just typical." She settled her head into the crook of his arm. "Although, if you really are a typical man, you're obviously wrong, too."

He gave her a nudge and turned his thoughts to getting enough capital to hold the office space over the weekend. She might be persuasive, but he was definitely determined.

Chapter Seven: Hensley

When Hensley heard the garage door open, he sprang from the recliner and peered through the plantation shutters. Davison fled with undue haste in a red Z-51 Corvette. Hensley smiled. A chariot fit for a prince of the realm. And three guesses as to his destination. That left adequate time for reconnaissance and strategic planning.

Despite the impression Hensley intentionally fostered, he was the most efficient person he knew. For example, he would never have saddled himself with this rambling suburban domicile, choosing instead to engineer a way to enjoy its virtues without circumscribing his mobility.

He had developed his personal philosophy—minimum effort, maximum pleasure—through years of direct research among the citizens of the world on every continent and in every social stratum. And he had discovered the key to implementing that philosophy with the three Ps: prioritization, positioning, and personality.

For example, a current assessment of priorities dictated another martini. As Hensley positioned himself at the bar, he noticed the coins scattered across the floor. They would have to be addressed, but not immediately. He assembled the requisite components for a libation adequate to restore the tissues, and then surveyed the room. Davison had achieved a modicum of success but radiated a commensurate lack of depth, a certain bourgeois superficiality.

He'd first noted the signs in the Tarrytown neighborhood where Ellis had said he would find Rex, but the house had been empty. He thought of waiting, but the neighborhood was infested with joggers with strollers and strollers with dogs and a lady inspecting her rose bushes for evidence of malfeasance on the part of her gardener. All paying particular attention to the guy in the Sherpa suit.

So he had moved on to Davison's house in Lakeway where the neighbors returned from work around sunset and drove straight into their three-car garages like Bruce Wayne into the Batcave, entering directly into their ozone-layer-depleting homes without the discomfort of interacting with the great unwashed, assuming one of that clan had the temerity to encroach upon their domain. Where an al-Qaeda cell could go undetected for years as long as they kept their hair and their grass cut, drove the right car, and didn't leave the recycle bin out overnight.

Finding the neighborhood deserted in the late afternoon sun, Hensley compromised the security system at his leisure, used the three Ps to run a quick inventory of the larder, and whipped up dinner.

But the gathering of the clans had not gone as anticipated. First, he had not planned for the presence of a third party, however welcome. And Davison had not been seduced by the well-placed word and the well-mixed cocktail. Hensley found himself nonplussed by the failure of the three Ps. He sat on the coffee table in the lotus position and searched his mind for an explanation.

It came to him almost at once. He lacked information. He had been prioritizing, positioning, and personalityizing, if he could use that word, in an informational vacuum. Or, to put it in the vernacular, he had no idea why he was here. And everyone could agree on the identity of the culpable party.

The telegram catches up with him in Nepal in a small village that's little more than a jumping-off place for intrepid thrill seekers on their way to the Everest base camp.

COME AT ONCE. SAY NOTHING TO DAVISON. —R

The contents seem plain enough on the surface, but Hensley takes nothing at face value, especially where family is concerned. He takes the paper and the envelope to the only bar in town. He greets Mingma, the proprietor, and orders a mug of *tungba*, the local liquor made by pouring hot water over fermented millet.

He focuses the insight derived from the first two mugs on searching for the message behind the message, and after a third mug, for the message behind the message behind the message. He studies the telegram like a fortune cookie, trying to decode it, but it fails to yield its secrets. He drags the bamboo mug across the rough wooden table and dips his head to the bamboo straw. The last of the liquor gurgles up the straw with a noise like radio static.

Hensley scans the room for Mingma, catches his eye, and nods. He sets down the paper and picks up the tattered envelope. International Telegram delivered it to the hostel in Amsterdam, but he hasn't lived there for almost two years. The markings on the front of the envelope chronicle its three-week journey through Europe and Asia, with three more addresses crossed out. On multiple occasions he has intended to apprise Ellis of his current address, but other priorities have superseded the thought.

Mingma arrives at the table, holding a kettle with a towel around the handle. "More water for you, Hensley." He pours steaming water into the mug.

"May your house be filled with joy and peace, Mingma."

"May your house be free of sorrow." Mingma bows slightly.

Hensley holds the telegram. "See this? The old man seems to be saying I should leave here immediately. What do you make of that?"

"Yes, sir," Mingma says, smiling.

"Not that it's a problem. I can leave at the drop of a hat." He picks up his Sherpa hat from the table and drops it on the floor. The soft thud is inaudible in the noise of the bar. "In fact, I frequently leave at the drop of a hat. Quicker, even."

"Yes, sir," Mingma echoes.

Hensley returns his attention to the telegram. "And I get the distinct impression that Davison should know nothing of this business. Which is rich because I've only talked to him twice in thirty-seven years." He looks up at Mingma. "Does that strike you as odd?"

"Yes, sir?" Mingma's smile fades slightly.

The thing that most puzzles Hensley is this abrupt summons from the old man. Hensley has been summoned by others, from a magistrate to a dominatrix, and any number of people in between, but never by the aging scion of the Stone tribe who seems content to let slumbering canines snore.

What does it mean?

He is due for a trip to the States. It's been more than ten years. Santa Fe and Chrystal and her kids. They are probably all grown and gone. He smiles, wondering what she is doing now. Perhaps he will do this thing, whatever it is, and then track her down.

After numerous hours of reflection and judicious application of multiple mugs of *tungba* and the three Ps, Hensley makes the journey by a circuitous route, the chief virtue of which lies in the contacts in each locale who owe him favors and can therefore finance the next leg in the trip. He actually comes out ahead.

———

Hensley came to the end of his martini without achieving enlightenment. Despite Ellis's assurances to the contrary, the one man who could decode the telegram was not in evidence in Austin. Perhaps if Hensley had come an hour or a day earlier, he might have discovered what Rex wanted. He had failed in that regard, but at least he had followed directions. Davison knew nothing about the telegram, just as Rex had intended for reasons that Hensley couldn't guess.

But what to do about Davison and his lack of the spirit of hospitality and cooperation? Should Hensley fold his tents and slip into the night, or stay the course and wear down his opponent through the sheer force of his considerable personality? He needed greater insight into the mind of his subject.

He popped off the table like a man shot from a cannon, gathered the scattered coins from the floor, and considered where to begin his search. In these cases, one must consider the psychology of the individual. Where a person stored an object depended on his attitude toward it.

A treasured memento might be displayed on a shelf or in a case. An object of value might be locked away. The flotsam of souvenirs that followed one about in the move from place to place might be in the garage or the attic or a guest room closet.

It came down to the question of how Davison regarded the object in question. Given his behavior this evening, Hensley doubted it would be on display. But surely Dave would not have tossed it into a box along with childhood diaries, the mortarboard tassel, the World Series ticket stubs.

He found it in the study, locked in a glass-fronted shelf along with an eclectic assortment of first editions—Robert Louis Stevenson, Daniel Defoe, and Ian Fleming. The lock wouldn't keep out the cleaning ladies, much less Hensley. He opened the door, pulled out a slim green album, and opened it to reveal a complete collection of

Liberty head dimes from 1892 to 1916. He checked the next, buffalo nickels, and an album of Indian pennies.

Davison had completed the few albums Hensley had left behind as a testament to the unbreakable bond of brothers and had expanded the collection to cover all the US currency and beyond. Evidently, he was not completely devoid of sentiment when it came to the token of Hensley's promise to return.

He emptied his pocket of the coins he had brought, filled in a few empty slots that matched, and put everything back, leaving the extra coins inside the case before he locked it. Then he returned to the den for a final drink.

The signs were favorable. Hensley would stay. Eventually Rex would surface, and they would discover what this was all about. But just in case, he collected the cash Davison had thrown at him before he exited stage left in a huff and a 'vette.

Enough to get out of town, but not enough to get very far. He needed either a better plan or better financing.

Day 2: Wednesday

Chapter Eight: Dave

Dave drove out to Lakeway with the sun at his back and an open road in front. At six a.m., the eastbound traffic was already starting to pick up. By the time he got a shower and a shave, MoPac would be a parking lot.

Angela was right; she was very persuasive on the matter of St. Croix. But he wouldn't leave town until he had the office space locked down. As he had lain awake, his brain spinning like a hamster wheel, it came to him. The coin collection. Ten years ago it had appraised at seventy-three thousand dollars. It might be over eighty by now. That and his other sources of capital should be enough to get things started, or at least hold the office space until next week, allowing him to take the trip after all.

He pulled into the garage and recalled the circumstances of his departure the night before. Hensley in his Sherpa glory. The last thing he wanted to see in the morning. Dave edged through the utility room into the kitchen and came to a dead stop. It looked like a model home staged for showing. He checked the cabinets and drawers. Everything where it should be, as if the night before had been a hallucination. He started the coffee and watched it drip, trying to remember exactly what had happened.

Knowing it would drive him crazy if he didn't, he searched the house, working his way from the kitchen to the bedrooms and opening every door, even the closets. His search ended in the third guest bedroom.

Hensley sprawled nude on the bed like a murder victim, twisted in the sheets. With a sudden snort, he turned over, entangling himself further. His pasty-white body was hairy and solid, not flabby as Dave had assumed. His duffel bag sat on the dresser, packed and zipped up like he was ready to go. The cash Dave had thrown at him lay on top in a neat stack.

Dave resisted the urge to drag Hensley out of bed and throw him out. Because he was technically family, at least as far as DNA was concerned, Dave relented to the point of conceding one night's stay. Plus, he didn't want to look at that hairy naked body any more than absolutely necessary. Less, actually.

He closed the door, went to his own bedroom, took a shower, and got dressed. In the study, he printed directions to the bus station on East Koenig. Then Dave unlocked the glass case and saw the stacks of foreign coins on the shelf in front of the albums.

Hensley had been in the case. Wasn't the cash Dave had thrown at him enough? He brushed the coins aside, pulled out a folder, and flipped it open. Nothing missing. He grabbed a box and transferred the folders to it, checking each one. Hensley hadn't taken anything. He'd found the collection and left the coins inside the glass, evidently banking on a decades-old appeal to sentimental value, unaware that the only value left in the red and green folders was strictly financial. It wasn't Hensley's first mistake and probably wouldn't be his last.

Dave scanned the shelf. There was room in the second box for some first editions, but he decided to hold the books in reserve. Before he headed to the garage, he grabbed the printout of directions to the bus station, slipped into the guest bedroom, and left it on top of the duffel bag. Hensley had not moved. Dave stopped at the door and took a last glance. It could be the last time he would ever see Hensley. With any luck. He didn't need the drama or the trauma.

On the way into town, he dialed his favorite numismatist, who worked by appointment only. He got voicemail and left a message asking for an appraisal as soon as possible. Now he would have to go to the office with the coins locked in the trunk.

At the office Dave went straight to Vanek's cubicle to confront him about Rivera, but found no hyena in evidence. He went into his office, booted up his computer, and checked his email. Inbox empty. He looked at his desk, also empty. Not surprising for a guy with three days left in his career.

He realized his trip downtown was essentially pointless. He might as well have stayed home, except that Hensley was there and the only thing Dave wanted to see when he got home was Hensley gone.

Dave leaned back in his chair, propped his feet on the desk, and surveyed downtown. If he stood in the corner on the other side of the conference table, he could see the capitol building, but he didn't bother. He'd seen it before.

The coin collection in the trunk of the 'vette in the parking garage worried him. He hadn't planned on leaving eighty grand just sitting there waiting to be taken. He'd expected to drop it off on the way to the office. Then he thought about why he had to sell the collection, about having to scrabble together capital from multiple inadequate sources.

Maybe he should cancel retirement. He was only forty-six. He could put in eleven more years before he was forced out, be careful with his expenses, build up the capital necessary to start the agency properly. But then he'd be starting up a new business at fifty-seven. He didn't like the sound of that.

Dave left. With Vanek MIA, he had no reason to be there. The elevator opened as he approached, and two men exited, the first tall, thick, and blond, the second younger, thin, and bald. Or at least shaved. They nodded as they passed. Then the blond stopped abruptly and turned back.

Dave stepped into the elevator and hit the button for the parking garage. The man stuck out his hand to stop the doors. They jerked back open. "Special Agent Dave Fletcher?"

"Yep."

"Can you spare a few minutes? In the office?"

With an ear-piercing buzz, the elevator complained about being held up. Dave stepped back into the hall. "And you are?"

"Special Agent James Johansson."

"Out of . . ."

"D.C."

"I'm not working any active cases."

"I know."

"What's this about?"

Johansson took a few steps toward the office. "If we could—"

The bald guy followed.

Dave didn't move. "What division are you from?"

"OPR." Johansson walked to the door.

Dave hesitated. The Office of Professional Responsibility, the internal affairs branch of the Secret Service. Vanek had gone full gonzo with his fabricated corruption conspiracy.

Johansson held the door open. "I have a room reserved."

Dave headed toward his office, but Johansson directed him down the hall to an interrogation room. It didn't have a view of the capitol or anything else. The walls were bare save for a whiteboard and a door and a projector hanging from the ceiling.

As he sat down, Dave realized they might be here about something else besides Rivera. He mentally ran through his twenty-five-year career. He might have occasionally erred on the side of justice as opposed to procedure, but nothing that would trigger an OPR investigation three days before retirement. At least he didn't think so, but they obviously did.

A phone conversation with Harris a few weeks ago popped into his mind. The call was unremarkable at first but descended into awkward silences rather than caustic repartee, the trademark Harris conversational style. Harris had wandered into a sentimental reverie of their prep school and university days. Dave had sensed an elusive subtext, an unasked question, but he had not pressed it. Now he knew what Harris had been hinting at.

Or maybe he was imagining the whole thing. Dave rubbed his face with both hands to clear his mind.

The bald agent took the chair facing the door. He opened a notepad and waited.

Johansson took the chair opposite Dave and dropped a file folder on the table. "How did you meet Güero Rivera?"

Dave leaned forward, his elbows on the table. "Did Vanek put you up to this? Because not only is he an incompetent idiot, he's making it up. There is nothing between me and Rivera."

"Just answer the question."

Dave let out a heavy sigh. "He's a small-time player. Sells arcade and casino games. It's all in the case file."

"How did he first come to your attention?" Johansson asked.

"That's in the file too."

"Let's say I haven't read the file." Johansson closed the folder. "Yet."

Dave shook his head and leaned back in his chair. This was even more ridiculous than he thought. "A few years back, I decided to get a biplane."

"You decided to get a biplane?"

If Johansson was going to question every sentence, this was going to take a long time. Dave sighed. "It's a hobby. You've heard of those, maybe?"

The bald agent stopped taking notes and raised an eyebrow, waiting for the response. Johansson smiled indulgently and motioned for Dave to continue.

"I drove down to check it out, took it for a test flight."

"How did you hear of it?"

"I know a guy who used to play golf with him." In response to Johansson's expression, Dave added, "Rex Stone."

The bald agent made a note.

"I said I wanted it. Rivera suggested a trade. His plane and Corvette for my Lamborghini."

An eyebrow inched up Johansson's forehead. "Lamborghini?"

Dave had no doubt Johansson knew everything about the Lamborghini, but an interview was a game and they had to play it, regardless of how tedious each found the other's responses. An agent owning a car worth several hundred thousand dollars would raise a few questions. The compensation wasn't that good.

"A gift from my uncle. It was more than ten years old when I traded it, but I kept it by the book." He ran an appraising glance over Johansson. Two could play this game of innuendo. "BMW. Leased. Am I right?"

Johansson didn't respond, which told Dave he'd made a direct hit, but the note-taker betrayed the ghost of a smile before concentrating on his pad.

Dave pressed the point. "I'm willing to bet my monthly expenses were cheaper than your car payment, and nobody's investigating you. Or are they?"

Johansson conceded the point with a nod.

"Three months ago, the Baton Rouge office popped a casino for passing counterfeit currency. The owner said it came from Rivera. But you already know this."

Johansson gestured for Dave to continue.

"He claimed total ignorance, of course. After a few hours, he gave me Woodstock Arcade Supplies in Atlanta. A one-time customer. Paid cash for a shipment of video poker machines."

"Video poker is illegal in Georgia."

"I checked it out. They bought the games for resale to the casino in Baton Rouge, a nice little circle. I passed it on to the Atlanta regional office, but there was no way to trace the actual bills from Woodstock to Rivera to Baton Rouge. Evidently, a lot of Rivera's customers pay in cash."

Johansson opened the file, flipped through a few papers, caught himself, and pushed it aside. "Tax evasion."

Dave reached across the table, pulled a cash transaction report from the file, and shoved it in front of Johansson. "All the cash deposits in his account were covered by a CTR. The federal prosecutor wouldn't touch it. Yet. You already know all this." Dave shrugged. "But we'll get him eventually. Or they will. I'm out in three days."

"How does the scheme work?"

Dave pushed the paper back at Johansson. "Were you ever a field agent?" He didn't bother to wait for an answer. "Most vendors discount their gaming machines heavily to gain or keep market share. Rivera probably charges full list price but throws in a suitcase or two of counterfeit bills, which the casino can use for payouts to rubes as they choose. Those payouts are basically free to the casino, and more than make up for the lack of discount."

Johansson skimmed the document briefly, put it back in the file folder, and closed it.

"Then what?"

Dave settled back into the chair. "Then nothing. No way to tie specific bills to a specific transaction in the chain."

"Then why did Rivera finger the guys in Atlanta?"

"Everyone else pays in bundles of hundreds. Woodstock had a lot of smaller bills."

"And the counterfeit bills—"

"All hundreds. Could have come from anyone."

"You dropped it."

"I passed everything to the interagency task force in case a connection to Rivera turned up in another investigation."

"And that was it."

"For me. I'm retiring."

Only that wasn't everything.

Chapter Nine: Dave

When Dave found out Rivera owned a piece of a casino in Cancún, he suspected the counterfeit cash had come in bulk from Mexico, not in singles from a dodgy customer. After all, Rivera couldn't operate down south without getting in bed with the cartels.

Dave's jurisdiction didn't extend to Mexico, but he couldn't let it go. He took some leave time and went to Cancún. He wasn't surprised when Detective Rafael Rodriguez of the Ministerial Federal Police seemed intensely uninterested in kicking over rocks at the Mayan Palace casino to see what crawled out. Dave visited it himself, without flashing his badge because it would get him nowhere in Mexico. He returned to Texas with a nice tan and no information.

None of that was in the file. The Service was not particularly supportive of agents freelancing.

"But you stayed in touch with Rivera."

He didn't say it as a question, but he should have. As a former suspect, Rivera was radioactive as far as the agency was concerned.

"No. Didn't see him again."

"But you talked with him on the phone."

Dave shook his head.

Johansson flipped through the file and pulled out a report.

Dave recognized it. A CDR, a call detail record from the phone company. If you wanted one of those, you had to get a warrant. Johansson was digging deep on this thing. Dave shook his head. He was drilling a dry hole and didn't know it.

"Three times this week. Eight times last week." Johansson locked up from the report and waited.

"He left me voicemails."

"About?"

"Said he wanted to buy the Jenny."

"Or maybe he arranged to meet you at Lakeway Airpark."

Did Johansson know they had indeed met, if inadvertently, at Lakeway Airpark yesterday? Or was he on a fishing expedition? "There was no plan to meet. I never said I would sell. I didn't even call him back."

Johansson opened the file folder like a weapon. "So you would be surprised to learn that Rivera claims you threatened to expose his activities if he didn't make regular payments to an offshore account set up for that purpose?"

Dave stiffened. How did this connect with Rivera in his hangar yesterday?

Johansson turned a page. "That for the past three years you have assisted him in structuring bulk cash transfers for the Sinaloa cartel to escape the notice of the FBI?"

"Sinaloa? If he's in bed with any of the cartels, it will be the Gulf, not the Sinaloa." As his pulse arced upward, Dave studied Johansson. He appeared to be serious, but there was no evidence. There couldn't be. "Rivera told you this?"

Johansson glanced through the statement in his hand and set it back down in the file.

Dave gripped the arms of his chair. "When?"

Johansson returned Dave's gaze without comment.

Dave thought so. He leaned back in his chair. "And of course you have me in here because there's some kind of evidence."

The bald agent stopped writing and looked at Johansson.

"We have the offshore account."

"And no evidence that I accessed it or am even connected to it." Although it would have been handy for starting up his new business.

Johansson pulled another paper from the file and shoved it across the table.

Without turning it around, Dave could see that Johannson had filed the forms to get access to his bank account. He snatched it from the table. The balance was a distressingly familiar low amount up until yesterday, when a $120,000 deposit appeared. A wire transfer.

Dave had no further interest in talking to Johansson. There were a few things he wanted to say to Rivera. He stood. "Keep in touch. I'll see myself out."

"I'm not finished."

Dave stopped at the door. "If you have faked enough evidence to convince a grand jury, go ahead and arrest me. Otherwise, I'm late."

"You have to read and sign the statement."

"Fax it to me." Dave opened the door and left.

Johansson stood, knocking his chair over. "But—"

Dave slammed the door on his "but."

As Dave approached the front door, Vanek shot out of the corner office where he had evidently been lurking.

"Hold it, Fletcher. As acting lead agent of the regional office, I need your badge until the investigation is closed."

"Check with Johansson." Dave crossed the distance to the elevator.

"You gave it to Johansson?" Vanek yelled from the office door.

Dave hit the button. He would be out of the parking garage by the time Vanek figured it out.

On the ride down, Dave thought of twenty ways to kill Rivera. Somehow he had got ahold of Dave's account number and wired the money from the offshore account. Probably connected to a cartel. Dave could say he knew nothing about it, but it was his word against $120,000 sitting in his checking account.

By the time he got to his car his boiling rage was reduced to a simmering anger. He called his boss in D.C.

He answered on the third ring. "McNeil."

"What do you know about this OPR investigation?"

"Dave?"

"When did you find out about it?" Dave had to know if his own boss had been holding out on him.

"Fifteen minutes ago."

"What do they have?"

"You know I can't talk about it. But I told them you were clean."

"And then you okayed the immediate transition to Vanek."

"No, that was just a few hours ago. Just a formality anyway. You're out in three days and Vanek has been acting lead agent for a month."

"Did they show you any evidence?"

"Of what?"

"Anything."

"They don't answer questions, they ask them." After a pause, McNeil said, "What they asked about, well . . . I told them they had the wrong guy."

Dave took a deep breath. "Thanks."

"No problem. I wouldn't worry about it. You're out and I don't think they'll mess with your retirement."

Dave's laugh was short and bitter. "I think they're aiming a little higher than that, Bob. Later."

Dave disconnected. He thought about calling Harris, confronting him, but the thought of the conversation made him tired. He dropped the phone in his pocket. Instead, he drove to the coin shop and had a long conversation about the best way to turn the collection into cash by Friday.

Then he made the half-hour drive down to Wimberley. Rivera had a lot to answer for, but he wasn't home. Estelle said he flew the Citation to Tucson for a client meeting. She didn't appear to be concerned or distressed. Dave doubted that she knew anything about the business, legit or otherwise. He pointed his 'vette north to the house for an overnight bag. His next stop would be the airport.

Rivera might actually be in Arizona, but Dave's money was on Mexico. Evidently one of the agencies brought him in two weeks ago. Based on what Johansson had said about the Sinaloa, the DEA probably had squeezed him, and Rivera had panicked. He decided to save his own skin by making up a story about a federal agent instead of ratting out the cartels, and the DEA had handed it over to OPR.

The phone calls from Rivera about buying the Jenny were strictly for the benefit of Johansson, a way to establish the appearance that he and Dave were in contact. Rivera probably opened offshore accounts under Dave's name for the same reason, everything a smoke-screen to cover his exit.

With this missing detail plugged into the puzzle, Dave reconsidered the scene with Rivera in the hangar. It still didn't make sense. He set that conundrum aside and considered where his quarry might be right now.

If Rivera wanted to disappear, one thing mattered more than anything. Liquid cash. He needed large quantities, he needed it now, and he needed it off the radar of law enforcement. And where was the best place to get that cash? Not in Tucson from a client. In Can-

cún from his partners in the Mayan Palace. When he landed his Citation at the Cancún International Airport, Rivera probably thought he
was home free, safely off the radar. He was mistaken.

Dave pulled into his garage, dashed into the house, and ran into
Hensley frying eggs in the kitchen. It jolted him out of his opera-
tional plan. "Why are you still here?"

"Fried egg sandwich?" The toaster popped up four slices. Hensley created two sandwiches, two eggs each, and held one out to Dave.
"A little something for the road?"

"You should already be on the road." Dave sniffed the sandwich,
which Hensley continued to dangle under his nose, and snatched it.
It was almost noon, after all.

Hensley poured a cup of coffee and handed it to Dave, then
took a sip from his own cup. Dave took a bite of the sandwich. Too
soon.

"Just off the grill," Hensley said.

Dave took a few breaths to cool his tongue. He looked out the
kitchen window and saw a scene from more than three decades ago.

Dave sits on a log at the edge of the Angolan jungle, near the river,
which is almost dry this late in the season. Hensley slowly turns the
breasts of two Namaqua doves on a spit above a bed of coals.

"What's he going to do if we say no?" Hensley asks. "Nothing.
He can't do anything."

"He would ground us," Dave says. That much is obvious.

Hensley shoots him the look that Dave hates. The one that says
he's an idiot.

"Then we say no. That's the point."

"Then he'd send us for the belt." Dave wants to hit Hensley with
the same look, but he doesn't know how Hensley does it.

"You're not getting it, Buckaroo. We don't bring him the belt."
He picks up the spit, examines the breasts, and nods. "It's no, all the
way down." He breaks the spit in the middle and hands one side to
Dave.

Dave takes the long end of the stick and raises the breast to his
lips.

"Too hot," Hensley says. Too late.

Dave snatches it away, his lips glowing. He takes a drink from his canteen and wipes his mouth with the back of his hand. "Then he'd get it himself."

"And what do we do then? Just bend over, admit defeat?" Hensley blows on the dove meat and bites it with his teeth bared to spare his lips. "Submit?" He swallows. "Figure it out, Buckaroo. We say no. What's he going to do then?"

Dave tries to work it out in his head like a double-digit multiplication problem, but he just can't visualize it. Some things don't change. The ebb and flow of the river according to the seasons. The phases of the moon. The serval hunting the springbok. The springbok outrunning the serval when it can, dying when it can't.

Saying no to Dad is like a springbok saying no to a serval. Dave tests the meat. It's cool enough. He takes a bite. Crunchy on the outside, moist in the middle. He's lucky to have a brother like Hensley. He smiles at Hensley across the fire.

Hensley finishes his portion. "He only has as much power as we decide to give him." He tosses the stick aside. "He knows it. And he's dreading the day we figure it out." He kicks dirt into the fire. "You can see it in his eyes. All we have to do is stick together."

—

Dave finished his egg sandwich and followed it with a gulp of coffee. Hensley had learned the ways of power in the jungle long ago. Dave set down his coffee cup and went to the study to book a late flight to Cancún.

Hensley was still teaching him this lesson, the one about saying no when it suited you. Only now, Dave was on the receiving end. He said no by not leaving, by treating the house as if it were his own. And like thirty years ago, Dave couldn't visualize his alternatives. How could he say no to Hensley right now? Physically throw him out of the house? Call the Lakeway police and let them do it?

First he connected with the coin shop and made an appointment. Then he scheduled a flight for after nine, packed an overnight bag, and locked his handgun in the desk. He found Hensley in the kitchen packing egg sandwiches in plastic bags. "I'll be back tomorrow. Don't be here when I get back."

"Where are you going?"

"It's business. Mine, not yours." Dave went through the utility room to the garage. "And make sure the security system is armed."

"You got it, Buckaroo," Hensley yelled as the door closed.

The first stop was the coin shop. Dave could get at least eighty if he was willing to break up the collection and wait for the right buyers, considerably less if he wanted to move quickly. He made it clear to the owner he needed as much cash as possible by close of business Thursday. He also got an advance against anticipated sales. He'd need it for the work he had to do in the next twenty-four hours, the kind where cash was king.

Then Dave went to the property manager of the building that housed his dream office and got a commitment that gave him until the Tuesday after Memorial Day to assemble the cash.

The next item on his list couldn't be done until after six. He killed time touring the capitol building, something he hadn't done for at least a decade.

He bypassed the metal detectors with his badge and strolled along with the tourists. It was late May. The legislature had let out just a few days before, so he went upstairs to the Senate chamber and studied the painting of dawn at the Alamo. On the south wall, Colonel Travis stood on the body of one Mexican soldier and fired his pistol at another.

Dave admired Travis and the few hundred Texians standing together against almost two thousand Mexican soldiers, but drawing that line in the sand was the next thing to suicide. By then he knew reinforcements were not coming from Goliad. On the other hand, what choice did he have? Could he surrender and still live with himself? Dave shook his head and left, glad he didn't have to make that decision.

He wandered around the chambers until they ran him out and closed the building. He stopped at the Clay Pit for happy hour. At seven, he went to the office. A lone agent sat with his feet up, talking on the phone and taking notes. Dave nodded to him and strode directly to the corner office. He unlocked the desk, removed a file folder, and locked it. The agent didn't return Dave's wave as he left. On the way to the airport, he stopped at Wal-Mart and bought a disposable phone. With OPR getting warrants for CDRs, he wasn't taking any chances.

Chapter Ten: Hensley

Hensley arrived in Philadelphia at nine p.m., took the train into town, the Thorndale line out to Villanova, and a cab to the Stone estate, arriving close to eleven. The housekeeper recognized him from the last time he was there, fifteen years ago, and let him in.

Rex wasn't at home, his return date unknown, but that didn't seem to perturb the housekeeper. She showed Hensley to a guest room. He left his bag and followed her down to the kitchen, where she made him a cold prime rib sandwich, poured him a glass of wine, and bade him goodnight.

The beef was good and the wine was better. He finished them off quickly, poured another glass, and wandered through the shadows of the ground floor rooms like an anthropologist exploring Tutankhamen's tomb. He had a ghostly memory of the place, as if from a previous life, which it was for all practical purposes. He was barely out of diapers when Mom got control of the trust fund and they moved to Angola.

Unlike Davison, who had been shipped stateside for proper training, Hensley had been allowed to flourish in the jungle wilderness, unmolested but haunted by the unspoken assumption that he shared in the altruistic vision of his parents, that he would joyfully shoulder the white man's burden among the benighted natives. He had certainly disabused them of that notion long before he slipped into the jungle and out into the world.

Hensley eventually found a familiar room, the study, the setting for the only real conversation he'd ever had with Rex. That was fifteen years ago, when Hensley came back from New Zealand for Mom's funeral.

Rex had planned a calm, staid affair, quite unlike the tribal spectacle of Dad's funeral in Angola with the drums, the procession to the grave, dancing, singing, praying, smashing bottles and dishes, and a meal that extended into the night. In the midst of all the passion and pathos, Hensley had remained aloof like a *National Geographic* reporter embedded with the natives.

After all, the old man was the reason Hensley had left, and nothing had changed in Hensley's mind. Dad lived in his own world and could go into the next accordingly as far as Hensley was concerned. He'd treated his sons like extensions of himself, automatons generated to expand his kingdom. Almost as if they should have been buried along with him, like some pharaoh.

Then, at Mom's funeral, Hensley had showed up in Philadelphia, ready to go through the motions, but he'd been dragged through the emotions instead. With no warning, he'd disintegrated like cotton candy in the rain while the few surviving members of the Stone family had stayed the course with a stiff upper lip.

Hensley still didn't understand why. They had been a team, Mom and Dad, a united front with a shared vision. Why would her funeral have been different? The tsunami of emotion that overwhelmed him came with no warning or explanation. He sat with the family, but at the end of the row, weeping silently.

There was no parade of memories, no sentimental vignettes to prompt the cataract of tears. Just a disabling sense of emptiness. The realization that something irreplaceable had been lost, something he hadn't comprehended, or even detected, until it was too late. It had left him empty and hoping desperately that he wouldn't have to repeat the experience.

All he could think was that he shouldn't have come.

It had taken hours to recover. He had walked away from the graveside service and hitched a ride into town, ending up in west Philly, where he found a corner bar that felt like home and got to know a few folks.

When he felt more like himself, he caught a train to the Main Line and took a cab to the Stone estate, much like tonight. Davison had already taken a plane back to Virginia.

Hensley squelched the memory, turned on a desk lamp, and strolled through the room in silence, stroking the oak paneling, the leather chairs, the leather-bound volumes in the lofty bookcases. He found a cigar and a bottle of scotch and sat in the same chair Rex had shown him to that night fifteen years ago.

Hensley lights his cigar as Rex pours a superannuated scotch as peaty as a fence post and as smooth as a used-car salesman's pitch. He guesses Rex is in his mid-forties. A little more than a decade older than Hensley.

Rex ignites his cigar and spreads a cloud of carcinogens into the room. "So, Hensley, how is it you keep body and soul together?"

Hensley takes in the opulent surroundings. "With innate felicity and grace." A sense of irony creeps in as he realizes Rex would never agree that they both live by their wits.

Rex takes a sip of scotch. Hensley does likewise. They sit in comfortable silence.

Hensley thinks back through the day, his arrival, the trip to town for suitable clothes courtesy of Rex, the memorial service. The last is better left alone, so he speaks to banish the demons. "I find my way among the great unwashed, communing with the spirit of mankind."

"The problem with the common man is that he is so . . . common."

Hensley tilts the tumbler of scotch toward Rex. "I submit to you, sir, that you speak from lack of experience. Scratch aside the topsoil of the laborer and you unearth a mine of nuance."

Rex nods, as if taking the possibility under advisement. "And does it pay well?"

"I live modestly, find simple, honest work."

"But you are a man in your prime. How can you be satisfied with a subsistence life? Have you no ambition, no desire to build something that will last?" Rex waves his hand, the cigar leaving a trail of smoke, to indicate the study, and by extension, the Stone family mansion and estate.

Hensley surveys the floor-to-ceiling bookcases filled with leather-bound volumes, the hardwood paneling dotted with oil paintings, the heavy leather furniture clustered in groups like contented cows seeking shade. "A monument worthy of Ozymandias himself." He watches the smoke from his cigar climb to the dim reaches of the ceiling. "As a great philosopher once said, there is no luggage rack on a hearse."

"Spoken like a son of Reggie Fletcher."

Hensley turns his head and blows out a column of smoke, annoyed by the comparison. Now that he thinks about it, Dad had said the same thing. But that doesn't mean anything. Nobody can deny that, while he may be a Fletcher, he is nothing like Dad.

Rex interrupts Hensley's thoughts. "But even Reggie had ambition, if of a different sort. He left behind a clinic in Angola."

"Each man takes the path that rises to meet his feet. You could no more walk my path than I could walk yours." Hensley finishes the scotch in a gulp. "Or Dad's," he adds grudgingly. He sets the tumbler on the desk with a thump. "But I could easily join you in a toast."

"To what?" Rex replenishes both glasses.

"Dealer's choice."

Hensley sat in the silent, empty study and held his glass aloft in a toast. "To you, Rex, wherever you've got off to." He drank the scotch, looked at the empty chair on the other side of the desk, and swapped places to take in the view from the side of the owner. At age fifty-three, he began to see the appeal of the well-stocked liquor cabinet, the well-appointed study, the spacious mansion, free and clear.

Why had Rex sent for him? Hensley had always assumed that Davison was the heir apparent, given his close relationship with Rex, but sitting here in this room, an interpretation of the telegram crept up on him. *Say nothing to Davison.* Could he be tossing over Davison and looking for someone on whom to settle the estate? He surveyed the room again. One could dare to dream, couldn't one?

Day 3: Thursday

Chapter Eleven: Dave

The phone startled Dave into consciousness, and the strange room disoriented him for a few seconds before he remembered where he was and why. Cancún. Rivera. Salvaging his career. Assuring his retirement. Staying out of prison.

Dave checked the caller ID and ignored the call. There was never a good time to talk to Vanek, but morning had to be the worst.

He heard the voicemail beep while he was in the john. Vanek demanded that Dave come in immediately and surrender his badge and the key to the corner office desk. Dave checked the time on his phone. Almost ten. He couldn't remember the last time he'd slept past seven. He grabbed breakfast in the hotel and then took a cab into town.

From the street, the Policia Federal building looked the same, but the inside had changed. Half a dozen hard plastic chairs crowded a small vestibule with brown tile floor, yellow walls, and the smell of stale cigarettes rising from an overflowing ashtray on a cracked Formica end table. A young officer in the blue and black uniform of the Policia Federal sat behind a bulletproof window, watching Dave as he came in.

Dave showed him his badge and spoke into the grate. "I'm here to see Detective Rafael Rodriguez."

The blank expression on the young man's face raised Dave's blood pressure a few millimeters. He asked again, this time in his halting Spanish, but language was not the difficulty.

"There is no Detective Rodriguez," the officer replied in English.

"I worked with him three months ago on a case. In this building."

The officer pointed at the empty chairs and picked up a phone.

Dave took a seat. The kid looked like he hadn't been on the force for three days, much less three months, but he ought to know who worked in the building.

Not that Rodriguez would welcome the visit. He'd been particularly unhelpful the last time around, balking at every question and annoyed when Dave pressed for answers. And of course the people at the Mayan Palace had been even less helpful and more annoyed when he came around asking questions. That's what they paid people like Rodriguez for, to keep people like Dave away.

After a frantic conversation, the kid behind the glass hung up the phone. "Someone will be down."

Dave nodded.

Twenty minutes later, the inside door buzzed and opened. A middle-aged man stepped out and appraised his visitor. Dave stood and returned the inspection. The man wore the uniform of his office: suit black, shirt white, tie thin, shoes polished, hair thick, short, and black with a dash of grey at the temples.

Dave displayed his badge. The man inspected it and motioned him inside.

"I am Detective Edgar Aguilar with the Ministerial Federal Police. You can explain in my office."

Aguilar led Dave through a warren of hallways, offices, and desks. They ended up in a small office with files piled on all available surfaces. Aguilar moved a pile to the floor, motioned for Dave to sit, and dropped into the wooden swivel chair behind the desk. He leaned back, rested his elbows on the arms, and interlaced his fingers across his appreciable gut.

"Now." He consulted his notepad. "Special Agent Fletcher, what is it you want with Detective Rodriguez?

"I worked with him on a case a few months ago. I have a new lead and wanted to know if he had any new information before I follow up."

"What case is this?"

Dave cataloged Aguilar. Mid-forties. Well fed. His half-mast eyelids and slow way of speaking made him seem arrogant. Or maybe he really was arrogant. He held the man's gaze as he said, "I'd rather speak with Rodriguez."

"I'm afraid that won't be possible."

"Why is that?"

"He's dead."

Aguilar studied Dave as he took a moment to absorb this information.

"When?"

"Last month."

Dave inclined his head and waited for details. Aguilar continued grudgingly.

"There was a sting. Airport police involved in drug trafficking. Rodriguez was present for the arrest. The suspects fired on the Policia Federal. Two officers died at the scene. Rodriguez died on the way to the hospital."

Perhaps Rodriguez wasn't in the pocket of the cartels after all. Or more likely the sting was a front for a turf war, a rival cartel edging in on Los Zetas territory. Perhaps the Sinaloa. There was bad blood between the two, and Cancún was only a hundred or so miles north of the Sinaloa territory bordering Belize and Guatemala.

Dave chose his words carefully. If Aguilar was dirty, he could be telegraphing his hand. "What can you tell me about the Mayan Palace?"

"You are looking for a particular individual? You have a provisional arrest warrant, of course?"

"Country clearance. I'm here to investigate, not arrest. At this time." Dave did have country clearance, but it didn't cover investigating Rivera or the casino. No need for Aguilar to know that. "The Mayan Palace?"

"It has nothing remarkable." Aguilar shrugged. "Live card games upstairs."

Casinos weren't legal in Cancún before 2010, and after then only for slots. However, sub rosa card games were common in most casinos up until the fall of 2011, when the government began auditing more closely after a fire in a Monterrey casino. The fact that the Mayan still ran card games indicated some kind of arrangement with the authorities. "Cartel involvement?"

Aguilar took a long time in answering, considering Dave as if attempting to determine if he was an idiot or a threat. "It is possible. These things, they are very hard to prove."

Especially if you don't try. Clearly Aguilar would be no more help than Rodriguez had been. "I'm more interested in the activities of one man in particular. An American."

Aguilar glanced at a notepad in the foothills of the mountain range of documents that covered his desk. "A Mr. Bill Sackett, perhaps?"

Dave frowned. Who was Sackett?

Aguilar smiled grimly. "Yes, these things do not go unnoticed. Cancún is not such a big town."

He decided to go along with it. "What do you know of Bill Sackett?"

Dave waited until Aguilar finally admitted he didn't know Sackett, either.

"Who owns the Mayan Palace?"

"It is a matter of record. I do not know offhand."

"I thought it was a small town."

"There are a number of owners. Señor Soto is the general manager."

"Any Americans?"

"Certainly not Sackett. I would remember the name. Why are you interested in the Mayan?"

"We have reason to believe a certain party is funneling counterfeit American currency from Los Zetas to the States, and laundering drug money the other direction."

Aguilar regarded Dave for a minute without speaking.

Dave finally broke the silence. "So you are not at present working any kind of case involving the Mayan Palace or its owners."

"I cannot comment on any cases we may or may not be pursuing."

Dave stood. "Thank you for your help, Detective Aguilar."

Aguilar shook his hand briefly. "I must warn you, Special Agent Fletcher, that asking inconvenient questions can be dangerous."

"Is that what happened to Rodriguez? Asked too many questions?" Dave spoke by reflex, but an afterthought chilled him. Despite the badge, he was here without authority. If his own inquiries awakened sleeping dogs and they came after him, the best he could hope for was sanctuary at the consulate as a citizen. If he got that far.

If Aguilar noticed Dave's discomfort, he didn't show it. "Rafael was an honest man, but he was not reckless."

Dave nodded as if the answer made sense. Aguilar ushered him out of the office and through the maze back to the entrance. Dave stepped through the door, and then stopped and turned back to Aguilar. "Did you get them?"

"Get who?"

"The men who killed Rodriguez."

Aguilar stared back a few seconds before answering. "No." He disappeared inside the building.

Dave grabbed lunch at a taqueria and took the number 27 bus down Tulum to the Mayan Palace, uneasy in the hard plastic seat. Talking to Aguilar might have been a mistake.

Chapter Twelve: Dave

The casino hadn't changed in the last few months. Flashy, Vegas-style exterior, with a lower profile than the behemoths in Sin City. Inside, it bore the mark of all casinos—florid carpet, indirect light, the pervasive smell of cigarettes, and the electronic cacophony of video games screaming for attention like spoiled toddlers in a day-care from hell.

Dave got an iced coffee and wandered the aisles, acclimating to the dim and the din. This early on a midweek afternoon, it felt deserted, but the tourists didn't even glance up as he passed by. In the center of the building, he found the twin spiral staircase twisting upward like a DNA ladder to the second floor.

The large, circular bar still dominated the room, surrounded by dozens of armchairs and bistro tables. He got a Dos Equis for show and wandered the room, coming to rest at a large wood and brass double door with a thug in an expensive suit standing beside it.

Dave nodded and reached for the door. The thug blocked his way.

"VIP guests only," he said in a local accent. He was the size of a telephone booth and had one of those haircuts that looked like his head had been buzzed and a muskrat pelt set on top.

"Detective Aguilar sends his regards," Dave said. It might work once.

Muskrat opened the door. Dave entered.

Leather couches lined the walls, interspersed with tropical plants. In one corner, a macaw paced a perch in a cage large enough for Muskrat to share without cramping his style or crowding the bird. Along one wall, a massive aquarium featured a range of species that would have gratified Jacques Cousteau. Round tables surrounded by leather chairs dotted the room, separated by seating areas sporting large ash trays on the end tables. Here, the aroma shifted to cigars and leather.

The room was empty except for a game in progress at a table near the aquarium. Five players, all focused on the hand. One of them was Guëro Rivera.

"Deal me in," Dave said, pulling up a chair.

Everyone looked up, surprised and a little annoyed. Dave ignored the others.

"Rivera! What a surprise to see you here. You still in the market for a plane?"

"Fletcher!" Rivera's smile didn't reach past his lips. He glanced at the door.

"I'll sell you the Jenny if you still want it. I'm looking at doing my own experimental kit." Dave scanned the table. "Texas Hold 'Em? What's the blind?" He pulled a stack of bills from his wallet. "I'll take $2,000 in chips for starters."

Dave smiled at Rivera and quickly assessed the others. Evenly split between Anglos and Latinos. Retirees by the look of them. Varying degrees of fitness. At least one of them armed, judging by the bulge under his jacket. None of them hurting for money. None appeared to be hostile. Yet.

He turned back to Rivera. "Just remember, I've done some improvements. I'm not letting it go cheap."

"I thought you were up in Austin."

Dave held Rivera's eye. "There's a lot of that going around."

"Have old home week on your own time. We got a card game going here." This from a guy with a ponytail who looked like a Hispanic Kenny Rogers.

The others grunted their assent. Dave held up his hands in surrender.

"Sorry. Carry on."

They played out the hand. Rivera placed bets without conviction and then gave up completely, folding. Kenny Rogers won and the dealer button passed to him. He sized up Dave.

"Still want in?"

"Sure," Dave said. "But first let me get a drink."

Kenny stared at Dave's beer bottle. "That one's full."

"I was thinking a good single malt."

"Andre will bring you one." Kenny twisted in his chair and gestured to a man sitting under a plant.

Dave waved Andre back into his seat. "That's okay. I want to see the selection. Rivera, why don't you let me buy you a drink?"

Rivera glanced around the table without meeting anyone's eyes. "Sure."

Dave walked out to the bar. Rivera joined him.

"What's your poison?" Dave waved to the bottles behind the bar. "Highland? Lowland? Islay?"

"Screw the scotch. What are you doing here?"

Dave looked at the bartender, shrugged, and turned back to Rivera. "How did you get down here? Didn't they tell you not to leave town, much less the country?"

"You're not the only one with a plane, my friend."

Dave had called it. Rivera was on the run. "What have you gotten yourself into?"

"This is not the place."

"Okay. What have you gotten me into?"

Rivera glanced away, unable to meet Dave's eye. "Nothing to worry about."

"You look worried enough for the both of us. And I'm worried enough for a dozen of you."

A few seconds passed before Rivera responded. "As I think on it, I will take that drink."

Rivera approached the bar like a horse scenting water. Dave followed. Rivera ordered a double shot of Pepe Zevada and downed it in two swallows.

Dave leaned in toward him. "Your little stunt could cost me a million in retirement income, not to mention a prison sentence."

Rivera took a deep breath with his eyes closed, evidently waiting for the tequila to do its work. He faced Dave. "This is the reason you're here? To clear your name?"

"That seem like a small thing to you?"

"No, no, no. But we can't speak of it here. Where are you staying?"

"I'm not leaving without something that will get OPR off my back."

"Want me to strip down again?" Rivera stepped away from the bar, back to the chairs. He dropped into one and stared off into a corner, shaking his head. "These amateurs, they know nothing of what they're doing. They have created a mess."

Dave sat down in the opposite armchair. "Which guys?"

"The Federales. They will get me killed."

"And how do I come into the picture?"

"You don't, my friend." Rivera's unfocused stare converged on Dave. "They inconvenienced me by looking too closely at a bulk transfer I did for Los . . . well, for certain individuals. They were willing to deal if I would cooperate. Get them to the next level."

Dave waited a good thirty seconds before prodding Rivera. "I'm not the next level. I'm not any level."

Rivera glanced at Dave and then away. "I gave them an acccunt number."

"And wired 120 grand to my checking account?"

Rivera shrugged. "I had to distract them with something while I made my escape."

"Who did you tell this to?"

"I forget the agent's name. But it is nothing to worry about."

"Tell that to Johansson. He seems to think otherwise."

"Who?"

"The OPR agent who caught my case. He's saving a cell for me."

Rivera shook his head. "Whoever he is, he knows nothing. He's fishing."

"Who does this offshore account belong to?"

Rivera's expression clearly said Dave was as astute as a paint huffer. "You want to also get me killed?"

"I want to make this whole thing go away."

"Take a number, my friend, take a number."

Dave eyed Rivera for a few seconds and then pulled out his phone. He found a number in his call history and hit send. He got voicemail. "Johansson, this is Dave Fletcher. I've got Guëro Rivera here. He's going to give you some information important to your investigation."

Dave held the phone up to Rivera's mouth.

Rivera grabbed it from his hand and ended the call. "Are you crazy?" He scanned the room. A few customers had arrived, but nobody paid Rivera and Dave any mind. "Let's go."

Dave followed Rivera down and outside into the warm, humid afternoon to a traffic circle a block north. They dodged the cars until Rivera stopped in the shade of stubby palm trees. He turned on Dave.

"These guys, they play for keeps, and they don't follow the rules."

Dave closed what little distance lay between them. "You're the one who signed up for this game. You can unsign me." He grabbed his phone from Rivera's hand. "You're going to tell Johansson you made the whole thing up and who that account really belongs to so he can verify it."

Rivera backed away and studied Dave. "How much is it worth to you?"

The sea breeze kicked up sand from the traffic island in the middle of the roundabout, coating them with a layer of grit. Dave squinted back at him. "I'm not financing your disappearing act, if that's what you mean."

Rivera shook his head in disgust. "You want me to give away that kind of information with no protection? Do you realize what a governor could do to me if I begin leaking names?"

"So it's a governor? Which state?"

Rivera looked past Dave and waved down a taxi. It stopped in the middle of traffic, precipitating a chorus of horns and gestures. Rivera pushed past Dave, who threw up a hand to stop him but thought better of it when he realized the size of the audience they had gathered. Rivera got in the back seat. "You have thirty-one to choose from. But leave me alone."

Chapter Thirteen: Dave

Dave caught a taxi to the airport and dialed Harris on his disposable phone.

He answered on the first ring.

"Did you lose something?"

"Fletch?" Harris sounded cautious.

"Maybe you should check. Largish guy, looks like a bear with a big belt buckle and sharkskin boots."

"How would you know that?"

"Let me tell you what else I know. He's not in the US anymore."

"Fletch? What are you mixed up in?"

"I think you owe me a little information, especially after what happened yesterday." Dave waited for an explanation or an apology but got only silence. "The information Rivera gave you, it's only half right. That account he gave you, it's legit."

After a pause, Harris responded. "Think what you're saying, Fletch."

"They're payoffs, but not to me. That's the part he lied about."

"Then to whom?"

"A state governor."

"Which state?"

"I'm working on it. But at least you can narrow it down to a finite set of people."

"Fletch." Harris drew in a deep breath. "Fletch, you're playing a dangerous game. Why don't you just cooperate and give us what you have?"

"Us?" Dave squeezed the phone like he would a serpent. "Us? Us used to be you and me. When did that change?"

"Maybe you should tell me."

"I'll tell you. I might lose my retirement, or guess what? I might go to prison. Why? Because the man who should have my back turned me over to OPR instead of coming to me to see if a CI was lying to save his own neck."

"Fletch, that's not what happened."

"Oh, what did you do, flip a coin first?"

"Okay, Fletch, I know how you feel—"

"You don't know squat, Harris."

"Let me rephrase. You're right. I should have come to you first."

As close to an apology as Dave would get. "You only have to pick from thirty-one, not fifty."

"Thirty-one?"

"States." Dave could almost hear the gears turning over the phone.

"Mexico? It's a Mexican governor? Did he say anything about Joaquin Guzmán?"

"I'd start with Quintana Roo and work your way out from there."

"You're not making it easy on me."

"I know the feeling." Dave disconnected the call.

Why did Harris mention Guzmán? He was the head of the Sinaloa cartel, and Rivera was in Los Zetas territory. He shook his head and pocketed the phone. That was no longer his problem. Let Harris deal with it.

At the airport, Dave worked his way through the layers of bureaucracy and finally made it to the airport manager. It took more than his badge to get access to the log of incoming traffic. The manager passed him on to Celeste, a young woman who spoke passable English. She found a desk for Dave and brought him the logs.

He found two Cessna Citations, one from Nassau with five people onboard and one from Brownsville with one person onboard, Bill Sackett. It seemed Aguilar had been tracking Rivera without knowing it. Dave wasn't sure what that meant, but he didn't take time to ponder it.

Instead, he used his smartphone to check the N-number against the FAA registry website. He wasn't surprised when it came back as an experimental single-engine prop owned by some guy named William McIntosh. Rivera probably picked it at random when he flew in and out of Brownsville and continued to use it when Cancún asked for his international flight plan. Towers didn't usually do a visual check to verify that the N-number matched what the pilot reported over the radio, but Immigration did.

He looked up from the log. Celeste was next to him in an instant.

Dave pointed to the log. "I need to see this plane."

The fading heat of the day radiated from the tarmac as Celeste drove him to the hangar in a service vehicle. The hangar door was open, and Dave saw the Citation before they came to a stop. It had the same color scheme as Rivera's jet. Dave circled the plane for a better view. Celeste followed. The N-number matched.

Searching the registry by name got him Rivera's Citation. He compared the N-number in the registry to the one on the tail. The last digit was different.

He moved around the wing to the tail, and saw the signs of a quick paint job. The white around the last digit was slightly brighter than the surrounding paint, and the edges of the number weren't as crisp. Rivera must have done it himself and failed to push down the edge of the tape properly.

But he had to make sure. He opened the cockpit door and retrieved the registration. Güero Rivera. Immigration would have checked it, but the name didn't have to match Rivera's passport. He could just be the pilot coming down to pick up his boss. And Dave had no doubt Rivera was carrying a passport with the name of Bill Sackett.

Dave was satisfied that he'd found Rivera's method of entry, but more importantly, his manner of exit. He placed a few large crisp bills in Celeste's hand, looked into her large brown eyes, and thanked her for her help. He asked her to call him the moment she heard anything about this plane being prepared for departure and said he'd find his own way out. She left, her reluctance mitigated by what was probably a month's salary in her hand. He watched until she got into the service vehicle and was out of sight and then turned to the jet.

With any luck the thing he needed would still be exactly where he saw it three years ago when Rivera gave him a tour. He opened the nose baggage compartment, pulled out the equipment bag, and rummaged through it. He found the battery lock, still in the box, grabbed it and a tool kit, and returned the bag to storage. Then he went to the aft baggage compartment, opened it, and removed the cover to the battery. It only took a few seconds to turn the knob on the quick disconnect, snap the lock in place, and turn the key.

Dave pocketed the key, slipped a business card out of his wallet, snagged a pen from the cockpit, and wrote the number of his burner phone on the card. He wedged the card between the lock and the battery.

As he closed the aft baggage compartment, the ringing of his personal cell phone caused him to drop the pen. He scanned the hangar, verified he was still alone, and checked the caller ID. The Stone family lawyer.

"Ellis, to what do I owe the honor?" He turned to leave but stopped halfway to the door.

"Died?" How was that possible? "When? Where? How?"

Dave paced around the jet, inspecting random objects as if something would help him make sense of the words coming through the phone. "I had dinner with him two days ago, and he didn't say anything to me about a brain tumor. Or that he was going to Cancún." He came to a stop by the fuselage. "Where did they take the body? Hang on." He found the pen he'd dropped and wrote an address on his arm. "I'll see you tomorrow."

He disconnected and shoved the phone in his pocket, staring at his reflection in the Citation window without seeing it. His mind bounced back and forth between two thoughts—that Rex was dead and that he had known he was dying for the last six months. Both seemed impossible, but evidently both were true.

Dave focused on one, trying to comprehend it and, failing, switched to the other, only to find it equally incomprehensible, and returned to the first. Around the time Dave was on the bus to the casino, Uncle Rex was drowning in a spring-fed pool two hours away.

As if the act of organizing them could help him organize his thoughts, he wiped down the tools, keeping cloth between this fingers and the metal, and put them back in the bag. At dinner Tuesday, Uncle Rex knew he had an inoperable, malignant brain tumor. And yet he said nothing of it. Suddenly the strange behavior made sense, all the talk of regret, the apology.

It hit him without warning, like a sucker punch to the gut. He threw the bag into the compartment, leaned against the fuselage, and took deep breaths as the tears brimmed and crawled down his face.

Uncle Rex would never join him for a birthday dinner again. Never talk to him. Never offer his thoughts on retiring, on how to launch the new business, on anything.

Dave suddenly wanted to ask Rex about Angela, about St. Croix, about how things had suddenly changed between them. Rex had never married, and Dave had never thought to ask him why. Maybe the answer to that question would have given him a clue about what to do next. Now he would never know.

Why had Rex done this thing this way? Fill the empty spaces with silence instead of explanations. Come down here with a secret. Die without warning.

Dave pushed the tears aside with the heel of his hand, feeling the empty place in tomorrow where Rex should have been. He slammed the baggage compartment closed and listened to the echo in the emptiness of the hangar.

The road to hell was paved with what-ifs. Dave knew that, but he couldn't stop. What if he had pushed harder at The Emerald? What if Rex hadn't died? What if Dave had a second chance? Would he have looked past his own problems to see Rex staring into the void, trying to make things right before it was too late?

His obsession with the OPR investigation—Rivera, Johansson, Vanek—seemed trivial now. Irrelevant. Stupid.

Dave threw the pen at Rivera's plane and escaped the hangar.

After a short conversation in broken Spanish, the coroner led Dave through double swinging doors into a chilled room with large drawers along one wall. The coroner consulted a logbook, located a drawer, and pulled it out.

Dave stepped forward. He was more composed now, moving on autopilot, acting like humans do in the presence of other humans.

He looked at the body in the drawer. Uncle Rex, or rather, what Uncle Rex had left behind. The coroner glanced a question at him. Dave nodded, confirming the identity, and the coroner returned to the desk, busying himself with paperwork. Dave turned back to Rex.

He thought he understood why Rex didn't tell anybody about the tumor. Some things are hard enough to confront without having to summon the energy for social effluvia. How do you tell someone you're going to die? How do you endure the inevitable pitying look, the inane comments from the terminally clueless adding insult to tragedy?

Regardless, Dave felt betrayed. Surely he could have been trusted to bear the news without responding with clichés and gaucherie. He leaned over Rex and whispered. "Why didn't you tell me?"

The coroner glanced up. Dave turned away, skirting the storm of emotion that threatened to overtake him again.

Day 4: Friday

Chapter Fourteen: Dave

Dave dropped into one of a pair of wingback chairs in a law office in Philadelphia. Opposite him, Ellis Thornton, looking, as always, like he was chiseled from a single block by Michelangelo himself five centuries ago, sat behind his old-money desk in his old-money office, surrounded by massive walls of law books both ancient and modern. He was as serious as an unopened bottle of thirty-two-year-old single malt and spoke in ponderous phrases as if he personally carried the weight of the entire canon of common law on his granitic shoulders.

"Davison, let me again convey my deep regret that we should meet again under such unfortunate circumstances."

"I'm still trying to wrap my brain around it." He'd spent the flight from Cancún to Philadelphia thinking about little else, Rivera, Vanek, and Johansson banished from his mind for now. Angela continued to impinge at discrete intervals. He wondered if he should have called her when he heard, but he never overcame the inertia to dial her number. No sense dragging her into family business. Not yet. Not when his future was so tentative. Best to wait until he had undone everything Rivera had done.

The door behind him opened, and Dave twisted in his chair.

The secretary looked in. Hensley entered, dressed in a tie-dyed t-shirt, jeans, and hiking boots.

Dave shot up out of the chair and turned to Ellis. The old man returned his gaze, then motioned Hensley to the chair next to Dave.

Hensley surveyed the office, grabbed a low-slung overstuffed leather armchair from a nearby coffee table, and shoved it in front of the desk, pushing aside the other chair.

"How did he get here?" Dave asked Ellis.

"Taxi." Hensley slouched into the armchair.

How did Ellis contact Hensley? Nobody knew where he might be at any given moment, probably not even Hensley himself.

With a vague sense of betrayal, Dave dropped back into his chair. Of course Hensley had every right to be here, but that didn't change the fact that Dave resented his presence. Over the years, as Hensley became most notable for his absence, Dave came to regard him as more symbol than substance, like the portrait of a patriarch over the mantle in a castle. And, like an ancestral ghost, he might make the sporadic appearance on occasions of significance, but he was otherwise irrelevant to the daily life of the family.

Although he had said nothing about it, perhaps Rex had summoned Hensley for reasons unknown and now unknowable, but Dave would be much happier when this day ended and Hensley, having no further reason to afflict him, beat a retreat to his nomadic existence.

Ellis leaned back into his leather swivel chair, resting his elbows on the armrests. "Two months ago Rex came to me and completely restructured his estate."

"Was that when he got the diagnosis?" Dave asked.

"Not long after. It took him a while to process it."

"Understandable," Hensley said.

"But I'm afraid I have disturbing news. Yesterday Rex changed his will."

Dave frowned. "Yesterday? From Cancún? Can you do that over the phone?"

"He set up a video conference from his laptop, created a holograph will, and signed it on screen, with a witness. The will, which was faxed to me later as per his verbal on-screen instructions to the witness, matched in substance and detail the directions he gave me on camera."

"Who was the witness?" Dave asked.

"One Acilino Vega. The driver of a limousine."

"What does it say?" Hensley grunted from his quasi-prone position in the overstuffed chair.

Ellis donned reading glasses and surveyed the faxed pages on his desk. "He left the total of his estate, some $200 million, to one Masie Wright, recently of Cancún."

"Who?"

Ellis opened the file on his desk and turned a few pages. "She appears to be a medical professional employed by Endless Vacations, the agency through which Rex booked the vacation."

"He left the whole nut to a nurse?" Hensley asked.

"That's the last thing he would do," Dave said.

"Evidently, it was the last thing he did," Hensley said.

Ellis looked over his glasses. "I questioned the decision. He was quite emphatic." He sorted through the papers and selected one. "But there are other curious aspects of his trip. A transfer of funds of five hundred thousand dollars to an offshore account held by AZ Limited."

"Who is . . ." Dave asked, hoping to accelerate the flow of information.

Ellis set the pages aside and slowly removed his glasses. "We haven't been able to determine that. Yet."

Dave considered the pages on the desk. The signature of Rex's career was the ability to instantaneously render an astute call and act on it. But this snap decision didn't feel like Rex. It felt more like a stranger using Rex's skills for his or her own purposes.

"So, that's it? Just like that he changed everything?" Hensley asked, evidently still a few steps behind.

Ellis shook his head. "You can, of course, contest the will. Considering the tumor, you certainly have grounds."

"Sound mind and body and all that. I'd say you're on the right track." Hensley turned to Dave. "You concur? Of course you do."

Dave waved his question aside. No way would the will stand. But that wasn't what bothered him. He leaned forward "Wait. What time did Uncle Rex call?"

Ellis donned his glasses again and pulled out a bound log book from a desk drawer. He flipped it open with a ribbon marker and ran his finger down the ledger. "Two twenty-seven p.m. Central Time."

"And the time of death?"

He consulted a faxed document. "Three nineteen p.m. Central Time. Ms. Wright reported the death."

Dave paced behind the chairs. "So, Uncle Rex suddenly changes his will in favor of this woman, and an hour later she is present at his death."

Ellis nodded his head thoughtfully. "I share your concern."

From his leather nest, Hensley snorted. "Concern? It's plain as pudding. Wright was after the money." He raised a hand for a second, pointing a finger at Ellis, and then let it drop back to the arm rest. "And what's more, she got it."

"So it would seem."

"I want an autopsy with a full toxicology report," Dave said. "There's more to it."

Ellis made a note. "There is more. Rex stipulated that you travel to Cancún, inform Ms. Wright, and award her the balance of the estate. Personally."

Dave stopped pacing and stared at Ellis.

Hensley stirred in this chair. "Me?"

"Davison." Ellis turned a searching gaze on Dave.

Dave stared back. "Go to Cancún and hand over $200 million to a complete stranger?"

"I objected most strenuously. But he was emphatic on all points."

The more he heard, the less he understood. Evidently Rex had fallen down a rabbit hole and was determined to drag Dave down it too. Definitely not Rex, tumor or no tumor. Two days before his death he had been completely lucid, if somewhat introspective.

Dave stared out the window into the manicured gardens Ellis kept in the courtyard of his office complex. The money was secondary. Somebody had manipulated Rex and that took unprecedented skill, undetectable finesse, and great force of personality. More importantly, somebody had just murdered Rex, the one person left on the planet to whom Dave owed his life as he knew it. And he would be damned if he would let her get away with it.

He strode to the desk. "I'm your man. Give me the details, and I'll book a flight."

Hensley stood. "That's the spirit, Buckaroo. I'll go with you."

Dave looked at Hensley, startled. He had forgotten he was there. "Like hell you will."

Dave spent his time in the Philadelphia airport learning what the web could tell him about Endless Vacations. He quickly learned why Uncle Rex had booked his vacation through them, given his condition. Special-needs people liked to take vacations as much as the next person, but a dialysis machine wouldn't fit in your carry-on. What if you needed access to specialized treatments or supplemental medication, or replacements if your bags were lost or stolen in a foreign country?

Full facilities for people with special needs. For a price, which had been no problem for Rex, who had booked the most expensive package. But what about the half-million dollar deposit to AZ Limited?

Did it have anything to do with Masie Wright's scam? He thought not. Scamming a guy to change his will and then hastening his departure was the work of an opportunistic hustler out for the quick payoff. Setting up a shell corporation to take payments required an infrastructure, a different skill set, and a bulletproof exit strategy. His money said they were two different things, and for all he knew, AZ Limited was legit.

He pulled out his personal mobile phone. Harris answered on the third ring.

"Fletch? Where are you calling from?"

"I'm giving you a shot at redemption."

"Do you know where Rivera is?"

"I can tell you that, but I need something in return."

"I can't arrange any deals, Fletch. You know that."

"I'm not looking for a deal. I'm looking for information."

"What kind of information?"

"A company called AZ Limited. Who they own. Who owns them." Of course, AZ Limited had nothing to do with Rivera, but if Harris thought so, he would check it out and report back.

"Arizona? We checked the Tucson lead. It's a red herring. Rivera didn't go there."

"I have reason to believe they're laundering money, and they have a facility in Cancún. It's a small town. There might be a connection."

"He's in Cancún?"

"You get me the file on AZ Limited, I'll tell you where Rivera is."

The line went silent for a second. The PA announced pre-boarding for Dave's flight. Harris was too sharp to miss it, even if he didn't mention it.

"Okay," Harris said. "I'll look into it. But if you find Rivera in Cancún, you tell me."

"Send the file to my personal email account."

Dave started to hang up but remembered the last call. "By the way, Harris, why are you asking about Guzmán?"

Harris paused several seconds before responding. "Rivera might give us a way into the Sinaloa."

That's the part that hadn't made sense before. "But he was based out of Matamoros, probably with the Gulf cartel. And now he's based in Cancún."

"Which used to be Gulf territory before Los Zetas edged them out."

It took a few seconds for the tumblers to fall into place. "Don't tell me he's playing one against the other."

Harris didn't respond. After a few seconds of silence Dave checked his phone. They were still connected.

"Harris?"

"Look, Dave, you didn't hear this from me, but Johansson found the money."

Dave slowed down. "The money?"

"At the hangar. Twenty grand stashed in the Jenny."

Dave came to a stop in the Jetway. The guy behind him ran into him and then shoved past, dragging his luggage over Dave's foot. Dave looked back at the passengers lining up behind him and hurried up to the door.

"What are you talking about?" He nodded at the flight attendant as he turned down the aisle.

"Counterfeit. The whole thing looks like a setup to me, and I told them that. I'm just saying, watch your back." Harris disconnected.

Somehow Dave found his seat and dropped in it. That's what Rivera was doing in the hangar, working overtime to convince OPR that Dave was in bed with the cartels. Who should he tackle first: Rivera or Wright?

He studied the paperwork Ellis had given him, files from Rex's doctor, receipts from the vacation he had booked. When he deplaned in Cancún, he powered up his phone and deleted three frantic voicemails from Vanek. He got a taxi and then dialed the Endless Vacations number. He got hold music. After a few minutes the music stopped and a female voice came on.

"Endless Vacations. How may I help you?"

"I'd like to book a vacation to Cancún. The Aztec Gold package."

"That program is only available through referral."

"Rex Stone recommended it to me."

After the sound of a keyboard, a pause, and more keyboard, "Okay. We'll need a fax of your medical forms."

"No problem."

"And a five hundred thousand dollar deposit for medical emergencies."

"I have insurance."

"This is a very exclusive package." She sounded bored, like she heard this all the time. She continued in an if-you-have-to-ask-you-can't-afford-it voice. "The deposit is not optional. It will be fully refunded if it isn't used. If that's a problem, we can book a less expensive package."

"What is the purpose of the deposit?"

"If it helps ease your mind, the deposit is held by an independent company with no connection to Endless Vacations."

AZ Limited.

"They can only release funds to us if we provide documentation of medical expenses not covered in routine care. And all non-routine procedures must be approved by you or your designee."

"I see." Dave paused, as if considering. "I'll book a standard package for now."

He settled the arrangements, hung up, and tried to connect the dots. The AZ Limited thing was a part of Endless Vacations, the Aztec Gold package specifically. If what the booking agent said was true, Ellis should see a refund come through soon. As he suspected, AZ Limited had nothing to do with Masie Wright and her murderous get-rich-quick scheme. He wouldn't let it distract him from his main goal, two goals as he saw it. First find out how she got Uncle Rex to change his will, then find out how she killed him.

He thought about calling Angela. It would be good to hear her voice right now. But when she heard what was going on she would want to come down, and he couldn't afford to turn his attention away from his new goal, not even for Angela. Besides, if he didn't clear up this Rivera thing, he would have to step aside. He wouldn't take her career down with him.

Chapter Fifteen: Masie

All of Masie's instincts told her to leave town immediately. Go now, get away, they said. Pay the difference and change your ticket. You're crazy if you stay.

Masie usually paid attention to her instincts. They had saved her in a tight spot more than once. She felt guilty for disregarding such intimate, lifelong companions, but she stuck to the plan. Leaving so soon would send the wrong message.

In four days, she would be in Aspen, reveling in the break from the heat and humidity of Cancún, soaking up the solitude in the off-season. All she had to do was keep calm and carry on. And ignore her inner friends.

But the thing with Mr. Stone kept haunting her. She'd barely got a minute's sleep last night, seeing his body floating like that every time she closed her eyes. Then today the morgue called to inform her that Mr. Stone's family had claimed the body and preparations were in progress for shipping the remains to Pennsylvania.

They had showed up barely twenty-four hours after his death, but not soon enough for Masie. With any luck at all, things would be taken care of before Tuesday and she could leave the whole sordid episode behind.

She took the elevator to Paco's penthouse office, smiled at the secretary, and walked past him without a word. That was the way to deal with that weasel.

"He's with someone," the secretary whined, but Masie turned the handle on the door and entered.

"That's a bit much, even for me," Paco was saying.

He sat, trim and compact, behind his massive desk, his back to the view of the Caribbean as if it were boring compared to the world inside his office. He stopped talking as the nasal drone of the secretary came over the intercom

"Mr. Torres, Ms. Wright is here."

Paco held up a hand. "I'm a little busy right now, Masie."

Masie followed his glance to the man sitting in the leather chair in front of the desk. Mr. Rivera, a man for whom she had little use and even less affection. She felt guilty for disliking him, so she compensated with manners.

"Sorry to interrupt, but I thought you would want to know that Mr. Stone's family has made arrangements to transport the remains."

Paco nodded and returned to his conversation, effectively dismissing her, but Mr. Rivera's reaction cut off his sentence and froze Masie in mid-turn.

"Stone? Remains?" Mr. Rivera swiveled his massive frame in the chair to face Masie. "Which Mr. Stone?"

"Rex Stone."

Rivera turned to Paco. "Our Rex Stone?"

Paco glanced at Masie and then back to Rivera. "Ironic but true. He died enjoying the very service he helped to create."

"You mean . . ." Mr. Rivera's voice trailed off.

Paco nodded.

Masie didn't want to spend any more time in the presence of Rivera than absolutely required, but she paused before escaping. "What does he mean 'our Rex Stone?'"

"Mr. Stone provided the seed money for Endless Vacations," Paco said.

"He didn't mention it to me."

Paco and Mr. Rivera exchanged a meaningful glance. Meaningful for them, at least. It didn't mean anything to Masie.

"Why would he talk about his investments with a nurse?" Paco asked.

"You would be surprised what people will tell a nurse."

The two men did the glance thing again. Mr. Rivera regarded Masie with more interest than he had ever displayed in her. It didn't give her a warm, fuzzy feeling.

"Did his family call?" Mr. Rivera asked.

"I think someone came to identify the body before making arrangements."

Mr. Rivera looked through her with a thousand-yard stare. Paco studied Mr. Rivera as if deciphering a puzzle. Masie left, tired of the game.

Maybe she would move her ticket up after all. She didn't know if she could take four more days of this.

Chapter Sixteen: Dave

Dave's reservation was ready before his taxi reached the hotel. He found his room, showered, and went down to the restaurant. The maitre d' showed Dave to his assigned table for group dining, a feature in all Endless Vacations packages, as he had learned when he checked in. It encouraged cross pollination among the tourists, like on a cruise. The table for eight was empty. Dave ordered coffee and took a seat with a view of the door.

The first order of business was to hunt down Rivera and beat a confession out of him.

Or maybe he should locate this Masie Wright woman first, learn what he could without revealing his connection to Uncle Rex or raising suspicion. This project would require finesse. She was at the most critical stage in her scheme, more unnerving than the actual murder. She had to wait around at the scene of the crime, the one place every instinct would tell her to flee from, and act normal. Waiting for a stranger who would show up holding her fate in his hands. Not knowing if he would award her $200 million or arrest her. She was probably as jumpy as a counterfeiter at a numismatist convention.

The coffee arrived, and with it, a middle-aged white-bread couple who looked like they were from Minnesota. They sat as far from Dave as they could. He smiled at them.

"Hello."

They whispered to each other without taking their eyes off him. Dave shrugged and turned to his coffee.

The maitre d' appeared. A man stepped from behind him and took the seat to Dave's left. Dave turned to greet the newcomer and found Hensley looking back at him, dressed in black slacks, a black shirt, and a black jacket.

Hensley held out a hand in greeting. "Reginald Kite of Bishopsgate. I assume you've met the Hendersons."

Dave brushed Hensley's hand aside. "What is this?"

The whispering from the other side of the table sounded like a slow leak in an inner tube.

Hensley unfurled his napkin. "It's dinner. Followed by a floor show by Henry the Horse."

Dave leaned over and whispered fiercely. "What are you doing here?" Now that he thought about it, he realized he should have expected Hensley to show up.

Hensley tucked the napkin into his shirt collar and responded in his typical, less-than-subtle whisper. "It's my money too. Potentially, of course, pending the original will."

"Shh." Dave looked around, but nobody was nearby, except for the Hendersons, who pointedly avoided eye contact. "What do you care about money?"

"Says the man with plenty of it."

The chair to Dave's right moved. A slim woman with long, dark hair sat down and held out a hand. "It's Mr. Fletcher, isn't it? You just got added to my list an hour ago."

Hensley interrupted Dave's response by leaning across him. He grasped the woman's outstretched hand. "Reginald Kite of Bishopsgate."

She took Hensley's hand. "Masie Wright of Detroit."

Dave blinked involuntarily at the shock. In the worst development in the worst of all possible worlds, Hensley was shaking the hand of the prime suspect. A sense of dread nosed about in Dave's brain. Like the moment Hensley offered a martini to Angela, Dave felt powerless to prevent the inevitable catastrophe.

Hensley's eyebrows arched like two black cats on Halloween. "Do tell." He pulled his hand away and shot Dave a look that employed all the subtlety of a water balloon. Dave sneezed loudly into his napkin to disperse the insinuation.

A voice from behind him said, "Bless you, young man."

Dave turned to see a woman with the Shar Pei aspect of an octogenarian in a voluminous, full-length, flowered dress.

"Oh, my, a crowd already." She held out a white-gloved hand. "Mrs. Beauregard Crenshaw of Alabama."

Such was the power of Mrs. Crenshaw's antebellum aura that Dave and Hensley immediately stood. Hensley helped her to the seat on his left.

Masie did the introductions. "This is Mr. Fletcher and Mr. . . . ."

"Kite," Hensley said.

"Yes, Mr. Kite and . . ." She looked at the whispering couple. They didn't respond.

"The Hendersons," Hensley said. "Late of Pablo-Fanques Fair."

A waiter appeared with a bottle of wine and proceeded to fill glasses until he got to the Hendersons. They shook their heads vigorously.

Hensley cleared his throat and spoke loudly to no one in particular. "Mr. Fletcher was just telling me of his vast commercial empire in the States." His gaze came to rest on Masie. He looked at her archly. "And him the last of his line, with no family."

Dave kicked him under the table. A tightening of the jaw muscles was the only visible clue of Hensley's pain.

"Indeed?" Mrs. Crenshaw said. "How sad. Captain Crenshaw, God rest his soul, always said 'What good is money if you can't share it?' I thank God for my grandbabies and great grandbabies, all twenty-seven of them. We almost lost Bess last month to a bee sting. Allergic, the poor dear."

"Davison almost died from a driver ant bite in Angola," Hensley said.

"Davison?" Mrs. Crenshaw asked.

"Mr. Fletcher. As a child. He was telling me earlier."

"Indeed?"

Everyone looked at Dave expectantly, even the Hendersons. He had no choice but to play along.

"I swelled up like a pumpkin. Luckily Dad was a doctor and had anti-venom handy."

Mrs. Crenshaw smiled. "There's a mercy."

The waiter arrived, took their orders, and left.

Mrs. Crenshaw indicated the empty seat beside Masie. "It appears that Mr. Stone is missing dinner."

"I'm sorry, Mrs. Crenshaw," Masie said. "You didn't hear? He died yesterday afternoon. At the ruins."

"Oh dear, then he's missing a lot more than just dinner."

Dave studied Masie. Her eyes were a little misty, but her voice was steady.

"Who?" Hensley asked.

"A guest at the resort."

"He seemed like such a nice young man," Mrs. Crenshaw said.

"He met his demise at the ruins?" Hensley asked. "Fall from a pyramid, did he?"

"No. He had a seizure while swimming in the cenote," Masie said. "By the time I got to him, he was already gone." Her voice broke slightly on the last word.

In his twenty-five years of law enforcement, Dave had seen some excellent actors, but this girl topped them all. Not a trace of anxiety. He caught her gaze and held it. "That must have been awful for you."

Masie's gaze turned inward. "I'll never forget it as long as I live."

"I feel just terrible," Mrs. Crenshaw said. "I'm the one who recommended he go see the ruins."

"It's not your fault, Mrs. Crenshaw," Masie said.

"And so young," Mrs. Crenshaw said, "and the picture of health. Apart from the cigars and whisky, of course."

Masie shook her head. "He was far from healthy. Inoperable brain tumor."

Dave wondered how she knew about the tumor but then recalled the request for medical records when he attempted to sign up for the Aztec Gold package. So Masie knew he was terminal, a ripe target.

Hensley weighed in. "Let me offer a précis of the situation. A fellow with an inoperable brain tumor goes swimming in a bottomless sinkhole. I must say it's hardly surprising that it didn't end well."

A certain hardness crept into Masie's eyes and voice. "Apart from the tumor—"

"Oh certainly, apart from that."

The look Dave shot at Hensley should have left an exit wound, but Hensley just raised an eyebrow.

"Your tone is—" Dave started.

"He was in good physical condition. I gave him a checkup myself when he arrived."

"And then catapulted him off the deep end, no doubt," Hensley said.

Dave attempted another surreptitious kick, but Hensley had moved his feet out of range. Instead, he reached for the wine and knocked over Hensley's glass. "Sorry."

As Hensley righted the glass, Dave leaned across with his napkin to clean the spill. In a harsh whisper he said, "Cut it out."

"I think it's going quite well," Hensley whispered back.

Dave retrieved the wine bottle, blocking Hensley from Masie's view. "Keep it up and you'll be wearing this bottle of wine," he muttered under his breath. He sat down and refilled Hensley's glass.

In the interim, Masie had regained control of her voice and spoke more calmly. "Do you not think that people should be allowed to make their own decisions about how they face the final days of their lives, Mr. Kite?"

"What exactly is it you do here, Ms. Wright?" Hensley asked.

Masie inspected him like a defense lawyer sizing up a cop on the witness stand.

"She takes care of everybody," Mrs. Crenshaw interjected into the silence. "She keeps all my medications up to date, and that takes some doing, I can tell you."

In the following silence, Masie finally spoke. "What is it you do, Mr. Kite?"

"As little as possible."

After a longer silence spent scrutinizing Hensley, Masie turned to Dave. "And you, Mr. Fletcher?"

"I'm retired." He noted her expression as she assessed his age and health and added, "I've been fortunate. So far."

"Unlike the unfortunate Mr. Stone, whose death seems . . . most untimely," Hensley interjected.

"You've said enough. I think you owe Ms. Wright an apology."

"Every death is untimely," Masie said. "Particularly for the person involved."

"Oh, dear. Oh, dear." Mrs. Crenshaw attempted to escape from her chair. "I'm afraid I must take my meal in my room. Most upsetting."

Hensley helped her get free from the table. Dave stood also, as it seemed indecent to remain seated when Mrs. Crenshaw made an entrance or exit.

"I'm sorry if we've upset you, Mrs. Crenshaw." Masie pushed back from the table. "I'll talk to Armando." She chastised Hensley with a glare and left.

"Oh dear," Mrs. Crenshaw muttered to herself as she tottered to the exit.

Dave and Hensley watched her until she disappeared from view out the doors that opened onto the beach. Then Dave turned on Hensley.

"We agreed I would do this, just like Uncle Rex stipulated in the will."

"The will stipulated what you should do. It didn't say anything about me. I'm a free agent."

"A loose radical is more like it. This isn't going to work with the two of us here."

Hensley held Dave's gaze for a long moment, then pulled out his chair and sat back down. Across the table, the Hendersons whispered like a convention of rabid lawn sprinklers, glancing obliquely when necessary at Dave and Hensley, but they didn't abandon their posts. Evidently dinner was a great motivator.

Dave stared at the back of Hensley's head, resisting the urge to grab a handful of the thick hair and drag him out to the ocean. Questioning Masie any further would be pointless with him around. He would have to get Masie alone.

Chapter Seventeen: Masie

Masie found Armando in the kitchen and asked him to send a dinner to Mrs. Crenshaw's room and another to her own room. Then she skirted the dining room where the odious Mr. Kite lurked and stopped at the lobby bar.

"Noah, how about a cranberry and ginger ale?"

The bartender, a lanky guy in his twenties from some rural town in the States, spun a napkin in front of her. "Coming right up."

"Make it a double."

Masie took three deep breaths to settle her mind like Pop always said to do. The whole business with Mr. Stone was enough to set anyone's nerves on edge, but then to be interrogated by a stranger about it, well, it was too much, wasn't it? She thought back on the conversation. Had he actually accused her of killing Mr. Stone, or just being negligent? Not that there was much difference. Both were dangerous to a woman in her situation.

Who was this Mr. Kite, and why did he care? He wasn't an EV guest. He'd probably booked his room directly with the hotel. If he even had a room. She would look into that. He seemed like the type who would crash a funeral on the off chance of snagging hors d'oeuvres at the after party.

Noah set the drink in front of her.

Masie took a long, refreshing sip and thought about those last few minutes with Mr. Stone. The promise. Life without regret. He had told her to call him Rex.

"There are no coincidences," she said to herself.

In less than twenty-four hours he had changed her life. They had climbed the pyramid, him refusing help, and the possibilities that he opened up to her were as limitless as the view from the summit. All she had to do was act on it.

But the waiting was murder. She couldn't get to Aspen to plan her new life fast enough. Just a few more days, she reminded herself.

From the corner of her eye she saw Armando push a room-service cart through the lobby. She put a tip on the bar, slid off the stool, and waved at Noah. "You're a lifesaver."

Noah waved back.

She followed Armando down the hall to her door, tipped him, and went inside to eat dinner, her thoughts lingering on the afternoon at the *cenote*. She seemed powerless to push the image from her mind, the sight of Rex face-down in the water. Would it forever haunt her like a curse in a Dickens novel?

Aspen, her inner friends whispered.

"Too soon," she whispered back.

Rex's death should not affect her this way. She was no stranger to death. She was a professional nurse, after all, an RN in Detroit before she caught Paco's attention and a position at the Endless Vacations location in Cancún. And many of the EV guests were well past their prime. Death followed them like a shadow, threatening to catch up at any moment. A few had even died in her care, and it had not affected her the way Rex's death did.

Her thoughts drifted further into the past, back to the first time she saw a dead body.

—

When Masie is five, Mom goes to the Henry Ford Hospital in Detroit. She's supposed to bring back a baby sister, but Dad says that Colleen went to live with Baby Jesus instead.

When Mom comes home, she stays in her bedroom with the door closed. When Masie gets hungry, she goes in the bedroom and asks Mom for lunch, but Mom just turns to the wall.

After a few months, Mom finally comes out of the bedroom, but now Masie is used to doing the chores and making simple meals, so Mom spends her time watching the telly and sampling from the small city of medicine bottles she keeps on the end table.

After a few years, Mom is pregnant with Corey. She retreats back to the bedroom. Sometimes when Masie brings her a tray and finds her sleeping, she studies Mom's face, wondering what it's like to have another person growing inside you. It makes Mom sad, but Masie knows that other mothers don't act the same way. But other mothers are different in a lot of other ways, too.

Endless Vacation

Every time Mom wakes up while Masie stands there, watching and wondering, her unfocused eyes converge, take in her surroundings, and change from oblivion to confusion or pain or disappointment or regret or anger. Like she resents life for intruding on her sanctuary. Eventually Masie takes to setting the tray on the bedside table and leaving before Mom wakes up.

This time when Mom goes to the hospital she's supposed to come home with a baby brother. But she never comes home. Neither does Corey.

It's late at night, and Dad retrieves Masie from Uncle Brandon's house. They drive into town, and he leads her down a hall in the hospital. It smells funny, and their shoes clack on the tile, echoing in the shadows. He stops at the door of a room and picks her up like he used to, even though she is nine and much too large to be held. She doesn't mind. She puts her arms around him and buries her head against his neck. He steps into the room.

She doesn't want to look, but Dad stands as still as a statue for a long time and finally she straightens up and turns around.

Mom is on a bed under a sky blue blanket, her eyes closed, her hands at her sides. Masie expects her to look like she is asleep, but she doesn't. Her eyes no longer seem like they will slide open at any moment. She studies Mom's face, searching for the difference, for why she doesn't look like Mom anymore. She looks like something that is designed to move but never will, like a ship in a bottle.

Masie's tears stop. Mom isn't going to wake up, but maybe that isn't so bad. Life will no longer intrude. Maybe Mom is happier now. Maybe she's finally in that place that she resented returning from every time she opened her eyes. Maybe Masie is being selfish, wanting Mom to come back.

She looks at Dad. Tears run down his face. He makes no effort to wipe them away. He squeezes her without taking his eyes off Mom.

Masie hugs him and says, "It's okay."

———

It wasn't okay, exactly, but in time she had come to realize that it might be the best outcome that could be expected. Even at nine, she had sensed that life had become a burden Mom could no longer sustain.

Now, as an adult, Masie realized that Mom wasn't made from the stuff of survivors. She had lasted as long as her kind could be expected to live, perhaps longer. Some deaths were simply meant to happen.

So why did Rex's death haunt her? He was sick. At the most optimistic, his future could be measured in weeks, not years. Life had become an unsustainable burden.

Then why had she panicked at that last moment? Why, instead of accepting his death as fitting, had she felt that an obscenity had been perpetrated upon creation? Why was she haunted with this final image?

Masie glanced at the clock. After midnight. She pushed her thoughts aside along with her unfinished dinner.

There were things that must be done tomorrow. She picked up a gym bag, left her room, and went to the medical supply room. She made sure she was alone, slipped the key into the lock, and let herself in.

Instead of turning on the light, she flipped on a penlight. Holding it in her mouth, she unlocked the cabinet that housed the meds, removed a few items, dropped them in the bag, and locked it again.

At the door, she turned off the penlight, checked the hall, returned to her room, and stowed the bag in the back of the bedroom closet.

Day 5: Saturday

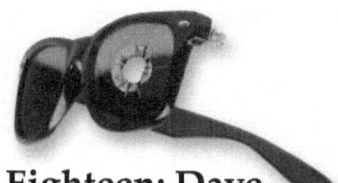

Chapter Eighteen: Dave

After a late breakfast, Dave found an umbrella table near the pool and sat down to figure out in which direction to focus his attention. He opened his laptop to check his e-mail. The first one was from Harris with a subject line of "AZ Limited." Dave smiled. Fast work. Harris must be desperate.

"Mr. Fletcher. How about a day excursion? Do you snorkel? Parasail?"

Dave looked up, saw Masie, and slammed the laptop shut. "Don't I need a checkup, first?"

Masie smiled. "Do you want one?"

Was she flirting with him? Was that how it had started with Uncle Rex? After all, Hensley had dropped a false lead the night before, that Dave was wealthy and single. He pushed the laptop aside. "I could use a break. Do you go along on the excursions?"

"No."

"But you went with that other guy. The one who died."

Masie squinted at him. "How do you know that?"

"You said you couldn't get to him in time."

She relaxed. "He booked a charter trip, just him and the driver. I had the time and thought he could use the company."

"Not because you were concerned for his safety?"

"No. He was in good shape. He dove right in and did laps."

Dave thought back to the diminished Rex who had bought dinner four days ago. She wouldn't have described him as being in good shape if she had known him in his prime. "That sounds strange."

"He brought his swimming trunks with him."

"No, I mean if he was in good shape and he's in a pool with no currents, how did he drown?"

"I didn't say he drowned."

True. She didn't. "Oh?"

Masie paused. "He had a seizure."

"And died instantly?"

"He dove in from a ledge several times, trying to swim down to the rocks. The water is as clear as air. You can see the bottom, but it's too deep to reach without scuba gear."

Dave pictured it—Uncle Rex in swimming trunks, maybe showing off for a pretty young lady who had spent the drive in the limo flirting with him. Maybe pushing himself too far. Or maybe he had some help.

"The last time he went twice as deep. Then he stopped by the dark side of the pool, where the cave opens up. For a long time, maybe ten seconds."

Masie took a few breaths and looked away, out toward the surf and the Caribbean. "He went rigid, jerked a little bit. Then he relaxed and floated to the surface."

She told a good story, rich in detail, like most lies. The image of Uncle Rex swimming one moment, floating lifeless the next, rushed uninvited into his mind. Dave closed his eyes and forced his mind away from Rex and onto Masie and what she had done, how she had convinced Rex to change the will, what she must have done to guarantee his death afterward.

He needed to keep her talking. "I can't imagine how that felt, a life-or-death situation miles from any help."

Masie nodded. "It was just . . ." She shivered. "I did what I could, but he was gone before I even got to him."

"That's right, you're a nurse. But you must be used to dealing with life-or-death situations. And he was a stranger, after all."

Her head shook slowly. "Actually, he didn't feel like a stranger."

Especially not after he made you a millionaire. "Why? What did he do?"

Masie sat down on the edge of the opposite chair. "We had a few hours to talk on the drive out. He asked me a lot of questions about myself."

Dave waited for the kicker, but that was it. He studied her face.

She blushed. "I felt a little guilty, but he seemed so interested."

Dave leaned back in his chair. She was very good. Was this how she did it? By being terminally cute? By reviving hope in a person who had no reason to hope? Perhaps she created an environment where a sucker felt like he had a chance after all. Then, with his emotions already out of control from riding the medical roller coaster, he would surf a wave of gratitude and be seduced into writing a large check or changing a will. It might work on some, but Rex was no sucker. How did she get past the defenses of a skeptical person?

"I'd consider an excursion if you came along. What do you recommend?"

Masie looked at him as if working a math problem in her head. Then, as she opened a brochure, a kid did a cannonball off the high dive, splashing water over them and the computer. Luckily, Dave had closed it.

Masie jumped up. "I'll get you a towel."

Dave watched her rush into the hotel. He felt his certainty begin to crumble. She seemed so likeable, so sincere. But she would, wouldn't she? He thought of Rex flying down here, alone, dying, full of regret, his guard down, his natural defenses obliterated. A Rex Stone no one else had ever seen. Dave had only caught a glimpse of it, and even then he had no idea what the man was going through. It filled Dave with sadness, but as he reminded himself of who was responsible, a thin wedge of anger crept in.

He wiped the laptop with his sleeve, opened it, and skimmed the email from Harris. "Shell corporations, subsidiaries . . . will take days to untangle. Great." Not that it mattered. Masie was the target, and she had nothing to do with AZ Limited.

A shadow fell across the keyboard. Angela stood across the table in a swim suit and a gauzy robe.

Angela! Dave jumped to his feet. "Angela. How did . . . What are . . . It's so good to see you."

He meant it, despite the complications it posed for his investigations. He didn't know how the hug looked to the tourists around the pool, but to him it felt like the best kind of medicine. A fraction of the weight of Rex's death fell away. He took a deep, shuddering breath and whispered into her hair. "I'm sorry I didn't call."

"You should be," she whispered back. "I had to hear it from your brother."

"Hensley?" The moment of relief faded. It seemed no aspect of Dave's life was immune to Hensley's interference. He pulled away and gestured to a chair.

Angela sat down. "I'm so sorry about your uncle. How are you holding up?"

Her sympathy exposed the raw nerves of Dave's grief. He took another deep breath and looked away to avoid cracking. "It happened so fast. He seemed fine on Tuesday, and then on Thursday he was dead."

Angela leaned across the table and took his hand. "I'm here now. We'll get through this together."

He wished it could be that simple, that he could spend the day with her talking about Rex, about the day he introduced Dave to the insider world of the Stone family, about the day he rushed a suit to the dorm so Dave could attend the St. Brigid Fall Mixer where Harris introduced him to Stephanie in his trademark James Bond manner, about the day Rex came to Warfield Hall to tell him that Dad had been killed by a stray bullet in Angola.

He wished he could just go to a funeral, say his goodbyes, and move on without the knowledge that Rex had kept secrets, that he had been killed for his money, that his killer would get away with it if he did nothing.

For the first time since he left college, he wished his life was different, that he was different. But the truth was that Angela's presence brought both relief and complications. She had a need to comfort him, and he had a need to expose Masie and avenge Rex's death.

She had come for his sake, but if he did what he needed to do, both for his sake and for Rex, it probably wouldn't turn out well. He wasn't sure how he would handle it, but the prospect was not promising, based on his track record.

As Dave struggled for a response, a hand holding a sweating glass of orange juice appeared between them.

Hensley offered the drink to Angela. "For you, my angel."

Chapter Nineteen: Hensley

Hensley opened his eyes and was immediately awake. It was a gift from his peripatetic life, the instantaneous transition from sleep to wakefulness, and from wakefulness to sleep. There had been many occasions in his journeys when total clarity and a rapid exit upon waking had been imperative.

But today there was no need for urgency. He was in a suite in a four-star resort and a *No Moleste* sign hung from the doorknob. He placed the time at 12:15, give or take, and sat up on the side of the bed. The alarm clock read 12:12. A fortuitous combination, an auspicious omen. He smiled and headed to the bathroom.

Sometime later he stood before the full-length mirror, evaluating his ensemble. He wore hemp sandals, white linen trousers, and a white linen V-neck shirt with loose three-quarter-length sleeves. The secret to traveling light was to trust that climate-appropriate clothing would be available at your final destination. A leisurely afternoon at the resort shop had provided everything he needed. Charged to the room, of course, which he had reserved using the credit card information he'd gleaned from Davison's computer after he left so precipitously.

Satisfied with his appearance, Hensley left the suite, flipping the *No Moleste* sign on the way out. Although he had learned to be content in all circumstances, there was no virtue in denying oneself fresh linens when they were there for the asking.

His first stop was the cabana bar. Nothing like a little fresh air and a nip of the hair. Being partial to juice in the morning, he ordered two large tequila sunrises from Noah, the lanky and accommodating bartender he had befriended the night before, and scanned the tables. Davison sat at a poolside table with Angela. Hensley smiled and added another drink to the order. Perhaps this would make up for the aborted tryst the night of his arrival in Austin.

Having devoted considerable thought to the issue of the will, Hensley looked forward to giving Davison the benefit of his advice on how to proceed with the mission. He thanked Noah for the drinks, writing in a generous tip on the ticket. Charged to the room, of course.

He circumnavigated a chaise lounge burdened with a middle-aged woman, a copy of *The Secret Life of Bees* lying on her face, and arrived at the table.

"For you, my angel." He handed Angela a sweating glass.

She smiled and took the drink. "Thank you."

He held out a glass to Davison. "Hey, you should put on some sunscreen."

Davison responded with more anger than one bearing the nectar of life would expect to encounter. He jerked the glass from Hensley's hand, took a drink, and coughed.

"What is this?"

"Tequila sunrise."

"I thought the orange juice had gone off." He looked at Angela and drank more deeply.

Hensley circled the table for a seat in the shade, passing between Davison and the roasting woman, when a bee swooped in and circled his head. Hensley swatted at it. It veered away, landed on Davison's back and crawled toward his neck.

Acting on instinct, Hensley snatched the book from the tanning woman's face, spun around and smashed the bee, slapping Davison in the back of the head.

Angela gasped.

"Hey!" Davison said.

The bee dropped to the poolside tile. Hensley squashed it with a hemp sandal and kicked it aside into a grate. He wiped the book on Davison's shirt and placed it back on the startled woman's face without comment.

Then he sat in the shade and sampled the sunrise. Quite good, that Noah chap.

Davison was wearing his tequila sunrise on his shirt and pants. A goodly portion had splattered on the laptop.

"Bee," Hensley said. "But don't worry, I got it."

"Gee, thanks." Davison wiped at the keyboard with his sleeve.

"Think nothing of it. What's a spilled drink compared to saving my brother's life?" He took another restorative draught and set the glass down. "I got up early so we could strategize."

Dave glanced at Angela and leaned toward Hensley. He spoke in a hoarse whisper. "Here's the strategy. You're leaving."

"Why would Hensley leave now?" Angela asked.

Ah. He had forgotten to brief her on the call. But of course, at that early date, he had not yet decided on his strategy or selected his code name. "Reginald," Hensley said. "Reginald Kite."

Angela frowned. "Not Hensley Fletcher?"

Hensley shook his head. "Down here it's Reginald Kite." He rested his forearms on the table and caught Davison's eye. "We have her precisely positioned for the psychological squeeze play. I'm proposing we employ the good cop, bad cop scenario. Which role do you prefer?"

"The only cop."

"Cop?" Angela studied Hensley. "Are you some kind of agent?" She turned back to Davison. "And you're retired. How could you be working a case? And in Mexico?"

Hensley realized he would have to read Angela into the case. Given her profession, she wouldn't be able to stop asking questions. He attempted to formulate an answer, but his gaze slipped past her to Masie, who approached with a towel, and he was forced to change tactics. He signaled Davison with a discrete wiggle of his eyebrows, with disappointing results.

"One more stupid comment like at dinner last night, and you'll blow the whole thing," Davison said.

Angela's gaze bounced back and forth between them and settled on Davison. "What's going on?"

Masie approached, regarding Hensley with a bemused expression. He calmed his eyebrows and smiled broadly as if nothing pleased him more than to see her right here, right now.

Davison stared at Hensley, unaware of Masie's presence. "You're getting on the next plane out of here."

Masie held out the towel to Davison. "Are you leaving us, Mr. Kite?" She looked from him to Angela with an appraising gaze.

Davison took the towel, surprised. "Something came up, and he has to go."

Hensley sat back in his chair and sipped his sunrise. Ultimately, Davison was powerless to force him out of the picture. He could afford to play it calmly. "Oh, I don't think it's finalized."

Davison wiped off the screen. "Oh, I think it is."

A chime sounded from Masie's pocket. She retrieved a phone and pushed a button. "Sorry, I have an engagement." She smiled and disappeared into the resort.

Hensley leaned forward again. "I have used my morning wisely in formulating a plan. First, to get the angel up to speed—"

Angela leaned forward to match his posture. "Is she the she in question?"

Davison tossed the towel aside and met Hensley's gaze. "This is the plan. I'll pay passage for you on that cruise ship over there." He gestured at the ship without breaking eye contact. "Unlimited food and booze. Cruise as long as you want. Final offer."

Angela spoke before Hensley could reply. "Nobody's going anywhere until you explain what you're talking about. Why did you call me? Is your uncle really dead, or is that just part of some kind of case?"

Hensley was saved from responding by the appearance of Mrs. Crenshaw, supported by a cane. "Good afternoon, Mr. Kite, Mr. Fletcher." She took in Angela with a long, disapproving stare.

Hensley stood like a schoolboy caught nicking the biscuits. Davison stood as well. Hensley didn't know why the woman made him feel guilty, but she did it without fail. He pulled back a chair for her.

"Good afternoon, Mrs. Crenshaw. Have a seat here in the shade. This is Angela Martini, official avenger of the aggrieved."

Mrs. Crenshaw nodded toward Angela with half-lidded eyes and sat down slowly, arranging a lumbar support pillow behind her back. "Thank you."

"Mrs. Crenshaw, are you familiar with cruises?" Dave asked.

"Oh, mercy, yes. I take a cruise every year. Sometimes two."

"Mr. Kite is dying to go on a cruise. I'm sure he'd love to hear all about it. I have to dry off this laptop before it shorts out."

Before Hensley could respond, Davison folded his tents and slipped into the offing. Angela followed. Hensley appropriated what was left of Davison's drink and turned to Mrs. Crenshaw. "Can I get you something to drink, dear?"

"I'd love a spot of English breakfast tea. With lemon."

Hensley strolled to the cabana, placed the order with Noah, refreshed his sunrise, and alighted on a bar stool to await the brewing of the tea. Much to Hensley's disappointment, Davison continued in taking a hard line, but Hensley had a purpose for being here. Yes, there was his half of the $200 million to consider, but more to the point, he'd been asked to come. By Rex, himself, may he rest in peace.

COME AT ONCE. SAY NOTHING TO DAVISON. -R

Although the reason was still a bit sketchy. Why come? Why keep it secret from Davison? Why had Rex summoned Hensley, the black sheep, in such a preemptory manner?

Despite the actual words of the message, Hensley sensed that it had nothing to do with him and everything to do with Davison. A distress signal. Hensley would stake his life on it. Well, maybe not his life, but at least ten bob or so. Twenty in a pinch.

But that was the rub. Davison was not in distress. In fact, he was sitting as pretty as any bloke in a catbird seat—great job, palatial house, sweet ride, hot girlfriend, if mismatched.

There had been a time when Davison clearly was out of his depth, a time when he needed a lifeline. Perhaps even a time when Hensley had failed him, although he would never admit it out loud.

———

Hensley is thirteen. The rainy season in Angola holds him captive in the clinic with the stifling scents of chlorine and ammonia. Hensley rolls up another bandage and tosses it on the pile.

Beside him, Davison carefully winds a bandage on itself, keeping the edges precisely aligned.

Hensley rolls up two more before Davison finishes the one. This will take all day if he keeps this up.

Davison clips his bandage and holds it up to Hensley. "Look, it's like the rings of a tree."

Hensley grunts and grabs another loose bandage from the basket.

Davison turns the rolled bandage in his hands. "I wonder how many people have gotten well because of this very bandage."

Hensley snatches it away and drops it on his towering mound. "Starting from now, none, if you don't speed up."

It's just like Davison to take an insufferably boring day and transform it into the world-class, Guinness-book-record-breaking most boring day in the history of the planet. Like rolling bandages is the most fascinating pastime in the world and each little ball of elastic a singular marvel.

The thing to do on a rainy day is read. If they can get through this pile of bandages, Hensley might be able to get in a few chapters of Sir Edmund Hillary's *High Adventure* before dinner.

Davison takes his perfectly wrapped bandage and places it carefully in his short but perfectly aligned row of other perfectly wrapped bandages. Then he watches Hensley roll up another bandage and toss it on his mound, which towers like Everest above the half dozen in Davison's row.

"That's not how you do it," Davison says.

"No, that's not how *you* do it." Hensley grabs another bandage. "This is the fast way."

"It's not supposed to look like a ball when you're done. It's supposed to look like a can of condensed milk."

"It unrolls either way." He tosses the roll on the mound.

"But Dad said—"

The door to the surgery bangs open. Dad walks in, drops a porcelain-coated tray filled with bloody instruments in the sink, and goes to the table where Davison and Hensley stand. He looks at Davison's row and Hensley's pile, then at Davison and Hensley.

Davison fidgets under the gaze, but Hensley returns it without flinching. The old man doesn't intimidate him anymore. He got over that on his thirteenth birthday, and he can tell that the old man knows it.

Without a word, Dad takes two bandages from Davison's row and returns to the surgery.

Davison opens his mouth, but Hensley cuts him off.

"Since you're so slow at wrapping bandages, why don't you clean that up and put it in the sterilizer?" Hensley nods at the bloody tray in the sink.

Davison glances at the tray and looks away just as quickly.

Hensley rolls another bandage as Davison closes his eyes and sways, his breath suddenly short and shallow. As Hensley tosses the bandage on the pile, Davison opens his eyes and grabs the table for support. Hensley's Everest quivers. Davison reaches to steady it, but the base shifts and the mound disintegrates under his hands.

Hensley stares at the balls rolling across the floor of the clinic. They will have to be unrolled, re-washed, dried, and rolled. At least an hour of work undone, obliterating his reading time. Well, not this time. He turns his fury on Davison, who looks back with a silent apology.

"I'm not washing those again."

He kicks aside the bandages on the floor and steps to the sink. He rinses the blood off the tray and instruments, rinses out the sink, plugs it, and fills it with water.

Davison drops to his knees and gathers bandages off the floor, still breathing quickly.

Hensley walks past him to get the antiseptic soap from the cabinet.

Davison frantically gathers bandages in his arms. He stands with a batch and sets them on the sideboard. Pointedly avoiding what is in the sink, he drops to his knees to gather more bandages.

Hensley lets out a breath. The poor kid is only seven and the old man works him like a galley slave, right in the surgery, even though he knows about the blood thing. He circles around Davison, pours in the soap, and swirls it into the water.

Davison stands and deposits more bandages on the sideboard without looking up. He kneels back down to get the rest.

Hensley reaches down with a soapy hand, leaving a smudge of pity on Davison's shoulder.

"It's okay, buckaroo. I'll take care of this. And you can teach me how to roll bandages when I'm done."

Davison nods, grateful and teary. He reaches for the last of the bandages. Hensley watches him, slowly realizing that nothing will ever change, that as long as he stays, the old man will work him like an indentured servant. Ten, twenty, thirty years from now he'll still be here, rolling bandages.

That's the day Hensley starts stockpiling provisions, smuggling little things over weeks and months like a prisoner in a concentration camp. He keeps them in a backpack under his bed, hidden behind boxes and books and stuff. Clothes, food, rope, matches, a knife, a compass, a little money, anything that would be useful on the road.

When he turns sixteen on their annual trip to the States, Hensley talks Mom into taking him to get his driver's license, not so he can run errands while in the States as he tells her, but so he will have some kind of ID when he finally leaves. He doesn't want to risk sneaking his passport out of the safe in Dad's office.

When they return to Angola, Hensley starts watching for his chance. A day comes when Dad is in the office catching up on reports for the Global Health Alliance, Mom is designing a better layout for the surgery, and Davison is trying to play soccer with the native boys.

Hensley stalks a Namaqua dove a quarter mile into the jungle, slingshot in hand. The sun bakes out the cool of the morning in wisps of steam, like clouds on the ground. He inches through the bush with the slow, steady movement of a minute hand on a clock. Two feet away, a sungazer lizard at the mouth of his burrow doesn't give Hensley a glance.

The dove flits down from a branch to a clump of turf next to the water and struts back and forth, picking at the grass. Hensley retrieves a stone from his pocket in a smooth motion. Dove breast makes an excellent brunch when roasted over an open fire, wrapped in banana leaves to keep in the juices. He lines up his shot.

Then, through what passes for silence in the bush, he catches the buzz of the prop plane carried on the wind in sporadic murmurs.

Hensley searches the sky. It seems too soon and not soon enough. Every day passing just like the last, working in the clinic, working in the garden, hunting, cooking meals, repairing things, slowly being absorbed by routine and vegetation and dirt and river, until he is invisible, just another vine, another tree, another ant bed, another sungazer. And then, just like that, it's time.

He lowers his slingshot and stands, sending the dove sputtering into the undergrowth and the sungazer scuttling back into his burrow. He lopes to the compound in easy, ground-eating strides and breaks into the clearing.

The sound of the plane catches up with Hensley. Mom comes out of the clinic. Dad stands in the door of his office and scans the horizon, shielding his eyes from the sun with a sheaf of paperwork.

The plane appears. The soccer players cheer and race to the airstrip, Davison trailing them gamely. Hensley stands in the shadows while everyone leaves whatever they are doing to watch the plane land and taxi in.

Once he's alone, he runs to his bedroom and pulls out the backpack. He slings it over his shoulder and takes a last look around the room. He's spent ten years in this place, more than half his life. Davison's bed is made, smooth sheets and hospital corners. His own bed is a rumpled mess of sheets and blankets.

Through the window, he sees the plane taxi to the edge of the clearing, the props spinning down and stopping. Mom is greeting the pilot. Dad directs the unloading. Davison dashes back and forth with boxes of supplies.

Hensley stares out the window for a long time and then slowly slips the backpack from his shoulder and lets it drop to the bed. Moisture fills his eyes as he returns the pack to its hiding place and goes out to unload the plane.

He continues this dance every two or three months—extracts the backpack from under the bed, stands frozen with fear, and then hides the backpack under the bed again—until one day when he doesn't slip the pack off his shoulder. Instead, he slips both arms through the straps.

He's still afraid to leave, but he's more afraid that if he doesn't leave now, he will never leave. He scans the room one more time and spots the red and green folders, faux-leather quad-fold albums with die-cut, coin-sized holes, one each for US pennies, nickels, dimes and quarters.

He shrugs out of the straps, unzips the backpack, slides the four albums in, and hoists it on again. He risks being discovered to pass them on to a bewildered Davison, not sure why he is doing it. A token? A payoff?

The sight of a tray with a teapot, a cup and saucer, and a lemon wedge startled Hensley from his reverie. He signed the ticket, leaving a generous tip, and threaded through the beach chairs to Mrs. Crenshaw.

It occurred to him that Davison did indeed need his help to extract the family fortune from the clutches of a charming scam artist. But he was still no closer to deciphering the meaning of the telegram. Rex couldn't have known about this situation several months ago.

Hensley could see now that things weren't going to be as simple as he thought when he booked the flight from Philadelphia. Davison was being stubborn, no surprise there, but this time it mattered. However, Hensley hadn't made it this far by sitting back and sipping umbrella drinks. Not all the time, anyway. Everybody had a weak spot. All he had to do was use the three Ps to find the one thing Davison wanted more than anything. Unfortunately, the thing Davison seemed to want more than anything was for Hensley to be on the other side of the planet.

Chapter Twenty: Dave

Dave scanned the lobby but didn't see Masie. He checked his laptop at the front desk, turned toward the shops, and ran into Angela.

She grabbed his arm. "Did your uncle really die or did you and your brother make it up?"

There was no way to explain, especially not standing in the lobby, and no time. As glad as he was to see Angela, this was why he hadn't called her. He was in investigation mode now. He had to move quickly without having to discuss everything before he did it.

Dave checked the area for Masie once more. "I need a shirt." He nodded toward a shop and ushered her in. He threaded through the aisles. "It's kind of complicated."

"There is way too much you're not telling me. Who is this guy? Hensley? Reginald? Why are you really here?"

Dave spotted a guayabera shirt in his size and pulled it from the rack. "Did he really call you?" He located the checkout counter, jerked the tag off the shirt, and handed it to the clerk.

"Yesterday. Said he was sorry for ruining our evening, that your Uncle Rex had died, suggested I come down."

Dave stroked her hair. "I'm glad you're here."

She hugged him, pressing the wet shirt against his body. "Me too. Now tell me what's going on."

He removed the wet shirt and put on the new one. They left the shop. Dave scanned the room again. No Masie.

He'd lost the trail already thanks to Hensley and his meddling. He turned to Angela, attempting to formulate some kind of story that would satisfy her. Laying out the whole Uncle Rex changing of the will story would take too long. "I need to take care of a few things."

"Of course. I came down to help you. What do you need?"

What did he need? A doppelganger, allowing him to be in two places at once. "This is something I have to do myself."

Angela laid her hand on his arm. "Dave, if you meant what you said Tuesday night, you're going to have to trust me. I'm through asking questions. It's time for some answers."

Dave opened his mouth to attempt an answer but caught a glimpse of a familiar figure passing by in unfamiliar clothes. Like Mrs. Crenshaw, she wore a flowing floral-print summer dress and a floppy straw hat that hid her face, but the similarity stopped there. Nothing could disguise that shape. Before Dave could react, Masie disappeared through the front door of the resort carrying a gym bag.

Dave regretted what he was about to do. He hoped Angela would understand later when he had time to talk. He shoved the wet shirt into her hands.

"Angela, I . . ."

He only had seconds, and a real explanation would take hours. He gazed into her eyes, squeezed her hand, and sprinted to the door. He arrived in time to see Masie get into a taxi. Dave ran to the next taxi in the queue, jumped in the back, and slammed the door.

The driver took a slow drag on a cigarette and regarded Dave in the rearview mirror with a sleepy expression. Angela rushed out of the hotel and looked around, still wearing the swimsuit, wrap, and sandals. Dave leaned forward, hiding behind a headrest.

"Can you follow that taxi without them knowing?"

The driver raised an eyebrow, glanced out the windshield at the departing taxi, and nodded slowly. "*No problemo, jefe.*" He lodged the cigarette in his lips and pulled out slowly.

Dave appreciated a greater sense of urgency in his taxi drivers, but he said nothing. As they accelerated, he glanced toward the hotel. Angela caught sight of him and they locked eyes as the taxi cruised out to Kulkulkan Boulevard.

Then she ran for the next taxi. He should have known Angela wouldn't go down without a fight, one of the many things he loved about her. But right now he had no choice. Either he followed Rex's killer or he briefed Angela on the whole mess. He couldn't have both.

Knowing he may have just alienated the one remaining person in the world that cared about him, he sat back in the seat with a loud sigh and glanced at the license on the front dash. Ernesto Garcia. The photo looked like a mug shot, but then so did the driver. A crucifix hung on a chain from the rearview mirror, along with a medallion bearing the likeness of Saint Christopher.

Ernesto kept well back from Masie's taxi on the long road from hotel row to downtown, letting a few cars get between them. He caught Dave's eye in the rearview.

"This woman, she is your wife?"

Dave ran his hand through his hair. "Is it that obvious?"

Ernesto shook his head. "It is the same old story."

Dave glanced behind. A taxi followed, too far away for him to identify Angela as the passenger, but he wasn't lucky enough for it to be someone else. Not this week.

In town, Ernesto expertly maintained a sightline with Masie's cab while keeping a few cars between them. Obviously this wasn't his first rodeo. They drove into an older section of Cancún. Adobe and stucco buildings lined the streets, interspersed with barren vacant lots where trash blew against the fences. There were no tourists.

A half block ahead, the taxi stopped and Masie got out.

Ernesto squinted at her and twisted in the seat to face Dave. "This woman, she is your wife, *jefe?*"

Dave pointed at the nearest corner. "I'll get out here."

Ernesto pulled the taxi to the curb and turned to look at Dave. "She is never your wife. Why do you follow her?"

Dave opened the door. "Long story. Thanks for the ride. How much?"

The driver gave him a long, hard look before responding. "Seventy. *Vaya con Dios.*"

Dave handed him a bill. "She's the one who'll need your prayers."

The third taxi stopped behind them. Dave darted into the nearest doorway, an appliance repair shop. He dashed behind the counter and through a door before anyone could object. A vacuum cleaner lay disassembled like a jigsaw puzzle on a workbench. The technician dropped a wrench and ducked behind a toolbox. Dave spotted a back door and headed toward it, grabbing a dirty, sky blue windbreaker from a hook as he pushed through the door to the alley.

He slammed the door behind him, lodged a trash can under the knob, sprinted up the alley to the cross street, and jogged back to the main street.

Dave paused at the corner to shrug on the jacket and look back to the shop entrance. The third taxi had already left. The driver rolled past, unaware of Dave's presence. Angela wasn't on the sidewalk.

He guessed she was in the repair shop, interrogating the clerk. She wouldn't last long. She was in swimwear after all. He'd lost her for now, and perhaps for good, but he couldn't afford to think about that now. He looked the other direction.

Masie was a block away. He eased into the flow of the foot traffic and followed her discretely, checking occasionally to make sure Angela hadn't picked up his trail. He wasn't too concerned. She hadn't spent twenty-five years as a field agent.

Masie glanced back frequently, as if worried someone might be following. But it wasn't Dave's first rodeo either, and he escaped detection.

He assessed his surroundings as Masie took a winding route, pausing at booths and shops occasionally and glancing back. She hadn't chosen a good part of town, but he'd been in worse. After a few minutes, she darted into a church.

Dave paused, evaluating his options. Going in the main door could attract attention. She might see him. He skirted the wall enclosing the grounds, searching for another entrance. On the side street he found a wrought iron gate opening into the courtyard.

Inside, children and adults stood in a line. A small girl sat on a table. Masie inspected the girl's eye, which was red and swollen. She took a small bottle from the gym bag, squeezed drops in her eye, and gave the mother the bottle and instructions on how and when to use it.

Dave had expected some kind of clandestine meeting. He watched as she treated several more patients. It appeared that this was exactly what it seemed, medical assistance to the locals. He would gain no more information covertly. Time to engage the enemy directly. He tried the gate. Unlocked. He pushed it open. The gate creaked and everyone turned toward him, including Masie. She didn't smile.

Chapter Twenty-One: Masie

Masie was surprised, not in a good way, to see Dave at the church. This could be a problem. She stepped away from the line to meet him in the courtyard. "Mr. Fletcher. Why are you here?"

"Why don't you just call me Dave?" He smiled and looked beyond her to the church. "Found it in the guidebook. Historic mission."

She doubted he had even seen a guidebook, much less read one. He probably followed her, but why? "It's a bit off the beaten path."

"That's what the book said." He nodded at the locals. "How about you? Why are you here?"

Masie hesitated. Her little friends, the instincts, told her to nip this in the bud. Nothing good could come of it. She studied him. He seemed nice, and she could use a friendly face right now, what with the little friends constantly harassing her.

"Children's clinic. Once a month." She returned to the table. Jose Luis sat on the edge, holding up his cast. She ran her fingers across it.

"Need some help?"

Masie inspected him. He had said he was retired. "Are you a doctor?"

"I spent a few years at a clinic in Angola."

"Angola?" Whatever she was thinking, it didn't include medical work in Africa. She had pegged him for the package vacation type.

"Global Heath Alliance. With my parents. It's been a few years, but I remember the basics."

Angola. Doctor. He said something about that at dinner. Masie shrugged, and he joined her on the other side of the table. Dave was a surprisingly able hand, even with the kids, and the afternoon passed quickly. The clinic was a welcome break from her usual duties, a small window of hope for the future sandwiched between weeks of patients for whom death was often a welcome alternative.

As the sun neared the horizon, the line finally dwindled down to a few, then one, then none, and she packed up her gym bag.

"Here, let me get that." Dave grabbed the bag. "Any good places to eat around here? I like getting out into the local scene."

"Actually, there's a good café just across the street. The *buñuelos* are excellent."

They left through the side gate, crossed the street, and found an empty table. Soon they had filled it with dishes.

Masie glanced at the mission wall. "I'd appreciate it if you didn't mention this to anyone."

He seemed puzzled. "Who are you, Mother Theresa?"

"I asked Paco to sponsor the clinic. When he said no, I just did it myself."

"Paco?"

"My boss."

"With supplies from Endless Vacations," he finally said.

She rushed to explain. "The cost is minimal. We waste more in a week than I use in a month at the clinic. But yes, it's not exactly allowed."

He continued to study her. "What happens if your boss finds out?"

Masie shrugged. "Maybe fire me. Maybe not."

He seemed surprised. "You risk your job for these people?"

"Jobs are replaceable. People aren't."

This guy was hard to peg. He seemed to be here on vacation with that Mr. Kite and the woman at the table, but here he was spending the afternoon working in a clinic miles from the beach. He seemed like a really nice guy, but then he treats the waiter with that attitude too many tourists had, as if they were servants, not people. And she still couldn't figure out why he was here. Was he flirting with her?

"What would you do with $200 million?" Dave asked out of the blue.

Masie laughed. "Go to Disneyland? It's not something I have to worry about, thank God."

"But if you did?"

"I don't know." Masie didn't waste time with what-if fantasies. Maybe when she was very young, but not since Mom died. "What does it cost to build a clinic?"

"It depends on where you're building. If you're not doing major surgery, it's probably cheaper to renovate an existing building."

At the next table, the waiter tripped, dropping dishes on the sidewalk. Masie jumped from her chair, knelt on one knee, and helped him gather the pieces. The waiter rocked back on his heels and shook his head.

Dave called from the table. "They have people to do that." He gestured at the waiter. "Him, for example."

Masie shrugged and continued cleaning. "I'm right here. I can help."

The waiter shooed her away. "*No problemo*. I take care of it."

Dave grabbed her elbow and pulled her back to the table. "If you're that concerned, just leave him a bigger tip."

Just as she had thought. A nice guy, but the kind who considered money to be the answer to any problem. "If you really want to help, you don't give money, you give yourself."

"But there's only so much of you to go around, and there's a lot of them."

Masie watched the waiter carry the broken dishes inside. "It didn't cost me a thing to help him, did it?" Her phone chimed. She checked the display. "I have to do rounds in half an hour."

They shared a taxi back to the hotel. Dave told her stories of stalking sungazer lizards and roasting Namaqua dove breasts over an open fire. Masie told him about the first time she tasted a strawberry.

It's her fourth birthday. Mom isn't feeling well, so Masie plays in her room. At lunch Mom comes out in her bathrobe, fixes Masie lunch, and goes back into her bedroom. Masie is through eating when Mom emerges, dressed to go out.

They carefully descend the outside steps to the bakery below their apartment. Mr. Byrne smiles when Masie comes in and calls to the back of the shop. His wife emerges from the kitchen with four cupcakes on a plate, each with a candle. The baker holds up a present.

Masie sits in the back of the shop with the baker's wife and eats cupcakes while Mom goes out. Then she opens the present, a doll with a bottle of milk. When she turns the bottle, the milk disappears, but it doesn't come out the nipple. When she turns it back over, there is the milk, again.

When Mom comes back, they go straight upstairs for a nap, but Masie can't sleep on her birthday. She plays in her room with the doll and the milk until she gets bored. She creeps out to see if there are more presents to open, like at Christmas.

The apartment is quiet. The afternoon sun slopes through the blinds, making stripes on the wall. Dust motes float in and out of the bands of light like microscopic faeries. Masie tries to catch them, but as slow as they are, they still slip between her fingers.

Then she hears footsteps on the stairs, and Dad stomps in, his lunchbox in one hand and a paper bag in the other.

"Daddy," she yells. "I got a doll."

He kneels down, and she collides into his arms. He sets the lunchbox down and opens the paper bag.

"Guess what I have, birthday girl?" He pulls out a large basket of red berries as big as her fist. He gives her one. It's shaped like a heart and has little black dots all over it, red and black like a lady bug.

"What is it?" she asks, dubious of the dots.

"It's a strawberry. Try it."

Dad takes a big bite out of one, and the juice runs down his chin.

"I don't like strawberries," Masie says.

"Have you ever had one?"

Masie shakes her head vigorously. "No, because I don't like them."

"Then how do you know?" He holds one up to her nose. "Smell it."

It smells wonderful, like a rose dipped in sugar. But the black dots worry her. She shakes her head, more slowly this time.

Dad smiles and gives it to her. Now she has one in each hand. "Just try one little pixie bite, and if you don't like it, I'll eat them all myself."

She reluctantly nibbles one. It tastes even better than it smells. She smiles and takes a big bite, the juice running down her arm to her elbow.

"There, you see?" Dad says, and then looks past her and his smile fades. He stands up.

Mom leans against the door to her bedroom. Her hair is messy, like she just got up, and her eyes are red.

"Are you feeling any better?" Dad asks.

"Look, Mama! Strawberries!" Masie says.

Mom gives her one of her smiles, the one where only her mouth smiles, but not the rest of her face, and looks at Dad. "Did you wash them?"

Dad doesn't answer. Mom walks across the room. Masie stuffs the rest of the strawberry in her mouth. Mom picks up the basket, takes the other strawberry from Masie's hand, and disappears into the kitchen.

"That's mine, for my birthday," Masie whines, following her.

Mom ignores her. She sets the basket in the sink and turns on the faucet. "I went to the doctor."

"What did he say?" Dad asks from the doorway.

Mom doesn't answer right away. She spreads the strawberries on a towel on the counter. "That we can't afford to buy strawberries out of season."

"It's her birthday, Caitlin."

"That this place is going to be too small," Mom says, starting to cry.

Masie wants another strawberry, but it doesn't feel like a birthday anymore. She stands in the middle of the kitchen, alone.

Dad puts his arms around Mom. "We'll get a bigger place."

Mom pulls free. "How? With what?" She gets a can out of the pantry and slams it on the counter.

"I'll tell Dad that we need—"

"What can he do?" Mom turns around. "Why are you home so early, Dec?"

Dad looks away.

She slams a pan onto the stove. "It's drying up, that's what. You can't see it. Brandon can't see it. But that doesn't change anything."

"I'll find something else."

"This whole town is drying up, Declan. There isn't anything else."

Masie begins to cry. Mom seems even sadder than she was before. Dad picks up a strawberry, sits in a chair, and pulls Masie to his lap.

"Look. It's all washed and clean."

Masie holds the strawberry, but she doesn't eat it.

Masie didn't tell him all of that, just the part about refusing to eat the strawberry, and then the joy of discovering that the world held such luscious surprises. But she remembered it all, the poverty, invisible to her in her innocence, the conversation she didn't understand until years later. The endless dance of affection and acrimony between Mom and Dad. The ebb and flow of crisis and celebration like the tides that determined Dad's schedule on the boat Uncle Brandon had inherited from Pop.

She glanced at Dave, who watched the boats of Nichupte Lagoon file past the right window as the cab approached Hotel Row. What was he up to, this tourist going off the reservation? Especially when, to all appearances, he had a companion back at the hotel? The mystery woman who wasn't at dinner last night but was at the pool today.

Masie decided to keep her distance. Whatever game he was playing, she couldn't afford to be part of it. Too bad, since he seemed nice enough.

Chapter Twenty-Two: Dave

Dave sat in the taxi and watched Masie go inside the hotel. It didn't feel right, his primary suspect a humanitarian worker who risked her job to help the locals. He had studied her the whole time but never caught a hint of larceny showing through the façade, much less murder. If it was a façade. Either she was good or she was very good. He couldn't decide which.

He told the driver to take him to the Mayan Palace. He hadn't heard from Rivera in forty-eight hours, and that made him nervous. Why would Rivera stay in town that long when he knew Dave was on his trail? And if he had tried to leave, why hadn't he called to get the key to the battery lock?

At the casino, tourists crowded the room like cattle in a holding pen waiting for the auction. Dave trolled through the ground floor before moving upstairs. Unlike Thursday afternoon, a crowd filled both floors. Fortunately, Muskrat still guarded the door to the private room. He recognized Dave and let him in.

A dozen illegal card games were in progress around the room. The fact that the Mayan had not been forced into compliance during the great purge of 2011 told Dave all he needed to know about cartel connections.

In the couches and armchairs, couples and small groups smoked cigars and cigarettes, drank their beverage of choice, flirted. Dave didn't find Rivera, but he did see someone winding through the crowd and the furniture toward him. The Kenny Rogers guy. He stopped in front of Dave.

"Didn't catch your name last time."

Dave held out his hand. "Dave."

"You're a cop."

No point in denying it. "Retired."

"How do you know Güero?"

"He sold me an airplane."

"The Jenny?"

Dave nodded.

Kenny gestured to an alcove that held a round booth. "We're blocking traffic." He signaled Andre, who came to the table with two tumblers of whiskey and two glasses of water.

Dave selected a glass of water and regarded it skeptically.

Kenny nodded. "It's safe."

Dave took a sip. Cold, crisp. Maybe he wouldn't regret it. "How do you know Rivera?"

"Part of the syndicate." When Dave raised an eyebrow, Kenny elaborated. "Investors for the casino."

"So you're an owner." Dave guessed he was Señor Soto, the manager Aguilar had mentioned. "You weren't here three months ago."

"Ah." He gave Dave a slow nod. "Was that you slinking around here asking questions? I was in Alaska hunting caribou."

Dave scanned the room, letting his gaze rest on the card tables.

Kenny shrugged. "You know how these things work. Some rules are more equal than others."

"So did the syndicate buy out Rivera's stake?"

It was Kenny's turn to raise an eyebrow.

"He's in a tight spot," Dave said. "He could really use the cash."

"If he got his butt in a sling, it's his own fault. It don't make it my emergency."

Dave nodded. "True, but he might not bounce back from this one."

Kenny set down his glass, picked up the whiskey, and took a sip without breaking eye contact. "You used Aguilar's name to get in here." He set the tumbler down deliberately. "Not going to have to do something I'll regret, am I?"

The ghost of a smile played across Dave's face. "You're from Texas."

"Texas, Mexico, who's counting these days?"

"But you live down here."

"Cheaper. Got everything I need."

Dave scanned the private room once more. He thought about the first floor, the public area outside the doors of the private lounge.

Kenny kept a clean establishment. The private room was a concession to American tourists who demanded more from a casino than pushing a button on a machine programmed to deliver a certain payoff down to five decimal points. Something with at least a touch of skill. He made the payments to Los Zetas, payments he would have to make anyway as the cost of doing business, and they made the private room possible.

The faces around the Texas Hold 'Em game from Wednesday flashed through Dave's mind. Older guys. Sixties and up. The syndicate was basically a solid, conservative retirement plan in a symbiotic relationship with the natural habitat. They didn't fancy a high-risk, high-growth portfolio.

Except for Rivera. The wild card. The kind you hope disappears. The geezers froze him out. No wonder Rivera hadn't left. He had no cash.

"What can you tell me about Aguilar?"

If a ponytail could prickle, Kenny's would have. He stepped out of the alcove. "I knew I would regret this."

Dave didn't move. "I'm just looking for help in finding Rivera. The question has to do with how much help I could expect from Aguilar."

Kenny hesitated.

"Obviously," Dave said, taking in the illicit room with a wave of his hand, "you must have an understanding with the local authorities." He shrugged. "Authorities of various types." Dave let that marinate for a second or two. "But I get the impression that Rivera expanded the understanding with certain types, perhaps beyond the scope of the original agreement. I'm asking if Aguilar might be part of that equation or if he would disapprove of it."

"I can't answer that question."

Dave nodded. "Fair enough. Let's bring this back to the Mayan Palace. I might be able to take Rivera off your hands."

Kenny sat back down slowly. "Thought you were retired."

"It's a favor for a friend. Another person whose life has been touched by the disaster with a belt buckle known as Güero Rivera."

The ironic smile spoke volumes. "Ain't it the truth?"

"But I have to find him first."

Kenny thought about this while he sipped the whiskey, then looked straight into Dave's eyes. "I ain't seen him since you left with him two days ago."

Dave set the water glass down. "Thanks for the drink." He slid out of the booth. "Good luck with the place."

Kenny climbed out of the alcove. "Stick around. Play a few hands. I'll comp the drinks, whatever you like."

"Tempting, but Rivera's out there, and he's not going to catch himself."

The smile spread across Kenny's face like spilled whiskey. "You get Güero out of my hair, you're comped for life."

Dave took a cab to the airport, but the Citation sat right where he had left it. Other than the casino and the Citation, he had no leads for locating Rivera. He'd have to wait for a phone call from either Kenny or Rivera himself. But that was fine. He had a killer to pin down.

Chapter Twenty-Three: Hensley

Hensley was the first to arrive for dinner. He sat alone at the table, sipping wine and wishing for the first time in his life that he had succumbed to the global craze and procured a cell phone instead of being reduced to spending half the day searching the resort for his brother. So far, Davison seemed to be getting the one thing he wanted most in the world, a complete and total absence of all Hensleys in his immediate vicinity.

Thirty-seven years was a long time to hold a grudge, but Davison had always been tenacious. And a little squeamish, but perhaps a career in the Secret Service had taken care of that. Then again, how often did a counterfeiting investigation require attendance at an autopsy? It wasn't like he was a homicide detective. Hensley wondered if he had done the right thing in coming.

He poured himself some more wine. The Hendersons arrived at the table, took their place opposite, and whispered between themselves like the endless waves outside the open veranda doors. Or maybe he really heard the waves. The other chairs were empty, the place settings untouched, the sculpted napkins still looking like salmon-colored cranes.

Mrs. Crenshaw arrived next in her antebellum glory. Hensley stood, Armando handed her off, and Hensley installed her safely in her usual seat to his left.

"Where is Mr. Fletcher?" she asked.

"Since last I saw you, it has been my sole endeavor to answer that question, but I fear I have failed." Hensley surveyed the room.

"And his . . . companion?" She said this as if the word hurt her tongue.

"I saw her after lunch, entering the spa. Said she needed some *me* time."

Mrs. Crenshaw's nostrils flared as if to say she wasn't surprised.

Hensley gestured to the table. "Maybe he's with the nurse, Masie, is it?"

"Oh, no," Mrs. Crenshaw said. "This is Masie's night to work the second shift."

Davison appeared, pulled out the chair on Hensley's right, and sat down. He picked up the menu and scanned it. "Did you order already?"

As cool as a cucumber in outer space. Well, Hensley could play that game. "Mr. Fletcher," he said as casually as a pickpocket. "Perhaps you could fill us in on how you spent your day."

"We can talk about it later over cigars." Davison leaned forward to look past him. "Mrs. Crenshaw, I've been meaning to ask you about the ruins you recommended to the unfortunate gentleman a few days back. Despite the tragic circumstances, I'd like to see them."

Mrs. Crenshaw's icy aspect thawed considerably. "Oh, they are wonderful, and not at all deadly under normal circumstances."

"Where are they located?"

"Captain Crenshaw and I always took a limo, and I paid no mind to the route. But Masie could tell you."

Davison shook his head. "I'd rather not discuss it with Ms. Wright. Do the ruins have a name?"

"If so, I've never heard it."

Armando arrived, escorting Angela. She wore a flowing white frock that contrasted nicely with her tan skin, still glowing from the ministrations of the spa gnomes. Hensley reminded himself that she belonged to Davison. For now, at least.

Davison stood to help with her chair. "I called your room. No answer."

Angela took the seat to Davison's right, where Masie sat the night they played good cop, bad cop. She looked at the Hendersons, who paused momentarily to assimilate her into the diorama and then resumed their clandestine conversation. Her gaze raked around the table, and she nodded politely. "Mrs. Crenshaw, Reginald."

She ignored Davison, grabbed a salmon crane, flipped it open, delicately smoothed it across her lap, looked at Hensley, and touched her wine glass. "Could you do the honors?"

Hensley poured the wine, a New Zealand Sauvignon Blanc as crisp as a head of iceberg lettuce. He held the bottle out to Mrs.

Crenshaw, who regarded Angela as if seeing the serpent in the vernal garden.

"No, thank you. I don't drink anything stronger than Earl Grey."

A sigh of satisfaction came from his right. Angela set down her glass and turned to Davison.

"I suppose you have what you think is a good explanation for this afternoon?"

From what Hensley could see, everyone wanted for the answer.

Davison glanced around the table before answering. "There were certain . . . details that needed attention."

The lines on Angela's face softened. "Oh, you mean Uncle Rex? I could have helped if you hadn't run off and—" A few lines reappeared. "And left me in the lobby holding a wet shirt."

"There were arrangements to make."

"But he died two days ago. What could be so urgent now?" She sniffed in his direction and leaned closer to his shirt. "And you reek of cigarettes. What kind of morgue has a smoking section?"

Hensley decided to intervene. The poor guy was twisting in the wind. "There have been some complications."

Angela regarded him with skepticism. "Of what nature?"

Hensley glanced at the Hendersons, their elbows on the table, leaning forward. They suddenly retreated into a hushed conversation. He turned to Mrs. Crenshaw. She studiously ignored him, evidently unwilling to get involved with anything that included Angela. He wasn't fooled. No self-respecting southern dowager would waste an opportunity to eavesdrop, but his code was sufficient to disguise the content.

"Nefarious complications. Questionable circumstances. Opportunistic outcomes."

Davison intervened. "Maybe we could talk about this after dinner."

"I thought he had a seizure while swimming."

"That is exactly what they want you to believe," Hensley said.

"They?" Angela asked.

"Hens—Reginald," Davison blurted.

"If I were to hazard a guess, I would suggest that Mr. Fletcher has been pursuing the prime suspect."

The frown lines on Angela's face vanished, replaced by a blank expression. "You don't mean . . ."

Hensley nodded. "Exactly."

"Not natural causes?"

The waiter arrived.

"Thank heavens," Mrs. Crenshaw exclaimed.

As she ordered, Davison stage-whispered, "We'll talk about this in my room after dinner. So let it go for now. Both of you."

Hensley nodded. A sound plan.

Angela didn't respond quite as graciously. She seared Davison with a glare, as if he were a filet of ahi tuna, and dismissed him by opening her menu.

Chapter Twenty-Four: Dave

In his hotel room after dinner, Dave flipped through the papers in the file Ellis gave him, searching for a name that might lead to information on what Masie did and how she did it. He found the revised will and held it up for inspection.

"Acilino Vega."

Hensley pulled his head out of the minibar. Eight miniature bottles of various kinds of liquor hung between his fingers like stalactites. "Try saying that after drinking one of these." He sat cross-legged on the coffee table, the bottles in a mound in front of his legs.

Scanning the room, Dave located Angela on the patio, leaning on the iron railing. He stepped next to her in the cool, humid breeze and watched the surf roll out of the darkness, beyond the reach of the hotel lights.

She spoke without turning her head. "I got the lagoon side. No waves."

"Nichupte Lagoon," Hensley yelled from the table. He opened one of the bottles and turned it up over his mouth.

Dave watched the wind rustle Angela's hair against her neck. He wanted to brush it back from her face, wrap his fingers around the back of her head, and kiss her. Instead he said, "King size. Plenty of space in the closet."

An empty whiskey bottle tumbled through the door to Dave's feet. Hensley's voice followed. "Nichupte Lagoon, Nichupte Lagoon, Nichupte Lagoon."

Angela cut her eyes toward Dave. "Don't press your luck. Right now in my book you're so low you need a ladder to tie your shoes." She glanced at the paper in Dave's hand. "So what's this?"

Dave pushed away from the rail, kicked the bottle back inside, and returned to the room. In his white linen clothes and wild hair, Hensley looked like a guru with a booze offering at his shrine.

Angela reached past Dave, took a bottle from the pile, twisted it open, and sat in the armchair.

Dave took the couch and held up the signature page from the will. "Acilino Vega."

Hensley downed another bottle. "Acilino Vega, Acivino Vega, Acivino Lega." He pointed the bottle at Dave, holding the neck like a chicken leg. "The limo driver."

Angela threw her empty bottle at Dave. "I file a motion to compel discovery."

"Rex was murdered," Dave said.

"But you said . . ." She looked at Hensley. "On the phone—"

"I was not authorized for full disclosure." Hensley opened another bottle. "I merely acted on my own initiative to issue a writ of habeas corpus." He waved the bottle at Angela. "And here you are."

"He changed his will an hour before his death," Dave said. "Leaving everything to Masie Wright."

Hensley nodded sagely, one finger alongside his nose. "The nurse." He emptied the bottle down his throat.

"Who was alone with him when he died," Dave said. "She told me so herself."

Hensley spread his arms, palms up, as if conferring enlightenment upon the world.

"Circumstantial," Angela said, although clearly she wanted to believe it.

"And now we come to Acilino Vega." Dave handed the signature page to Angela.

"The limo driver," Hensley said. "Acilino Vegas, Acili—"

"I get it," Angela said. "He drove the limo."

Dave smiled. Hensley's old-world charm was beginning to pale. Good. "And he witnessed the will. And he brought the body back to Cancún."

"But was he present at the death?" Angela asked.

Like Dave knew it would, her prosecutor's mind immediately ferreted out the holes in the case. But Dave's investigator's mind searched for the possibilities. "That's what I intend to find out. When I hire him for an excursion to the same ruins."

"And Bingo was his name. Oh." Hensley reached for another bottle.

Dave leaned forward, snatched it from his hand, and appropriated the pile. "Raid your own minibar."

Hensley shrugged. "It's all the same in the end."

"What exactly are you hoping to accomplish?" Angela asked.

"Evidence that she coerced Uncle Rex into changing his will and then murdered him."

"*Exactamente*," Hensley said. He regarded the bottles in Davison's hands with longing and took a deep breath.

"Evidence?" Angela said. She nailed Davison with a steely glare. "You're retired as of yesterday, and even if you weren't, this isn't an official investigation. You have no jurisdiction in Mexico. Any so-called evidence you discover is useless in the States."

Hensley whistled. "Could you say that a little slower? And pull my hair while you do it."

Dave extended a foot, shoved Hensley off the coffee table, and watched him roll to a stop against the door. Angela smiled with obvious satisfaction.

"I'm going for actual justice, not playing the odds in the justice system." Dave might not be able to get a murder conviction, but surely whatever he turned up would be sufficient to invalidate a last-minute will, and he had no doubt that a gold-digger would find the loss of $200 million a fate worse than death.

"And how are you going to enforce this actual justice of yours?" Angela asked.

From his place on the floor, Hensley slapped his hands together and rubbed them vigorously. "That's settled. Now let us adjourn to the cabana for libations and cerebrations. I'm buying." He arose from the floor with ease, despite the fact that he was in his mid-fifties and had recently folded his legs into a pretzel.

"I'll give it a miss," Dave said. Hensley would find some way to stick him with the bill if he came down.

"And you, milady?" Hensley bowed and held out a hand to Angela.

Angela looked at his hand, then at his face. "What am I supposed to call you, anyway? Hensley Fletcher? Reginald Kite? Mickey Mouse?"

"In Cancún, it's Kite. In the hinterlands, it's Hensley. Shall we?"

"She'll catch up with you if she wants to," Dave said. "I'd like a word with her first."

Angela cast a curious glance at Dave.

Hensley straightened up. "I shall number the moments and shower you with the same number of tokens of my undying affection when you arrive."

"So the longer I wait, the more I get?"

Hensley considered the question. "Perhaps the incentive is poorly constructed, but I trust you to discern the sentiment." He left, but not before liberating a miniature whiskey from the minibar. Dave made a note to ask housekeeping to empty his minibar until Hensley left town.

Angela sat back down in the chair and tucked her feet under her. "Was he flirting with me?"

"Hensley flirts with Mrs. Crenshaw, too."

She arranged her skirt, covering her legs.

Dave sat on the edge of the couch cushion and drank in the sight. The light fabric of the white dress just touched her knees, her calves and feet hidden, her hands tucked together in her lap. He thought back to the Amicus Curiae, his decision to change things. To avoid the mistakes he'd made with Stephanie. If they were to be together, they should do this together.

"I wanted to apologize for the last few days, ruining the weekend, abandoning you here all day."

Angela waited, watching him.

"And now I'm in the middle of this . . . investigation, and I can't say when it will be done. If you want to go back, I understand. But maybe you could come with me tomorrow. If you want."

"I don't know what you hope to accomplish. Anything you find—"

"I just have to know. Even if it doesn't change anything."

Angela nodded. "I can understand that. When do we leave?"

The relief melted the tension from Dave's body. "One o'clock. But if you're staying, you might as well move in with me. It's paid for."

"I said I was staying. I didn't say I was easy."

Chapter Twenty-Five: Hensley

Hensley found a seat at the cabana bar and signaled to Noah. In ninety seconds, he had a top-shelf margarita at his disposal. He didn't find himself conflicted as to the proper disposal of the contents. He took a long, appreciative sip, graced Noah with a Boy Scout salute, and settled in to wait.

Angela would be down within a few minutes. Of this he had no doubt. Davison was many things, but it could not be said that he charmed the ladies. He was less of a hale-fellow-well-met sort and more of a cut-to-the-chase-and-get-things-done type. Women found that appealing when they were ready to settle down and raise a family, but Hensley didn't peg Angela as that sort. She was a career girl all the way. As he saw it, he would do Davison a favor if he removed her from the roster. Entirely unsuitable was his verdict.

Hensley sampled the drink again, verified its value, and considered his plight. He was in a premier resort in the Caribbean with an unlimited expense account. All to the good. But he hadn't survived four decades as a citizen of the world by resting on his laurels. Like a good chess player, he always thought several moves ahead. From the beginning, he had been forced to learn urban survival skills to match his knowledge of the jungle.

After Hensley left Davison behind in Angola, he had traveled through a dozen countries, circumnavigating the Mediterranean from Morocco to Portugal the long way, scraping together a meal and a bed the best he could.

He quickly learned that the road to starvation was paved with sullen teen angst. In Tunis, a woman who took in laundry took him in as well, out of pity for his emaciated frame. She taught him French as a second language and extroversion as a third. He used his new-found fluency in both languages to cajole his way beyond odd jobs to a regular gig in a vegetable market. It lasted a month, longer than any job he had held.

As his urban survival skills increased, so did the length of his residency in any given location. After a few years he had progressed from weekly stays in hostels and flop houses to subletting a room from a coworker. His transportation evolved more slowly, from walking to hitchhiking to bicycle to motorbike.

When he felt time had insulated him from a repatriation attempt, he sent a postcard to Mom with his current address. She responded with money and a plea for his return. He sent the money back. He wasn't above charity. In fact, he would take money from anyone. Anyone except them.

The next time he moved, Hensley kept in touch with the family through Uncle Rex, who could be trusted to leave him to his own devices instead of tracking him down and forcing him to return. Subsequent envelopes from Mom, channeled through Uncle Rex, contained letters, primarily about Davison's exploits at boarding school, since life at the clinic was a static quantity.

A few years later, after an extended twenty-first birthday celebration in a Paris bistro, Hensley reevaluated his choices. He felt that this important milestone demanded a response on his part. Perhaps he should take life more seriously. No more living day-to-day, taking whatever came to hand. A thought formulated in his mind, crystallized into a vision. He would celebrate his next birthday in Scandinavia. With this long-term plan in place, he began working his way north.

Hensley is in Le Touquet, France for his twenty-second birthday when the telegram arrives. It reaches him at the resort hotel where he washes dishes when he isn't training for the Enduropale du Touquet, the three-hour off-road motorcycle race open to all comers, professional or otherwise.

His plan for today is to get in a few hours of riding between the lunch rush and dinner, but the telegram finds him first. He sits at a two-top in a corner of the deserted dining room, drinking brandy. When the bartender hears about the telegram, he hands Hensley the bottle and leaves him alone.

Transportation has already been arranged. If he wants to, he can get on a plane in a few hours and be back at the clinic in time for the funeral. If he wants to.

Hensley sips brandy and argues with the better angels of his nature. He escaped once. Is it wise to return? He tries to conjure the desperation that fueled his flight, but six years of survival against the odds has blunted the sense of injury and urgency he felt at sixteen. Why not return? After all, this moment isn't about the old man anymore. Now it's about Mom. And Davison. It was time he kept his promise.

He takes a final drink and carries the snifter and bottle back to the bar. The bartender nods.

Hensley slaps a ten franc bill on the counter. "Give me change. In coins."

The bartender places two five-franc coins on the counter. Hensley shoves one back at him. The bartender regards it blankly for a second, then replaces it with two twos and a one. Hensley shoves one of the twos back. The exercise continues until Hensley has at least one of every French coin in circulation.

He rakes them off the bar and deposits them in a pocket. "Tell Bernard I'll be back in a week."

In Angola, Hensley stands among the villagers when Davison gets off the plane. He hardly recognizes the fifteen-year-old in the salmon lacrosse pullover and Dockers dragging his luggage from the cargo hold. Hensley pushes through the crowd, approaching Davison as the natives shoulder the bags, and hugs him. Davison returns the hug awkwardly and pulls away. In that moment, Hensley knows Davison is lost to him.

For Davison's sake, Hensley goes along with the cover story of the stray bullet in a distant skirmish taking Dad by chance, but one look at the wound tells him it is little more than a polite fiction for the sake of appearances. He's surprised. Maybe the old man was hardest on himself. Is it possible that even Dad couldn't live up to his own expectations?

He reluctantly joins the tribal funeral, but even in the midst of it, he isn't a part of it. He's never really been a part of this place. It is one reason he had to leave all those years ago, to find his true home.

The ritual lasts most of the day—drums, procession to the grave, dancing, singing, praying, smashing bottles and dishes, and an extended meal that goes into the night, the warthog on a spit, the palm liquor.

Looking past the firelight, he sees Davison sitting on a stump, facing the field where he used to muddle through the soccer games.

Across the way, the clinic door stands half open, a dark spot in the shadow of a half moon.

Hensley sits on the ground next to him. "Remember how we used to roll bandages?"

Davison's head nods in the gloom.

Hensley does his best impression of the old man. "When done properly, they should look like a can of condensed milk." He laughs.

Davison shrugs. Hensley studies his profile.

"You remind me of him a little," he says. But only in looks.

From the day he was born, Davison has followed the rules, rolled the bandage in the accepted manner. He isn't the type to launch into the middle of nowhere and start a clinic, to follow a vision into the unknown, to brazen it out in the face of criticism and disdain at every turn.

Just look at him. A few years of prep school, and he has already morphed from Junior Explorer into Alex Keaton on *Family Ties*. He's not even Davison anymore, much less Dad.

The next morning, Hensley leaves before dawn, happy to quit the place he never belonged to and return to his native land, the rest of the world, where he lives by the law of the urban jungle—survival of the cleverest.

—

Hensley signaled Noah for a refill. Despite his personality, his position at the cabana bar, and prioritizing her at the top, Angela had not shown up. Perhaps he had misjudged her. She might even be moving into Davison's suite at this very moment. He forced his hyperactive imagination away from the scene and its implications and returned to the matter at hand.

Two things competed for his attention. First, as always, the practical—the possibility of a portion of $200 million. Not that he was feral, but neither was he daft. If a fellow had a shot at $100 million, making the questionable assumption that Rex liked him as much as he liked Davison, then he could afford a few days of effort to see if it could be had.

Then there was the telegram. Like thirty years before, Rex had summoned Hensley in his laconic style for a reason. And $100 million or not, Hensley would ferret out the reason. And perhaps snag the $100 million in the process. It wasn't exactly an either/or thing.

Day 6: Sunday

Chapter Twenty-Six: Dave

At the crack of ten, Dave ordered breakfast in and spent the morning tracking down Acilino Vega over the phone. He booked an afternoon excursion to the ruins. Next he called room service and arranged for a picnic lunch. Then he called the Mayan Palace. Rivera was still conspicuous by his absence. He dialed Rivera's cell from the burner phone. He got voicemail.

"Rivera, give me a call, let's settle the final details, and you can be on your way." He moved his thumb to disconnect the call but stopped. "One way or another, you're going to have to talk to me."

He disconnected, confident that Rivera wouldn't leave a multi-million-dollar jet behind in his mad scramble to South America.

Dave checked his email. Nothing more from Harris about AZ Limited, but it had been only twenty-four hours since the last email, and on a holiday weekend. Harris probably had a life and a wife. The third? Fourth? Dave had lost count.

At one o'clock, he slung his bag across a shoulder, went to the front desk, checked with the concierge about the picnic lunch, and surveyed the lobby. Angela sat at the circular bar drinking white wine. She wore a halter top and shorts.

Dave joined her, wondering again why a woman like her put up with him. He vowed not to make the same mistakes as he had with Stephanie. He moved the large sunhat from the adjacent stool to the bar and climbed on.

She leaned over, bumping his shoulder without looking at him. "Is it just the two of us?"

Dave noted a man with the appearance of a driver talking to the concierge. "That's the plan."

The concierge pointed toward Dave. The driver approached. A busboy emerged from the restaurant with a picnic basket, and the concierge directed him to Dave as well.

"Prepare for departure," Dave said, pushing back his stool.

The driver arrived first. "Señor Fletcher?"

"Acilino Vega?"

Vega nodded.

The busboy arrived. "Mr. Fletcher?"

Vega saw the picnic basket and took it. "Okay. This way." Vega led them out the front door to the limo next to the valet station.

Third back in the taxi queue, Dave saw the driver who had tailed Masie leaning against the hood of his taxi smoking a cigarette. He waved, trying to remember the name. Ernesto, that was it.

Vega opened the back door, motioned Angela in, and opened the trunk.

"We might want that on the way," Dave said, motioning to the basket.

"We will definitely want that on the way," a voice said from behind. Hensley approached in a safari outfit—khaki shirt and shorts, pockets everywhere.

"Good timing," Dave said.

"So it would appear."

Dave took the basket from Vega and climbed into the back seat with Angela.

Hensley stuck his head in and studied the arrangement. "I'll ride shotgun." He closed the door and climbed into the front seat.

Angela had the basket open already, digging through the contents. She pulled out a foil bundle and tore it open. "Tamales!" She grinned at Dave. "Early breakfast, working on briefs all morning." Reddish oil oozed down her fingers as she peeled back the cornhusk.

In the front seat, Vega argued with Hensley. Evidently he didn't want a copilot. Hensley overpowered him in his usual style and rapped on the glass partition. Eventually it slid down.

"What did you find?" Hensley asked.

"Tamales," Angela mumbled.

"Excellent." Hensley snagged a couple from the pack. "Any *cerveza* back there?"

Dave dug through the built-in cooler and found him a Corona.

"*Gracias.*"

Dave tossed a linen napkin from the basket over the seat and, not content to take the first thing he came across, dug deeper for the barbacoa soft tacos he had ordered.

Vega surveyed the lunch orgy, shook his head, and pulled onto Kulkulkan Drive.

Dave didn't know what he expected to find at the cenote where Uncle Rex died. It wasn't like he could detect a telltale footprint in the water. If Masie was involved, she probably had full knowledge of and access to drugs that would make it seem like a seizure. He hadn't seen any obvious puncture wounds on the body in the morgue, but he hadn't had the opportunity for a proper search. He had to wait for the tox report, but that was six to eight weeks out and he didn't have the authority to expedite it.

And there was the nagging thought that he might be on the wrong track. All the circumstantial evidence pointed toward Masie, but all the personal experience contradicted his suspicions. His twenty-five years as a special agent didn't settle the issue. His instincts had been wrong about as many times as they had been right. Experience had proved that there was no substitute for evidence, no matter what happened in the movies. Evidence for, intuition against, go with the evidence, even if circumstantial.

Regardless, Dave was certain somebody killed Rex. He thought back to their last conversation. At the end, he spoke in riddles, called him Davison. His last words were an apology. Dave wished he had argued, forced him to speak plainly. Then he might have understood instead of being left behind with a lingering sense of regret and bewilderment.

His thoughts turned to the first real conversation he had with Uncle Rex—the day he transferred from Braithwaite to Warfield. That led by stages back to the reason he changed schools, to the reason he was sent to boarding school in the first place.

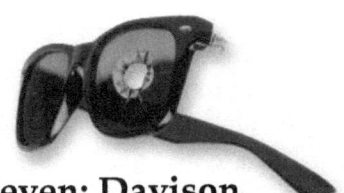

Chapter Twenty-Seven: Davison

Davison tries to stock the supplies that the natives have carried in from the plane, but he is only nine and most of the crates are too heavy.

Dad says, "Let Hensley get it." Then Dad glances around the clinic, and a hardness creeps into his face, the expression that often surfaces when he talks to Hensley. "Why isn't he helping?"

Davison ignores the question, his face suddenly burning, probably as red as a baboon's butt. He wrestles with the box.

Dad takes it from him. "Go find Hensley and tell him to get in here now."

Davison runs from the clinic without a word and slips into the jungle. He wanders aimlessly, knowing the search is pointless. Hensley said to tell no one, and he won't. Hensley is almost twice as old as Davison, and the only true companion Davison has ever known. He will tell no one, and Hensley will come back. Maybe not soon, but soon enough.

Later, in camp chairs under the pavilion canopy, Mom and Dad hold council over coffee, silhouetted by the sunset. Davison cleans up after supper, lingering near the window. He catches a phrase here and there, a parry, a thrust.

Too easy on him . . . pushed too hard . . . *when he gets hungry* . . . what if . . . *can't search the whole* . . . but the civil war . . . *made his choice* . . . just a baby.

Davison has no trouble hearing the last comment. "He's sixteen. And he's a Fletcher, not a Stone. He lives with the choices he makes."

Mom retreats to her bedroom. Dad storms to the clinic and slams the door. Davison sits at the kitchen table and looks at the gaps in the coin collection, careful not to stain the cardboard pages with tears.

Despite Dad's final word, the men of the village come together for a search the next day. One tracker finds a trail as far as the river, but loses it after that. Davison knows they won't find him. Nobody can find Hensley when he doesn't want to be found.

Three weeks later, he is still gone. Davison spends more hours in the clinic to pick up the slack. It takes a while, but eventually he is able to rinse the bloody utensils from the surgery without dizziness.

Mom cleans the house, turning it upside down and putting it back together. She does the same with the surgery. Then she takes to sitting in a camp chair, drinking tea and staring at the shadows in the jungle. Dad spends most of the time in the surgery, speaking only when asked a direct question, and then only in monosyllables. Eventually the cold front weakens. The late night conferences under the canopy resume, equally intense but less volatile, as Davison eavesdrops from the kitchen table.

Then one day as Davison works in the clinic, Mom comes in. The small row of correctly rolled bandages shrinks faster than he can fill it as Dad pops out of the surgery, grabs a handful, and pops back in.

Mom takes a clean bandage from the basket and rolls it as quickly as Hensley, but as neatly as Davison. The next time Dad pushes the surgery door open and reaches for a bandage, he stops and looks at Mom. Davison senses a conversation in the silence, Dad with his searching gaze, Mom with an almost-smile ghosting the weary expression she wears these days. She nods slightly, and Dad disappears back into the surgery.

Mom picks up another bandage and rolls it in a fluid motion. "Do you like working in the clinic?"

Davison shrugs. "It's okay."

"Would you like to learn how to do more?"

"Sure."

They work in silence for a while. He thinks about things. Mom in here, doing a job reserved for the boys. Asking questions. It probably has something to do with Hensley and the late night conversations just outside his range of hearing, but he doesn't know what. He likes the idea of doing something more important than rolling bandages and cleaning up, preferably something that doesn't involve blood.

"It's time we got serious about your education."

Davison stops, a half-rolled bandage in his hands.

Three months later Davison and Mom fly to the States. Davison feels a little more important than on previous trips to the big house where Grandmother and Uncle Rex live. No Dad. No Hensley. Just him and Mom.

There are more conferences, the adults ignoring him, involved in grownup talk while he explores the grounds. He circles the lake, feeding bread to the ducks and avoiding the nasty-tempered swans. A whole infrastructure exists out here, essential to and invisible from the main house. Beyond the landscaping and fountains and riding stables, vegetable gardens, orchards, chicken coops, goats, cows, any number of interesting things grow, eat, poop, live.

He pesters the help, and they accommodate the scion of the estate, allowing him to tag along with varying degrees of forbearance. Soon he is a part of the regular routine, enthusiastically doing chores the others dislike.

After a month or so, the day arrives when Davison discovers the implications of getting serious about his education. A series of shopping trips culminate in a drive to Braithwaite Academy, a boarding school that caters to the socially proud but financially embarrassed. His immediate family doesn't suffer from the first ailment but qualifies for the second. As long-time representatives of the World Health Alliance, Mom and Dad fall in the lower economic quintile of those aspiring to a private education for their children.

After a visit with the headmaster and a tour of the facilities, Davison stands in a dorm room with four beds. Uncle Rex stands outside the door in the hallway, studiously ignoring the scene within. Davison's trunk sits at the foot of his assigned bed.

Mom settles on the edge and catches him in the eye. "You study hard so you can come back and help your father. He's counting on you."

Davison doesn't respond. They probably counted on Hensley, but that is no longer an option. Now they're stuck with him.

"We'll come visit." She straightens his jacket and adjusts his tie.

Hensley's last words come unbidden to Davison's mind. *One day I'll be back to check on you.* But Davison has waited and watched, and Hensley hasn't come back. Davison is here in this room today because of him.

Later, Davison stands by his bed, the coin albums in his hands. At the window he watches Mom and Uncle Rex disappear through the trees flanking the long driveway. He spends the afternoon exploring the campus, the only boy here a day early. He finds the library and settles on *Treasure Island* to fill the time. As he reads, he becomes Jim Hawkins, at sea and fatherless.

The next day, as Davison reclines against the headboard of his bed and reads the part where Jim meets Ben Gunn, a chunky boy strolls in, a slim plastic box hooked to his belt. A wire snakes up from the box, splits at his chest, and extends to his ears. A tinny noise, like the dry-paper rasp of jungle insects in the summer, but more rhythmic, ekes out. The porter wheels in a stack of suitcases and leaves them just inside the door.

Davison closes his book on his finger to keep his place and swings his feet to the floor, sitting on the edge of the bed in anticipation of a greeting. The boy looks at Davison, eyes lingering on his clothes.

The boy is a catalog model in loafers, slacks and polo shirt. He has a sweater tied around his neck, the arms knotted across his chest. Davison sees his frayed cotton shirt, khaki shorts, and boots with the other boy's eyes and suddenly hates them.

Davison stands and holds out a hand. "Davison Fletcher."

The boy regards his hand the way he would a dog humping his leg, crosses to the other bed, and plops down on it, closing his eyes. Davison retracts his hand self-consciously, sits back down, and returns to his book. He finds it hard to concentrate on the story with the boy across the room so pointedly ignoring him, the scratching sounds coming from his ears.

Several minutes later, as Davison re-reads the same paragraph for the third time, another boy appears, a tall, skinny kid with flaming red hair that fights with the pastel orange Tommy Hilfiger shirt.

Hilfiger gives Dave and his outfit a cool appraisal and dismisses him. He turns to the other boy, the one with the ear buds. Davison watches them over the top of his book.

"Homeslice! Who's the narbo?" Hilfiger indicates Davison with a sideways nod.

Davison doesn't know what a homeslice is, or a narbo, for that matter, but evidently it is good to be the one but not the other.

Homeslice shrugs. Hilfiger points at the plastic box on his belt. "Is that a Discman?" Homeslice nods calmly. Hilfiger steps closer. "Trunkicular! What's the jams?"

Homeslice hits a button on the Discman and the buzzing stops. "Bangles. 'Walk like an Egyptian,'" he replies in a tone that drips with boredom. He turns to Davison.

"New Coke or Coke Classic?"

Davison blinks at him. "What?"

"Where do you come down on the question?"

"The question?"

Homeslice looks at him for a second and turns back to Hilfiger. "We have tickets to the premier of *Phantom of the Opera.*"

"No way."

"Way," Homeslice replies. He turns back to Davison. "I can't place the accent. Where are you from?"

"Angola," Davison replies. Perhaps he exists after all. He closes *Treasure Island* and sets it aside.

"Angola?" Hilfiger says. "Isn't that some kind of goat?"

Homeslice drills him with a weary expression. "It's in Africa, nimrod." He turns back to Davison. "Why?"

"What?"

"Why were you in Angola?"

Davison doesn't know how to answer. Why is anybody anywhere? You are where you are.

"What's that book?" Homeslice asks.

Davison holds it up. "*Treasure Island.*" He feels more like Jim Hawkins than ever. "Have you read it?"

Homeslice stands and walks to the door. "Come on, Mansfield. Let's get out of here."

Variations of this theme replay like a summer rerun throughout the next five years. Thanks to Uncle Rex, Davison adjusts his wardrobe to provide protective coloration, but due to Dad's no-charity stance, an economic divide denies him entrance to the fraternity of personal electronics, upscale hair products, and disposable income. Most students get a car the nanosecond they turn sixteen. Davison rides the bicycle he keeps chained to the back stair railing of the dorm.

In his isolation, Davison turns to the Stone family motto: I shall not be moved. He writes it across pen-and-ink renditions of the Rock of Gibraltar in his notebooks. He repeats it to himself when he becomes the butt of the inevitable social slight or practical joke targeting the narbo.

Five years later and three months into his freshman year at Braithwaite, Davison answers a summons to the headmaster's office. The administrative assistant gives him a smile of pity as she opens the door to the inner sanctum, but that doesn't give him a clue to the reason for the summons. She does that every time she sees him. When he enters, the headmaster looks up from his desk, nods, and gestures to a leather wingback chair reserved for visitors.

A man sits in the matching chair. He turns toward the door, sees Davison, and stands. It's Uncle Rex. He places a hand on Davison's shoulder and squeezes it slightly.

Uncle Rex delivers the news quickly, with a kind but businesslike air that makes Davison feel more grown up than he is. He doesn't even cry. He just sits there in the chair that is too large for him, listening, arms lying limply on the red leather and brass studs.

Dad is dead, killed in the renewed Angolan civil war.

From the newspapers and the letters from Mom, Davison knows about the peace treaty signed last year and how it disintegrated after the presidential election. It had never bothered him. The civil war dates from before Davison was born, but it has no effect on the clinic. Dad treats all comers and takes no sides.

Unfortunately Dad's neutrality didn't protect him from fate, which as Davison has learned in his science class, is really a word for the randomness of the universe. A minor skirmish erupted when a passing gang of MPLA soldiers stopped by the clinic for medication and stumbled upon a company of UNITA soldiers bringing their wounded for treatment. A stray bullet made it into the clinic. After two decades of patching up the locals, Dad found that all the revolutionaries' soldiers and all the president's men couldn't patch him up.

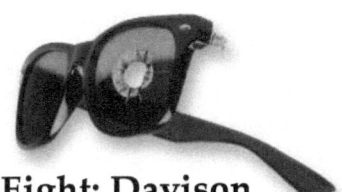

Chapter Twenty-Eight: Davison

Davison makes the trip alone—fifteen hours on a transatlantic jet to Johannesburg, three hours on a commuter turbo prop to Luanda, and four hours in a twin-engine cargo plane to the dirt runway in the clearing near the clinic.

As usual, the entire population waits at the end of the runway. Mom grabs him before his feet are on the ground. They hug for a long moment. The villagers watch in silence, the only sound the dying roar of the props as the pilot cuts the engines. Davison hugs her tightly, but he doesn't share in her tears.

As they approach the house, Davison sees a stranger towering above the natives, a tall, solid young man in his twenties with shaggy hair and a scraggly goatee. He is startled when the guy holds out his hand, smiling. He is shocked when the guy says, "Hey, Buckaroo."

Neither Mom nor Uncle Rex had said anything about Hensley.

The handshake becomes an embrace as Hensley pulls Davison in and swings an arm around his shoulders, squishing their hands between them. Davison hugs him lightly and pulls away, following the villagers with his luggage to the house.

The bedroom hasn't changed in five years—a dresser, a desk, a chair, and two single beds. An olive-drab duffel bag explodes with clothes in the corner by Hensley's bed, which is still rumpled from the previous night.

Davison unpacks, brushing his hands over the shirts and hoping the humidity will steam out the wrinkles.

Davison wonders how Hensley has survived on his own the past six years, but he doesn't ask. As far as he's concerned, Hensley walked out of the village and into oblivion. The thread that connected them has frayed and broken, along with his promise to come back.

He is here now, but it doesn't count. It isn't Hensley who has come back. It's a twenty-two-year-old stranger, smiling like nothing has changed, like he hasn't disappeared for the last third of Davison's life, left him alone to face the New World and its hostile natives.

The day after Dad's funeral, Davison awakes in his old bedroom, sticky from the humidity of the jungle and taunted by the aroma of bacon and coffee. He kicks the sheet aside and looks at Hensley's bed. Empty.

Davison swings his feet to the floor and rubs the sleep from his eyes. He sees something on Hensley's pillow. He stands, stretches, and investigates.

It's a pile of coins—pennies and dimes and a rainbow of other currencies. He sits on the bed and examines them. The years and markings for the US coins match gaps in the folders locked in his trunk at the foot of his bed at Braithwaite Academy.

He glances around the room. Hensley's duffel bag is gone.

That answers one question—what will Hensley do now that Dad is gone? Other questions remain unanswered, such as what will Mom do? And what will she do with Davison?

He dresses quickly and finds Mom in the kitchen, sitting at the table drinking coffee. She stares out the open door, absently fiddling with the rock necklace she always wears, a chip from Gibraltar. He sits in front of a plate and picks up a piece of bacon.

Mom smiles. "Morning, honey." She studies him. "It'll take a few days to catch up with the time zone."

"Hensley's gone."

She looks at him without seeing him. From her expression, he concludes that she didn't know. After a while, she exhales loudly and picks up her coffee. "He'll be okay."

"Where did he go?" Silence. "Where has he been all this time?"

She pinches a bite from a crumbling muffin and washes it down with coffee before she answers. "We have to let him find his own way, Davison."

He eats his breakfast. Hensley was about Davison's present age when he disappeared into the jungle. How did Hensley know what to do, what his journey should be? How will Davison know?

"Why did you marry Dad? Why did you come out here?"

Mom doesn't answer for a long time. He starts to wonder if she has even heard him, when she begins talking.

"He was different from anyone I knew. He was so . . . passionate. Unspoiled. Like a fresh apple in a bin of culls." She smiles absently, lost in memory. "And confident. He knew what he wanted."

Davison wonders how Dad knew. Did he see the possibility of what eventually happened and decide to do it anyway?

"When are we going back?" Davison asks between bites.

Mom watches him a moment before answering. "I'm not going back."

Davison stops with his elbow on the table, his fork in the air. "But it's dangerous. And if Dad isn't here you could . . . " He can't bring himself to finish the sentence, or even to imagine what would come next, in the sentence or in life.

She looks at the pendant she has been turning in her fingers, lets it drop to her chest, and reaches out to grab his hand. "Davison, you can't escape danger. But nothing is greater than the power of love." She brushes his fork aside and takes his other hand too. "That is the world I choose to live in, and if this is not such a world, I won't regret leaving it."

Davison is not reassured. His experience at Braithwaite Academy doesn't corroborate her worldview. The last six years have taught him that there are the few who matter and then there are the others. The ones who enjoy the largess or suffer the disdain of the whimsical few.

And as far as he can see, Dad is dead because of what happens when guns rather than social rank differentiate the few from the others. How did love figure in when Dad caught a random bullet? How did love figure in when Hensley left him behind?

Two weeks later, Davison is on a plane. Mom stays to keep the clinic going. At least until they can get another team in place.

Back in the States at the end of twenty-four hours of travel, Davison stumbles off the plane. Uncle Rex meets him at the gate, and they drive to Warfield Hall, where his trunk already rests at the foot of the bed. New school, new dorm, new room, new roommates.

It is Mom's one concession to the family now that Dad is gone. Davison will follow in the path of his Stone ancestors to the family alma mater, Warfield, and then Harvard.

Uncle Rex doesn't say much on the drive until they approach the school. "Davison, you're the last man in your family. Your life has changed in ways you don't fully understand yet."

He pauses as they turn into the school grounds. Davison's years at Braithwaite haven't prepared him for the stately grandeur of Warfield, some of the buildings over two hundred years old. As he stares out the window at the oaks lining the drive, Uncle Rex resumes.

"There are many ways to fail in life but only one way to succeed. Be true to yourself, discover the one thing you were made for, and then go do it." He glances at Davison briefly as if to gauge his reaction. "Reggie was a great man of high principles, maybe higher than he could live up to. But you are not your father. Bridget wants you to carry on the work in Angola. She . . ."

He falls silent, perhaps searching for the words. Davison pulls his gaze from the grounds, wondering what Uncle Rex will reveal about his own sister.

"She means well, and maybe she's right, maybe that is exactly what you should do. But only you can decide that, not Bridget, not Reggie, and not me."

Davison doesn't find any comfort in his words. Everyone else seems to know what they should do, and even what he should do. Maybe one of them is right, but which one?

They pull into a parking space with a sign that says *Reserved for Alumni of Warfield Hall*. Uncle Rex turns off the car.

"Now that you're at Warfield, keep your eyes and ears open. The most important things you learn will not be in the classroom."

Uncle Rex gets a box from the back seat, and they approach the admin building. If the grounds have not clued Davison into the differences between Braithwaite and Warfield, the entrance into the headmaster's office removes all doubt.

Dr. Sumner meets them at the door of his office as if he has been watching them from the window. His eyes bounce from Davison to Uncle Rex to the box. He holds out a hand. "Rocky! How did you know that a Cohiba was calling to me in the night?"

Uncle Rex shakes his hand and passes him the box. "Isn't it always, Gordon?"

"And this must be Bridget's boy. How was your trip, Mr. Fletcher?" He shakes hands like he's coaxing a particularly troublesome pump to cooperate.

"Fine, Dr. Sumner," is all Davison gets out before they are whisked into the office.

Once the box is opened and they all take their seats, Uncle Rex asks, "With whom do you have him rooming?"

"Harry's boy," Dr. Sumner says. He finishes lighting his cigar and tosses the cedar shaving into a large ashtray. "Remember Harry? He was a few years behind us."

"Right, the ambassador at large. Is he still in Moscow?"

"No, no, no. He's in D.C., grooming himself for a cabinet position in case his man wins this fall."

"I'll have to look him up. He owes me a steak dinner or two."

Dr. Sumner smiles. "Take a number, Rocky, take a number."

Davison's first extracurricular lesson at Warfield is in how long it takes two old school chums to catch up on old times and smoke a cigar. About an hour is his estimate, give or take. He sits through it all, trying to absorb the cataract of personal information for future reference, especially references to Harry and his son, Davison's new roommate.

Uncle Rex says his goodbyes to Davison on the steps of his dormitory. "Remember what I said. Call me if you need me, but only if you really need me."

Davison watches him return to his car and drive away, once again on his own. It seems the last few years have been spent watching someone leave him behind. He trudges up the steps, into the dorm, and finds his room. The door stands open. He enters. His trunk sits at the foot of his bed, his clothes already hanging in the closet.

There are two desks. The one near his bed is empty. A tall, slender boy sits at the other desk typing on a MacIntosh Powerbook 170. He studies Davison.

"Fletch, I presume, recently of Angola?" he says with a raised eyebrow.

Davison nods.

"I'm Harris." The boy stands and holds out his hand. "You're Rex Stone's nephew, right?"

Davison nods, again.

"So, which is your favorite Bond?" He waits a microsecond for an answer. "Not Roger Moore. Say it isn't Roger Moore, or I'll toss you right out."

Chapter Twenty-Nine: Dave

Dave stared out the window as the desert vegetation of the Yucatan peninsula flashed by the limo—stunted trees, cactus, agave. Thirty years ago, Uncle Rex had implied that Dad and Mom were well-meaning but deluded. Five days ago, Uncle Rex had said outright that Dave's parents had it right all along.

Who should he believe? The man in his prime or the man with the brain tumor? Which was more accurate, the euphoria of success or the ruminations of the dying?

Or the directives of the dead?

Dave wiped his hands on a napkin from the picnic basket and tossed it aside. "Señor Vega." The glass partition was still down. Angela and Hensley had finished their meals.

Vega glanced over his shoulder, then adjusted his mirror to meet Dave's eyes. "*Si, señor?*"

"On Thursday you took a man and a woman to these same ruins."

The eyes in the mirror were uneasy. "*Si, señor.*"

"The man died."

Dave felt Angela stiffen. Hensley leaned against the door, watching both Vega and Dave. But Dave kept his eyes locked on the man in the mirror.

Vega glanced at the road ahead and then back at Dave. "*Si, señor.*"

"What can you tell me about that trip?"

Vega waited a long time before answering. Eventually he shrugged. "It was much the same, *también.* I drive. They eat. They talk. They see the ruins."

Dave waited, but Vega was done. "And then?"

The driver let out a long breath. "And then he die. *Lo siento.*"

"But before he died, he talked to you."

Vega nodded but said nothing.

"About what?"

Vega crossed himself and muttered, "*Madre de Dios.*" He glanced back at Dave and then held his gaze in the mirror. "I do not kill him, Señor Fletcher."

Dave nodded slowly and deliberately. "I know you did not kill him. But I also know you talked to him. You signed your name." Dave pulled the signature page of the revised will from his bag and handed it to Hensley, who held it so Vega could see it.

Vega crossed himself again. "He talk to someone on his computer. He show a paper, ask me to sign it to say I see him." He shuddered. "This is all I do."

Dave nodded again to show he believed the man. "What happened next?"

"The man go to the cenote. I stay with the car. Smoke. Wait." Vega shrugged as if to say this was his job. To wait. To smoke. To drive.

"And the woman?"

"I do not see the woman until she come to tell me the man is dead."

"How did she seem, this woman?"

"*Cómo?*"

"The woman. How did she act? What did she say?"

Vega nodded eagerly. "Yes, this woman, she is . . . wet and she is very . . . *agitate. Lagrimas.* Crying."

Angela raised an eyebrow raised. "Crying?"

Hensley waved her concern away and turned to Vega. "*Cuánto tiempo?*" He made a writing motion with his hand. "How long after you signed the paper?"

"*Una media hora?*"

"Half an hour. Plenty of time to do the deed and then compose herself for her performance."

"Really?" Angela asked.

Dave didn't answer.

"Years ago I was living in a tent in a patch of woods in Bulgaria when winter hit," Hensley said. "The nicest woman I ever met took me in. I later learned she had ten children and sold them all into prostitution."

"Is he serious?"

Dave shrugged. Who knew when it came to Hensley?

"In China I saw a monk who lived peaceably in poverty for decades almost kill a man over a bicycle. When he found out the man hadn't eaten in three days, the monk sold the bicycle to buy him a meal. Seemed like a nice guy."

Angela looked from Dave to Hensley and back to Dave.

Hensley half-climbed over the seat and dug around in the cooler for another beer. "The moral of the story is 'Don't mess with a man's bicycle.'" He grabbed another Corona and settled back down into his seat. "So the question is, did Uncle Rex mess with her bicycle?" He took a long pull from the bottle and wiped his mouth with the back of his hand. "Or, in the vernacular, did she have a long conversation on the drive to the ruins and see her meal ticket?"

The turnoff to the ruins took a narrow dirt road that cut through the vegetation like a ditch. After a few miles, the scrubby plants gave way to sparse, thirsty grass and larger trees, ten to twenty feet tall. Beyond, a pyramid rose above the horizon, gradually emerging into full view as they came to rest on the edge of the clearing.

At the ruins, Vega got out of the car, leaned against the front fender, and lit a cigarette, but Dave asked him where he first saw Rex's body. Vega led them to a gap in a cove of trees.

The pines on the outer perimeter stopped on the brink of the sinkhole. Dave looked down into the exposed interior of a karst cave, the limestone roof worn away by millennia of running water until it collapsed. The passage of time had created a grassy bowl with stone outcroppings poking through, rimmed with pines and willows, sloping down to a rocky bank. Some kind of aquatic grass choked the shallow water at the near end. The grass faded as the bottom dropped away. On the far side, a wide rock apron provided the launching platform that Masie had spoken of.

In his mind, Dave saw Uncle Rex diving off the rock ledge, swimming deep as Masie watched from the hill. In the last few hours, the sense of loss he felt when visualizing Rex's death had slowly been replaced by a controlled anger, a fierce determination to bring retribution on the head of the person responsible.

Vega pointed to the pebble beach on the shallow end. "*Allí.*"

Dave slowly descended the slope. The two stories matched, Masie's and Vega's. Masie pulled him to the shallows and then ran for help. But what happened while Vega leaned against the car, smoking a cigarette after signing the will?

"Thank you, Señor Vega," Dave said, waving him back to the limo before continuing down the slope.

He set his bag on a rock, stripped down to a t-shirt and a swimsuit, trotted around the edge to the rock platform, took several deep breaths, and dove in.

According to Masie, Rex dove off here, went down twenty feet or so, and examined the side of the pool. Dave did the same, pushing and clawing with powerful strokes until he noticed a dark spot to his right. A tunnel. Dave swam toward it and felt cold water pushing back, the underground stream that fed the cenote.

Dave did his best to keep his depth while staring into the black hole. Had Rex seen something here? His own death, coming for him, overtaking him seconds later as he tried to outrun it? Deep into the blackness of the hole, he saw a flicker of light distorted by a current.

He tried to swim toward it, but he was out of breath. He shot to the surface and sucked in a lungful of air.

"I thought this was an investigation, not a pleasure excursion." Hensley sat cross-legged on the diving rock.

Dave caught his breath and searched the banks for Angela. He found her wading in the shallows. He swam toward her, his feet eventually reaching solid ground, and pushed through the grass to the bank. Then he took a towel from his bag and dried off.

"I was checking Masie's story. Rex dove from that spot, stayed under looking at the back wall where that dark spot is, and then had his seizure."

"Find anything?" Angela asked.

"A tunnel, the spring that feeds the pool."

"And what does that get us?"

"I don't know."

"Nothing," Hensley said.

"Perhaps," Dave said.

He pulled on his shirt, focused on a spot on the bank above the spring, and circumnavigated the pool until he reached that spot. Then he examined the ground and began to climb the slope of the sinkhole. He topped the edge without seeing anything and edged down the other side. The slope was shallow, of course, since there was no sinkhole on this side. The ground leveled off, and he followed the slope around to the right. That got him back to the gap that Vega had led them through. He kept going, circling the crater. At the three-quarter point, he found something. A hole.

Chapter Thirty: Dave

In a cluster of yucca at the base of the outside slope of the cenote, a crack in the ground about three feet long and two feet wide revealed the black ripples of the underground spring that fed the cenote. Dave knelt and submerged his hand in the water. Icy cold.

"What's that?" Hensley asked.

The others had followed him. Dave pulled his hand out. "The spring."

Hensley circled around for a better view, but Dave stopped him with a wave of his arm, releasing a spray of water.

"Wait."

Next to the crack, the dirt was disturbed. Dave searched for a pattern in the chaos. He squinted, saw the repetition of curves scattered through the random smudges. Like a snake. He rocked up from kneeling to crouching and widened his perimeter. An unnatural shape came into view. Straight lines. Ninety-degree corners. A rectangle about one foot by two feet, give or take.

"Somebody put something heavy right there," Angela said.

"And a bunch of round things over there," Hensley said.

Round things. Coils, but not of a snake. "Cable," Dave said. "And—" He pointed at the rectangle.

"A generator?" Hensley asked.

"Too noisy," Dave said.

"A battery. A big one," Angela said. "Still circumstantial but more compelling. Not that it matters, since it's all unusable."

"And what looks exactly like a seizure?" Dave said.

"An electrocution," Hensley said.

Angela leaned in for a better view.

"She's good." Hensley observed Angela as she inspected the evidence. "Very good."

Dave shoved him back a few steps. "You may have a few pounds on me, but I can still take you."

Hensley staggered backward. "No, not her." He caught his balance. "Although she is good, no question. I meant Masie."

Dave waited for the explanation.

"Who else knew Rex's medical history?" Hensley gestured to the prints in the dirt. "Who else knew how to reproduce the same symptoms as his disease to get a fortune without having to wait for natural causes?"

"Yes, but . . ." The pieces didn't all snap into place. There were annoying anomalies. "This requires preparation and premeditation on a pretty grand scale. Getting the equipment out here without anyone noticing, including Vega."

"Unless she cut him in on it."

"But she didn't know about the money ahead of time. Rex didn't change the will until they were already out here. Until just before he died. No time to set it up."

"Advance planning. The price of financial freedom is eternal vigilance. She played the odds, got the infrastructure in place in case she got lucky. Which she did."

Dave shook his head.

"Who else had the knowledge?" Hensley asked.

"Ellis. And Rex's doctor."

Hensley surveyed the desert surrounding the cenote. "And the opportunity? And the motive? My money is on the money. No need to look any further than the one who gets $200 million out of the deal."

Dave locked eyes with Hensley. "Would you kill for $200 million?"

Angela studied the prints in the dirt. "Immaterial. He's not the suspect." She joined them. "But it seems possible that somebody killed your uncle, and Hensley is right. The prime suspect is the beneficiary."

"Thank you, ma'am," Hensley said.

"But all this is academic. It would be nearly impossible to prove." She gestured to the evidence, such as it was. "You need a whole department to run this down, find out where she got the battery and the wire, how she got it out here, and where she took it after. You are no longer an agent, and even if you were, you have no authority in Mexico and anything you discover can't be used in court."

"I don't care about what can be used in court. Whoever killed Rex is not going to get away with it. I'm not leaving until I know."

"I'm with you. What do we do next?" Hensley asked.

Angela shook her head and turned away, muttering something like, "of sound mind."

"We don't do anything," Dave said. "You can go back to the resort and continue running up your bar tab or go home, wherever that is."

"Whether you like it or not, this concerns me just as much as it does you."

"You're just here for the money. You didn't care a thing for Uncle Rex, or anyone else."

"You may recall that I arrived when there was no discussion of money or wills, because Rex was still alive."

"Broke and looking for a place to stay. What happened? Took you forty years to burn every bridge in the world, one at a time? Did you decide to start back at the beginning for another round? What did you think, that we'd forgotten?"

Angela reappeared in the periphery of Dave's vision. He ignored her, focused on Hensley. The expression on Hensley's face could have been remorse or empathy or something else. Dave didn't care which. He didn't want an apology or pity. He just wanted Hensley as far away as possible, as soon as possible.

"Davison, I—"

"It's Dave," he shouted. "Nobody's called me Davison since Dad died. If you had stuck around, you might have figured that out."

"I did what I had to do. You know what it was like. Dad and his—"

"You never meant to come back, did you? You said that just to keep me quiet, to give yourself more time to get away."

"I was going to—"

"I kept quiet for weeks, months, just a dumb kid believing his brother would keep his promise. I never told them. Never."

"Davison—"

"It's Dave! And it's too late to come back now. When you burn a bridge, it stays burned."

"You know what Dad was like. Nothing was ever going to change while he was there."

Dave's hands tightened into fists. "Dad didn't care if you came or went. You didn't leave him. You left me."

Dave lunged at Hensley, hitting him in the chest with his shoulder like a linebacker, wrapped his arms around him.

Angela shouted, "Dave!"

He barely heard her above the sound in his head like rushing water, the backside of the cenote a blur in his vision as they staggered to the ground and rolled against the yucca. Dave pulled back to punch Hensley, the body beneath him convulsed, and he suddenly found himself tumbling back.

As Hensley struggled to his feet, Dave rolled, attempting to knock his legs out from under him, but he did a forward roll over Dave, who hit the trunk of the yucca instead. Dave scrambled to his feet to see Hensley come up from his roll and spin around to face him.

"Boys," Angela shouted. "You're wasting your energy on the wrong enemy."

Dave closed the distance in two steps and feinted a left to the chin. Hensley dodged it without appearing to do anything more than slouch to the side. Dave followed with a right uppercut, but Hensley batted it away. Dave lashed out with a kick and caught him in the gut. Hensley staggered back, stepped on a dried ocotillo branch, and went down.

In a split second Dave was on him, one knee on his chest, his arm cocked back for the strike. A kick to his side knocked him off Hensley and the breath out of his lungs.

Angela stood above him. "If you want to walk back to the hotel, keep at it. But I'm leaving." She disappeared around the curve of the banked wall of the cenote.

Dave pushed to a sitting position and tried to regain his breath. He glanced at Hensley, who sat pulling ocotillo spines from his sandal.

"You keep away from me," Dave said, favoring his ribs as he climbed to his feet. "I'll deal with Masie." He pointed a shaking finger at Hensley. "You just keep away." He held his hand against the pain in his side and followed Angela to the limo.

The drive to Cancún seemed twice as long as the drive out to the ruins. No one spoke. Halfway back, Dave's phone beeped. A voicemail. Only one bar of service. No way of knowing when the call was attempted. He hit the button and listened to the voicemail.

"Very funny, my friend. Okay, I'll play your game. A trade. But maybe not the trade you imagine."

Evidently Rivera wanted to leave. Did that mean the syndicate had finally bought him out? Dave called the Mayan Palace and navigated through the gatekeepers to Kenny.

"You have good news, I trust," Kenny said. "Is the package taken care of?"

"As near as dammit. One question. Did he shake any cash loose from the partners?"

"Easier to get milk from a milkstone."

"All I needed to hear. Thanks." Dave smiled and disconnected.

Dave saw the unspoken question on Angela's face from the corner of his eye, but he had no desire to discuss Rivera with her. If things went as planned, the OPR investigation would go away and no longer pose a threat to her career or their relationship. If it went off the rails, there would be nothing to talk about.

Rivera must be insane with desperation by now. He needed two things—cash and the key to the battery lock. If he had somehow scored the cash from Los Zetas, he'd be highly motivated to disappear before they realized he'd crossed the aisle to work with Guzmán.

Dave dialed the phone.

Rivera answered on the first ring. "Where are you?"

"Here's what we're going to do. You're going to contact Harris and provide whatever information is required to discredit your previous statements and establish the real nature of that account."

"I do not think it will work that way, my friend."

"When I get confirmation from Harris, I'll call you at this number and tell you where to find what you need."

"No, here is the way it will work. You will bring me the key, or I will call Harris and give him certain information about Rex Stone."

It took Dave a few seconds to overcome his confused silence. "What information?"

"Information that could have his accounts frozen, perhaps have his estate confiscated."

"Don't talk nonsense. There is no such information."

"Quite to the contrary, *mi amigo*. For many years, I have assisted Mr. Stone in certain, shall we say 'investments' in varying shades of legitimacy. Some high risk, high reward. Some of the kind that could interest our mutual friend Harris. For example, he provided the original seed money for Endless Vacations."

It had to be a bluff. Rivera was desperate. "I don't think so. If you want that key, you'll make that phone call."

"If I make that phone call, it will not make you, it will break you. If you need verification, ask your lady friend."

Dave glanced at Angela. She squinted at him with suspicion. He looked away. "Who?"

"The nurse. Masie Wright."

Chapter Thirty-One: Masie

Like every Sunday afternoon, Masie sat in the front seat of Ernesto's taxi surrounded by cloth bags. But as Ernesto drove her to the market, she couldn't stop thinking of Rex in the cenote.

Her instincts continued to beg, to plead with her to change the ticket, as they had done continuously for the past four days. She had become adept at ignoring them by thinking of other things, and the more she thought of Rex, the more her mind wandered back to Pop and Lake Erie and model ships, back when Dad drove her out to stay with her cousins while Mom was in the hospital.

The cousins have all gone to school, Uncle Brandon is out on the boat with Dad, and Aunt Dana is busy with the laundry. The big gloomy house is like a cave. Masie explores the grounds and ends up at the little gingerbread house in back where her grandfather lives.

The door stands open. The smell of Pop wafts out—pipe tobacco, coffee, and donuts. Masie stands on the threshold, curious but cautious. Then a voice calls out.

"Well, come on in, then, but keep your hands in your pockets."

Masie doesn't have any pockets, but she enters. There is an old rug on the floor and even older furniture. The pictures on the wall are black-and-white photographs of people dressed like in the old movies. The men have black suits, white shirts, skinny ties, and hats. The women also wear hats, with little fishnet veils in front.

"Back here," the voice says.

She finds a doorway. Pop, wearing half spectacles low on his nose, sits behind a desk. He holds a bit of wood in a set of long tweezers. In front of him, a large bottle lies on its side, a half-built ship inside, just hull and deck.

"Sit there." He gestures to a chair in front of the desk.

Masie climbs in it and sits down. She watches as Pop smears glue on one end of the piece of wood and then sticks it into the bottle, slowly and carefully positioning it on the deck of the ship. He holds it in place for a long while, then just as slowly pulls out the tweezers.

"There." He sets the tweezers aside. "That's the mizzenmast. You know what that is?"

Masie shakes her head.

"Hasn't your Dad taught you anything?"

"A rhinoceros has a horn, but it doesn't honk," Masie volunteers.

Pop smiles. "Oh, so he told you that one, did he?"

"A full house beats a flush," Masie continues.

"Oh," Pop says in a different voice.

"And you can use the top button to mend a shirt because nobody uses it anyhow."

"Don't they?"

"No, it's an extra." Masie looks at Pop's top button. It's fastened.

Pop leans forward with a serious expression. "Here's a bit of advice, little sponge. Listen to everything your Dad tells you, because he's your Dad. But always verify it."

Masie has never considered the possibility that Dad might be wrong about something. She finds the thought disturbing. She looks at Pop's top button as if it has betrayed Dad.

Pop continues to study her. "Do you mend your Dad's shirts?"

Masie nods. Once, Masie asked Mom if she could help, and she's been doing it ever since.

Pop stands, shuffles to a cabinet, grabs a box with a puffy lid, and brings it back to the desk. Needles and pins stick out of the top. He opens it, removes a spool of thread and a button, and sets them in front of her. He picks up a small white triangle of cloth sitting next to the ship-building materials and sets it beside the thread.

"Show me how you sew on a button."

Masie picks up the spool, measures a few arm lengths of thread, and bites it off. She sticks one end in her mouth to wet it, twirls it into a point, and threads the needle on the first try. A few minutes later, she has the button on. She ties it off and clips it with her teeth.

Pop inspects it, turning it over and over. His hands are brown and wrinkled and rough, like the saddlebag on Dad's bike. "Do you like sewing buttons?"

Masie nods. Pop carefully pushes the ship in the bottle to one side, goes to a shelf lined with bottles of various sizes, and selects the largest one. He sets it on the desk.

"Come around here and sit in this chair," he says. He takes a tool—a wooden handle with a long metal rod flattened on the end—and dabs it with glue. Then he slides the tool into the neck of the bottle and paints the beams on the back of the ship inside the bottle. "This here is where the poop deck goes." He sets the tool aside, selects a small piece of wood, grasps it with the long tweezers, and gives it to Masie. "This side is the top."

Masie looks at Pop, then at the wood, then at the ship. She slips the tweezers into the opening, keeping it away from the sides, and moves the chip of wood over the back of the ship. Her hand quivers with the strain of holding the tweezers closed. A muscle spasm causes her to drop the chip into the hold of the ship.

Pop takes the tweezers from her and positions the decking across the bow where she can retrieve it.

"Try again."

Masie takes the tweezers, picks up the wood, hovers above the spot, and then sets it down squarely in its place.

"Steady, now," Pop says.

Masie releases the wood and slowly pulls the tweezers out. Pop takes them from her, picks her up, sits down in the chair, and sets her in his lap.

"My oldest grandson can't do that, and he's three times your age."

The Pop aroma envelopes her. It's like the smell from the bakery on the first floor under their apartment, like a spirit that fills her room and wakes her up when it's still cold and dark and makes her snuggle down into the blanket and dream of cupcakes and cookies.

Pop picks up a pipe, strikes a match, and puffs on it. When he has it going good, he holds it in one hand and looks at her. "How would you like to build your own ship, Sponge?"

"Yes, please," Masie says. Dad sometimes plays with her in the evenings, after his shower, but during walleye season he always smells like fish. And since her birthday and the strawberries, Mom spends most of the time in her room, reading magazines or sleeping and sometimes crying. And there is no one else to play with.

"First we have to find the right ship."

Pop sets her on the desk and searches through a bookshelf. He doesn't even tell her not to meddle with the tools and glue and wood and cloth next to her, like grownups usually do. He slides his finger along the spines and selects a big picture book. He clears the desk and takes her back in his lap.

Before he opens the book, Masie says, "I want to make a boat like the one Dad works on."

"Oh, that's an ugly thing," Pop says.

Masie frowns.

"But it's a good one," he adds. "I bought it when your Dad was no bigger than you. But it's not pretty enough to put in a bottle." He opens the book and flips through the pages.

"That's pretty."

"Yes, it's very pretty. That's the *Queen Margaret*, built in Scotland. A four-masted barque. But it's not a good starter ship." He flips the page. The next one has twice as many sails. He flips the page. "What about this one? The *Minotaur* from Australia."

It's a small boat with two masts and red striped sails. Masie shakes her head and he turns the page.

"I like that one."

"The *HMS Revenge*. Very famous, that one. Sir Francis Drake's flagship. You'll need help with the sails and rigging, but you might be able to do it."

"That one," Masie repeats.

"The *Revenge* it'll be, Sponge," Pop says. "But it will take a long time. How old are you now?"

"Almost five," Masie says.

"You might be six before we're through."

"When I'm six, I get to go to school," Masie says.

Dad doesn't come to get her that night or the next one. Masie spends her time with Pop picking out the wood and helping him cut it into miniature planks for the hull. He tells her of the exploits of the *Revenge* against the Spanish Armada in 1588 and of her final battle in the Azores in 1591.

When Dad finally comes to get Masie, he says that Colleen didn't come home. She went to live with Baby Jesus instead. When they climb the stairs to the flat, Mom is asleep with the door closed. The next day Mom stays in her bedroom. Dad makes Masie breakfast before he goes to work, fried eggs and tomato on toast, his favorite. When she gets hungry, she goes in the bedroom and asks Mom for lunch, but Mom just tells her to go away. Masie finds some sausage in the refrigerator and eats what is left.

In the coming months, Masie spends the weekdays fending for herself and the weekends with Pop building the *Revenge*, dreaming of adventure and glorious battles at sea.

———

Twenty years later Masie took her first voyage on a freighter from Detroit to Cancún for her new life as the medical liaison for the new Endless Vacations destination. Paco sent her an airline ticket, but she exchanged it for passage on a cargo ship.

It was nothing like she imagined sailing the seas on the *Revenge* would be, more like inching across the waves on a floating warehouse, but she started every morning on the deck with the sun at her side and the wind in her face, bound for paradise, smelling the brine and imagining Spanish treasure ships laden with gold returning from the New World only to be met by privateers and broadsides and bounty lost and won, the silly dreams of a twenty-four-year-old-girl liberated from her dreary past by a chance meeting.

But reality had a way of asserting itself, even in paradise. She enjoyed her work, even eight years later, but lately she had the growing sense that despite her escape from Detroit to paradise, she had not escaped her father's fate as a wage slave. The dream she had brought with her on the ship along with her luggage, the vision of doing something large, something grand, had gradually faded into background noise, obscured by daily rounds and managing meds and arranging excursions for the guests of Endless Vacations.

Until she met Rex. He had awakened the dormant dream, opened the possibility of reaching beyond her raising to grasp for something more. The brief hour at the ruins had changed her life. Like Pop, but on a scale she had never imagined, Rex had opened her eyes to what could be. What would be, if only she would reach out and take it.

He was right. And her friends, the inner voices of her instincts, were right. She would change her ticket, go to Aspen two days early, and start planning her new life, regardless of appearances. Which meant she didn't need groceries.

The taxi pulled up at the market in Old Town Cancún. Masie turned to Ernesto with the realization that she had spent the entire drive absorbed in her own concerns and now she was going to confuse him. "Ernesto, I've made up my mind. Take me back home."

Ernesto flinched. "*Pero . . . sí, señora.*"

Chapter Thirty-Two: Dave

Dave used a generous tip to dispense of Vega. The nervous chauffeur was gone before Dave had his wallet back in his pocket.

There had been a few ticklish moments on the drive from the cenote when Angela asked about the call from Rivera and Dave dismissed it as last minute work stuff, and Hensley pointed out it was Sunday and wasn't his last day on Friday. Dave had muddled through somehow but hadn't been able to meet Angela's steely gaze.

In the thick silence of the last hour, Dave had pondered Rivera's allegations regarding Uncle Rex. Could it be true? Dave considered what he knew of the family history as related by Mom. In his early twenties, Rex had taken charge of the declining Stone fortune and, in a few years, had reversed the tide, eclipsing its former glory over the next three decades. Could that be done legally? Sure, if you were lucky. That reminded Dave of a favorite saying of Uncle Rex. *You make your own luck.*

How far had Rex gone to make his own luck? Far enough that, as he stared at the abyss of eternity, he had regrets?

The nephew in Dave cried out, "No!" The investigator in Dave wanted more evidence. But Rex was dead, and Dave wasn't willing to take Rivera's word. Maybe as the family lawyer, Ellis would know. No, if Rex had done anything the slightest bit off plumb, he would have hidden it from Ellis. Considering Rex's skill with corporations and contracts, it would take some serious financial investigation to find out, and now that he thought about it, Dave wasn't sure he wanted to.

Instead, he turned his sights on Masie. There was no moral ambiguity about killing an old man for his money.

As the limo drove away from the hotel, Dave turned to Angela. "I'm going to find Masie and get to the bottom of this. I'll see you at dinner."

"I'll come with you," Hensley said.

Dave blasted him with a glare that could skin a rhino at fifty paces.

Hensley looked past Dave, through the doors to the bar where Noah set drinks in front of a blonde and a redhead dressed for a night on the town. He shrugged. "As you wish." He walked away.

"You're pretty harsh on him," Angela said.

"Let's just say the last thing I have right now is time for his nonsense. If you knew the whole story, you wouldn't have stopped me back at the ruins. You would have piled on. But he's not worth even the time it would take to explain it."

"That clears it up wonderfully, thank you," Angela said.

That hadn't quite come out the way Dave had meant it. She deserved an explanation. About Hensley, sure, but a lot of other things too. About how Dave thought he was finally ready for a real relationship, perhaps even marriage, this time for keeps. Without reservations or conditions.

Not about Rivera though. Or Johansson. If Dave could manage that particular nightmare, it would fade away, and there would be no need to ever mention it.

But Masie must be dealt with first. "I'll provide full disclosure at dinner. I promise."

Angela considered him with narrowed eyes. "Tell me you're not as clueless as you sound."

She didn't have the best conviction rate in the state for nothing. There was no good way to answer the question and to respond would lead to a long conversation. He smiled. "I'm not as clue—"

"I'm serious, Dave."

"So am I. As soon as I get the truth out of Masie, we can go somewhere nice for dinner, and I'll tell you everything." He kissed her quickly on the forehead and left before she could answer. He didn't look back.

In his room, Dave took a quick shower, donned slacks, and grabbed a guayabera shirt, buttoning it on the way out. As he passed the bar, he noticed a small humidor. He picked up the note resting on top.

MR. FLETCHER. COMPLIMENTS OF ENDLESS VACATIONS.
ENJOY YOUR STAY.

He opened the lid. A dozen Cuban Cohiba Churchills. If he didn't know better, he would have thought Uncle Rex sent them. He slipped one into his shirt pocket and began his search for Masie. He roamed the resort with no result. He returned to his room, grabbed the flowers from the vase on the dining table, and went to the concierge.

"Can you tell me the room number for Masie Wright?" He smiled sheepishly.

The concierge regarded Dave with a dubious expression and held out his hand for the flowers. "I can see that she gets them."

"It's very important that I deliver them myself," Dave said. He slipped a twenty discretely under a map next to the concierge's hand.

The concierge nodded and divulged the room number. Just down the hall from Dave's room. On the way, Dave ditched the flowers in a trash can. He knocked on Masie's door, got no answer, and tried the handle. Locked, of course.

Banking on the likelihood that her room was similar to his, Dave went out the back, counted his way down from his room, and slipped over the railing that separated the patio from the beach. He tried the sliding door. It slid. He was inside in a second.

As he expected, Masie had an upscale suite like his own, with a full kitchen and at least one bedroom. A ship in a bottle and a row of framed photos sat on the counter by the kitchen. He flipped on the light switch and picked up the closest photo. A much younger Masie Wright stood with her arms around an older man, probably her father, on a green hill overlooking a lake, an old tower in ruins behind them.

He put the picture back. The next photo showed a teenage Masie and several boys, all holding what looked like a cheesewheel made of metal with three wheels protruding from the bottom and a crane-like arm that terminated in a buzz saw. He'd seen something like this before in a show about robots that fought to the death, guided by teams of geeks. The boys in the photo certainly looked the part. Masie smiled along with the geeks, obviously a part of the team. He shook his head, confused, and continued his search.

Against the far wall, a PowerBook sat open on a desk next to a filing cabinet. Which one would have information about Uncle Rex? He could probably skim through the filing cabinet quickly. The computer could take forever.

He pulled open the top drawer and leafed through the files. Medical records. He flipped to the back. It ended at the letter P. He closed the drawer and opened the next one, thumbing back to the letter S when he heard the noise of a key card swiping through the reader.

As the lock clicked, Dave searched for cover and dove behind the couch. He crawled to the end where a plant gave him cover and a view of the door. It swung open, and Masie entered, reaching for the switch with the hand that held her key card. She stopped, looked up at the light, surprised to see it on, and then around the room. She took a few steps in.

"Hello?"

Dave held his breath. Masie glanced about the room and closed the door. Her other hand held an empty shopping bag. She set it on the counter next to the photos, picked up a knife from the counter, and crept into the bedroom, flipping on the light.

He waited until he saw the bathroom light come on. Then he scrambled up, leapt to the door, slipped out soundlessly, and retreated down the hallway.

After a dozen yards he stopped, returned to her room, and raised his hand to knock, but just then Masie jerked the door open and rushed out. She ran into his fist, catching it in the eye.

"Ow!"

"Sorry!"

He reached up to do something, but there was nothing for him to do. She had a hand over one eye and a question in the other. This wasn't how he had envisioned the encounter.

"What are you doing here?" Masie asked.

Dave peered in the door. Across the room, the second file cabinet drawer was open, a folder hanging out.

"I just wanted to ask you something."

"Okay."

"Well . . . Don't you want to do something about that eye?"

Masie shook her head. "I need to talk to security. Somebody's been in my room."

"Really?"

Masie didn't answer. They walked down the hall.

"Look, I'm sorry about your eye."

She pulled her hand away and blinked a few times. "I think it's okay."

They passed his door. If he could get her inside, he could buy some time to ask her a few questions. "Here's my room. Let me get you some eye drops." He pulled out his key card.

Masie seemed reluctant. She stopped a few feet past his door and looked down the hall.

Dave started to swipe his card but hesitated with the card above the scanner. The door was ajar. He pushed it. It opened a few inches. The light was on. He knew he had turned it off when he left. He pushed it harder. It swung open silently. He took one step into the room. The smell of a good cigar and burnt fabric met him.

Güero Rivera lay sprawled on the floor, surrounded by a nimbus of cigars. One smoldered on the carpet near his right hand. The coffee table was demolished, the small humidor resting in the ruins.

Rivera must have bribed someone to find out where Dave was staying, come for the key to the battery lock, and run up against someone. Maybe the cartel thugs had followed him and roughed him up as a warning. With any luck, Dave could revive him and make the trade, keys for information, and have this part of his trip settled.

Masie peeked around him, saw Rivera, and gasped. "Mr. Rivera!"

"You know Rivera?" He found this unexpected piece to the puzzle unsettling. How did she know him?

She rushed forward, but Dave held her back.

"Hold on. Whoever did this might still be here." He scanned the area. In the middle of the room, a centipede ran straight for him. He stepped forward, and it veered away, making straight for Rivera. Dave sprang after it.

Masie called from the door, "No! Don't! You're allergic!"

Dave stomped the bug. It bounced up, curling back, landed on the carpet and kept running. He stomped it again, but it had no effect. The carpet pad was too thick. He kicked it away from the body, grabbed the empty vase, and trapped it. He heard it hiss from under the glass.

Masie ran to the body and knelt beside it. Dave slid a brochure under the vase and lifted the whole thing up, looking at the centipede.

"He's dead," Masie said.

Dave peered at the centipede. Something was strange about this bug. "He's . . ." The word registered. "Dead?" A hole opened up in

Dave's gut, and his heart dropped through it like an anvil through a tub of warm butter. His last chance to clear his name had just died.

"Yes." She checked for a pulse. "He's still warm. It must have happened just a few minutes ago. We should call Dumont."

"Who's Dumont?"

"Hotel security."

Dave set the vase holding the centipede on the table. He approached the body. Rivera was as dead as Dave's chances of clearing his name. Rivera's days of playing both ends against the middle were over. Dave picked up the smoldering cigar and rubbed out the embers with his foot.

Dave heard another hissing sound. The Hendersons peered through the door. Dave slammed it. He considered the tableaux before him.

Rivera dead on the floor. Masie hovering above him. All the data points Dave had compartmentalized into two cases, Masie and Rivera, broke out of their neat containers and ran amok in his brain. Maybe Rivera hadn't been killed by a cartel thug. "You got to your room a few minutes before I knocked on your door. Where did you come from?"

Masie wasn't listening. She inspected Rivera's skin.

"And then you came out almost immediately. Where were you really going?"

Masie gestured to the swollen features. "It looks like anaphylaxis. He was bitten by something." She nodded at the vase. "Like a centipede. But I can't find a mark."

"That's what it's supposed to look like, isn't it?" He saw it now, the genius all the more stunning due to the sheer improbability of it. She didn't run a one-time scam on Uncle Rex. She had partnered with Rivera, maybe even with the cartel, and his sudden flight put her at risk. "How do you know Rivera? Were you getting a cut of the action? Get too greedy? Panic when he decided to run?"

"What are you talking about?"

Dave went through Rivera's pockets. Billfold with a decent amount of cash, US and Mexican. A passport. A folding knife. A lighter. "And you just happened to be on hand to discover the body. Just like the last time. How convenient."

"Last time?"

A loud knock startled them. They looked at the door and at each other.

A voice with a strong accent came from beyond the door. "Hotel security. Open at once."

Dave hesitated.

Masie said, "It's Dumont."

A louder knock shook the door. Dave opened it. A small, middle-aged man with a military bearing pushed past. A young man with the physique of a cement truck and the demeanor of a demolition derby filled the doorway.

Dumont saw the body and pursed his lips. "Mr. Rivera. What have we here, Miss Wright?"

"We think it's an allergic reaction to a centipede bite."

Dumont noticed the passport in Dave's hand. "May I?" He took it and held it next to Rivera's face. "It is not the good likeness. How does he come to be in your room, Monsieur . . ."

"Fletcher."

"This is your room, is it not?"

"Yes, but he was here when we got here. Like that."

"Yes," Masie said. "The door was open and he was on the floor, just like you see him. We didn't move anything."

Dumont studied Dave closely. He took in the situation, the ruins of the coffee table, the scattered cigars. His gaze came to rest on the centipede in the vase.

"I see." He turned back to Dave. "May I see your passport?"

"I don't see—" Dave started.

"Dave didn't— " Masie started.

They were both cut off by an irritated wave of Dumont's hand. "Please, the passport. Let us not engage the assistance of Monsieur Finney."

Dumont indicated the mountain that filled the doorway. Dave went into the bedroom and returned with his passport. Dumont slipped it into his jacket pocket and held out his hand.

"Your room key."

Dave hesitated. Dumont glanced at Finney. Dave gave him the room key.

"*Merci*. We shall now proceed to my office."

He strode to the door. Finney stepped back to allow them to pass.

On Dave's list of things to avoid while on vacation, being rail-roaded into a Mexican jail on circumstantial evidence ranked right up there with being framed by a cartel stooge, but Masie followed Dumont. Seeing no way to take on both Finney and Dumont, Dave followed. Finney brought up the rear.

Walking down the hall sandwiched between the captain and the goon, Dave wondered about Masie's willingness to go along with them. How did this fit into his new theory? Maybe they were in the pocket of Los Zetas too. A dozen yards down the hall, he realized how absurd the Masie-Rivera theory was. If he didn't watch out, he'd be no better than Hensley, suspecting everyone from the management to the wait staff.

As they approached the lobby, Dave searched for some way to extricate Masie and himself from this death march, but nothing suggested itself.

Chapter Thirty-Three: Hensley

Hensley changed from the safari outfit to the man-in-black style he sported on his first night and set up camp at the bar. The stinging in his right foot had abated to a tolerable level. The ache in his gut didn't bother him. Much.

At the other end of the bar, Angela checked her emails on her phone. He had been right about her. She was no good for Davison.

On the drive from the ruins, Hensley had debated with himself about leaving, but he figured Davison may have gotten it out of his system with the fight, and things would get better. Besides, there was the $100 million to consider. Then the girls came over and turned his thoughts in another direction. In seconds he had their hands filled with fruity drinks garnished with plumeria and had drawn them in with a story.

On his right, the blonde looked like her day job involved presenting giant golden trophies to NASCAR winners. On his left, the redhead looked like she spent her time on photo shoots sprawled across the hoods of restored muscle cars. They leaned in toward Hensley, their shoulders grazing his.

"So," Hensley said, "I opened the briefcase and showed her the money and said, 'Here it is. Bring out the cocaine, and let's get this done. I have a taxi waiting.' And she said, 'How do I know you're not a cop?'"

"Oh!" squealed the redhead. "But you are a cop!"

"Precisely, my succulent munchkin. I was knee deep in the soup. I had to think fast. I said, 'Scout's honor.'" Hensley held up three fingers in the Scout salute.

"Did that convince her?" the blonde asked.

"Almost. But she leaned in real close to me, nibbled on my ear, and whispered, 'I know how you can prove it to me.'"

The redhead squealed again. "You mean—"

"Yes, my little passion flower, I'm afraid that's exactly what she meant. You see, she was a woman of dubious virtue."

"But," the blonde said, "you were wearing a wire."

"Ah." Hensley gave her an appreciative nod. She was the sharper of the two dull knives in the drawer. "You apprehend the difficulty of my position." He took a long, slow drink of his refreshing beverage.

At that moment, Hensley glanced across the way and saw a strange procession. A short, self-important martinet strode from the north wing of the resort across the cabana side of the lobby to the south wing, followed by Masie, Davison, and a thug the size of the Isle of Guernsey, in the order named.

Davison spotted Hensley and made a surreptitious sign with his right hand. He hadn't seen it in thirty-five years, but he recognized it immediately as the distress signal they had worked out in Angola, useful in all manner of social situations. This appeared to be a situation of the more serious sort.

The redhead bounced her shoulder against his. "What did you do?"

Hensley finished his drink in a gulp and pushed his stool back. "Buy me another drink, and I'll tell you. But it will have to wait. I'm afraid I have an urgent appointment with a Neanderthal."

"A Neanderthal?" the redhead said, her brow knitted in a charmingly vacuous expression.

Hensley loped across the lobby without a backward glance and rounded the corner to the south wing. He was met with an imposing set of metal doors that seemed strong enough to withstand a siege. The right door was swinging closed. Hensley got his foot in the gap and pushed it open.

Isle of Guernsey was about twenty meters away. Hensley closed the distance silently and delivered a roundhouse kick, bouncing Guernsey's head off a fire extinguisher with a satisfying clunk.

Guernsey staggered in the hall, arms flailing from the elbows. A punch to the kidney put him on the ground, safely out of consideration for the nonce.

Dave spun around, grasped the situation, grabbed Masie's upper arm, and pulled her toward Hensley. They navigated around Guernsey.

"What are you doing?" Masie asked.

"Want to go to prison? In Mexico?" Davison said over his shoulder.

"But we didn't do anything."

Hensley moved aside to let them pass, stepped over Guernsey, and advanced on the martinet, assuming a martial arts stance.

Hensley glanced meaningfully back at Guernsey. "We're leaving now. Any objection?"

The martinet dispassionately regarded Guernsey splayed across the hall. "None at present."

Hensley bowed. "Well done." Then he dashed down the hall and through the metal door. He caught them up in the lobby.

Masie pulled away from Davison. "This is a bad idea."

Hensley watched the entrance to the south wing. Guernsey was probably out for the duration, but there was no use taking chances. Some of the more industrial-grade thugs had amazing resilience. "Perhaps this isn't the best spot for this discussion, love."

Angela joined them. "Done so soon? Where shall we go for dinner?"

Hensley suspected the question wasn't completely sincere. Perhaps a bit on the sarcastic side. Or a lot.

Davison pointed to the front entrance. "The best place to be right now is not here." He strode out to the taxi queue.

Angela stalked after him. Masie reluctantly followed.

Hensley served as the rear guard, keeping watch over his shoulder. When he got outside, he caught up with Davison, who passed by the first two taxis to the third.

The driver leaned against the fender, smoking. When he saw Davison, he smiled, flicked away his cigarette, and ran around to open the door.

The doorman shouted. "Ernesto! No jumping in line."

The driver waved his objections aside. "Friend of the family, *señor.*"

"He's my half-brother," Hensley said.

The doorman inspected at him doubtfully, but Angela, Davison, and Masie were already in the back seat. Ernesto held the front door open for Hensley. He got in.

Ernesto ran around the car and jumped behind the wheel, cranking the engine. He caught sight of Masie in the rearview, raised an eyebrow, and then turned to Davison. "Where to, *jefe?*"

"Somewhere else," Davison said.

Ernesto nodded and calmly pulled away from the resort.

"What's going on?" Angela asked.

Dave looked at Hensley. "The ninja skills?"

Hensley shrugged. There was much Davison didn't know. "Three years in Guangxi under a wing chun master," he answered while watching the palm trees on Kulkulkan whiz past.

"Is there any place you haven't been?" Angela asked.

Hensley considered the question, skimming through his wandering past like viewing a travelogue. "Duluth."

Masie said, "We should go back right now. We've done nothing wrong."

Hensley glanced over his shoulder. "That's exactly what Dreyfus said just before they hauled him out to Devil's Island."

Masie ignored him. "This is going to turn out badly."

Davison waved her comment aside. "Ernesto, where can we go for the night where no questions will be asked?"

"I know a place," Masie said. "*Iglesia del Cristo Ray.*"

Ernesto nodded. "I know of it."

Angela punched Davison in the arm. "What happened in there?"

Hensley twisted around in the seat so he could see Davison. He waited.

Davison studied each of the people in the cab before he answered. "I'll tell you over dinner."

Chapter Thirty-Four: Masie

Masie didn't say anything during the drive to the mission church. She tried to make sense of the last few minutes. Someone had been in her room, snooping through her files. Dave had come to ask some undisclosed question. And then Rivera. Why did Dave suspect her of killing him? And why did Mr. Kite attack Finney when things were under control? And how did this woman fit in? And why had Masie got into a taxi with them when she should be changing her ticket and flying to Aspen tomorrow?

Father Roberto would take them in. He would do it because of all she did for the children at the clinic. In fact, he would probably take them in even if he had never met her.

Ernesto stopped in front of the church, but she directed him around the corner to Father Roberto's living quarters. She left them waiting in the car as she knocked on a wooden door older than all of them put together.

It took a few minutes for him to answer. He was seventy and didn't move that quickly. The door opened and a rectangle of yellow light spilled out onto the street and across the taxi.

"Masie, what brings you here at this hour?"

"Father, I have some friends in trouble who need a place to stay tonight. Do you have room?"

"Of course." He opened the door wider and gestured.

Dave dismissed the taxi, and they came in. Father Roberto got them settled, opened a bottle of wine, and disappeared.

Masie sat at the kitchen table, facing the doorway. Mr. Kite sat to her right, drinking deeply from the glass. Dave sat to her left. He spun the wine glass by rolling the stem between thumb and fingers, and stared at the ripples on the surface as if they held a message. And then there was the woman across the table, the one who had been with the other two at the pool yesterday. She was attractive, beautiful even, in a hard kind of way.

"I don't believe we've met. I'm Masie Wright."

The woman studied Masie as if she were an exotic species of spider. "Angela Martini."

"And how do you come to be mixed up in this?"

"How about you go first?"

Masie had no idea what that meant. She turned to Dave. "Perhaps you can tell me why you dragged me out here."

Dave pulled his gaze from the wine glass to Masie, then glanced away. "It's hard to know where to start."

Masie could take it no longer. "Let's start with Mr. Kite. Why did you attack Finney? Who are you, really?"

He stared at her as if waiting for her to break first. "The wild card," he finally said.

The man was infuriating. He had no right to interfere, place them at risk, and then act like it didn't concern him. "How do you know Dave?"

"It's a Zen thing."

This was clearly going nowhere. She turned to Dave. He would at least talk sense. "And how did Mr. Rivera's body come to be in your room?"

Angela's head jerked toward Dave. "Body?"

Mr. Kite set his glass down. "You're holding out on us."

"Güero Rivera?" Angela asked, her voice moving up an octave. "Dead? In your room?"

"Who is Güero Rivera?" Mr. Kite asked.

Dave waved the question aside. "The important question is—"

"A suspect in a federal investigation," Angela said. "But he's supposed to be in custody."

Suspect? Federal investigation? Masie's instincts had been right about Rivera. "But why was he in your room?"

"He owns a casi—That doesn't matter. How do you know Rivera?"

Masie was more interested in a different question. "What about what you said back there? When I told you Rivera was dead?"

Dave shifted in his chair. "What did I say, exactly?"

"That I killed him for his money."

Mr. Kite leaned forward. "Did you?"

Masie looked from Mr. Kite to Dave. "Is he serious?"

Dave fixed Mr. Kite with an expression Masie couldn't decipher. "Not usually."

Masie stood up. "This is going nowhere. We know how Mr. Rivera died, from anaphylaxis due to a bite from a centipede. We had nothing to do with it. Running away just makes us seem guilty. I'm going back right now to straighten this out." She turned to leave.

Dave stepped to the door, blocking her exit. "If he died from a centipede, why didn't you find a wound?"

"I didn't have time to do a full examination. It could be under his clothes."

"What about the cigars?"

"What about them?"

Mr. Kite butted in. "Why don't you both sit down and tell us about the cigars?"

Masie moved to pass around Dave, but he blocked her again. They stood inches apart and stared at each other.

Dave glanced at Mr. Kite and back to Masie. He motioned to the table. "What do you say?"

"Either answer my questions or get out of the way."

Dave studied her for a bit. "Fine."

He returned to his chair and sat.

"What's all this about cigars?" Mr. Kite asked.

Dave raised an eyebrow at Masie.

She returned to her chair. She needed to find out how things stood so she would know what to do next. "There were a bunch of cigars scattered around the room."

"From a box with a card," Dave said. "Compliments of Endless Vacations."

"We don't give cigars to guests."

"And Rivera had smoked one. It was still burning."

"What are you saying?" Angela asked. "The cigar killed him? Why not the centipede?"

Masie took a long sip of wine, wondering just how crazy this group was and what had focused their attentions on her.

Dave leaned forward, his arms on the table. "The centipede have been in the box when Rivera opened it. But she couldn't be sure it would actually bite him. On the other hand, he would probably smoke a cigar. No bite, no problem. The cigar takes care of it."

"She?" Masie asked. "As in me?"

"Like that one?" Angela pointed at Dave's shirt pocket. The rounded end of a cigar poked out the top.

Dave pulled the cigar out. "I forgot about it. It's a good thing I didn't smoke it."

Angela's brow furrowed, evidently trying to determine whether he was serious.

Masie shoved back her chair and stood. "You're all crazy. I'm going back."

Dave rolled the cigar in his fingers. "Maybe we can get it tested. My money says it's laced with a toxin that mimics an allergic reaction to venom."

"Rivera was Davison," Mr. Kite yelled.

Masie stopped halfway to the door. All eyes converged on Mr. Kite.

"Somebody plants a box of poisonous cigars in your room, with or without the complimentary centipede inside. Rivera goes in your room for reasons, and via methods as yet undetermined, opens the box and wins the prize—a free boat ride on the river Styx."

Masie turned to leave but stopped again. She didn't like this theory. It raised questions instead of settling them. And one question in particular bothered her. "Are you saying Mr. Rivera was murdered, but Dave was the target?"

Mr. Kite poured more wine. "That much seems obvious."

"But who would want to kill Dave?"

Mr. Kite studied at her over his wine glass. "You don't know?"

Masie shook her head and started toward the door.

Angela called out from the table. "Consider this. If Rivera was murdered and Dave was the target, then now you're in danger too. They have no way of knowing whether you're in on whatever it is that drew their attention to Dave. You might want to stay out of sight for at least a day."

"Who is they? And why do they want Dave dead?" Masie didn't like this woman, but she couldn't leave. Too many unanswered questions filled the air, and who knew where they would lead.

Masie's internal friends reminded her of the promise to leave for Aspen. She told the voices she would stay the night and leave for sure tomorrow, if for no other reason than to shut them up.

Chapter Thirty-Five: Dave

Dave's room was more like a cell with two single beds that were not much more than cots. The only other furniture was a massive chest of drawers in the corner and a crucifix on the wall. Not a problem, really. They had no luggage.

He left Hensley testing out the beds, went down the hall past Masie's room, and glanced in the next door. Angela sat on the bed, checking email on her cell phone.

He leaned against the doorway. "What's your take? Did she do it?"

Angela looked up. "Do you have a phone charger?"

Dave shook his head.

Angela shoved her phone into a pocket and jabbed a finger at his chest. "You have a lot of 'splaining to do, mister."

"You heard most of it. I did get a short look at her room, got a glimpse of Rex's medical file in her cabinet, but nothing suspicious."

"I don't care about that. I want to know why Güero Rivera, wanted by the FBI, comes down to Cancún to see you and comes to an untimely end while relaxing with a cigar in your hotel room."

Not the topic at the front of Dave's mind and the last thing he wanted to discuss with Angela. "I didn't know he was there until we found the body."

"How did he know you were down here and not in Austin?"

Dave hesitated. If he told her about the casino, he would have to tell her about Rivera. He hesitated only a second, but she didn't need more.

"Don't even think of denying it. I'm not some floozy nurse with a flawed exit strategy. You're hiding something."

Dave took it as a life lesson. Think twice before dating a prosecuting attorney. "Maybe we should go outside to discuss this."

"I'll go to wherever it is that gets me to the truth."

Dave led her out to the courtyard where he and Masie had treated the local children the day before. The moon loomed large above the steeple, almost full. Under different circumstances this would be a romantic evening—the courtyard of an ancient mission church in the tropics, with a beautiful woman in the moonlight. But it wasn't different circumstances. It was the worst of circumstances.

"I came down here to find out who killed Uncle Rex, but I also came to find Rivera." He moved so that the moonlight fell on Angela's face. He wanted to see her expression, and he hoped she couldn't see his.

Pale shadows lined her forehead as she frowned. "Why? It's not your case. It's not even your agency. Former agency."

"When the FBI pulled Rivera in, he cut a deal to stay out of prison."

Angela considered this. "Who did he give them?"

"Me."

In the moonlight her eyes glinted like steel. "You?"

"He faked evidence to make them believe I was taking a cut of his money-laundering operation."

"What did you do for your cut?"

"Theoretically I ran interference. Showed him how to stay under the radar."

"And they took the deal?"

Dave nodded. Harris took the deal. He couldn't bring himself to say it out loud.

"How did you find out?"

"OPR showed up at the office Wednesday." There. He'd said the O-word. Let the dominoes fall where they may.

"So you're suspended, under internal investigation. With possible criminal charges to follow."

"Unless I break Rivera's story."

"And if you don't?"

"All they have is Rivera's testimony and some bogus account numbers. And the fact that Rivera wired $120,000 to my checking account last week."

"And his body in the hotel room of the one person who stood to gain from his death."

"Gain? Now I can't get him to testify and clear my name."

"And they can't get the evidence to convict you. Rivera didn't need your complicity to wire money to your account. They were counting on his testimony to seal the deal."

In the last few hours, things had happened too fast for Dave to analyze them, but as usual, Angela cut straight to the most vital fact. His first reaction had been panic that Rivera's death had slammed the door on the evidence proving his innocence. But now he saw that it would likely make it impossible to convict him, while also making it impossible to clear his name. He might not go to jail, but Rivera's ghost would follow him into retirement and the rest of his life.

Angela squinted at Dave in the silvery light. "But why do you think Masie had something to do with his death? He's mixed up with the cartels. Isn't that why he's under investigation?"

"When he was seventeen, he disappeared into Mexico. The best intel says he slipped across the border to Matamoras."

"Gulf cartel."

"But now he has a casino in Cancún. Which means he has to deal with Los Zetas."

"That can't be easy for a guy with old-school ties to the Gulf cartel."

"Harris picked him up because of a connection with Guzmán."

"Sinaloa cartel? That's the other gulf, Gulf of California."

"Guzmán has been gunning for Los Zetas ever since the Beltrán Leyva brothers split with him and joined forces with Los Zetas. Rivera probably had a grudge against Los Zetas for taking over most of the Gulf cartel territory. He may have been working as a mole for Guzmán. I get the impression he was always available to the highest bidder."

"But you don't think Los Zetas killed him?"

"A cartel hit usually sends a message in large, bold letters. They don't try to make it look like natural causes."

Angela tilted her head, unconvinced.

Dave took a deep breath. "Masie knows about Rex's tumor and its symptoms. Rex dies by electrocution made to look like a seizure. Masie knows I'm allergic to venom because Hensley mentions it at dinner. A man in my room tries the complimentary cigars and dies by poisoning made to look like anaphylactic shock. With a bonus centipede thrown in to make it more convincing."

"That brings us back to why Rivera was in your room. How he knew where to find you."

"Well . . ." Dave wasn't sure how much he should tell Angela about his investigation. "I tracked Rivera down to his casino and demanded he recant his claim to settle the OPR investigation. Since he was fleeing the country, most likely headed to South America, the state's evidence deal didn't matter to him anymore."

He looked to Angela for confirmation. She just stared back, waiting.

"He gave me a little, but not enough," Dave continued. "So I fixed it so that he couldn't leave without seeing me first."

"How did you do that?"

"The details don't matter. He left me a message while we were at the ruins. Agreed to meet."

"The phone call in the limo."

Dave nodded. "There was no plan. Somehow he figured out where I was staying."

"And caught the bullet meant for you."

Dave nodded.

"Better to be lucky than good."

She had a point. Dave had been good, and look where it had gotten him. But he hadn't been particularly lucky, either. "Maybe so. If things fall right, I could be cleared." He let it hang there. Maybe that would be enough. Maybe she wouldn't leave.

Angela stood silent for a long time, looking first into his eyes, then at nothing in particular.

The silence proved too heavy for him. "Is there still a chance? For us?"

She looked back to him.

"If I'm cleared, I mean," he finally said.

Angela shook her head. "You'll be cleared. That's not the problem."

Not the answer he wanted. "Then—"

"Dave, everyone knows you're a man of integrity. You're practically a Boy Scout. But you don't really love me."

She held up her hand to quiet his objections. "You like me. You might even love me the best you can. But that's not good enough. Not for me. Not anymore."

"Angela, I was going to . . . When this was over I—"

"Exactly. When this is over. And then when the next thing is over. And the thing after that. Then you'll become available. It won't be a case to solve next time, but it will be something. A key business deal with your new agency. A mid-life crisis."

Anger at the unfairness of her statement enveloped him like a bonfire. How could she treat this like just another case? His life was on the line. Their future together. He had kept her out of it to protect her. Her career. Her life.

He calmed himself with a deep breath. "You have no idea—"

"It's not something I think. It's what I know. I asked you to St. Croix to talk about our future. About us. And you just blew it off. Then Hensley tells me your uncle died, your mentor, and I cut you some slack. I know what that's like."

Her voice broke on the last word, but she cleared her throat and powered through. "I came down here to be with you, to help you through it." She crashed to a stop, blinking rapidly and glancing away. Her next words were barely louder than a whisper. "And we both know how that turned out. You ran off after that . . ." Her voice took on an edge. "After her the minute I showed up."

Her words were painfully accurate but infuriatingly wrong. "But I had to—"

"Exactly." Angela trained a fierce stare on him. "We've established how it works. You have to take care of one more thing, something that is not us, and then things will change."

Her words struck him mute. She'd emasculated any possible response. He finally said, "Angela, if you only knew . . . I've been thinking the same thing, about you, about us, almost constantly since you mentioned the trip to St. Croix."

"That's the problem, Dave," she said quietly. "It's not what you think that's important. It's what you do. And you do what you've always done." A tear brimmed and spilled. "You don't know how many times the last few weeks I wanted to call Stephanie, ask her what happened fifteen years ago, why she—"

Angela shuddered, shook herself into a determined stance. "No, that doesn't matter. What matters is that I'm ready for something more, but you're not."

"But I am—"

"Despite what you think." She stepped toward him. "Because all you do is think. I need someone, no, I deserve someone who acts on those thoughts. Acts today, not someday." She slipped her arms around him, melted into him for a fleeting second. "And I wanted it to be you," she whispered.

He wrapped his arms around her, willing her to understand, but she pulled away.

"Goodbye, Dave. Don't call me."

She disappeared into the mission.

Dave stared into the moonlight, seeing nothing. He thought he had changed. He had tried to do the right thing, but it seemed he was genetically incapable of turning off his tunnel-vision focus.

When he had a goal, everything else disappeared. And he had learned too late that if you do that enough, everything else really does disappear. It was Stephanie all over again, only this time he had nothing left, not even Uncle Rex.

Only Hensley, and that was worse than having nothing.

Day 7: Monday

Chapter Thirty-Six: Masie

Masie waited until everyone was asleep. Then she waited two more hours.

When the noise of the guys settling in their room had faded into the night, so did their fantastic speculations. In the following hours of silence she realized that she was right to trust her instincts. They smiled silently, obviously wanting to say, "I told you so."

She stole through the priest's quarters and used the phone in his office to call a taxi. Then she slipped outside and waited in the shadow of the narthex until the taxi came to a stop in front of the mission. On the twenty kilometer drive to the hotel, she finalized her plan.

She had a job and solving this mystery was not it. She would pass the information on to the people paid to figure out such things, give them the facts free of speculation, and change her ticket to leave for Aspen as soon as possible.

Ultimately the police would get involved, but Masie suspected they were as trustworthy as Mr. Rivera. If something really was rotten in the Yucatan, going to the police would be the same as walking into the clutches of the bad guys.

Bad guys? Clutches? She was starting to sound like the inmates of the traveling asylum back at the mission.

But the question of what to do remained. She was fairly certain that Dumont was trustworthy, but the cigars and the note made it an EV matter first and a hotel problem second. She would contact Paco Torres.

There was no telling what time zone Paco was in. He had been in Cancún on Thursday, but he could be anywhere in the world today. With resorts on every continent, he rarely spent two consecutive weeks in the same hemisphere. She didn't have to wait until morning to call, as it might already be afternoon wherever he was, but she was afraid she might not be completely coherent in her current condition. First a shower and a few hours of sleep.

When she opened the door of her suite and turned on the light, she could see that someone had been in her room. Again. She left it last night because of an open drawer with a paper sticking out. Now several file drawers stood open, folders were stacked on the desk, and her laptop had disappeared.

Could it be the same person, just come back to finish the job? Was he still in the suite? Masie left the door open, grabbed the knife still lying on the counter from the night before, and searched all the rooms until she felt confident that she was alone. Then she closed the door, turned the deadbolt, slid the chain in place, and told her inner friends to quit saying that they knew all along something bad would happen if she stayed.

What was the burglar looking for? Did it have anything to do with Rivera? Maybe Dumont did some investigating after they ran. If so, who broke in it the first time?

A chill crept over Masie. She remembered Dave's question from a few hours earlier. Why did Rivera choose to smoke a cigar in Dave's room? Perhaps he had visited her room first. If so, why? Did he plant a deathtrap in her rooms too?

She shook her head and laughed nervously. She needed a hot shower before she turned into Mr. Kite. Time to get some rest and follow the plan.

She loitered in the shower for an eternity and let the steaming water pour over her. The grimy feeling that comes with sleep deprivation, the feeling that even your eyeballs are gritty, your eyelids sliding over them like sandpaper, gradually washed away. She lathered her hair with a shamefully extravagant dollop of shampoo and used the mountain of suds to clean her whole body.

After drying off, she wrapped herself in a towel, got some aspirin from the medicine cabinet, went into the kitchen for a glass, and screamed, dropping the pills on the floor.

Two men sat in the living room, one on the couch, the other in an arm chair. They both stood as she approached, no more than dark silhouettes in the shadow cast by the kitchen cabinets, which blocked the light above the stove.

On the kitchen counter a few meters away, the knife lay where she left it, hidden from their view by the bar rising from the counter. Beyond the bar she saw a third man standing by the front door. A large man. Finney.

She looked back to the living room and recognized the diminutive shape of Dumont by the chair. Her heart still racing, but no longer in fear for her life, she flipped a light switch. The man by the couch was Paco Torres.

"Sorry to startle you, Masie," Paco said. "I just wanted to make sure you were safe."

The three men stood staring at her as if unsure what she would do next.

"Why wouldn't I be safe?"

"After what happened to Güero, when I heard you were kidnapped, naturally I feared for your safety."

"I wasn't kidnapped."

Paco turned to Dumont.

Dumont glanced with slight irritation at Paco. "Ms. Wright, do you give me to understand you went with these ruffians free of your will?"

Masie paused. That wasn't exactly the case either. "I was . . ." Then she realized she was having a conversation with three men while wearing nothing but a towel. "I have to ask you to leave. I'm not in any state to discuss this."

There was a short moment of tense silence before Paco spoke. "Of course. We can talk about it over breakfast. My treat."

Masie checked the clock above the stove, which read 4:17.

Paco followed her gaze. "Let's say five o'clock in my suite, shall we? Finney will bring you."

"And of course," Dumont said, "at a reasonable hour we must also have the conversation with the Ministerial Federal Police. There is still the matter of the body."

Paco waved a dismissive hand. "Of course."

Masie didn't know why she was uneasy. This was, after all, the reason she came back, to tell everything to Paco and then get out of town. The fatigue? Maybe the adrenaline from thinking she was alone only to discover three men waiting in the shadows? Or maybe the fact that her rooms had been searched more than once, and she didn't know who to trust.

"Somebody went through my files while I was gone."

"I'm afraid I'm the guilty party," Paco said. "Since the kidnappers didn't phone with demands, we were looking for some clue that might help us find you."

"I wasn't kidnap—"

"Of course. We know that now," Paco said, holding up a hand apologetically. He stepped back and gestured for Dumont to leave with him. "But we can cover all that at breakfast. Finney will wait outside."

They left without waiting for a response. The door clicked closed, and she crossed the living room to do the locks. Was Finney there to protect her? Or to watch her?

Her hand froze as she slid the chain latch into place. She had locked the knob, the deadbolt and the chain before she took the shower. They were all undone, with no trace of forced entry. Her sense of unease increased.

She did all the locks again, then dragged a chair from the kitchen table and wedged it under the knob.

The bed beckoned to her. Just fifteen minutes, it said in a soft feathery voice, but she knew that if she closed her eyes, they wouldn't open until hours later. The shower would have to do.

As she pulled on her clothes, she tried to separate the facts from Mr. Kite's conspiracy theories. That brought her mind back to the one question that defied explanation. Why did Dave, and Mr. Kite, now that she thought about it, assume she was involved in Rivera's death? It seemed as if Dave expected a dead body to turn up in his room, maybe even expected it would be his own body. And he expected it to come at her hand.

She pondered this mystery as she worked through her normal morning routine. A few minutes after five, as she swiped makeup containers into the drawer, she still hadn't come up with a sensible explanation.

She removed the chair from the door, unfastened all the locks, and opened it. Finney stood immobile, impassive, imponderable. She hadn't seen him in full light since the flight of the night before. He had a black eye and a bandage on his head. He turned to go without a word. Masie followed.

Chapter Thirty-Seven: Masie

In Paco's penthouse suite, a table on the balcony faced the Caribbean. Dawn was an hour away. The horizon was a division of the blackness of the water from the gradual graying of the sky. The moon had long since set, the stars like shards of a shattered goblet flung across velvet.

A feast of eggs, meats, breads, cereals, fruits, coffee, and several juice carafes crowded the table. Paco gestured to a chair and assisted her as she sat down. Then he took the opposite seat.

The aroma of fresh fruit, bacon, and coffee made her suddenly weak. When was the last time she ate anything? Must have been lunch yesterday, because this whole circus began as she entered her rooms after her aborted trip for groceries.

But she left the food untouched. Instead, she looked at Paco. "What happened to Mr. Rivera?"

Paco loaded his plate with bacon, a slice of ham, an egg over easy, an English muffin, and five strawberries as he talked. "I'm more interested in what happened to you."

"What was he doing in Dave's room? How did he die?"

"I was hoping you could answer those questions. You or Mr. Fletcher." He stopped with a coffee cup halfway to his mouth. "Where is Mr. Fletcher, by the way?"

"I don't know." Not necessarily a lie. He could have left the mission by now. Possibly. But what bothered her more than the deception was the sudden sense that the truth might be dangerous, although she wasn't sure why or to whom. Perhaps her association with Mr. Kite had induced paranoia. Perhaps her inner friends were whispering to her.

"Didn't you leave with him?"

Masie looked away. The sky was noticeably lighter. She could make out the stripes on beach chairs and umbrellas stacked against a shed below them. She suddenly felt foolish. She'd defied Dave and

Mr. Kite, slipped out and come back for the express purpose of setting the record straight. And here she was playing some kind of cat-and-mouse game with Paco.

She piled food on her plate and told him the story as she ate, starting with her return from shopping and the suspicion that some-one had been in her room, ending with the moment that Mr. Kite exploded in a flurry of fists and kicks at Finney while Dave dragged her away and shoved her into a cab.

"He was afraid of being put in a Mexican jail," Masie said in an-swer to a question from Paco.

"Where did you go?"

Her decision to clear things up didn't include selling out the oth-ers. She answered without hesitation. "He told the driver to take us to a place in Old Town. We had a drink and argued about what to do next. I said I was coming back here to clear everything up and get back to work."

"Did they stay?"

"I don't think so. Maybe they came back too."

Paco shook his head. They sat in silence for a while.

"There was one thing," Masie said. "Dave seemed to think I had something to do with what happened to Mr. Rivera."

"Why?"

"I don't know. He said I was the first to discover the body, just like last time."

The sun crept above the horizon. Out past the balcony a golden road led across the sea to the unknown, the sky burnt white at the horizon.

Paco studied her with an expression she couldn't decipher. Like he had mistaken her for someone else and was still searching her face to identify the points of similarity and difference. A mixture of pondering and recognition. He leaned forward, resting his elbows on either side of his plate.

"Can you get in touch with Mr. Fletcher?"

"Why?"

"He knows more than he's telling. And the other fellow, what was his name?"

"Kite. I don't recall his first name. He's not an EV guest."

"I think they have something to do with this. In fact, it might be some kind of scam. Blackmail."

"Dave? He's not like that." Mr. Kite, maybe.

"Agents are quite adept at hiding their true intent. Where was this bar you went to? Would you recognize the taxi driver who took you there?"

His interest in Dave was understandable, but it made Masie uneasy. "I didn't pay much attention. I was pretty shaken up." Her first true lie. It didn't feel right coming out of her mouth.

Paco searched her face for a moment and then leaned back in his chair. "Of course. That's a lot to process in twelve hours. And I didn't help matters by terrifying you in your own living room." He poured a cup of coffee and set it down in front of her. "I want you to take the day off. Relax. Get some rest. Pat can cover your shift."

Masie tasted the coffee. Like sipping velvet. "I'd rather check on the guests. I may leave for my vacation a day early." She took another sip. "But you can do one thing for me."

"Anything," Paco said.

"This is the best coffee I've ever had. Can you tell me where to find it?"

"I fly it in from Southeast Asia. I'll have some sent to your rooms."

Masie thanked him and stood to leave. Paco leapt to his feet and escorted her to the door.

"One moment," he said. He stepped to a desk near the windows and returned with her laptop. "Sorry for the intrusion, but my first priority was delivering you from the hands of your kidnappers, as I understood them to be. Finding a clue on your computer was unlikely, but I wouldn't be able to forgive myself if something unfortunate happened and I hadn't explored every possibility."

"Thank you." Just as on the day she met him, Masie was touched that Paco Torres, CEO of Endless Vacations, took a personal interest in the welfare of his employees. But even as she took the laptop, the unease resurfaced. And despite the embarrassment at her ungracious reaction, she couldn't dispel it.

She thanked him again, awkwardly, and left. Back in her rooms, she booted up the laptop and checked her schedule. Nothing demanding. She needed to confirm that Mrs. Crenshaw's medication had been delivered and that Mr. Polanski had been scheduled for dialysis.

As she updated her schedule with new arrivals, a knock came at the door. She peered through the peephole. Finney stood outside, holding a pound of coffee. She removed the chair, undid the locks, and opened the door.

Before she could speak, Finney shoved the bag toward her. "Mr. Torres sends this, with his regards."

The words seemed incongruous with his hulking presence. She had never heard him speak. She looked at the large, serious man standing in the hallway, holding out a bag of coffee with an apologetic air, and smiled.

"Thank you, Finney." She started to close the door, then pulled it back open. He had already turned to go but stopped when she said, "Are you a coffee drinker, Finney?"

"No, ma'am," he said, with a trace of a drawl. He faced her awkwardly. "I prefer tea," he finally said. "Orange Pekoe."

Her smile broadened. "I sometimes like a cup of tea myself." She waited, but he avoided her eyes and didn't speak. "Give my thanks to Paco," she said, and closed the door.

Masie set the coffee on the bar separating the living room from the kitchen. The knife still lay on the counter from the night before. She remembered the near paralyzing fear that gripped her while she searched the suite, flipping on lights and peering into and under things, not knowing that Paco had been the one in her rooms, searching for clues to rescue her from danger.

She put the knife away, gathered the file folders from the desk, put them back in the cabinet, and set to restoring the room to its natural order. This accomplished, she surveyed the living room, satisfied with her efforts. Still a bit early, breakfast time for people who had not been occupied most of the night by corpses and conspiracy theories. She still had time for a power nap.

But first she called the travel agency. It would cost a hundred dollars to change her flight to tonight instead of tomorrow night. She paid it gladly, unwilling to wait another twenty-four hours. She was far past caring if it appeared unprofessional to leave so soon after a patient died. She just wanted to get to Aspen before something else happened.

Chapter Thirty-Eight: Dave

Dave woke to a soft grey dawn shining just enough light to give a shape to objects in the room. He threw his legs off the cot and sat up. Four feet away in the other cot, Hensley slept on his back, his hands folded outside the counterpane like a corpse.

The memory of the night before swept through him like a fever. Angela was gone. Even if she was still in the room down the hall, asleep, she was gone.

Dave stood, tried to smooth the wrinkles from his shirt, and gave up. He slipped out the door and down the hall to Angela's room. The door stood open, the room dark and empty.

Dave found the old priest in the kitchen pouring coffee into a cup. He handed it to Dave with a nod, poured another, and sat at the table, gesturing to a chair. Against the opposite wall, an ancient television with rabbit ears sat on a stool. The priest watched the news with the sound off.

Dave sat and sipped his coffee. He forced his mind away from Angela and onto the problem of Masie. Bodies seemed to pop up wherever she went, and the thing with Rex's will was very suspicious. But her denial of any knowledge of the cigars and centipede was convincing.

And there was the fact that she hadn't tried to cash in on the will. And the more time he spent with her, the more innocent she seemed. But that left the problem of Rex and the will. He wanted to come right out and ask her, but he knew it would be a mistake. It would blow his cover, and if she was guilty, she would escape before he had proof. And there was the question of who or what killed Rivera.

Dave took his coffee outside and pulled out the burner phone. His first call caught the casino manager in bed. He powered through the "sorry to wake you" and "I'll just take a minute" and went for the information. "Did Los Zetas have anything to do with Rivera's death?"

"What?" Kenny's voice blended fatigue and confusion. "Rivera's dead?"

"How deep was Rivera into the cartels? Did he know enough to make him dangerous to them?"

Dave could almost hear the head shaking itself awake on the other end of the line. "Okay, so Rivera is dead. He didn't volunteer information about his outside deals and I didn't ask. He could have been a player or a gopher. I wouldn't know." He coughed and cleared his throat. "How did they do it?"

"Looks like natural causes. Allergic reaction to a centipede bite."

"I don't know how the gangs do it up in Austin, but down here, they don't mess with appearances. Empty a clip into the body is more their style."

"Thanks."

"Hey, thank you for getting rid of Rivera. You need anything, you come ask me."

Dave disconnected and made the second call. It rang four times.

"Aguilar."

"Detective Aguilar, this is Special Agent Fletcher. I visited you a few days ago."

A long silence followed. Dave opened his mouth to speak, but Aguilar finally responded.

"Where are you, Special Agent Fletcher?"

"I've been out of touch. Something came up."

"A body came up, Special Agent Fletcher. In your hotel room. Perhaps you can come in and help us with the details?"

It was Dave's turn to pause. Aguilar was remarkably well connected. Did he hear it from Dumont? Los Zetas?

"This is the man you asked about, is it not?"

Dave hadn't named the body and when he visited the federal building, Aguilar had used the name Sackett, the alias Rivera used to enter Mexico. How did Aguilar know Rivera and Sackett were the same man? Maybe the passport Rivera was carrying identified him as Sackett. He should have opened it instead of interrogating Masie at the scene. Either way, Dave would have to tread lightly. He decided to rely on the caller ID of the burner phone, which had a US number.

"I just wanted to talk to him. That didn't work out, so I'm back in the States. But I'd like to know who would want him dead. Can you help me with that?"

The sound of typing on a computer keyboard came across the line. "Which flight did you take?"

"I'm working a possible connection to a case here in the States. All I need to know is whether the death is related to the cartels. You answer yes, I close my case. Answer no, I bring in my suspect. One word. That's all I need."

"You presume too much, Special Agent Fletcher. We are speaking of a murder. In your hotel room. And you were present."

"Not for the murder. I found him later. I'm willing to help you with that investigation, but first I'm asking for a professional opinion. I trust that a man in your position is qualified to pass judgment."

A short silence, and then, "No, this death is not a cartel matter. It seems more like a personal matter."

Aguilar would be no help if things went south. "How certain are you?"

"Quite certain."

"That's good enough for me. Thank you for your assistance, Detective Aguilar."

"It is nothing. Now, about your cooperation."

Dave disconnected, hoping he would not find himself in the same room with Aguilar in the future. That left one suspect, even if his instincts said otherwise. He returned to the kitchen. Empty. He refilled his coffee cup and padded down the hall to Masie's room.

He knocked on the door. "Masie, it's Dave."

He waited, listening for the noise of her stirring. He knocked a little louder. No response. He tested the handle. It turned. He pushed the door open an inch.

"Masie?"

All his doubts about Masie echoed in the silence. He pushed the door fully open. The room was as empty as Angela's. Her bed was made. Feeling uneasy, Dave explored the living quarters until he found the priest in his office. He rapped on the doorway. The priest looked up.

"Father," Dave said, "where is Masie?"

"She is not here?"

Dave returned to his room. He shoved the door open and rattled Hensley's cot with his foot. "Hey."

Hensley opened his eyes immediately and looked at Dave without moving. "This better be good, Buckaroo."

"Get up."

"Really good. Like Luwak coffee good."

"Masie is gone."

"That's not good."

Hensley sat up. Dave handed him the mug. He took a tentative sip and nodded.

"Pretty good. Not Luwak, but good. When did she leave?"

"No idea."

Hensley shoved his feet into his shoes. "In that case, we have to leave now. We're sitting ducks."

"We don't know for sure that she's the killer."

Hensley's clothes seemed strangely wrinkle free. "You're welcome to test that theory by sticking around, Pollyanna." He shoved the coffee cup into Dave's hands and headed out the door.

Dave followed him down the hall. "I'm just saying we don't have enough information, and disappearing won't tell us anything." He left the coffee cup on the table in the kitchen and poked his head in the office. "Thanks, Father." He pulled out a wallet. "What do we owe you?"

The old priest waved the money away. "Put something in the collection box in the mission if you want."

Hensley was already out the door. Dave jogged to catch up. They circled around to the front of the mission. "We don't run. We get breakfast at the *taqueria* and watch the mission to see who shows up."

"Where's Angela?"

"Gone."

Hensley stared at Dave wordlessly for a few seconds, then across the street at the little café. The aroma of freshly made buñuelos, with a hint of cinnamon and anise, permeated the morning air. He grunted his approval.

"Get us a table," Dave said over his shoulder. "I'll be right there." He pushed open the massive wooden door. Inside, the cool air stirred dust motes in and out of the shadows. An aisle between wooden pews led to prayer rails and a dais, a crucifix looming behind it on the back wall. To one side, an altar buried in a mountain of candles stood before a brightly colored painting of the glorified Christ, God the Father above, the Virgin on his right, St. John the Baptist on his left.

Dave never had much occasion to visit a church, but thanks to an art class at Warfield Hall he recognized this painting as a detail from a larger work. He couldn't remember the title or the artist. Next to the altar was a basket of votive candles and a box with a slot to drop in a coin.

He slipped in several bills. He turned to go, but thought again. He took a candle from the basket, lit it from another, and set it in a clear space. He watched the flame sputter and settle into a steady light.

The silence of the sanctuary soothed the controversy raging in his head. Maybe that was why people came to places like this. Maybe when he got back to Austin he'd try it out. But the thought of going home reminded him that he had no reason to go back. Sure, there was the agency to start, but it didn't hold the excitement for him that it once did.

Uncle Rex had the right idea about living without regret, but sometimes it seemed like the only option was to choose which kind of regret you could live with. He'd chosen losing Angela over letting Rex's killer go free. In this moment, he wasn't sure Rex would have approved of his choice.

He thought about Masie patching up kids in the courtyard. He sat in the last pew and tried to lay out the case in his mind—the death of Rex, the changing of the will, the death of Rivera. How did Masie fit in? Why did she sneak out this morning? But the longer he puzzled on it in the quiet of the church, the more he felt like he was shouting in the middle of a prayer, and he gave it up.

He emerged from the sanctuary, squinting in the morning light, and crossed the street to the table where Hensley sat peering from behind a large sidewalk sign with the menu on it. Dave took a seat and sipped the coffee Hensley had ordered. Cold, but rich and slightly nutty. He decided he liked it cold.

"I didn't realize you were religious," Hensley said. "I would have waited to order your coffee."

Dave took a bite of a *buñuelo*, a warm, deep-fried ball of dough with a coating of cinnamon and brown sugar. It went nicely with the dark coffee aftertaste. "Why did she leave?" he asked.

"Which one?"

"Masie."

"Even you should be able to figure that out. To get her drugs so she can finish the job."

"There's no point in killing me until I decide to leave her money, which she hasn't asked me to do. So what's her motivation?"

Hensley dug into a buñuelo like the answer might be inside. He chased it with coffee and signaled the waiter for more. "She figured out who you are and why you're here. She has to take you out before you blow the whole thing wide open."

"How do you explain Rivera?"

"They're partners. She sets up the marks, he does the dirty work."

That made no sense. Rivera wouldn't work a low-grade scam like this one. "So if he's the hit man, who hit him?"

"Masie. She saw the size of the score from Rex and didn't like the idea of giving away $100 million."

"Did you sit up last night working it all out?"

"I'm just making it up as I go. What's your theory?"

"I don't have a theory. I have questions."

"So I've noticed."

"Like why she never contacted anyone about receiving the inheritance. Like why Rex insisted I deliver the estate to Masie." Dave considered what Rivera had said about Rex. That put a new complexion on the problem. "Like what if Rex's death isn't connected with Masie at all? What if it's not connected with the change of the will? Who else would want to kill him?"

"The Hendersons!" Hensley shouted, causing the waiter leaning against the door to jump and drop a menu. He lowered his voice. "I didn't trust them from the beginning. Always sneaking around and whispering."

"Could you at least pretend to take this seriously?"

"I do take it seriously, which is why you need to call your travel agent. But first call Ellis. The way things are going, we might need a lawyer to get out of the country."

Dave nodded. A phone call was in order. He pulled out his cell and dialed. He might have had the lead all along and never realized it. "Harris, did you get anything else on AZ Limited?"

"Harris?" Hensley muttered. "Who is Harris?"

"You said you could deliver Rivera," Harris said. "I can't string this out much longer."

"I can tell you exactly where Rivera is, but first AZ Limited."

A long sigh and the clattering of a keyboard came across the line. "Evidently it's a fund used for international currency speculation. We had to dig deep to connect a name to it. Paco Torres. Some Colombian entrepreneur."

Dave thought back to the phone call when he booked the trip. The girl said the $500,000 deposit went to an independent fund. Torres was working both sides of the street.

Harris interrupted his thoughts. "So where can I find Rivera?"

"The city morgue."

"What? In Austin?"

"Cancún. Somebody took him out last night."

"Who?"

"I'm working on that. Pretty sure it's not the cartels, any of them."

"This is not good. Not for me and especially not for you. Unless he told you which governor is on the make."

"Are you serious? You don't still believe I was working with him."

"No, but OPR doesn't give up easily."

"Even they have to admit their case is all circumstantial without Rivera's testimony."

"Unfortunately, they don't play by the same rules."

At this point, Johansson was so low on the list of Dave's problems that he had practically forgotten about the OPR investigation. There were so many front-burner issues that it became hard to prioritize them. The attempt on Dave's life that took out Rivera instead. Rex's murder and the changed will. The implication that the resurrected Stone fortune was built on dirty money. Angela.

"You still there, Fletch?"

"Yeah, I'm here. Listen, thanks for the info. I'm in a tight spot, and it might make the difference."

"No problem. And sorry to hear about Rex. First him, then Rivera. Is that place cursed?"

"Yeah, it's the curse of the Aztec gold." Dave stopped and stared at Hensley. That was it. Then another thought hit him. "Wait a minute." He disconnected and stood up.

Hensley remained seated. "What?"

Davison dialed. "It's not Wright," he said while the phone rang.

"What's not right?"

The call went through. "Ernesto. It's Dave. Come get me at the church. Thanks." He hung up and looked at Hensley.

"Why would Masie kill me? I haven't put her in my will. It's Torres."

"Who's Torres?"

"Paco Torres. CEO of Endless Vacations. He's the killer."

"But why Torres? He won't get any of Rex's money."

"He didn't kill him for the estate. Here's how it works." Dave ticked off the points on his fingers. "Rex books the Aztec Gold package, very exclusive. It requires a refundable $500,000 deposit to an independent fund. Rex dies of natural causes. I try to book the same package. They ask for medical records and the same deposit."

"And that leads to Torres how?"

"Torres owns both Endless Vacations and the independent fund. I bet the small print says that in case of death, the deposit is forfeited. If I had booked the same vacation, I would have died of natural causes."

"But you almost did die of natural causes without booking the vacation."

"Because I came back and started asking questions. Torres is the one trying to kill me, not Masie."

"Let's back up to how you got this revelation. Who is Harris?"

"My roommate from Warfield. He's now the Undersecretary of Terrorism and Financial Intelligence at the Department of Treasury."

"Oh, that Harris," Hensley sipped his coffee and pondered for a bit. "If this Torres was bumping off his own tourists, you would think somebody would notice after a while."

"It's like you said. Rex's medical forms show he had a terminal condition. They only kill people who everyone expects to die. Soon."

Hensley nodded solemnly. "Or people who want to die, perhaps."

Dave sat down. His thoughts drifted from Torres to dinner with Rex. He toasted to life without regret. He knew then, at dinner, that he would not be coming back. Rex died because he paid Endless Vacations to kill him.

Perhaps the tumor had affected his judgment after all. The old Uncle Rex was not a coward. He would have never given up. In business Rex played to win. He overwhelmed any obstacle by whatever means required—charm, cunning, intimidation, brute force. Even by illegal means, if Rivera was telling the truth.

Uncle Rex had the vision to see things others didn't, to anticipate the endgame and make unexpected moves to turn it to his advantage. Now that Dave thought about it, maybe that's what Rex was doing down here, making a preemptive strike against the Grim Reaper. The thought rippled through Dave's consciousness like a revelation. Uncle Rex had not run away from death. He'd turned the tables on death, forced the old specter to meet him on his terms. Did that make him brave or just a different kind of coward?

Not for the first time, and probably not the last, Dave wondered why Rex didn't tell him that night at dinner. Perhaps he was brave enough to face death head on but not brave enough to face his nephew with the truth of his own mortality. In a way, Dave could understand that. Much easier to carry the battle to the enemy than to compromise your defenses by opening the gate, even for a friend.

So the old man had not gone gentle into that good night after all. He'd gone down swinging, laughing in the face of death. It began to make some kind of sense, but it didn't explain everything, like the will. On the other hand, it did clear Masie from his murder. Dave's instincts about her had been right about one thing at least.

A taxi pulled up across the street in front of the mission. Ernesto cut the engine and relaxed with his elbow out of the window. Dave stood up.

"Where are you going?" Hensley asked.

"To nail Torres."

"That's not a plan. That's a reaction. Sit back down." Hensley leaned around the sidewalk menu sign, whistled at Ernesto, and waved him over.

Dave didn't sit down. "Torres gets the money from the Aztec Gold package, not Masie. And she obviously didn't know she would get money if Rex died. She didn't set up the deathtrap at the cenote. Torres did."

"That's a lot of speculation on very little evidence. Let's examine the facts. Masie works for Torres. For all we know, she's in on it. And, if I were you, I'd take the battery out of your phone."

Dave felt a strong urge to adjust Hensley's attitude with the sidewalk sign. Dave was confident in his analysis, but he removed the battery from his phone and the burner phone anyway.

"When you found Rivera's body, she went along with the goon squad willingly. She resisted when we rescued her. And the first chance she got, she went back."

"Fine. What if she is working for him? The point is that Torres is the guy behind AZ Limited. He arranged for Rex to die to get the half-million."

"How does the will fit in?"

"It doesn't." Dave wished it would fit in somewhere, but trying to make it fit was like finishing a jigsaw puzzle only to discover an extra piece in the box.

Ernesto approached the table. He looked from Dave to Hensley and back to Dave. "*Jefe?*"

Hensley shoved a chair back from the table with his foot. "Sit down, Ernesto. Have a buñuelo." He signaled the waiter.

Dave stared at Hensley, breathing heavily through his nose. Ernesto waited for a sign.

"Dammit, Davison," Hensley barked, slapping his hand on the table. "You are not a Secret Service agent anymore, this is not an operation, and you don't have authority. You don't even have a plan. Now sit down and talk sense or give me your phone, and I'll call Ellis, and you and Ernesto can drop me off at the airport on the way to your suicide mission."

"Suicide?" Ernesto said, even more confused.

Dave sighed and sat down. He motioned to the chair. Ernesto sat. The waiter arrived with another cup and more coffee for everyone.

Hensley passed the buñuelos around. "Ernesto seems to have a substantial amount of good sense. More than some I could mention. I propose we enlist him as a disinterested party to arbitrate this dispute."

Dave agreed, thinking it might not turn out as Hensley expected. He told the story, with color commentary from Hensley. At the end, Ernesto sat in silence for a long while. "So *Señorita* Masie is not your wife?"

"She's not even my girlfriend."

Ernesto shook his head. "She is a good woman. But it does not matter if she is on the good side or the bad. If you go in there, you will not get Torres. Torres will get you."

"Good man," Hensley said. "Always trust the instincts of the proletariat, I say. Survivors to a man." He leaned forward. "Now let's give Ellis a call and go home."

Ernesto shook his head, his eyes still on Dave. "You have no home, now, *jefe.*"

"What?" Hensley squeaked. "Of course he does. A nice one. Professional kitchen, sixty-inch flat-screen TV, security system. Well, strike the security system."

"They cannot let you leave now that you know."

"It doesn't matter," Dave said. "I won't leave until I take down Torres. And get Masie out of there."

"But she's one of them," Hensley said with infinite exasperation.

"Either way, she's coming with me. If she turns out to be one of them, she's going down. And if she isn't one of them, I won't abandon her."

Ernesto nodded with a grim smile. "*Exactamente, jefe.*"

Dave returned his smile. Ernesto was a romantic driving a cab, just as he had begun to suspect. Exactly the kind of man required for the circumstances.

"Unbelievable," Hensley said. "Neither of you has any sense of self-preservation."

"Always trust the instincts of the proletariat," Dave said.

Hensley shot him a look that would have curdled the milk in his coffee if he hadn't been drinking it black.

Dave sat up, suddenly revived. He decided to trust his instincts. If he had done that earlier, they might not be in this predicament. At this point, it might be their only hope. "We'll need a base of operations."

"I know of a place," Ernesto said.

"And a lot of cash."

"There I cannot help you, *jefe.*"

"Don't look at me," Hensley said.

"I have cash hidden in my hotel room," Dave said.

"That's helpful," Hensley said.

"And I know how we can get it."

Chapter Thirty-Nine: Masie

Masie awakened in a panic and checked the clock on the nightstand. Only fifty minutes had passed, but she was wide awake without a hint of fatigue. Experience told her that she would be good for the rest of the day. She got up and took another shower, trying to remember what had awakened her. She remembered a sense of alarm, like a light shining in her eyes.

While she was in the shower, the alarm clock went off. The buzzing grated on her nerves, and she rinsed off impatiently, wrapped herself in a towel, and went to turn it off. As she pushed the button, two mental images emerged in the sudden silence. The first one of her walking into the kitchen wrapped in a towel to find three men in her living room. The other of Paco leaning forward over breakfast saying, "Agents are quite adept at hiding their true intent."

Dave's occupation wasn't on her laptop. It wasn't in the medical file. Even she didn't know what he did. So how did Paco know he was an agent? What kind of agent? And what else did he know? She had told Paco that they found Rivera together, still warm, but he ignored that and zeroed in on Dave, which was completely wrong. Dave didn't have anything to do with it. He was as mystified as Masie herself.

She had come back to make sure Paco knew all the facts and to get out of town for a while, but now it seemed that Dave was a suspect. She knew instinctively that he was not a murderer. She couldn't just go about her day, abandoning him to fate. She had to warn him.

Her instincts told her not to make it her problem. She told them to shut up. She picked up the phone and dialed a number from memory. Father Roberto answered.

"Father, it's Masie. Can I talk to Dave? The tall one."

"He is not here. They left not long after sunrise."

Masie paused, not sure how to proceed.

"Masie?" Father Roberto said. "Who are these men? Are you in trouble?"

"Do you know where they went?"

"No, I'm sorry. I do not."

Masie thanked him and hung up. She dressed, trying to work out a way of locating Dave and Mr. Kite. As she left, she realized that Paco was trying to do the same thing. The thought did not give her comfort. She made sure the door was locked and closed. Not that it made a difference to anyone who wanted in.

As she walked down the hall, she heard a male voice say, "House-keeping." She rounded the corner in time to see a man in a hotel uniform enter a room. He looked familiar. She checked the room number. A spike of adrenaline coursed through her as she realized he had gone into Dave's room. Was this the man who had searched her rooms yesterday?

She rushed down the hall, but he closed the door before she got a look at him. She came to a stop in the hall. What did this mean? The door remained closed. She was sure that whatever his purpose, he didn't work for housekeeping. Did he work with Dave? Had he searched her rooms as Dave's accomplice? Or was he working against Dave? Perhaps the person who had planted the cigars?

Either way, maybe he could lead her to Dave. She continued down the hall to the lobby and took a stool at the bar, which commanded a view of the front and rear exits from the hotel and the entrances from both wings.

Noah stepped up to her, tall and lanky, with a carefree sincerity that no doubt earned him large tips from the guests. "Masie, you're starting early. What'll it be? A mimosa?"

"Morning, Noah," she said. "Black coffee. It's been a long night."

"Black coffee it is." He shoved a mug under a carafe.

At that moment, the man in the hotel uniform passed the bar and left through the entrance facing the lagoon. As Noah filled a mug, Masie jumped up and dashed past him.

"Sorry, Noah. Have to run."

Noah shrugged and sipped the coffee.

Masie paused at the entrance and peered out. The man bypassed the queue of taxis for the cab at the end. Masie stepped out and caught the eye of the doorman.

"Segundo, I need a taxi."

Segundo whistled the first cab in the queue up to the entrance. He opened the door and Masie got in. "Thank you," she said as he closed the door.

As she leaned forward to talk to the driver, the other cab drove past them, the man in the hotel uniform behind the wheel. The sight struck her momentarily speechless. Ernesto. She found her voice. "Can you follow that taxi without him knowing it?"

The driver's grunt was his only answer to this insult. He pulled away. She glanced at his license on the visor—Cesar. At this hour, there were few cars on the road. Cesar kept a respectable distance between them on the long drive to the mainland.

Masie thought about her conversation with Paco, about the possibility that Dave was mixed up in Rivera's death in some way. She replayed the discussion last night in the mission. She was pretty sure Dave was hiding something, but she didn't have enough to suspect him of murder. On the other hand, if she was wrong, following Ernesto to Dave was a mistake.

Once in the city, Cesar had to close the gap. As Ernesto wended through the city and Cesar kept a car or two between them, Masie realized that they were taking the route to the mission. Maybe Dave was still there.

Then Ernesto turned abruptly down a side street. To make the turn Cesar had to cut off a car, which formally registered a protest with its horn. Now they were right behind Ernesto and Cesar held back, but the direct route had turned into a complicated series of turns down side streets and alleys.

As Cesar followed Ernesto down a narrow street lined with shops that had living quarters on the second floor, he looked an apology at Masie in the rearview. "He knows we follow."

As if to illustrate the statement, Ernesto circled through a roundabout and headed back toward them. He locked eyes with Masie as they passed. She saw a look of surprise flash past as he sped back to the corner.

"That's okay, Cesar," Masie said. "Stick with him."

They circled the roundabout and met another taxi entering as they exited.

"Now he follow us," Cesar said, nodding toward the taxi.

Masie watched the taxi circle the roundabout and emerge behind them. Finding Dave was the primary goal. She would worry about the other taxi if it became necessary.

Ernesto suddenly accelerated, putting a few blocks between them, and took a hard right. When they made the turn, Masie saw Ernesto a block away, standing next to his cab, which was at the curb. He glanced back at them, slammed his door, and darted into a passageway between buildings.

Masie scrambled to get the cab fare. "Let me out there," she said, shoving bills over the seat.

Cesar stopped behind Ernesto's cab and took the money. "You want I wait for you?"

Masie was already out the door. "No. Thanks, Cesar."

As she crossed the sidewalk, she glanced back. The third taxi rounded the corner. She darted down the passageway, a wide sidewalk between shops cut off from the sun, searching for Ernesto. He had vanished. She rushed forward, intent on the sunlight at the end, when an arm thrust out from a doorway and pulled her in.

She was dragged into a dark room, an arm around her waist, the other hand over her mouth.

A voice rasped in her ear. "By the Virgin, I beg your forgiveness, *señorita*. If you will keep quiet, I will let go." She could feel the warm breath on her neck. "*De acuerdo?*"

Masie nodded as best she could and felt the grasp around her waist relax. The hand fell from her mouth. In the gloom of the room, Ernesto stood before her, his finger to his lips. She took in her surroundings, a cantina, empty except for a man cleaning glasses behind the bar, studiously unaware of the events at the front of the room.

Ernesto turned her toward the windows. Above the café curtains she saw the shoulders and head of a man following the same path she had taken. Ernesto performed the sign of the cross and picked up a chair. He waited for the man to pass the door, and then stepped out. Masie heard a noise. Before she could run to the window to see what had happened, Ernesto returned, set the chair inside the door, and motioned for her to follow.

A body lay sprawled on his face on the sidewalk. Ernesto pushed him over with his foot. "You know this man?"

Masie nodded. "Finney."

"Do we bring him?"

Masie knelt down and checked his pulse.

"He will be okay." Ernesto said.

Masie stood. "No," she said, slowly. "We don't bring him."

"Okay. This way."

Ernesto led her back to his cab, and a few minutes later, he parked the car in an alley a block from the mission. He led her to the café where two days ago she and Dave talked over tacos. Mr. Kite and Dave now sat at a table, not talking to each other.

Dave saw her and stood up. "Masie!"

Mr. Kite looked up. He didn't seem pleased to see her.

"She followed me," Ernesto said.

"Paco is looking for you," Masie said.

"Paco Torres?"

"She was followed," Ernesto said.

"Finney," Masie said.

Ernesto shrugged. "He is not following us any longer."

"Did you get the cash?" Dave stuffed the bundle Ernesto handed him into his pocket. "Let's go."

"You have Masie, and you have the cash," Mr. Kite said. "Everybody in favor of going to the airport indicate by a show of hands." Mr. Kite raised his hand. No one else did.

Masie looked at the group, confused. If they wanted to leave, why did they need her? They could have been gone hours ago.

"You forget that Torres knows where we live," Dave said.

"Correction," Hensley said. "He knows where you live. He doesn't know squat about Ernesto, and he doesn't want Masie." Then, almost as an afterthought, "And I don't have an address for him to track down."

Dave looked at Mr. Kite with an expression Masie couldn't interpret. There was sadness, impatience, resignation. The expression hardened. "You know what? You're right." He pulled the bundle out of his pocket, counted off some bills, and held them out to Mr. Kite. "Here's two thousand dollars. Do what you do best."

Mr. Kite looked at the money. He glanced at Dave. To Masie, he seemed to shrink for a second. Then he straightened up and looked Dave in the eye. He snatched the money from Dave's hand, extracted a single bill, and slapped it on the table.

"You heard the man. Let's go."

Chapter Forty: Dave

Dave tried to get a sense of where Ernesto was taking them, but his ignorance of Cancún made it impossible. Once they arrived, he would get Ernesto to show him their location on a map, but for now he would have to trust him. It seemed an acceptable risk. After all, he returned with the money. And Masie.

As on the previous night, Hensley rode shotgun and Dave and Masie were in the back. Dave looked at Masie. She studied him back. Despite Hensley's opinion, Dave rejected the idea that she was part of the suicide vacation scheme. He still didn't understand the thing with Uncle Rex and the will, but that could wait until they figured out what to do about Torres.

Ernesto took them to an apartment building deep inside old-town Cancún across from a café. The structure was built in a hollow square. Breezeways on each side lead into a large courtyard shaded with ancient palm trees and local plants that looked like they were made of wax. They followed him up the stairs to the second floor balcony.

"My cousin," Ernesto said as he opened the door. "He works for the oil company. He won't be back until next week."

It didn't have a large footprint. The door opened onto the kitchen, which was divided from the living room by a bar. To the left, French doors and a shallow balcony overlooking the street. Straight ahead, a tiny bedroom.

Hensley went straight to the small television in the living room, flicked it on, and dropped onto the couch. He picked up the remote and began flicking through the channels. "What's for lunch?" he hollered over his shoulder.

Ernesto opened the refrigerator. "*Nada,*" he said, and closed it.

Dave peeled a bill from the bundle from his pocket and peeled off a bill. "Could you get us something from the café? We'll have whatever you like."

Ernesto took the money and left.

Dave pulled a chair from the table and dropped into it. He motioned Masie to another chair and she sat.

"Why did you—" they both said at the same time and then fell silent.

Dave smiled. "It seems like we have the same question. You first."

"Why did you run? If you had nothing to do with Mr. Rivera's death, why not talk to the authorities?"

"I said I was innocent, not naive." He waited for a response, but didn't get one. "What about you? Why did you leave? And why did you come back?"

"Paco thinks you're involved in some kind of scheme to blackmail him."

Dave smiled. She had known the answer to her question, although she didn't seem to realize it. If a man like Paco Torres wanted you in jail, or worse, the fact that you were innocent wouldn't matter. Especially in Mexico.

Seeing Masie sitting across the table told Dave two things, that she didn't believe he was a blackmailer and that she was not involved in Torres's illicit activities. But even as he came to this conclusion, he heard Hensley's voice in his head. She was here to lead Torres to them. After all, Finney followed her, perhaps with her knowledge. Probably at her request.

He wanted to ask her about Uncle Rex. Knowing the truth about her would make dealing with Torres much simpler. But Hensley's voice in his head also sounded like the voice of Harris, his old partner. You can't run a case on intuition. You never know when an informant is playing his boss and when he's playing you.

But at least he could get her to say it. "And you?"

She studied him, then looked at Hensley, who was watching a Mexican soap opera, all drama and machismo and cleavage.

"I think you're hiding something, but not blackmail. Or murder."

"Everyone has secrets," Dave said, holding her eyes with his.

"Hey," Hensley yelled from the couch. "You might want to see this."

They joined him in the living room. He turned up the volume.

Dave's passport photo filled the screen before it shrank into the inset behind the anchor. The Spanish was too rapid for Dave to follow, although he did pick out the word *homicidio*, which didn't sound promising. The shot cut to the morgue where a body lay on a slab, the neck and face purplish and swollen.

Hensley squinted at the TV. "That thing is Rivera?"

"Used to be," Dave answered.

The door opened. Ernesto entered and set the food on the table. He joined them in the living room, holding out the change. Dave waved it away and turned back to the TV. Passport photos of both Dave and Masie replaced the morgue shot.

"*Madre de Dios*," Ernesto said.

The picture switched to a live shot of a reporter at the entrance of the resort, talking with Torres. He was slim but muscular, self-assured and in control.

"Who's that?" Hensley asked.

"My boss, Paco."

"What's he saying?" Dave asked.

Masie listened for a minute. "He says I'm his best employee and that it's probably just some kind of misunderstanding and not to be alarmed because he's sure I'll come in and help them sort it out."

"I thought you went in already," Dave said. "You said you talked to him."

"I did."

The on-location reporter handed off to the anchor, who said a few things, probably something like, "We'll keep you informed." Then the daytime drama returned.

Dave snatched the remote from Hensley and hit the mute button.

"This changes things. We need to get Masie out of the country."

"Masie?" Hensley asked. "What about—" He held up a hand. "Okay, fine. As long as we all get out, I don't care about your priorities."

Masie stared at the TV, not seeing the program. "But he knows . . I told him . . ."

"There's no time. We just lost our only advantage."

Hensley barked out a bitter laugh. "Advantage? We had an advantage?"

Dave was in no mood to spar with Hensley. "To operate under the radar." He turned to Ernesto. "How fast can you get us to the airport?"

Ernesto looked back at him with an expression of confusion and caution. "What have you done, *jefe?*"

Hensley jumped up. "The airport? They'll be watching the airport."

Dave didn't take his eyes from Ernesto. "It's a long story, my friend, but you must believe me when I tell you that none of us had anything to do with that man's death."

Ernesto waited for more.

Dave could just call for a taxi if Ernesto refused, but getting a flight out was a long shot. He suspected that if he could win Ernesto's confidence, they would have a significant advantage in formulating a backup plan.

"You know the man at the resort, Paco Torres?"

Ernesto nodded. "He is a very powerful man."

"Yes, and he is the man responsible for this murder." Dave ignored Masie's questioning cry of protest. "And he has the power to make it look like we did it."

Ernesto seemed to be considering his words.

"We both know how powerful men become powerful. They do not suffer the consequences of their own mistakes. That is for others."

Ernesto nodded.

"We need a ride to the airport. You are just a taxi we hired to take us there. And you will be well compensated."

At this last statement, Ernesto's expression changed. He pulled back slightly and looked at Masie as if embarrassed. "If I do it, it is not for money."

Dave nodded, keeping his eyes on Ernesto. "I understand, my friend. You are a man of honor. But there is some risk." He stepped to the kitchen. "I will put the money on the table. What you do with it is your decision." He placed a stack of bills on the table.

"They'll be watching the airport," Hensley said again, slowly, as if explaining the obvious to a small child.

"Very likely," Dave said. "But there is a chance that we can slip through before they get organized."

"Why?" Masie said.

Dave looked at her, startled. So did the others.

"Why is Paco doing this? What's going on?"

Hensley opened his mouth, but Dave cut him off. "I can't answer that question, but I will find out, no matter how long it takes. That's what I've been trying to do for the last twenty-four hours. But now that Torres has played his hand, it's too risky to stay in Mexico while we find the answers."

Masie seemed confused and hesitant. Dave put his hand on her shoulder.

"Masie, I know this is a lot to process, but at this point, your life is in danger. There's no time to figure it all out. Once we're in the States, we can work out those details. And then, if you want, you can come back."

Masie searched his face, and then turned to Ernesto. He nodded once. She shrugged. "I'm booked on a flight to Aspen in a few hours anyway."

Hensley raised his eyebrows.

On the drive to the airport, Masie asked one question. "Why do you think Paco is responsible for Rivera's death?"

"It's a long and complicated story," Dave said. "Let's save it for the flight."

As they rounded the corner approaching the departures area, Hensley said, "Let's take a slow pass. If it looks clear, we can circle around."

Ernesto checked the rearview. Dave nodded and he kept to the outside lane.

Dave searched the crowd and noticed a policeman. Then another. This one glanced from a printout to the faces of people emerging from vehicles.

Then Masie gasped. "There's Finney."

Finney, with two black eyes and a bandage on his head, scanned the crowd from a position near a doorway. His eyes drifted to the road and locked on their car. He squinted at them as they drove past.

Hensley laughed. "That's a man who should have taken a sick day."

Ernesto drove on without changing his speed and they exited the airport.

"Next idea?" Hensley asked.

"The bus station," Dave answered.

Hensley snorted. Ernesto turned to the north. Fifteen minutes later they found police standing at all the entrances to the bus terminal. They drove past without slowing.

"Maybe we could hire a rowboat," Hensley said.

Hensley's sarcasm was usually unhelpful, but this time it started Dave thinking. They could charter a boat and sail it to the Caymans, or even Miami, which wasn't that much farther. But that would require hiring a skipper along with the boat. Dave's experiences with sailing were limited to a few weekends on a friend's boat on Chesapeake Bay when he was stationed in D.C. He wasn't competent to make a three hundred mile cruise on open seas. And varied though Hensley's skills seemed to be, he wasn't about to trust him for the job, even if he claimed expertise.

But a four-seat Cessna would easily get them to US soil much faster than a bus, a car, or a boat.

"Ernesto, is there a private airstrip nearby that charters planes? Maybe someplace that does sky-diving trips for tourists?"

Ernesto nodded. "I know a place."

Chapter Forty-One: Dave

Booking a plane required a bit of negotiation. Even with Ernesto's help as translator, it took an hour for Dave to convince the owner of the sky-diving business to allow them to charter the plane for a day trip to Cozumel. That was the easy part. The ticklish part was opting out of using their pilot. As Dave expected, cash eliminated the obstacles. A surcharge, kind of like a corking fee, took care of the pilot issue by paying him anyway. A look at Dave's pilot license and a deposit big enough to buy the ancient Cessna 172 Skyhawk outright settled the issue of allowing a stranger to fly the plane without a chaperone. Ernesto suggested an additional gratuity to make the authorities look the other way if they didn't happen to return. Fitting, since Dave had no intention of flying it back from Miami.

Given the urgency of the situation, Dave was tempted to do a cursory "kick the tires and light the fires" preflight inspection and get going. But this was an old plane and they'd be crossing three hundred miles of water. While everyone else stood by impatiently, he took the time to do a proper pre-flight.

With full tanks and three adults, they would be at max gross weight, which was not a problem. The runway was long enough, and the airstrip was free of obstacles that would require a steep climb.

He declared the plane airworthy. As Hensley and Masie climbed in, Dave held his hand out to Ernesto.

"Thanks, Ernesto."

Ernesto grasped it firmly and looked Dave in the eye. "You be careful, *jefe*."

Dave got in and secured the door.

"What happens when we get to the States?" Masie asked from the right seat.

"Buckle up. We'll talk when we're in the air." Dave continued working through the checklist.

"Life vests?" he called over his shoulder.

Hensley dug around behind the rear seats. "Four."

Dave nodded and started the engine. It roared to life with a puff of smoke. It had been a while since he'd flown a 172, but it came back to him. He completed the after-start checks and taxied out.

The old plane rumbled down the runway. It took more speed to get it off the ground than the Jenny, but it also had a lot more power. Nobody spoke as they lifted off and headed southeast. Dave wanted to give the impression he really was going to Cozumel, which was due south. Once out of sight over the water, he would turn north toward the tip of Cuba.

Out here they saw scrubby vegetation and rocky soil, for the most part. As they approached the coastal highway, small commercial buildings appeared, then smaller resorts and beach houses.

Once they were past the coast, Masie yelled over the engine noise. "Can we talk now?"

"Sure."

"What about passports?"

Dave checked his altitude—1500 feet, still in range of a signal. "Harris will handle it." He pulled out his cell, clicked the battery into place, and dialed the number.

"You can cross the border without a passport?" Masie asked.

Just as Harris answered, a puff of smoke came out of the engine cowling, and the engine sputtered. The propeller spun idly. For a moment, the only sound was the whistling of the wind and the voice of Harris saying "Hello? Hello?" from the phone. The noise of panic followed.

Masie was the first to speak. "What happened?"

Hensley was next. "Don't tell me you're pulling over to make a call."

Dave was last. "Hang on." He dropped the phone and checked the instruments. He was doing 85 knots, which was about 100 mph, and they were at 1500 feet. He immediately started a gentle turn back toward the shore and raised the nose to slow his speed to maximize gliding distance. He checked both ignitions and selected the opposite wing fuel tank. With the prop windmilling, the engine should start. But it didn't.

"Hensley! Life vests!"

"What happened?"

"We lost power. I'm turning back to the airport."

"Then why am I getting the vests?"

"Because we might not make it. Now shut up and let me concentrate."

Dave banked away from the open sea in a slow, silent, graceful turn above the sparkling turquoise waters. Ninety degrees into the turn, he saw the surf on the white sand beaches of the island of San Miguel thirty miles dead ahead. He could even make out the cruise ships docked at Cozumel. It would have been lovely if they weren't about to die.

White smoke billowed from the engine. Probably fuel in contact with the engine and exhaust manifold. He cut the fuel, turned off the master switch, and closed the cabin air vents.

Hensley pushed a vest at Dave, but he shook his head.

"Put it on. I'm busy."

Hensley handed it to Masie and got another for himself. They fumbled frantically to get the vests on.

Dave had no desire to attempt a water landing. If they hit the water at 50 knots, which was about 60 mph, the stall speed of a 172, they could flip and sink. His best bet was to reach land.

He checked the instruments again once they had completed the half-minute turn and were headed directly toward the coast. It had cost them 500 feet of altitude and 20 knots of speed. The good news was that they were now at the optimum gliding speed for a 172. The bad news was that they had two minutes before they hit the ground, and the airport was four minutes away. The best he could hope for was Highway 307. Or, if they couldn't get that far, the beach. But he preferred a hard surface with perhaps a few cars to a soft surface crowded with sunbathers.

Highway 307 ran down to Playa del Carmen, a mile from the beach, two lanes each direction with street lights down the middle and power lines on either side. It would be a tight squeeze for the thirty-six-foot wingspan of the 172, but he might be able to keep it centered. If there weren't too many cars. If they made it that far.

They were heading southwest now, getting closer to land. Farther south, 307 ran closer to the beach. Unfortunately, that wasn't because the highway was closer but because the beach angled away from their position, back to the west toward the highway.

Dave checked the altimeter. Five hundred feet. One minute to impact. He checked the highway. No cars, but they weren't going to make it. He banked left and lined up with the harder wet strip between the water and the dry sand.

Early in the afternoon, plenty of tourists enjoyed the beach, unaware of the silent metal bird approaching faster than they could run. Kids built sandcastles a few yards from the surf, but Dave had no way to warn them.

They were seconds from touching down. Given the tourists, he would have to land on the dry sand, a much riskier alternative for everyone.

"I know you'd love to watch this amazing landing, but you might want to assume the crash position here pretty soon."

Dave didn't take his eyes off the job at hand. He couldn't see Hensley, but in his peripheral vision, Masie didn't move. She seemed unable to tear her eyes away from the ground as it rose to greet them, and the people enjoying their vacation on the beach, unaware.

A woman wearing a huge sunhat looked up. Her mouth opened in a scream Dave couldn't hear, but others could. More heads turned. People scrambled. The plane dropped lower. Dave went to full flaps.

"Like soon," Dave yelled. "Like right now."

Masie finally leaned forward, head between knees, arms over her head, hands on her neck.

Although the 172 could be converted to a tail-dragger configuration, this one had the standard nose wheel, not the best for landings on soft surfaces because the nose gear could dig into the sand and flip the plane. Just before they touched down, Dave eased back on the yoke. The tail dropped, plowing sand and reducing their speed before the main wheels hit.

People dove out of their path, their faces flashing by the windows.

Since they had no cargo, most of the weight was at the front of the plane. When the main wheels touched the sand, the plane settled on the nose wheel. But before it buried itself in the sand and flipped the plane end-over-end, a palm tree loomed into view and clipped off the left wing. That slowed them a little. The right wing dipped into the sand.

The plane cartwheeled. Even strapped in, Dave felt like a chew toy shaken violently by a gigantic dog. An angry dog. Then like a tennis shoe in a dryer. He lost all sense of orientation or direction. Just an eternity of kaleidoscopic images and the noise of buckling metal. Then a sudden stop and the pinging and popping of settling metal.

As Dave slowly regained coherence, he tried to assess the situation. As far as he could tell, he had survived. The other wing was gone and the plane listed to the right at a 45-degree angle. Masie leaned against the door, cushioned by the lifejacket, apparently unconscious.

Dave took several deep breaths to clear his head, with marginal success. He wedged his right leg against Masie's seat, released his seat belt, and eased over to check on her. She was breathing. No visible wounds. With deliberate effort, he let his hand drop against her neck, snaked two fingers out to check her pulse. Her eyes opened. She turned her head, confused to see him looming above her, and tried to pull away, but there was nowhere she could go. Dave braced his arm against her seat and tried to push back. He heard his voice ask, "Are you okay?"

She shook her head slowly, as if to verify that it was still attached. "I think so."

With a tremendous effort, Dave twisted his head to look into the back seat. Hensley listed at an angle with the plane, staring at Dave, one eye bruised. "I'm fine. Thanks for asking."

"Yeah. Me too."

Dave tried to open the door, but it didn't budge. He scanned the cabin. The windshield had popped out. "Looks like we're taking the front exit." He climbed over the instrument panel and put his hand on the engine cowling, but drew it back immediately. Too hot. He eased back down into his seat. If he could trip the window latch, he might be able to force it open all the way. On the fourth try, it cracked open, and he pushed. It stopped halfway, held in place by the retaining bracket.

A small crowd surrounded the front of the plane. A tall, tanned guy with grey chest hair and a massive beer gut hanging over his swimming trunks helped Dave pry the window open. He tossed it aside. Dave crawled out and slid to the ground. He tested his legs to see if they would hold him, then walked a few steps.

Dave scanned the crowd. "Anybody hurt?"

The big guy shook his head. "Not that I know of. How about you all?" He had a drawl as thick as crankcase oil.

Dave shook his head. "I think we'll walk away from it."

"Well, sir, they say any landing you can walk away from—"

"Can you give me a hand with the passengers?"

Masie was already halfway through the opening. He steadied her as she got her feet under herself and then handed her off to the tall guy. Hensley poked his head out of the opening, staring at Dave with his one good eye.

"You might want this." He held out Dave's cell phone.

"Oh, is that what—"

"Yes, now get out of the way."

Dave took the phone. Hensley slid out of the plane.

While Dave checked his phone, the tall guy looked at Hensley and whistled. "Let's get you some ice for that shiner." He scooped some ice from a cooler into a plastic grocery bag.

Hensley held it to his eye gingerly. "Thanks."

Chapter Forty-Two: Hensley

Hensley sat on one of the main wheels, held the ice to his eye, and pondered the odds of the engine failing all by itself.

Masie asked the obvious question. "What happened to the plane?"

Davison borrowed a beach towel to protect his hands, pried off the mangled engine cowling, and poked around inside. Hensley heaved himself to his feet, walked up, and looked over Davison's shoulder. A tube with a three-inch section missing caught his eye, the area around it charred. "What did that used to be?"

"Fuel line," Davison said.

"What could cause that? Wear and tear? Poor maintenance?" Masie asked.

Davison shook his head. "Looks like an explosion."

"You're calling it sabotage?"

"Somebody waited until we were too far to come back and then blew the line."

"But . . ."

Hensley turned from his study of the engine to catch Masie's performance. She had just realized that her partners had written her off as an expendable member of the team, that they considered her loss an acceptable cost of doing business.

"But they would have to know in advance that we were chartering a plane at that airstrip. And which plane we would take. How is that possible? Even we didn't know until the moment we did it."

Hensley detected a note of hysteria in her voice.

"The technology and logistics are pretty simple," Davison said. "Plastic explosive. Cell phone."

"Plastic explosive?" Her gaze bounced back and forth between Hensley and Dave. "You can arrange to cross the border without passports? Mr. Rivera dies in your room? The *Federales* have your picture at the airport and the bus station? Who are you?"

"What about the phone call?" Hensley asked. That got their attention. "Five minutes after we got there, the owner took a phone call, and suddenly he couldn't rent a plane to us."

Davison nodded. "It took an hour to bring him around. Plenty of time to rig the device."

Hensley held Masie's eye. "Do you know anyone who could do that?"

"No," she said immediately. "Of course not."

But before she turned away, Hensley saw the furrows on her forehead go smooth and her eyes go blank as she realized she did indeed know a specific someone who could. He pulled Davison to the other side of the plane.

"She knows," he hissed in Davison's ear. "She's just realized that Torres has left her hanging in the wind."

"You're turning into a paranoid with your conspiracy theories, Hensley."

Hensley pushed him away. "A paranoid?" He kicked the fuselage of the destroyed Cessna. "Look at this. I'm not a paranoid. I'm a target." He moved back to Davison and lowered his voice. "And she knows who pulled the trigger, because she's one of them."

Davison glanced over his shoulder. The crowd had grown. "Time to make ourselves scarce." He struck a track between the dunes to the beach houses.

Masie hurried after him. Hensley brought up the rear and watched Masie for signs of bolting.

Davison led them between the beach houses to a road that ran parallel to the beach. It took a few minutes to find an access road that headed west. He made a phone call as he turned north. "Ernesto will pick us up on the highway."

They had made it a mile toward Cancún when the taxi pulled up.

In the car, Davison filled Ernesto in on the most recent developments and launched into his next plan. "We can drive to Laredo."

"Buses, planes, cars. What else? Burros? If I had just changed my ticket a day earlier, I wouldn't be in this mess."

Davison ignored her. "Ernesto, how far is it to Laredo?"

"It is a very long road, *jefe*. About two thousand kilometers. Through the desert. Very lonely."

"Perfect. The last thing we want is company."

"We can go to Brownsville. Better road. I have a cousin in Matamoros."

"How many cousins do you have?" Hensley asked.

"Many," Ernesto replied. "Very many."

Hensley didn't offer his opinion on Davison's latest plan. Why should he? Davison had ignored everything he'd said to date. Hensley reflected that, like Masie, if he had taken his own advice and left last night, he'd be back in the States now.

At some point, one had to recognize that one had crossed the line from supporting a brother to enabling self-destructive behavior, and Hensley had come to that point. All Masie had to do was wait until they were in the desert, hundreds of miles from any form of sanctuary, alert Torres and his minions to their location, and leave before she became collateral damage. Davison's plan amounted to nothing more than removing all the obstacles to Torres's plan.

Back at the apartment, Davison spread a roadmap on the kitchen table, and everyone gathered around it.

Ernesto pointed to the highway leading west. "We take 180 to Merida and follow the coast all the way to Matamoros."

Davison shook his head. "They've been one step ahead of us so far. If they think we're driving, that's the road they'll monitor. Let's take 307 south to Chetumal and cut across to Escarcega on 186."

Ernesto grunted.

"What about the cab?" Masie asked. In answer to their blank expressions, she said, "Finney saw the cab. They know what to look for. It might be how they found us at the airstrip."

Hensley nodded, impressed by this play to remove any lingering suspicion about her involvement.

"My cousin has a van we can use, for a small consideration. It looks like—" Ernesto glanced at Masie. "It does not look nice, but it runs very well."

"Good idea," Davison said. "If you can get the van this afternoon, we can get some sleep and leave at sundown."

"Which cousin is this, Ernesto?" Hensley asked. "The one who lives here or the one at the border?"

"No, it is a different cousin. He works for a large farm. Very big. In the offseason he sometimes uses the van to make deliveries. And it has the reserve gas tank."

Davison nodded. "Good. We might make the whole trip with only one stop." He studied the map. "Say, in Veracruz."

Ernesto made a call.

Hensley opened the refrigerator. Except for a few non-perishable items, the shelves were bare. "It's five o'clock somewhere. Anybody else want a beer? I'm buying."

"Get us some food while you're at it," Davison said.

Ernesto, the phone to his ear, nodded. Masie caught Hensley's eye, as if daring him to speak his suspicions aloud.

Outside, he crossed the street and entered the café. The tables were empty. The air was close, almost stifling. A man behind a counter punched numbers into an old adding machine.

"*Tacos?*" Hensley asked as he approached.

The man nodded. "*Pollo o carne de vacuno?*"

"*Carne. Tres. Para ir.*"

The man called out the order. An answer came from the kitchen.

"*Y una cerveza,*" Hensley said.

Hensley took the beer and sat down at a table near the door. He watched the entrance to the apartment. He was halfway through the beer when Ernesto emerged, got in his taxi, and left. A woman came out from the kitchen and set a greasy paper sack on the table. Hensley finished the beer, set the bottle on the table, picked up the sack, and crept out, keeping an eye on the window to the apartment. He took the first corner that presented itself and trotted a few more blocks to a main road, where he flagged down a taxi.

As he headed to Hotel Row, Hensley ate the tacos. He had no doubt that Masie was involved in this scam, but it would take more than common sense to get Davison to admit it. With her safely holed up in town, he could search her rooms for the evidence without fear of interruption.

At the hotel, he lurked around her door until a maid rounded the corner pushing a cart with bedding and towels. He slapped his head like he had forgotten something, turned around, dug in a pocket, then another pocket, searching frantically.

The maid hesitated, and he turned as if he had just seen her. "Great! I locked my keycard in the room. Can you open it for me?"

She edged back with a mixture of fear and suspicion.

"Locked out," he said loudly and slowly. He pantomimed running the card and opening the door, then pointed inside. "My card. Inside."

"Front desk," she said uncertainly.

"No time," he said. "And you're already here." He held out a twenty dollar bill. "It would be a great help to me."

Her gaze drifted from the door to the money, her resistance melting. Then she checked up and down the hall, snatched up the bill, pulled out her card, and opened the door.

Chapter Forty-Three: Dave

Dave had done his best to hide it from the others, but the plane crash had shaken him up, and not just physically. Evidently Torres had an extensive network of resources, exceptionally efficient resources. Hence the suggestion to stay under the radar, to take a private car instead of buying a ticket or renting anything.

He felt better once they got back to the apartment and a solid plan began to form. His attitude improved even more when Hensley left to get food. His brother's normally annoying personality became insufferable when he turned paranoid. With the wisdom of hindsight, Dave realized he should have made an immediate departure a condition of taking the money.

After Ernesto left to swap out the taxi for the van, Dave charted a route on the map while Masie marked it down. He pointed out alternate routes in case they met up with difficulties along the way, and together they worked up a list of things to buy before they set out.

Dave called Harris, brought him up to speed, and arranged their entry at Brownsville. Harris wanted them to go to the consulate, but Dave refused. He wouldn't trust his fate to some third-level functionary who was nothing more than an extension of the consulate in Merida, which was not exactly Mexico City. In Davison's estimation, actual US soil in the Brownsville customs office trumped symbolic US soil at an office in the hotel zone. After a long argument, Harris reluctantly agreed to facilitate their entry to Brownsville in two days.

When Ernesto arrived with the van and asked about the food, they realized Hensley hadn't returned. Ernesto checked with the café and reported that Hensley had left hours ago with three tacos. Masie wanted to cancel the trip, but Dave stuck to the plan—get some sleep and set out after dark.

Dave insisted Masie take the bedroom. He stretched out on the couch with a washcloth on his eyes to block the light of the afternoon sun. But he couldn't stop his mind from retracing the events of the day.

Despite what he told Masie, he couldn't figure how Torres was able to predict their movements and sabotage the plane before they even chartered it. But it showed the measure of the man's despera-tion that he was willing to accept both Masie and Hensley as collat-eral damage in his attempt to eliminate Dave.

He had known a few people like Torres, successful business-men who had a name for people who played by the rules: losers. They didn't see success as a good behavior award for the timid. They claimed it as the birthright of those with the will to possess it at all costs.

In Torres's mind, he probably placed himself in the pantheon of iconoclasts responsible for human progress, from the first man to feed a village for the winter by bringing down a mastodon to the men who defied the chains of gravity and put a golf ball on the moon.

Dave finally gave up on sleep. He tossed the washcloth aside, opened the French doors, and leaned on the balcony. The surround-ing neighborhood wasn't prosperous by US standards, but it wasn't a slum. The businesses across the street appeared to be stable, even thriving.

He heard a noise, and Masie stood beside him on the balcony. He smiled at her. "You couldn't sleep either, huh?"

She shook her head. "Every time I close my eyes, I see the beach rushing up at me, the plane hitting the ground and rolling." She gripped the wrought-iron railing until her knuckles were white. "I've had one hour of sleep in the last forty-eight hours, but I'll have to be a lot more tired before I'll be able to keep my eyes closed."

Dave understood the feeling. For several months in Angola, ev-ery time he closed his eyes, he saw Hensley backing away into the jungle. Even years later, whenever he felt unsure or conflicted, the dream would return.

He looked down at the café across the street, the location of the last sighting of Hensley. For a few hours, between the buñuelos and the crash, it had seemed that Hensley might stick it out. As much as Dave resented Hensley's philosophy of self-interest, he couldn't find it in his heart to hold it against him this time. If ever there was a situ-ation where it was every man for himself, this was it.

Thoughts of Hensley brought to mind the issue of Masie's allegiance. Hensley wasn't completely off the rails in his suspicions, but whether she be friend or foe, the best thing was to keep her close.

"You never said how you know Rivera."

Masie regarded him with hazel eyes that seemed to know too much about the world for one lifetime. "Neither did you."

"I bought a plane from him."

"That woman, last night, said something about a federal investigation. And Paco seems to think you're an agent of some kind."

So much for a low profile. "Retired." He was giving more than he was getting. "And you? How do you know Rivera?"

This time she didn't hesitate. "Paco does business with him sometimes. Or did." Although the afternoon sun warmed them, she shuddered. "I spend as little time around him as possible. When he looked at me, it felt like that centipede had crawled up my back."

"What kind of business?"

Masie shrugged. "No idea. He would come by the office a few times a year."

"I got the feeling he worked the shady side of the street. Was he with the cartels? Los Zetas maybe?"

Her eyes narrowed. "Are you sure you're retired?"

"Sorry." Dave gestured with his palms up. "Occupational hazard."

As far as he could tell, she knew nothing about Rivera other than that he gave her the creeps, which spoke more for her character than against. As he attempted to distill his experience of Masie into its essence, he realized that the only thing he had against her was the fact that Uncle Rex had changed his will. If that fact were removed, her presence at his death wasn't unduly suspicious, and everything he knew from personal experience was uniformly positive.

It all came down to the will. If she truly didn't know about the will, then she didn't kill him for it. The one thing he needed to know and the one thing he couldn't ask her. But how else could he make sense of Rex changing the will? Was Rex of unsound mind, caught up in some kind of second adolescent obsession?

He glanced at her. It would be understandable if it were true. Although she was evidently of Irish descent, the warm glow of the late afternoon sun glistened on her black hair and painted her fair skin a golden hue.

Dave tried to imagine her as a local girl, but the longer he looked at her, the more it seemed as if she could belong on any continent, in any setting. In the South Pacific, in the Middle East, in his home in Austin, Texas. That last thought sent a frisson of electricity through Dave's frame.

He saw her in the kitchen, laughing as he juggled spices while making dinner. He saw her on the deck, reading a book in the hammock while he made margaritas. In the den watching Hitchcock movies, in the bedroom. He stopped himself.

Dave wondered what Hensley would say if he brought Masie home to Austin. Fortunately, Hensley had acted according to type and vanished, so Dave didn't have to listen to his inflated oratory.

"Do you have any brothers or sisters?" Dave asked.

Masie hesitated. "No."

"Lucky you."

She looked away, her eyes glistening, her black hair like a moonless night.

He tried to imagine Masie as a child. In Detroit. Wasn't that what she said on that first night? Growing up in the declining years of a crumbling city. He wondered if she had been happy anyway. She seemed like the type who could make the best of any situation.

She must not have been a child of privilege, or she wouldn't have ended up as a nurse, even if she had been lucky enough to land in a tropical climate.

The thought hit him like the train at the end of the tunnel. Mom. Child of privilege. Nurse. Tropical climate. Who was he to make pronouncements about Masie's origins?

"How—" he started, but had to stop to clear his throat. "How did you end up in Cancún?"

She took a long time to answer. "Fate. Destiny." The sun slipped behind the building, casting her face into shadow. "Do you think that things are meant to happen?"

Right then, Dave wished he believed in such things, that fate had led him to Masie. He wanted to twist his fingers in her hair, pull her to him, kiss her. But like a fool, he told her the truth. "No. I think it's the other way around."

"Is that supposed to be a joke?"

"I think things happen and we add the meaning."

"I believe that when two people meet, destinies intersect. The future is changed."

"Okay." Dave leaned back from the balcony against the stucco wall and watched her. It was a nice way to see the world, but self-delusion was dangerous, regardless of how much he wanted it to be true.

"You want to know how I met Mr. Rivera?"

The edge in her voice was new, like a challenge.

"When Mom died, we moved to the city. I got into the robotics club in high school and decided to apply to the Carnegie Mellon Robotics Institute for a degree in medical robotics, but we didn't have the money. I studied nursing and took a job at the hospital to save for college. I was working ER, and Paco came in with food poisoning. He thought he was dying." She smiled. "In a way, he was right. Ultimately, everything that is living is dying. It's just a question of when and what you do in the meantime."

"Paco hired you from his deathbed?"

"He gave me a ticket out of Detroit. Dad drank himself to death to spite my mother, who died because she couldn't stand the thought of living."

"So you met Paco, your destinies intersected, and your future was changed."

"Yes, and maybe his future was changed too."

"This is the story of how you met Rivera?"

A hazel fire flashed in Masie's eyes. "Haven't you been listening? If Mom hadn't died, we never would have left Erie, so I wouldn't have heard of robotics, so I wouldn't have picked Carnegie Mellon, so I wouldn't have gone into nursing, so I wouldn't have been in the ER when Paco came in, so he never would have hired me, so I never would have come down here and met Mr. Rivera. Destiny. Fate." She looked out over the city. "I don't expect someone like you to understand."

That last sentence was a slap. "Like me?"

"You've seen man at his worst and written him off. You think the world is like Mr. Rivera." She speared him with her eyes and held him there. "You're not the only one who has seen people when they're down. I've seen people at their most desperate, facing eternity or whatever is on the other side. Sometimes that fire burns away the impurities and reveals the gold."

As she stared at him, practically daring him to disagree, he suddenly wanted to tell her who he was, why he was here. He wanted her to explain why she hadn't asked about the will, hadn't tried to claim the money. Most of all, he wanted her to say that she didn't know. About Rex, about the will, about the Aztec Gold package, about anything evil in the world. That she was as unspoiled as she seemed. But how likely was that?

Something, perhaps Hensley's voice whispering in his mind, said to wait until they were safe on American soil where she couldn't run, slip from his grasp and disappear forever. He didn't know if it was because of the money or because he couldn't bear the thought of never seeing her again.

"I'm glad you took the job," he said after a long silence.

Masie looked at him with a puzzled expression, and he held her gaze as the last rays of the sun faded away, wishing that he dared to kiss her.

In the twilight, Masie and Ernesto packed provisions in a suitcase while Dave went across the street for takeaway. He bought enough for Hensley, sensing the futility of it even as he paid. Hensley most likely had used his two thousand dollars to disappear in a manner more to his liking, sans Masie.

As he crossed the street with the food, headlights suddenly blinded him.

Chapter Forty-Four: Hensley

Hensley closed the door and began his search. A series of framed photos lined the counter—Masie in various locations and groups of what he took to be friends and family. The last showed her kneeling next to an old man in a wheelchair, her arm draped around his shoulders. Her father? Or her first victim? Maybe she had trophies from other victims as well.

He scanned the room. His gaze fell on the laptop.

After an hour he gave up and expanded his search to the filing cabinet. Thirty minutes later he was no further along, other than finding Uncle Rex's file, which contained nothing but details about his secret medical condition. He was amused to run across Vera Crenshaw's file. It revealed that she was in as good a shape as one could reasonably expect when one was seventy-eight and grew up in the South. Adult onset diabetes, high cholesterol, osteoporosis, and other typical ailments of old age, which required a whole cocktail of medications.

He abandoned the files. Whatever he was searching for was probably not a document, anyway. Maybe something more personal. Hensley passed through the kitchen into the bedroom. He started with the dresser, tossing the clothes on the bed in a pile, checking the drawers for false bottoms. Checked under the bed. In the night stand. He worked methodically through the room and into the closet.

His search finally brought him to an engraved wooden box with a lock. He remembered seeing a key in a drawer earlier, but he couldn't be bothered to dig through the clothes to find it. He got a knife from the kitchen and broke the clasp. Inside he found jewelry. He dug through it, curious whether it all really belonged to Masie, when he saw a small manila envelope tucked into a corner. He opened it and poured the contents into his hand.

His heart stopped when he saw it. A silver chain with the Rock of Gibraltar hanging from it. He flipped it over, knowing what he would see—a silver scroll bearing an inscription.

I SHALL NOT BE MOVED

He hadn't seen it for over thirty years. Not since he left the village in Angola. Although he was certain of finding evidence that Masie was involved in Rex's death, the necklace stunned him. Rex must have taken possession of it when Mom died.

His mother was the one good person Hensley had known. A lifetime of experience had burned deep the lesson that she was unique. But standing here in Masie's rooms, the woman he thought was an assassin and that Davison thought was a saint, he sensed a similarity between the two women, the one he had abandoned and the one he had accused.

He'd always considered Davison to be the primary casualty of his decision to leave. Dad was so focused on his mission that Hensley's absence would be little more to him than a passing disruption in the routine of the clinic, a temporary labor shortage. He realized Mom would be hurt, but she was forgiving by nature and as an adult was used to compromise and sacrifice. In contrast, Davison at nine years old was by temperament and lack of experience singularly unequipped to deal with such abandonment and it had preyed on Hensley for years.

But now, as he held the pendant in his hand, he wondered about the woman who had welcomed him back at her husband's funeral without a word or look of reproach. Had her manner masked a wound that he had never suspected? Had his sin against her been the deepest betrayal?

These were unwelcome thoughts, introspection at a level he had learned through the decades to avoid. He shook them off and returned to the business at hand. Once Hensley showed this to Davison, he would be unable to deny Masie's complicity. Why else would she hide this trophy in a locked casket in the back of a closet?

Hensley shoved the necklace in his pocket and left the hotel. The lights of Cancún winked across the lagoon in the falling dark. He'd been gone longer than he realized. Surely they would wait for him. Or perhaps Davison would take his disappearance as a final abandonment and proceed without him.

He hailed a taxi, pointed the driver to a bar on a busy street several blocks from Ernesto's apartment, paid him, and hurried down the sidewalk, emerging briefly into the glow of the occasional street-light before slipping back into the dark. A block from the apartment building he noticed that the sound of a motor idling had accompanied him for a while. He glanced back. A large black SUV lurked twenty yards behind him with only the parking lights on, keeping pace.

It could be local thugs or it could be Torres and his henchman. Regardless, he wasn't excited about the prospect of meeting them on a dark street. He quickened his pace to the awning overhanging the sidewalk on the next block. Plunged into the shadow, he took advantage of his dark clothing and slipped into the deep doorway of a pastry shop.

He was certain he was invisible, now. The SUV idled past without changing its speed, evidently expecting to see him emerge from the shadows into the murky illumination of the streetlight at the other end of the awning. When he failed to do so, the brake lights flashed on.

Hensley turned to run the other direction, when beyond the SUV Davison exited the café and stepped into the street. The brake lights on the SUV flashed off and the headlights flashed on, lighting up Davison in the middle of the street like a convict in a prison break movie. He squinted into the lights, holding up a bag of takeaway to shield his eyes.

The engine revved and the SUV shot forward. Hensley shouted and sprinted toward him. Davison paused and then broke into a run. The SUV arced to cut him off before he got behind the cars parked on the street. At that moment, Masie appeared in the apartment breezeway with a suitcase.

Hensley was still half a block away when the SUV hit Davison. He flew over the hood and slammed into the windshield, enchiladas and tortillas tumbling from the bags as they fell. The SUV stopped abruptly with a piercing screech of tires and Davison rolled off the hood onto the street, unconscious.

Masie screamed, dropped the suitcase and ran to Davison.

Still a quarter block away, Hensley felt like he was in a dream, running under water. From what seemed like the far end of a tunnel, he watched Masie kneel next to Davison, peel back his bloody shirt, and then stare at him, suddenly still.

The two driver-side doors of the SUV opened. Finney slowly unfolded from the front door. From the back, a small nimble person jumped out. He was dressed in black leather that shone dully in the streetlights, head covered in black like a ninja. With no apparent effort, he grabbed Masie from behind, dragged her to the door, and tossed her in like a bag of groceries. At the same time, Finney stepped to Davison, pulled a gun from under his jacket, and pointed it at Davison's head.

Hensley yelled, still too far away to stop him. Finney looked up. Not only was Hensley bearing down on him, but a crowd had emerged from the café, other nearby establishments, and the apartments. Curtains brushed aside and people peered out windows. Ernesto appeared on the balcony of his cousin's apartment.

At a barked order from the SUV, Finney retreated to the car and roared away, scattering citizens in his wake. Hensley arrived as the SUV departed, falling to his knees next to Davison, searching for a wound. The first thing he saw was the tattoo over Davison's heart, a copy of the pendant in his pocket. He smiled sadly and shook his head.

Davison pushed himself up to one elbow and squinted down the street. "Where's Masie?"

"First let's get you in the house and see how badly you're hurt," Hensley said. "Then I have something to show you."

Chapter Forty-Five: Dave

The immediate roar of the SUV told Dave everything he needed to know. Somehow Torres had found them. He dashed across the street, knowing he couldn't outrun the car. At the last minute, he leaped over the grill of the SUV, rolled across the hood, and smashed against the windshield. Finney glared from behind the wheel, his two black eyes gleaming with satisfaction.

Then Masie knelt beside him, tearing away his shirt and calling his name. She stopped, stared at his chest, and said in a frightened whisper, "Where did you get that?"

Before Dave could ask her what she meant, Masie was whisked away and replaced by Finney, who pointed a gun at his forehead with a grim smile. Then he too was gone and Hensley appeared, also smiling, but differently. Dave asked about Masie, but Hensley put him off and, with Ernesto's help, dragged him upstairs.

The damage assessment revealed a bloody nose from when he hit the windshield and a few contusions on his arms and head from when he hit the street, nothing more. Throughout the process, he continued to ask about Masie, with increasing volume.

"She left with Finney," Hensley said.

Dave couldn't believe the woman who had just spent the afternoon planning their escape, who had bared her soul to him on the balcony, would willingly go back to Torres.

Ernesto shook his head. "A small man in a black suit and mask took her in the car. She did not choose to go."

Dave lurched from his chair and confronted Hensley. Too fast and too soon. He grabbed the edge of the table, sat back down, and waited for the room to settle.

Hensley shrugged. "It's true, she went with Finney. It appears that she went unwillingly, but things are not always as they appear." Hensley pulled a necklace from his pocket and placed it on the table.

Dave looked from the necklace to Hensley, his anger mounting. "Where did you get that?"

"From a jewelry box in Masie's closet."

"How did you . . . why—"

"Davison, the point is not how I found it, but where I found it. If she was not involved in Uncle Rex's death, what is she doing with this locked away in her closet with her?"

"Maybe he gave—"

"Gave a complete stranger the last remaining tie to his dead sister?"

Dave picked up the necklace and read the inscription.

I shall not be moved. The motto had carried him through boarding school and college, through a decade of impossible cases with the service. When he felt hopeless, when the only reasonable act was to cut your losses, to give up, to admit failure, it always came back to this. I shall not be moved.

"Maybe not," Dave said. "Maybe she wasn't a complete stranger. He only knew her for a few days, about as long as we've known her and I don't think we can call her a stranger."

Hensley pushed away from the table. "I shouldn't be surprised. You quit making sense long before you hit your head."

Dave turned to Ernesto. He was comparing the necklace to the tattoo on Dave's chest. He reached out his hand. Dave gave him the necklace. Ernesto inspected it. "He only is my rock and my salvation. He is my defense; I shall not be moved," he said quietly, as if to himself.

"What?" Dave and Hensley said together.

"It is from the Bible. David wrote this when the king searched for him, to kill him."

"Well that's bloody fitting," Hensley said. "But in this case, you'd better be moved. Out of the country as quickly as possible."

"No. I won't leave without knowing Masie is safe." He turned to Ernesto. "This man who took Masie, what did he look like?"

"He was small, but very strong. He wore a black costume, fitting tight. He had a mask that covered his head, like a wrestler, but all black."

"Could it have been Torres? Paco Torres?" Dave turned to Hensley. "Did you see him?"

"Yes," Hensley admitted. "Black leather outfit, a mask like a ninja. I've never seen Torres in person, only on the telly this morning. I guess it could have been him."

Ernesto shrugged in provisional agreement. Dave pulled out his phone with one hand and the battery with the other. "Harris should have some assets in the area. If nothing else, he can give me a contact that can provide mercenaries." He slid the battery into place.

Hensley put his hand over the phone. "Hold on, there, mate. You can't go in there with an army."

Dave jerked his hand away. "We'll keep it covert."

"Davison, listen to yourself. You're talking about an assault on a resort hotel in a foreign country. You, a foreign national with no authority or jurisdiction. It's suicide. Back away. It's over."

Hensley had gone from ranting to pleading. Dave saw that look in his eyes, of Hensley kneeling next to him on the street. Of Hensley holding out a coin collection. Dave couldn't hold his gaze.

Ernesto caught his eye and nodded. "The writing on this." He held out the necklace. "The writing over your heart. David said he would not fight the king's army with his own army." He placed the necklace in Dave's hand. "He would not be moved from trusting in God to save him."

"Great," Hensley said, shaking his head. "Thank you for that feast of reason." He stood. "As America's greatest writer once said, 'The race is not always to the swift, nor the battle to the strong, but that's the way to bet.'" He glanced at Ernesto. "No offense. And while we're doing sayings, here's one we can all get behind. 'He who fights and runs away, lives to fight another day.' And that's vintage stuff. Tacitus, from around the time of Jesus himself."

Dave hardly heard what Hensley said. Instead he heard the words of his mother the day after his father's funeral, struck down by a stray bullet in the civil war. The day he begged her to leave Angola and return to her home.

Nothing is greater than the power of love. That is the kind of world I choose to live in, and if this is not such a world, I won't regret leaving it.

"So, here's what we do," Hensley continued. "We go south, as planned, but we keep going south. Because now that Masie has reported back to headquarters, they know the Brownsville plan."

Hensley began pacing the floor, warming to his scheme. "Scratch that. We eschew travel by plane, train, or automobile. Too predictable. We hire a charter boat, slip over to the Caymans, lay low for a few weeks, maybe hop over to Jamaica, hit the Virgin Islands, then up through the Bahamas. I know a girl in Miami who might put us up for a week or so. Assuming she's forgotten a few things."

Suddenly it all came together for Dave. Hensley's words. Ernesto's words. His mother's words.

"Hensley, you're a genius," Dave said, shouting him down.

"Of course."

"We will leave by sea, in a manner unforeseen by those who trust in armies."

"Davison," Hensley exclaimed and opened his arms. "Welcome back to reality."

"First, we get a room in a dive somewhere. Now that Finney has tracked us down, he'll come back and I don't want to be here when he does." Dave ignored Hensley's confused expression. "Then I make a few phone calls. Ernesto, I have a few errands for you."

Chapter Forty-Six: Masie

Masie emerged from the apartment just in time to see a black SUV run Dave down in the street. She dropped the suitcase and ran to him as he bounced off the windshield and fell to the pavement.

She had barely knelt down beside him before someone dragged her away and shoved her in the car. Finney got out of the car. She caught a brief glimpse of her attacker, really nothing more than a black hood, before being overwhelmed. The unknown person pulled a black cloth over her head, cuffed her hands behind her back, and snapped her into the seat belt. With her hands cuffed, she couldn't sit up. By then the vehicle was in motion and she struggled to keep vertical on the turns. She leaned her head against the headrest in front of her to stabilize herself.

"Why are you doing this?" she demanded, hoping Finney would answer even if the ninja guy didn't. But her question was met with silence. They sped through the streets as Masie peppered Finney with questions that brought no answer. After a few minutes they came to an abrupt stop at what Masie assumed was a traffic light. She heard a door open and close, and the car lurched forward.

"What was that?" Masie asked to the empty air. "Who's there?" The cloth over her head was thin enough to allow her to discern the passing of streetlights and other sources of illumination, but no shapes. She leaned her head against the window on the chance that someone would see her and intervene, and tried to figure out what was happening.

She saw the SUV hit Dave, but she wasn't sure whether it was intentional or accidental. Her abduction, on the other hand, was quite unambiguous. Who would want her handcuffed and blindfolded? Dave seemed to think Paco was behind Rivera's death, but that made less sense than Paco thinking Dave was responsible. Nothing made sense anymore. If she needed proof of that, all she had to do was come back to her present condition, handcuffed with a hood over her head, speeding through the streets of old town Cancún.

Another question teased her adrenaline-addled brain. The tattoo on Dave's chest. It was the same as the pendant Rex gave her. Too bizarre to be a coincidence. She thought back on what she knew of Dave. Appeared at the resort the day after Rex died, along with Mr. Kite. Followed her to the clinic. Came to her room just before they discovered Rivera. And they'd been on a roller coaster ever since.

However, despite him having accused her of complicity in Rivera's death, despite him dragging her out of the hotel and then interrogating her at the mission, she realized that she liked him.

The first time they met, he had defended her against Mr. Kite's nasty questions about Rex. He'd helped her at the clinic for an entire afternoon and then bought her dinner. And the next day, he came to see her in her room. And throughout the chaos of their escape attempts, he'd tried to protect her. From what she thought at the time was an imagined threat.

Well it was real enough, now. But the thing that stuck in her mind above all others was the feeling that overwhelmed her when she saw Dave sprawled on the street. More than concern. More like a sense of loss.

For a moment while they stood on the balcony overlooking the city she had come to love, she thought he was going to kiss her. She wished he had but she was glad he didn't.

Sitting handcuffed and blindfolded in the back of an SUV speeding through Cancun to God knew where, she had an epiphany. If she ever got out of this mess and back to the States, if she ever got the chance to start the new life she'd been thinking of these past few days, she wanted Dave to be a part of it. But she knew it wouldn't work, not with his utilitarian, materialistic approach to life. They didn't want the same things, didn't see the world the same way.

The car rolled to a stop in a dark area, bringing her attention back to her current dilemma. A door opened, a body rustled against the seat in front of her, and the door closed. A hand whisked the hood from her head. Paco Torres twisted in the passenger seat, his back against the door, watching her. Finney sat behind the wheel, facing forward as if he were alone in the car.

"What is this, Paco? Kidnapping? Really?" She struggled to sit up, but with her hands cuffed behind her, she was forced to lean forward. She had to cock her head to the side to see him.

"It's complicated," Paco said. "If I remove your restraints, do you promise to behave?"

"If I promise . . . Are you serious?" She glared at him.

"I'll take that as a yes." Paco leaned between the seats and released the seatbelt. Masie held her hands toward him. He unlocked the cuffs and pocketed them.

Masie leaned back and rubbed her wrists. She peered out the side window, but the tinting made it impossible to see more than a few lights a distance off. She tried the window. Nothing. The door handle. Nothing. "Paco, what is—"

Paco held up his hand. "All your questions will be answered. I apologize for my methods, but the circumstances demand it."

Masie stared at him, seeing no reason to comment.

"I need you to contact Mr. Kite and ask him to join us."

"What about Dave?"

Paco paused. He glanced Finney. "Yes, and him, too, if he is available."

"Why? Why are you kidnapping your own employees?" She felt the edge of hysteria creeping into her voice and stopped to compose herself, inches from breaking down in tears. She summoned up outrage to carry her through. Despite her efforts, her voice shook with the next statement. "Somebody tried to kill us in that airplane. What do you know about that?"

He waited again, but she fell back against the seat, suddenly exhausted and nauseated from the adrenaline washing through her system.

"Masie, I understand your confusion. But you must understand my concern that Mr. Fletcher, who was present at the death of Mr. Rivera, and Mr. Kite, who assaulted one of my employees, refuse to come forward. I have cooperated with the authorities and taken private measures to resolve this incident, but still the principal parties refuse to do the proper thing." He looked at her in an appeal. "It is distressing and suspicious."

Paco's speech made Masie even more tired. She was tired of the subterfuge, innuendo and mind games. She just wanted to get the facts out into the open and settled. So she hit Paco with the question that had bothered her since she rushed to Dave's side.

"What does all this have to do with Rex Stone?"

Paco's face went blank. "Why do you think this has anything to do with Mr. Stone?"

Only that Dave has a tattoo of the Stone family motto on his chest. Only that what Dave said to her over Rivera's body finally made sense. Just like the last time. The last time she found a body. Rex Stone. This was not a coincidence.

"Because you do," she answered, suddenly sure that this thing about Rex was the reason for everything that had happened in the last forty-eight hours. And sure that Paco had made the connection over breakfast.

Paco's face melted from the mask it had assumed to an expression of concern. "It's late and you must be exhausted. You should get back to your room and get some rest. I'll get the door."

He exited the car and opened her door. She got out and glanced around in the dark.

"Where are we?" She suddenly realized Paco had not responded to her question about the plane crash. Hadn't even acknowledged it.

"Near the service entrance to the hotel," Paco said.

A hand pressed down on the base of her neck. She tried to jerk free, but could barely turn her head. She caught a glimpse of Finney in the corner of her eye before losing consciousness.

She awoke on a metal cot in a small room that was little more than a cell and pushed to a sitting position. Her head throbbed and her arm felt numb. The cot was bolted to the floor. The room contained a metal table, also bolted to the floor, a metal chair, and a small bathroom without a door.

She pushed herself to her feet, crept to the door, and tried the handle. Locked. She slapped her palms on the door repeatedly. "Paco! You can't do this! Open this door!"

Her feeble outburst was met with silence. All she could see out the steel mesh window was the opposite wall of the hallway. She leaned against the door. All the frustrations of the past few days, the past weeks, the past years, surged forward. She began to cry.

Chapter Forty-Seven: Dave

By midnight, Dave was ready to make his last call. He left the dingy hotel room in old town Cancún, took a circuitous route to a small plaza several blocks away, and leaned against a large plastic porpoise on a giant spring. He assembled his burner phone and dialed the number Harris had tracked down earlier. The number of Torres's cell phone.

Torres answered on the third ring. "Who is this?"

"Where's Masie?" Dave asked.

"How did you get this number?"

"I have something for you, but first I have to talk to Masie."

There was a short pause. "Why don't you come into the office, Mr. Fletcher, and we can all talk. You, Mr. Kite, Masie, and me."

"I'll come in, Torres, but not until I hear Masie."

There was a longer pause and then the noise of a phone ringing and a quick answer by a gruff voice. Evidently a speaker phone. "Yeah?"

"Finney, put Ms. Wright on the phone," Torres said.

Another pause and Masie's voice came on the line. "Yes?"

"Mr. Fletcher is concerned for your welfare. How are you feeling?"

"Like filing a lawsuit for wrongful imprisonment."

"Masie?" Dave said. "Are you okay?"

"She can't hear you, Mr. Fletcher, but as you can hear, she's fine."

Masie called out. "Dave? Where are you?"

"I want to know that she's okay," Dave said.

"Have you been harmed, Ms. Wright?"

"No. Where is Dave—"

Her voice was cut off with the click of a phone. "Satisfied?" Torres asked.

"I'll be in touch."

Dave disconnected the call, disassembled his phone, and pocketed the pieces. He was teasing the line between prudence and paranoia, but given what had happened so far, it seemed likely that Torres could track a cell phone if he wanted to.

He sat on the porpoise, looking through the trees at the sky. Despite the clear night, most of the stars were obscured by light pollution. A yellowish moon, one fingernail shy of full, had just cleared the buildings and loomed unnaturally large over the playground, rendering the brightly colored equipment in grayscale.

The call confirmed his suspicion that Masie had been abducted and settled the matter in his mind. If Masie was part of the scam, Torres would have left her in place. But Finney obviously reported back that he'd been assaulted while following Masie this morning, a lifetime ago. Torres would have concluded that she represented as much a threat as Dave did.

Hensley was right about one thing—all the signs pointed toward flight, not fight. And the plan Dave had in mind sounded crazy, even to himself. But playing it safe meant abandoning Masie. If the only way to get her out of there was to go in without a net, then that was exactly what he would do.

Day 8: Tuesday

Chapter Forty-Eight: Dave

An hour after sundown the next day, Dave stood outside the fleabag hotel waiting for Ernesto. He'd spent the morning catching up on three days of missed sleep. During the afternoon he found a net café and did more research on Torres. The Endless Vacations empire was expanding.

Beyond the medical vacation, specialty packages catered to a broad range of interests, from the predictable, like extreme sports and eco-tourism, to the more exotic, like a Holidays in Hell package modeled after the PJ O'Rourke book of the same name.

One bothersome flaw in his theory about the Aztec Gold package was that eventually someone would notice the high morbidity rate of Aztec Gold clients in Cancún, but he had come to the conclusion that the assisted suicide clients were booked in widespread locations, reducing the incidents at any one site. Until Dave showed up asking questions.

In the hours since Finney had run him down, Dave had come to realize that his actions were responsible for Masie's abduction and, when it came to it, Rivera's death. In the first case, if Masie was part of the Aztec Gold scheme, Torres wouldn't have snatched her. He would have allowed them to disappear into the wilderness, waiting for Masie to betray their location far from civilization and help. Torres had sent Finney after Masie because she was a threat, not an accomplice.

Regarding Rivera, well maybe he did deserve what he got, or maybe not, but there was no question that he had caught the metaphorical bullet meant for Dave. And he wouldn't have been in the hotel room searching for the battery key if Dave had not crippled his plane.

Initially Dave had been focused on bringing Torres down for the death of Rex and who knew who else, at half-a-million a pop. But in the small hours of the night, Dave realized that bringing Torres to justice could jeopardize Masie. He had to choose between nailing Torres or saving Masie.

Given the largely legitimate nature of the business model, Dave banked on Torres being open to negotiation. They would come to an understanding that an honest mistake had been made. Based on a long phone call with Ellis, who agreed to divert some funds from the estate for the purpose. Dave would offer two million dollars in exchange for Masie, with the understanding that it would go no further on either side. A gamble, but he couldn't leave Masie to the mercy of Torres. Despite Masie's view of the world, Dave doubted Torres came down on the side of mercy.

Hensley stepped out of the hotel and joined Dave at the curb. They waited in silence for a moment.

"We can still walk away from this," Hensley said.

"And Masie? What will she do?"

Hensley lost his detached demeanor. "Regardless of whatever is going on in that naïve brain of yours, Masie is not your friend. She's playing a role. And it's working."

Before Dave answered, a beat up VW minibus whipped to the curb in front of them. Dave opened the side door and jumped in, sliding over to make room for Hensley.

Hensley looked at Dave for a long moment. Then he slammed the door and got in the front. Ernesto waited for instructions. When none came, he pulled into traffic.

They moved through town in silence. Ernesto studied Dave in the rear view. Dave ignored him. As they approached the coast, Hensley said, to no one in particular, "It's a lot easier to go in a lion's den than it is to come back out."

Ernesto nodded. "We have a saying. When you dance with a bear, you don't stop until the bear is tired."

Dave watched the hotels pass by, their facades lit with flood lamps. "Greed is a very powerful motivator."

"So is self-preservation," Hensley said. "Although not necessarily in our family."

Time to get down to business. "You know the plan?" Dave asked.

Ernesto said nothing.

Hensley snorted. "Yes. You go in with two million dollars and magically come out with Masie. We just don't agree with the plan. Some of us are opposed to suicide, assisted or otherwise."

As they approached the resort, Hensley said, "Let me out here."

Ernesto checked with Dave in the rear view. Dave nodded. In a poorly lit area between hotels, Ernesto pulled over. Hensley held out a hand. "I want my badge now." Ernesto again checked with Dave. He let out a breath and nodded. Ernesto reached into his shirt, retrieved a cruise ship badge on a lanyard, and held it out.

Hensley grabbed it and got out without a word, slamming the door. He faced the minibus, locking eyes with Dave. Ernesto pulled away and Hensley disappeared from view.

Dave felt an unexpected sense of relief. Now it came down to him against Torres. He could focus on getting Masie free and not worry about how his actions might endanger Hensley. Ernesto caught Dave's eye in the mirror, a thousand questions on his face.

Dave shook his head. "He's not our problem. Hensley will take care of himself, like he always has. We stick to the plan."

Ernesto didn't say anything, but Dave sensed his disapproval.

The cab swung into the semi-circular drive of the resort. The doorman stepped forward to open Dave's door as they stopped under the canopy. Dave put one foot out. "Stick with the plan. If I'm not at the meet point in an hour, it's time for the nuclear option."

Ernesto grunted an acknowledgement.

"Ernesto," Dave said. He waited until Ernesto met his gaze. "Thanks, *amigo*."

He held his hand out over the seat. Ernesto grabbed Dave's hand and shook it, firmly.

"Don't make me regret this, *jefe*. I am not good with regret."

Dave smiled, held his hand for a last second, and let it go. He got out of the car, entered the hotel, passed through the lobby, turned right down the hallway, and walked through the metal door to Dumont's office. Finney stood outside the door like a lawn jockey. The bruises around his eyes had faded to purplish green.

Dave stopped in front of him. "I have an appointment."

Finney opened the door. Dave walked in and Finney closed it behind him.

Torres sat behind a desk with Dumont's nameplate on it. Masie sat in a chair in front of the desk. She jumped up.

"Dave! Why did you come here?"

Torres didn't move. "Sit down, Masie." He gestured at the other chair. "Have a seat, Fletcher."

Dave didn't bother. "I won't be here that long."

Torres smiled as if he thought otherwise. "You were supposed to bring your brother."

Dave was surprised, unsure how Torres had discovered this in so little time.

Masie turned to him, still standing. "Your brother? Reginald Kite is your brother?"

"Sit down," Torres said, with a hint of menace. "I insist."

Masie kept her gaze on Dave. He nodded at her and they sat down.

"Reginald Hensley Fletcher," Torres explained to Masie. "Named after his father, Dr. Reggie Fletcher of Texas, late of Angola."

Dave didn't give Masie time to respond. "Look, Torres. This thing has been a misunderstanding from the start. I'll give you two million dollars as a sign of goodwill and I leave with Masie. End of story."

Torres regarded him for a long moment. "But it won't be the end of the story, will it? Not when you tell the authorities about Rex Stone."

Dave closed his eyes. Torres was not going to negotiate. His gamble had failed.

"What about Mr. Stone?" Masie asked.

Dave opened his eyes.

Torres still looked at him. "Yes, we dug a little deeper after the incident with Rivera. It seems he failed to mention that our Mr. Stone had a nephew in the Secret Service."

"Rex was your uncle?" Masie asked.

Dave kept eye contact with Torres. It appeared hopeless, but he would not relent until he had a decisive victory or defeat. "He had a seizure while swimming. Masie can verify that."

Masie stood, again. "Of course I can. I was there."

Torres ignored her. "But you don't believe that, do you, Fletcher?"

Everything hinged on him convincing Torres of this point. "I have no reason to contest that, on or off the record. He was unwell. Not fit to travel. It's not surprising the stress was too much for him."

Torres chuckled unpleasantly. "Of course not. Because if you did suspect things were not what they seemed, what would you do?"

Masie seemed confused. She sat back down and reached out for Dave's arm. "Dave, what is he talking about?"

Dave reverted to his original bargaining chip. "Two million dollars, Torres. Tax free. Off-shore account. Right now."

Torres continued. "Because if you didn't believe it, you might come back and start asking questions. Go to the Ministerial Federal Police."

Dave frantically searched for another way into this deal, some other nugget to convince Torres that he didn't pose a threat. "As the executor for Uncle Rex's estate, I am familiar with his investments, some of which are . . . shall we say, structured in a manner that might raise a few eyebrows with regulatory bodies. I am prepared to be flexible and turn a blind eye to . . . irregularities."

"A convenient change of heart considering the circumstances, Mr. Fletcher."

"I was not initially aware of the special circumstances of the Aztec Gold package, or Rex's involvement with it."

"And you, a Secret Service agent—"

"Retired," Dave interjected.

"Are going to turn a blind eye to the entire operation?"

Dave leaned forward to emphasize his sincerity. "We can all walk away from this." And he meant it. If the only way he could save Masie was to let Torres escape justice, he would do it. But evidently Torres didn't believe that.

"Not all of us." Torres called, "Finney."

The door opened. Finney entered.

"Show our guests to their rooms."

Masie stood. "Paco, this is insane. What are you doing?"

"Correcting a small mistake."

Dave rushed Finney, hoping to make an opening for Masie to follow. But he had underestimated the reaction time of the hulk of muscle. Finney felled him with a single punch.

Chapter Forty-Nine: Dave

Dave regained consciousness face down on a cot in an antiseptic cell about the size of the monk's quarters at the mission, but the difference could not have been more dramatic. He was not greeted by adobe walls, hand-crafted furniture, and the soft illumination of a lantern. Instead, the glare of fluorescent lights blared like a vuvuzela over metal furniture and fabric-covered walls designed to minimize sound.

Cutting through the cacophony he heard a whisper.

"Dave."

He lifted his head and squinted around the room. He was alone. He let his head drop back to the cot. His jaw felt like it had been used to drive railroad spikes.

He had clearly underestimated the sense of personal threat Torres would feel. The open question was whether Torres would make a definitive move without all the threatening parties. It could be that the only thing keeping them alive was the fact that Hensley was a self-centered prick. Dave smiled, and then regretted it.

"Dave, are you okay?"

He forced himself up on his elbows and gave the room another inspection. Next to the bed at floor level, he spied a ventilation grate. "Masie?" he hissed, moving his mouth as little as possible.

"Yes."

Dave tried to rise to a sitting position, but the effort was too great. He collapsed on the cot and slid to the floor, dragging himself up against the grate.

"I'm here."

"Is your jaw broken?"

His fingers explored the side of his face that wasn't leaning against the wall. "I don't think so. But I think my kids, if I live to have any, will be born talking out of the side of their mouths."

"Was that all true? What Paco said?"

Dave tried to remember the conversation, but couldn't get past the fog. "Most of it," he guessed.

"Why did you come down here?"

He shifted to a position that didn't have his cheek pressed against the grate. "I couldn't leave you behind."

"Not that. Why did you come to Cancún at all?"

Dave closed his eyes to block out the shout of the lights. How much should he tell her? Evidently Hensley had been right about Torres, but Dave was betting that Hensley was wrong about Masie.

"I thought you killed Rex."

"What? Me? You thought—"

Dave shook his head, much to his regret. "Forget that. We have a bigger problem." He pressed his left hand against his jaw to reduce the movement and talked through his teeth. "Hensley is the last loose end. Once Torres finds Hensley, he'll kill all three of us."

"How could you think I would—"

"Masie, listen." She wasn't seeing the larger picture. "Torres killed Rex."

"Paco? We were miles away from the resort."

"Think back to Rivera. They made a mistake with the cigars. If you hadn't been there to point out that EV never gives cigars to guests, we would have assumed he died from natural causes. Just like Rex. I have an idea of how he killed Rex, but I can't prove it. But if we can get the cigar back to the US for testing, we might have a chance."

"You thought I killed Rex. How do you know you're not wrong about Paco, too?"

Dave could hear the doubt. She didn't believe what she was saying. "He's the one who put our faces on the news, got the entire police force searching for us, kidnapped you and now me."

He didn't mention the plane crash because there was no way to tie it directly to Torres, but who else could have done it? A long silence told him Masie was not yet convinced. He changed tactics. "How many Aztec Gold packages do you see in a year?"

"Not many." There was silence while she thought. "Not even one a year. Rex was the second one in five years."

"Do you remember the one before Rex?"

"I think it was a heart patient. Yes, an old woman. Italian."

"She died?"

"Yes. Heart failure."

"That's the Aztec Gold package. Assisted suicide made to look like natural causes. Nobody asks questions because the victims are practically dead when they show up."

"You didn't sign up for it."

"No, but I showed up asking questions and he came up with a plan that would look like natural causes. Rivera was snooping in my room and Torres got him by mistake."

"He was snooping in my room, too. I found a file cabinet open." She fell silent for a moment. "But why?" she asked.

Dave took a deep breath and sat up straighter. The fog was clearing. "No, that was me."

"You searched my room?"

"Trying to find evidence, find out how Rex was killed."

"Why did you suspect me? You didn't even know me."

They were back to the beginning. But they didn't have time to go into it. They had to make a plan and get out before Torres or his minions intercepted Hensley as he tried to get out of the country.

"Dave?"

There was no way around it. Masie wouldn't leave it alone until she knew. "Five days ago Rex changed his will to leave his entire estate to you. An hour later, he was dead."

"And you think I. . . How could he do that?"

"He knew he wasn't coming back. He'd paid money to make sure he didn't."

There was silence. Dave waited.

Masie finally spoke. "Oh. That's what he meant."

———

The midday sun beats down on the coastal plains of the Yucatan peninsula. A limousine sits parked in the shade of stunted trees at the end of an unimproved road. The driver leans against the fender, smoking a cigarette.

Beyond the ring of vegetation enclosing the site, Rex and Masie stroll through Mayan ruins, a smaller site not frequented by tourists. They pass by tumbles of overgrown stones and approach a pyramid that juts four stories above the trees.

"In the Mayan calendar," Masie says, "the last era ended on December 21, 2012. Some people thought the world would end. But I think something new began."

Rex nods. "Maybe you're both right."

They arrive at the base of the pyramid. It looms before them. The steep climb is intimidating.

Masie reaches out to Rex's shoulder. "We don't have to climb it."

"Oh yes we do," he replies.

He steps onto the first stone and then the second. Masie keeps pace easily, holding out a hand to steady him. He doesn't shrug her help off like he would have in former days, taking comfort from her touch.

A third of the way up, a piercing pain at the base of his skull rocks him. He reels, reaching for support to the stone near his face, so close on the steep incline, but no sound escapes his lips. His eyes squeeze shut.

"Maybe we should go back down."

"No," Rex rasps, not looking at her, or anything else.

He takes noisy breaths through his nose, his jaw clamped shut, until the spasm passes. Then he opens his eyes and starts climbing again. Masie follows, looking back to appraise the risk. A fall half this distance would likely kill him.

Rex presses on, reaching for the stones above him, almost crawling to the top. Halfway, two thirds, three quarters, almost there.

Masie stays behind him, ready to catch him and push him against the steps if he should fall.

Then they're at the top and Rex holds his arms away from his body like the statue of Christ the Redeemer towering above Rio de Janeiro and turns slowly around, surveying the wilderness that stretches before him to the horizon, a single road cutting through an endless expanse of sand and brush.

He makes one circuit, two, and then drops his arms and sits on the top step. Masie sits next to him.

"You're a strange one, Masie," he says. "Young, living in a tropical paradise. But you spend your time nursing old sick people."

"You're not so old."

He smiles back. "And not likely to get much older."

Masie assesses him, makes a decision, and takes his hand. She holds it in hers and looks at it. "In the hands of the right person, one day can count like a year if you use it well." She raises her eyes to his. "You have this day. How will you use it, Mr. Stone?"

Rex stares into Masie's eyes as if she can grant meaning to his life. "Rex," he says, softly.

"Rex," she says softly back to him. "You're a rich man. You've done great things. But you don't have to give up, now. There are greater things for you to do."

He surveys the ruins, at the consuming desert, at the road that leads to something he will never see. Then his gaze is suddenly focused outside of himself. "And what great things will you do?"

Masie withdraws her hands from his and avoids his eyes. After a long silence she says, "I'm just a girl from the projects, a welder's daughter. I do small things. A cup of water for parched lips. A familiar voice, a comforting touch in the darkness."

Rex retrieves her hand. She allows it, reluctantly. He gazes at it, so soft and smooth, nestled in his wrinkled fingers. "Not so small for the one who receives it. You remind me of someone. Someone I knew long ago."

Masie stands, brushes the dust from her clothes, and clears her throat. "It's warm up here. The cenote isn't far. See those trees?"

Rex smiles. She has misunderstood him, but it is of no moment. He stands. "You think a fortune is made of million dollar bills? No, a fortune is millions of one dollar bills, gathered one at a time."

He crouches down to rest his hands on the step at his feet and slowly descends. Masie follows.

"This pyramid isn't made of a few large stones," Rex says, his voice coming to him in snatches of breath as he continues down the incline. "It's made of thousands of small stones."

Halfway down, Rex clinches his eyes shut and falters. Masie comes alongside and steadies him. After a minute, he recovers and resumes the climb.

"You think a great person does great things. But the greatest things are made from small things. And the greatest person is the one who does the small things faithfully."

At the bottom, he reaches into his shirt and pulls out a necklace. He looks at the pendant, a chip of limestone from the Rock of Gibraltar. He slips the silver chain over his head and holds the necklace out to Masie.

Masie takes it and reads the inscription. I shall not be moved. "It's beautiful," she says. She holds it back out to him.

Rex pushes her hand away. "I want you to have it."

"Oh, no," she says. "It's too valuable."

"When the time comes, I want you to remember what we said here today."

"When what time comes?"

"You'll know," Rex says, smiling.

Dave sat with his back against the grate, the vision of Rex climbing crablike down the pyramid vivid in his mind. The mystery of the will unfolded before him. It wasn't about the money. It was about Masie.

"He went back to the limo," Masie said, "and made me stay outside. He called someone with his laptop. They argued for a long time. I took a walk around the ruins and then went down to the water. That's when I saw him."

Dave pulled the necklace from his pocket and rubbed his finger over the inscription. He whispered, so softly Masie could not have heard it. "He knew. That's why he changed the will. He knew about you."

Chapter Fifty: Hensley

Hensley watched the taillights of the minibus disappear into the circular entrance drive of the hotel as Davison went on his fool's errand.

For a while there, after he had come to Davison's rescue and they were tag-teaming Masie at the mission, it seemed like they might actually bridge the decades-old chasm. But then Davison refused to face reality, not at the café, not in the apartment, not after the plane crash. The situation was hopeless. Davison was hopeless. He was a good guy, but perhaps too good for his own good.

He ruminated in the darkness at the base of a clump of palm trees until a solid thud a few yards away convinced him to find another place to make his plans.

He headed north, away from the resort and toward the cruise ship. Life was tough life for do-gooders. Tough for everyone, really, but do-gooders, especially. There were hard cases all over. His travels across the continents had long ago convinced him that no man could redress every ill he encountered. There were cases where a timely hand made the difference, but more often lasting help lay outside the means of even the most selfless interventionist. And how many of those could you find?

When it came to helping your fellow man, best choose your battles carefully. In Hensley's experience, intervention inevitably led to complications and ultimately to the law of unintended consequences. What help was it to the fellow man if all you accomplished was to land yourself in the soup right next to him, doubling the work for the next well-meaning do-gooder?

No, he would leave this one to Davison. Perhaps with his experience as a special agent combined with the backing of the Stone fortune, he would pull it off. More likely he would find himself surrounded by people who felt uncomfortable with his level of knowledge about their affairs. People with the power and resolve to put their minds, and Davison's body, to rest.

But that was Davison's issue to sort out. Hensley had done all he could to dissuade him, to protect him from himself. Davison made his choice. But Hensley also had the freedom of choice and he chose not to stick his neck in a noose. He had a cruise ship badge. That would keep him in food and booze until the ship returned to port in the US. Then he'd figure it out from there.

At that thought, Hensley stopped. And what would happen when he tried to disembark? No passport. No ID. He didn't fancy spending the next few months until his deportation hearing date came due sharing a cell with a tattooed repeat offender named Ben Dover.

He retraced his steps toward the hotel. It had only been forty-eight hours since the fracas with Guernsey. His photo hadn't been on the news. Maybe they didn't even know who he was. Maybe his keycard would still get him into his room. Maybe he could slip in without being noticed and get his passport. Or maybe he would walk into the freight train that Davison had prepared for them.

He kept to the shadows as he approached the hotel. The front entrance was brightly lit with a glow that invited people like the doorman to inspect your face as you strolled nonchalantly past. Hensley skirted the grounds and approached from the beach where tiki torches and patches of romantic illumination were more accommodating.

A party was in full swing at the cabana bar. A dozen college girls in various degrees of beach dress, and undress, partied like it was 2999. He was so distracted that he forgot to turn his head before Noah, the uber-bartender, saw him.

"Hey, Mr. Kite. Your usual?" Noah yelled over the noise of a dozen alcohol-magnified voices talking simultaneously.

Hensley started to wave him away and proceed with his plan, but he couldn't be sure that Noah hadn't been enlisted to report sightings of the suspects. He decided to have a quick one and sound out Noah for hints that he was working undercover for Torres.

He squeezed into the only free seat at the bar on the perimeter of the celebration. "Certainly, my good man. Make it top shelf." If he was going down, it wouldn't be with cheap tequila.

Hensley admires the view close at hand. He noticed the girls all wore cruise ship badges on lanyards or clipped to a bikini bottom. His cruise ship. Here was a stroke of luck. He pulled his badge from his pocket and draped it around his neck. Fate had dictated the positioning and the priority, but it lay within his power to use the third P, personality, to alter the balance of power.

Noah delivered a tequila sunrise and a ticket with blanks for him to sign it to the room. Hensley took a sip. The master had outdone himself. Fresh squeezed orange juice, premier grenadine and tequila so smooth it would make a baby's butt feel like sandpaper. Forty grit. Hensley glanced at the price on the ticket, which was as elevated as the drink.

"You, sir, are a gentleman and a scholar," he exclaimed, loudly, cutting through the cacophony of chatter from the celebrating cruisers. "I shall dance at your wedding and sing at your funeral, may that day be far from us." He noticed, without looking, that the din had died away as all available eyes turned in his direction. He slid the ticket back to Noah, holding out the pen. "I shall require your autograph on this document to memorialize this occasion as the day the perfect tequila sunrise was born, and proclaim your name throughout the land as a benefactor to mankind."

Noah smiled, took the pen, and signed across the middle of the ticket with bold strokes. He pushed the ticket back to Hensley, who slipped it into his pocket.

"But wait," he said. "Before you print another ticket . . ." He gestured to his audience, pouring on his pan-European accent to maximum effect, "perhaps one of you ladies would care to share in this experience?"

He paused a moment to increase the tension while they looked at each other and back to him, trying to decide if he was too cool to be creepy, or the other way around. But before they could come to a conclusion, he made a flamboyant gesture.

"Dash it, Noah! Top shelf tequila sunrises for all, on me!"

A unanimous cheer erupted from the crowd and those with drinks quickly finished them off in anticipation of the upgrade. Hensley struck up small talk with the nearest vixens until everyone had been served. Then he held his glass aloft and shouted over the crowd.

"To young women and old tequila!"

The shout of acclamation was deafening. Hensley made his way through the throng, clicking glasses with every recipient of his largess before commanding the floor, again.

"Friends," he said in an intimate shout, "I have it on good authority that Brad Pitt is staying at this very resort." Now he had their attention. "Like Brad, I am a Sagittarius. I'm sure you know what that means." He flared his eyes knowingly at the nearest vixen. She giggled. "In fact, it may surprise you to learn that Brad and I were born on the same day. We are the same age." They looked at him, some skeptically, some appraisingly. "Of course, he has a better makeup artist than I do."

Hensley scanned the crowd. "How are we doing? Time for another round?" He glanced over the heads of the cheering girls and nodded to Noah, who was leaning on the bar, listening to the story. He snapped to and began squeezing oranges.

The cheering attracted attention in the pool area and the crowd began to swell. As they awaited refills, Hensley circulated among his shipmates, making maritime small talk, pairing names with faces and using details he learned at one end of the crowd to invent stories of his onboard experiences for those at the other end of the crowd. Once supplies were replenished, he led the crowd in raised glasses.

"As Kristen and Kayla have so sagely observed, in Cancún, calories don't count. Drink up!"

On the heels of the cheers, he resumed his story. "In 1980, before any of you were born, I spent a summer in France. A glorious time. Seventeen and the world was my playground. I met Brad there. In fact . . ." Hensley lowered his voice to a breathy stage whisper, "and this is something few people know. You won't find it on imdb. com or Wikipedia. Brad doesn't even know it, but . . ." He looked around slowly as if gauging whether to reveal this information. Everyone leaned in.

"I had a thing going with Brad's mother." The reaction ranged from amazement to amusement. Hensley shouted over the noise. "Yes. That's right. I'm not ashamed to say it. I was her love slave."

The crowd continued to grow. Hensley directed newcomers to Noah for complimentary drinks. The top shelf bottle had long since run out, but nobody seemed to mind, or even notice. Hensley made sure that the new arrivals were integrated into the crowd and the gossip of his torrid affair with the much maligned Mrs. Pitt, who was an upstanding Southern Baptist and family counselor at home in Springfield, Missouri, during the time in question.

Endless Vacation

Hensley assessed the crowd. A good two or three dozen, all well-oiled and ready for gentle guidance. The time had come. He climbed on a stool, towering above the revelers, and held up a fresh glass.

Chapter Fifty-One: Dave

Dave pushed himself up into a sitting position and opened his eyes. The roar of the lighting had abated from oppressive to annoying. "Masie."

"Yes?"

"How long have I been in here?"

"Half an hour? Three quarters of an hour, maybe."

Dave tentatively flexed his jaw. Moving it seemed to have helped. Still painful, but manageable. He crawled to the door and reached up to the knob. Locked. He pulled himself up and looked through the chicken wire of the reinforced-glass window. A bare hallway.

By leaning his head against the door he could just catch a glimpse of a metal security door to the left. They were in some kind of holding cells in the hallway by Dumont's office.

He performed the same maneuver the other direction, pressing the bruised jaw against the cool metal door. He could see a pair of combat boots leading to beefy legs and a hand with fingers like bratwurst holding the left side of a comic book.

Finney. Minding the guests.

Dave returned to the cot in a controlled fall and did the math. Brute force was not an option, even if he hadn't felt like he'd drawn the short straw at the running of the bulls. Perhaps some clever ruse could result in trading places with Finney, but the sucker punch had left his brain feeling like oatmeal with too much water. He could barely remember what had happened, much less formulate an elaborate scheme to outmaneuver Finney, extract the keys, and lock him in the cell.

Fortunately, Dave had made provision for the worst-case scenario. Unfortunately, they had landed in the worst-case solution.

He returned to the grate. "Masie."

"Still here."

"In about fifteen minutes they're going to open the doors. Don't worry about what happens next. The goal is to get away from Torres. Say as little as possible. Once we're out of here, we'll worry about the next step."

After a long moment of silence, Masie said, "This sounds like a frying pan-fire kind of thing."

"It could be. But Torres turned down two million dollars to let us go. I don't want to hang around to find out what he has planned for us. If we can trade Torres for someone who is willing to negotiate, we might get out of here alive."

"And who would that be?"

Raised voices coming from the hallway rendered a response unnecessary. Dave pushed himself to his feet and leaned against the wall. The door opened and Dumont entered. Not the face Dave expected to see.

"And how do you come to be here?" Dumont demanded.

"I'm a guest of Endless Vacations. At the personal invitation of the CEO."

Dumont shook his head. "First you have a dead body in your room. Then you incapacitate Mr. Finney and make the escape." He gestured to the room. "And now this." He fixed a disapproving stare on Dave.

The door opened wider and Detective Aguilar stepped in. "So it is true, you have usurped a suspect in a murder investigation."

"I usurp nothing," Dumont replied. "I find him here the same time you find him here." He motioned toward the door where Finney hulked. "This is the doing of Mr. Torres and his associate."

"Maybe we should call Mr. Torres," Finney said.

"I will most assuredly contact Mr. Torres in due time," Aguilar said. "But first I must take this suspect into official custody."

Dave stepped away from the wall. "Ms. Wright is also unlawfully detained. In the next room."

Aguilar looked from Dave to Dumont, who shrugged as if to say he could not be held accountable for the lunatic behavior of Mr. Torres, to Finney, who nodded reluctantly, and back to Dave. He grabbed Dave by the arm. "You will not give me any trouble, will you?"

"It's the furthest thing from my mind," Dave said.

Aguilar escorted him to the hall and waited as Dumont opened the next door. Masie stepped out tentatively.

"Ms. Wright, please accept my sincerest apologies," Dumont said. "I was unaware of this situation until a few minutes ago."

"Thank you," Masie said.

She glared at Finney. He blushed and fumbled with his comic book. Then she noted Aguilar's hand on Dave's arm. "And you are?"

"I am Detective Edgar Aguilar of the Ministerial Federal Police. You will come with me to give a statement on the death of Mr. Bill Sackett."

"Who?"

Masie's response was cut off by a commotion coming from the steel security doors at the end of the hall.

Chapter Fifty-Two: Hensley

Hensley maintained his balance on the bar stool and shouted over the heads of the roiling crowd he had carefully brought from a simmer to a boil through skilled application of his not inconsiderable personality and liberal doses of top-shelf tequila.

"To vacation romances!" Everyone cheered. Everyone drank. In the temporary lull, he launched the final shot. "I say we go party with Brad Pitt! What say you?"

This was his most popular suggestion to date. "Follow me!" he cried and sprang from the chair. The crowd parted, and he led the throng to the rear entrance of the hotel, to the edge of the lobby, past the Hendersons, who pointed and whispered in a scandalized frenzy, and turned left down the hall toward the martinet's office.

As they pushed through the double metal doors, Hensley spied a knot of people in the hallway turning to the source of the noise. Reading from left to right, the cast included the martinet, Finney, Masie, and what could only be a cop holding Davison by the arm.

Hensley fell back, allowing a dozen Angelina wannabes to press into the lead. All around him people snapped photos with their cell phones, shot video, tweeted, and Facebooked.

"That's his bodyguard," Hensley shouted above the crowd. "He's at the end of the hall."

Dumont held up his hand. "This is a secure area."

The crowd swelled forward and engulfed the group like a tsunami overwhelming an outrigger.

"You must leave this area at once," Dumont shouted.

As the crowd pressed down the hall, the revelers surged around the target of Hensley's scheme. Hensley reached through the bodies, locked arms with Davison, and anchored himself in the doorway to the cell. The cop lost his grip on Davison's other arm and was swept away.

"What did you say about self-preservation?" Davison asked.

"Just a little party with our shipmates. An alternative ending to the nuclear option."

Hensley loosed his hold on the door and allowed himself to be pulled along with the tide. "Work your way out the back door. I'll direct the cataract as desired."

Davison nodded and began pushing forward, shoving past bodies in an Australian crawl style.

Hensley jumped on the chair outside of the cell and yelled above the crowd, "Keep going!" He pointed farther down the hall, which had several doors labeled such things as EQUIPMENT ROOM, MAINTENANCE, and LAUNDRY. At the end, a brown crash door marked EXIT had a sign across the handle reading ALARM WILL SOUND.

The crowd tested the various doors and continued down the hall. Hensley jumped off the chair and pushed forward as the leading edge turned to the only untested option, the emergency exit.

He pushed through the crowd as they crashed through the door and out onto a loading dock. The momentum carried the front rank, including Dumont and Aguilar, over the edge to the concrete four feet below. The unstoppable force quickly disintegrated into a milling assemblage of tourists.

Hensley caught up with Davison and Masie.

"Back to plan A," Davison said. He pulled Masie down the stairs at the end of the dock and headed down a utility road.

Hensley followed. In a dark patch behind a wall enclosing dumpsters, a minibus waited, lights off, engine running. Hensley opened the front door. Davison opened the side door and stepped aside to let Masie in.

"She's coming?" Hensley asked.

Masie looked from Hensley to Davison, confused.

"That was the plan," Davison said.

Hensley examined Davison's battered face. "From the looks of it, things didn't go according to plan. Maybe you were wrong about a few things."

Davison kept his eyes on her as he spoke. "I was wrong about a lot of things. But Uncle Rex wasn't." He turned back to Hensley. "She's coming."

Hensley shrugged. "It's your nickel." He slid into the front seat and slammed the door. He nodded to Ernesto, who didn't respond. "Good to see you again. We're in a bit of a hurry."

Ernesto disregarded Hensley. He checked the mirror as the back door closed.

"Can you take us to the docks, Ernesto?" Davison asked.

"*Si, como no?*" Ernesto replied. He released the hand brake and pulled away from the dumpsters. He didn't turn on the lights until they were down Kulkulkan a goodly distance.

"Where are we going?" Masie asked.

Hensley kept silent, awaiting Davison's explanation.

"We have badges to get on a cruise ship leaving for Galveston tonight. Once we're in the States, my connections with the Feds will help us get to the bottom of what is going on."

Ernesto handed the other two badges over the seat to Davison.

Masie took the lanyard Davison handed to her. "But my passport is back in my room."

"So is mine. And Hensley's."

Hensley smiled to himself. Davison didn't know how close he came to being wrong about that point.

"Harris will meet us in Galveston and take care of it," Davison said.

Chapter Fifty-Three: Dave

Dave looked up at the cruise ship towering above them like a sky-scraper. The minibus pulled up to the loading zone. A steady stream of cruisers flowed down the pier to the gangways, swiping their badges and boarding.

Dave opened the door, stepped out, and scanned the area. No Torres. No Finney. No Dumont. No police. It looked like they would make it. He helped Masie exit and closed the door. Hensley ambled toward the ship with his hands in his pockets.

Dave opened the front door and sat down. "I'm sorry, but Finney cleaned out my pockets, and Hensley never has cash."

Ernesto shook his head. "*No problemo, jefe.* Your wife . . . okay, she is not your wife, I know, but last year she saved my daughter's life. She wouldn't take money. I did all of it for her."

Dave held a hand out to Ernesto. He grabbed it firmly, hold-ing Dave's forearm with the other hand for several moments. They looked into each other's eyes. Neither broke the silence. Then Dave got out and closed the door. Ernesto pulled away, and Dave watched until he disappeared down Kulkulkan.

Masie waited for him by the gangway. They boarded together and badged through security without incident. After a lengthy search, they found Hensley in a booth in the café at the stern, on the prom-enade level. They picked up a couple of sandwiches from under a heat lamp and joined him.

Masie turned to Dave. "How is it we have badges to get on the ship, but we don't have staterooms?"

"I didn't get the full story, but it has something to do with a flag in the system when an empty room suddenly shows it's booked half-way through a cruise."

"But it doesn't care if somebody without a room checks in?"

"Technically, the cards are connected to a room, only somebody is already sleeping in that room."

"And that doesn't trip a flag?"

"Hey, I didn't write the system. I just found a guy who knew the loopholes."

Masie looked around the café, which was practically deserted. "So we're living in booths and bars and stage shows for the next two days?"

"Don't forget the casino," Hensley said.

"Think of it as a weekend in Vegas," Dave said.

"Are you going to eat those fries?" Hensley asked.

Masie pushed the basket away. "They have beds in Vegas."

Hensley pulled the basket to his side of the table. "And I noticed they had beds in those cells. It's not too late to go back."

The ship horn sounded three times, making conversation impossible for a moment. Dave glanced out of the window. The lights of Cancún began to move slowly past, although he hadn't felt the ship move.

Hensley snagged the last of the fries. "Strike that. Looks like it's too late."

Masie slid out of the booth. "I want to see Cancún one last time."

Dave followed. "Me too."

"I'll be in the casino," Hensley said.

They took the stairs up six levels. There wasn't much on the top-most deck—the stack, antennas, several rows of deck chairs, a hot tub containing a couple oblivious to anything except each other. The lighting was minimal, a few strings of anemic bulbs stretched above the wooden slats, leaving the deck in a romantic semi-gloom, like a VFW hall dance floor. A bloated orange moon inching above the horizon to their left limned the wake in a soft glow. Venus descended upon the city, merging with the lights of Hotel Row.

Dave followed Masie to the stern. She leaned on the railing, watching the lights recede. Dave ignored Cancún, his eyes on Masie's profile, barely visible in the moonlight.

When Masie told him the story of the pyramid, Dave realized that Rex was behind the whole thing. Masie said enough for him to read between the lines of their conversation, to hear a continuation of the promise Rex extracted from him at the birthday party. It started then. Maybe even earlier.

The will was just an elaborate ruse to force Dave to abandon what he was doing, go to Mexico, and meet Masie. Rex knew that he wouldn't take it at face value, that he would dig deeper, trying to find out why he awarded a multimillion dollar estate to a stranger. An outsider. Like his sister, Dave's mother, who scandalized the family by choosing an outsider, rejecting the values of the family for something they couldn't see.

On that pyramid, Rex had seen something he didn't see a generation ago when Bridget made her choice, something Dave didn't see until today, something he left behind in a village in the Angolan bush without even knowing it. Something that stood next to him now, staring back wistfully at a town that tried to kill her.

Masie spoke without looking at him. "Do you really think Paco wanted to kill us?"

"I offered him two million dollars to let us walk away. You saw what happened."

She watched the lights for a while longer. "And you think he killed Rex?"

"He basically confessed. And we both know Rivera didn't die of natural causes."

"But I just can't believe that Paco . . ."

Dave leaned on the rail so he could see her eyes. Sometimes you couldn't admit what stared you right in the face. "When Uncle Rex said you reminded him of someone, he was talking about his sister."

She met his gaze. "Your mother?"

Dave nodded and looked away, at Venus slipping behind the world and at something else. "She was beautiful, intelligent, compassionate. They say she was the darling of the family. A rich family. But she fell from grace when she ran off with a nobody doctor who died penniless in the third world."

"How did he die?"

"It was random. A stray shot from some border skirmish. I was fourteen, in boarding school in the States. They sent me away after Hensley left, afraid I would end up like him if I grew up in the bush."

"The plan seems to have worked. You're nothing like him."

It seemed meant as a compliment. He took it as such, but he knew he didn't deserve it. "Not really. Dad wanted us to follow in his footsteps. Hensley basically went native. He adopted the culture of the locals. Live for today."

"So they sent you back to get a proper education to prepare you for your life's work."

"Exactly. Only I also adopted the culture of the locals. Boarding school kids. Uncle Rex. Family. The old family. I never went back."

"But I bet she was still proud of you."

"She was proud of me, but she wasn't . . ." Dave searched for a word to describe it. His mother had never reproached him for his choices. She had celebrated his success. But there was always the sense that she had hoped for something else. Something more. "She was proud, but she wasn't pleased."

"It's not easy to watch someone you love make bad choices."

They stood in silence for a long while, the lights barely visible across the expanse of the gulf. Rex had spoken about regret at The Emerald. He'd had the courage to say the thing Mom had left unsaid.

Dave had made the wrong choice. In fact, by taking the benefits of the education and then going his own way, he had betrayed the family far more than Hensley, who had never pretended to anything other than self-interest. Why had he never seen it? Did Rex really have to die, to give away $200 million, for Dave to get the message? He was late to the party, as usual, but maybe it wasn't too late to do some good in this world.

He broke the silence. "She was a nurse, a nobody, but there were hundreds of people at her funeral."

"I wish I could have known her."

Dave studied her profile in the orange light of the moon. You are her, he wanted to say. You are the best of what she was. Rex knew it, and now Dave knew it. But he couldn't say it. When they made port, things would change. Perhaps she would go home to Detroit.

He looked away. He of all people had no right to hijack her future. He was nothing more than a disgraced agent who was just now figuring out what was important in life, thanks to Uncle Rex's crazy scheme. He'd managed to drive away two women already, women who deserved much more than what he gave them. And as he watched each of them leave, Stephanie a long time ago, Angela a day ago, he thought only of what they had done to him instead of what he had done to them.

When it came to things of substance, what did he bring to the table? Nothing. Making some declaration of love or devotion to Masie would only amuse her. Or confuse her.

In the suddenly awkward silence, he picked the one sure thing in her future. "You must be excited."

Masie seemed puzzled. "Why?"

"Everything will be different now."

She searched his face, as if trying to decide between conflicting interpretations of his words. "How is it different, Dave?"

"Well, you . . . The inheritance. You can build that clinic. Or do the robotics thing. Do the things Uncle Rex talked about."

"Rex gave me everything I needed to change my life on that pyramid."

"Two hundred million dollars might come in handy while you're changing the world. I know my parents could have used it."

She avoided his eyes. "I can't take that money."

"Why not? You deserve it."

Masie skewered him with a glare. "Nobody deserves a million dollars. But even if I did, he was on medication for a brain tumor. He wasn't in his right mind."

"Oh, he knew what he was doing, all right. I, Rex Stone, being of sound mind and—"

"He was a sweet man who met me by coincidence at a weak moment."

"You heard what Torres said. Maybe Rex wasn't as nice as we all thought he was." Dave thought back to an earlier conversation. "Did you say coincidence? What happened to that 'destinies intersecting' thing? People meet for a reason. Futures change."

"That money should go to his family, wherever they are."

Dave spread out his arms as if making a target of himself. "You're looking at it. All the family he had left is on this boat. I can live without it, and Hensley would just blow it. But you, well, you might actually do something good with it, for a change."

Her eyes flashed. "Oh, might I? What is that supposed to mean?"

"I mean the money, for a change, not you for a—" He gestured surrender. "You know what I meant. Just take the money."

Dave turned away in frustration and almost ran into Mrs. Crenshaw. She tottered toward them, the rail in one hand, her cane in the other.

"Well, bless my soul," Mrs. Crenshaw said. "What are you two doing here?" She caught sight of Dave's face. "Oh, my, Mr. Fletcher. What have you been up to?"

Dave smiled. "You should see the other guy."

She swatted at his arm. "I didn't know you were on this cruise. Captain Crenshaw's favorite, you know."

Masie pushed past Dave. "Mrs. Crenshaw. How did you get all the way up here by yourself?"

The ship rolled slightly, and Mrs. Crenshaw slipped. She steadied herself with the rail and her cane.

Masie reached out a hand. "Here, take my arm. Let's get you back inside."

Masie handed Dave the cane. Mrs. Crenshaw put her arm through Masie's, grabbing it with both hands. They moved at a glacial pace back toward the stairs, Dave behind them.

"I'll be fine. Captain Crenshaw always said, 'Beatrice, you can't make an omelet without breaking a few eggs.' Beatrice was his first wife. He called me that sometimes, when he was feeling regretful."

Then, before Dave knew what was happening, Mrs. Crenshaw wrapped her arm around Masie's shoulder and jerked, rolling Masie over her hip, over her head, and over the rail. Masie disappeared into the darkness with a scream that was abruptly silenced.

Chapter Fifty-Four: Dave

Dave rushed to the railing. "Masie!" Down below, Masie lay sprawled on the tarp covering a life boat.

As he looked down at Masie, Mrs. Crenshaw grabbed his legs and cartwheeled him over the edge. He got his left arm looped on the railing before he plummeted after Masie. "What are you doing?" he screamed at her.

Mrs. Crenshaw picked up the cane, which had fallen to the deck, and began beating his arm with it furiously.

Dave reached across the rails with his right hand and grabbed Mrs. Crenshaw's dress at the collar, smashing her against the railing. "Come here, Beatrice. Let's make an omelet."

The cane clattered past him to the lifeboat. Mrs. Crenshaw clawed at him, and he lost his grip on the railing. His weight pulled her down, and they both plunged to the tarp. Dave expected to hit Masie, but she was on the deck now, Hensley kneeling next to her. Dave scrambled to his feet but before he could take a step, his feet were swept from underneath him.

Dave fell backward, tumbling toward the seaward side of the tarp. He landed and rolled to his hands and knees.

"Dave, behind you," Hensley yelled.

Dave jumped up and spun around facing the cruise ship. A crowd gathered, holding drinks, watching the show. Hensley knelt on one knee, supporting Masie against his other leg. Mrs. Crenshaw took a martial arts stance on the middle of the tarp, edging toward him slowly to keep her balance, her hair askew on her head.

Dave grabbed the cane lying on the tarp. Mrs. Crenshaw reached to her misplaced hair and pulled off a wig, revealing a shaved head. She flung it out to sea. Then she peeled off a latex mask, revealing the pale face of a very fit and very focused young woman. The crowd gasped.

"Crikey!" Hensley said. "It's Sinead O'Connor!"

Endless Vacation

Dave tightened his grip on the cane and swung it before him like a bat, trying to keep her at bay. Undeterred, the thing that used to be Vera Crenshaw approached slowly, her legs hidden by the voluminous flowered skirt that was her trademark. A leg whipped out and sent Dave sprawling off the edge of the lifeboat. He got a hand around a support cable, the only thing that kept him from following the cane down to the inky water roiling past fifty feet below.

On the unsteady footing of the tarp, Vera approached him cautiously. Dave struggled to get a leg up over the edge of the lifeboat. He felt the boat shift and saw Vera stabilize her stance. Hensley was on the opposite side, creeping toward her. She turned slowly. Hensley straightened up slowly. They faced each other, both with practiced stances, each waiting for the other to make a move.

Dave got both hands on the cable and swung a leg up. The boat rocked, Vera glanced back for a fraction of a second, and Hensley struck with a kick to her shoulder. She saw it just before it connected and ducked to the side, grabbing his leg as it glanced off and turning it with her as she used the momentum to do a quick roll.

The roll slammed Hensley to the tarp. He kicked her hand with his other foot and broke free from her grasp. She was already moving toward him by the time he got back to his feet.

Dave pulled himself up to the tarp, climbing to hands and knees and keeping an eye on the fight. Hensley and Vera traded a few sparring punches and then Vera unleashed a flurry of feints and thrusts. Hensley warded them off, but he was clearly outclassed. She maneuvered him toward Dave and staggered him back with a kick.

Then there was a flash of movement on the other side of the lifeboat. Vera spun around as Masie rushed forward, screaming. She dashed a bottle of rubbing alcohol in Vera's face, blinding her. Vera stumbled back, her arm guarding her eyes too late. Masie grabbed the loose skirts and swung Vera around, sending her careening off the lifeboat onto the deck.

On the deck, the crowd, consisting largely of Hensley's new friends in various forms of beach attire, screamed and dog-piled Vera.

Hensley pulled Dave to his feet, and they staggered to Masie, all holding each other as they reached the safe side of the lifeboat. Two security officers arrived and cheerfully sorted through the young bodies to uncover the subdued Vera.

A crewmember helped Masie down to the deck and draped a blanket over her shoulders. Dave and Hensley jumped to the deck and declined a blanket.

As they were escorted past the dog pile, an officer cuffed Vera's hands behind her back. She looked coldly at Dave, ignoring the others. "I told Torres this was a mistake."

The officers hauled her away to the brig. Crew members escorted Dave, Hensley, and Masie to the sick bay.

Masie had a cut on her temple. A nurse took her into another room. Dave and Hensley declined treatment. A doctor arrived and joined the nurse.

Dave and Hensley sat at a table, filling out forms, then waited. After a long while, the nurse came out. They pushed the forms toward her. She scanned them.

"How is Masie?" Dave asked.

The nurse looked up from the forms and regarded them suspiciously. She evidently disapproved of brawlers. "She has a concussion. We'll keep her under observation tonight."

She gave them the back copy of the forms and stared at them until they left. Dave followed Hensley to the casino.

Hensley weaved through the machines, coming to a stop at a video poker game facing the window. He picked up a bucket of tokens from the carpet and inspected it. Evidently satisfied, he sat on the stool, fed five tokens into the machine and resumed his play.

Outside, a crowd milled on the deck next to a lifeboat. Security personnel mingled among them. Dave recognized it as the location of their recent battle. That explained how Hensley got out there so quickly. He'd been gambling at the scene of the crime.

Through an unlikely series of events, it appeared that the hand that actually killed Uncle Rex was now in custody. Mrs. Beauregard Crenshaw was not what she seemed. But then, evidently neither was Uncle Rex. Dave was forced to face the possibility that his mentor, the man who had single-handedly restored the Stone family fortune, had done so through shady, and sometimes illegal, deals. At least in part.

Dave had abandoned the life choices of his own father and mother because of the influence of his uncle. An uncle who had achieved his goals by subverting the system, perhaps even subverting justice, and then in the end had renounced it all and endorsed the very thing he had turned Dave against.

It would take him a while to figure out what that meant, both for the past and the future, but the trajectory of Rex's life had culminated in giving $200 million to an obscure nurse at a Mexican resort. Perhaps as a way to atone for his transgressions, perhaps as a ploy to force Dave to reevaluate his own choices, or perhaps both.

Dave watched Hensley play the machine, annoyed that he could return to the game as if nothing had happened, ignoring the implications for the whole purpose of the trip. Maybe he didn't consider the attempt on Masie's life as proof of her innocence. Perhaps he thought that Torres was tying up loose ends, reducing risk by disposing of an expendable operative.

"Masie refused to take the money," Dave said as the machine announced that Hensley lost the hand.

Hensley fed it tokens. "Am I next in line, or do you get it all?"

"She wasn't in on it. She didn't know about the money and didn't want it once she found out."

"I inferred as much when Sinead threw her overboard." Hensley lost again and fed in more tokens.

"So you were wrong about her."

Hensley looked up from the screen. "What is this, an elaborate form of 'I told you so?'"

Dave returned his stare. Hensley quickly tired of the contest and went back to his game. The sound of the casino rang around them like a three-alarm fire. Hensley fed more tokens into the machine.

"That means we both were wrong. Uncle Rex wasn't coerced into changing his will."

"Well, he did have a brain tumor."

Dave didn't respond. Hensley was taking this as seriously as he took everything, which was to say not at all. Now that the money was not in jeopardy, he had no interest. Besides, there was no point in discussing the issue of why Rex changed his will. Dave understood why, but Hensley never would. The real question was why Masie became so angry when he tried to convince her to take the money.

"We were having an argument when Mrs. Crenshaw showed up."

Hensley fed the machine. "About?"

"She refused the money. I told her she should take it, do something good with it."

"Davison, you're an idiot," Hensley said without looking up.

Dave watched him play another losing hand. "Right. I'm not the one playing against the house."

"With other people's money. You're on the top deck of a cruise ship in the moonlight in Cancún, and you talk to the girl about money? Now I see why Rex wrote me. You shouldn't be allowed to leave the house by yourself."

"Rex wrote to you? Why?"

"Masie doesn't want the money."

"Then what does she want?"

"You. Or, rather, the you that you would be if you weren't the idiot that you are right now." He dug into the bucket and came up empty. He tossed it aside. "Let's get out of here."

The deck outside the window was still crowded with Hensley's posse, so they took the stern stairwell to the upper deck. It was deserted, even the hot tub. Hensley strolled to the back rail, staring into the wake foaming behind them like a con trail. The moon rolled across the Milky Way like a soccer ball in gravel. They were too far out to see any city lights.

They leaned forward onto the rail, the wind at their backs masking all other sounds. Dave waited. After a long time, Hensley broke the silence.

"Rex was worried about you."

"Me? I'm doing fine."

"Yeah," Hensley responded. "That's what he said. You were doing so well that, unless something happened, you would end up like him."

"You could do a lot worse."

"Evidently he didn't think so. Why else would he write the telegram?"

"Where's this telegram? I want to see exactly what he said."

"I memorized it and ate it. What do you think? I read it and threw it away."

"But—"

"Look. I don't know why he thought I could help." Hensley turned back to the water. "I can't save myself, much less you."

"Who says either of us needs saving?"

Hensley grunted. Dave started to say something but thought better of it. He leaned back against the railing, facing the wind and their destination. Here on the abandoned deck, a twilight desert island in a sea of blackness, he found it easy to forget the thousands of people below, to imagine that they were two lost souls alone in the dark, escaping from nowhere, fleeing to nowhere.

Out to the east, he saw the lights of another ship, not a cruise ship. Maybe a tanker or a container ship.

Hensley finally broke the silence. He spoke into the darkness, looking behind them. "How much do you remember about Dad?"

"Some. Enough."

"How many times did he play ball with you?"

"None. He wasn't into sports."

"Read you a book?"

Dave shook his head. "That was Mom's thing."

"Do anything with you?"

Dave thought back. More than three decades had passed since he had seen his father. How much did a nine-year-old really know about his parents?

"He let me help in the clinic. Cut bandages. Sterilize things."

Hensley leaned on the railing like Dave.

"Precisely. The truth is, he was a pathetic father. A bit of a jerk, actually."

"I don't—"

"He had no idea what to do with a kid unless his arm was broken or his appendix was about to burst. But when he was in the clinic, he was like a god." Hensley gestured, as if to clarify. "The good kind," he said. "He really cared about those people, the nobodies in the middle of nowhere, the can't-do-jack-for-themselves broken people."

"They both did."

"Outside the clinic, it was like he was from another planet. Inside was the only time he was fully human. And then, he was as satisfied as a man could be. Do you remember that?"

The expression on Hensley's face was a look Dave had never seen on him. Open, honest, vulnerable. "Is that why you left?" he asked quietly.

Hensley responded with an intensity that obliterated the question. "Have you ever been that fulfilled? That genuinely happy?"

"No," Dave said. "I don't think I have."

"That's why we need saving." Hensley leaned back on the railing and seemed to coast to a stop, deflating.

Dave let the statement hang in the air. He kept his eyes on Hensley. Then he asked the question again. "Why did you leave?"

Hensley turned to watch the wake, his back to the wind. "I wasn't broken enough."

The silence following that confession grew as they both stood in the false gloaming of the upper deck facing opposite directions, until neither of them could break it. Then a clutch of teenagers appeared at the top of the stairwell and broke the spell in a noisy maelstrom of insecurity and invincibility, flashing dismissive glances at Dave and Hensley.

Dave watched them wander around the deck, searching for a diversion in the long, final leg of the cruise. A skinny, short kid skittered to the hot tub and stuck a foot in, testing the waters. A brassy girl pushed him in. Dave shook his head. He wasn't alone in the universe any more than the kid crawling out of the hot tub, sodden clothes dripping as he complained shrilly to the laughing crowd. He wanted to go over, to deliver some sparkling words of wisdom, but he had nothing to say. And, he realized, even if he did, it wouldn't change anything. The kid would figure it out, perhaps decades from now. Or not.

Hensley straightened up and headed to the stairs. "I need a drink."

Dave followed him down. They stopped at the first bar they found. A neglected piano trio played standards in a corner. Hensley walked directly to the bartender.

"Dustin," he said. "I am in need of sustenance to restore the tissues. The usual, please."

Dave betrayed no reaction when the bartender, evidently named Dustin, smiled and immediately gathered the ingredients for a gin martini. As Dustin rattled the cocktail shaker with a cheerful ferocity, he raised an eyebrow at Dave.

Dave scanned the shelves. "Glenmorangie 18."

Dustin nodded, poured the martini through a strainer into a glass, dropped in a swizzle stick with three olives, and pushed it across the bar to Hensley.

Hensley took a long and deep sip and popped an olive into his mouth. "If you don't go down to the sick bay and tell Masie how you feel, you're a bigger idiot than either Rex or I thought."

Dave hid his shock by accepting the scotch Dustin slid across to him with a nod. He hadn't said anything to Hensley, or anyone else, not even Masie. If even the self-absorbed Hensley saw it, that was not a good sign.

"Maybe you should tell her, since you're the expert on my feelings," he said, and then tossed back half the shot in a gulp.

"I'm about to become the expert on throwing you overboard."

"You saw what happened to the last person who tried that."

"Yes, I did. Masie dealt with her. This time she might change sides and help me."

Dave swirled the scotch in his glass. "She's not my biggest fan at the moment. I might screw it up."

Hensley shrugged. "Then you come back here, and I'll buy you another scotch, and you'll buy me another martini, and we'll talk about the good old times."

"We don't have any good old times."

"We'll make up some. Now go."

Chapter Fifty-Five: Dave

Dave took the elevator down to the deck that housed the infirmary. He poked his head in the door. The same nurse sat behind a desk, reading a magazine. She frowned at him and went back to reading. Dave slipped past her to the door of the inner room.

Masie sat in bed, reading a novel from the ship library. She looked up. "Hey."

"Hey," Dave said.

She set the book down in her lap, open. He moved closer to the bed. She had a bandage on her head but otherwise seemed the same as when they came onboard. He was here on a mission, but had no idea how to accomplish it.

He gestured to the bandage. "Does it hurt?"

"Only when I think. Which is not often."

She was the real deal, the genuine article. He'd never felt this way before, but that wasn't surprising. He'd never met anyone like her before, not as an adult. He wondered what would have happened if he had met her in college. Would he have had the vision to see what was right in front of him? Or would he have continued in the way he had gone for all his life, focusing on the wrong things? He was pretty sure he knew the answer and it didn't give him comfort.

He cleared his throat, suddenly nervous. He had to say something before it became irretrievably awkward. "I brought you this." He pulled the necklace from his pocket and held it out to her.

Masie took it. "How did you get this?"

"Hensley found it."

She looked at him, annoyed. "Is there anyone left who hasn't searched my rooms?"

The awkward silence returned. Dave realized he had to treat it like the first swim of the spring. He just had to jump in. He crept to the edge of the precipice.

"When I went over the edge of that lifeboat, I thought it I was gone."

Masie didn't comment.

"When I was hanging on that cable, swinging sixty feet above the ocean, certain I would fall, my only thought was, 'No, not now. Not when I finally . . .'" He fell silent, doubtful of the wisdom of taking the final step.

"Finally?"

He stepped over the edge. "Finally . . . I found you."

Masie seemed puzzled. "You found me? What were you looking for?"

Dave inched close enough to touch her, although he didn't reach out his hand. "No, that's not right. I wasn't looking. I was found." He placed his hand on hers.

She shook it away impatiently. "It sounds like you're the one with the head injury."

"Masie," he responded without thinking. The words flowed without plan or thought. "I know this is going to sound weird, but Uncle Rex changed his will so I would come down here and find you. I came for all the wrong reasons, but in the end . . ." His brain caught up with his mouth and he stopped.

Masie looked at him, no longer impatient.

"Forget all that. There's only one thing, really. I love you. I can't imagine spending the rest of my life without you."

She didn't say a word. Her face betrayed nothing.

Dave gestured to the pendant. "Uncle Rex said you would know when the time came. It's here. You can do one more small thing."

Masie raised an eyebrow.

"You can save me from myself. I'm going down for the third time."

"Finally," Masie said.

"Finally?"

Masie smiled at him. "The first time we talked, I knew the real you was in there, somewhere. Finally, we meet."

She held out a hand. "Masie Wright."

Dave took it. "Dave." He squeezed harder. "Davison. Davison Fletcher."

They shook hands. Then he leaned in and kissed her.

Day 9: Wednesday

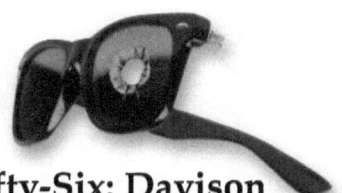

Chapter Fifty-Six: Davison

At the port in Galveston, Davison, Masie, and Hensley squeezed down the ramp past all the other passengers. At the end of the line, just before the final checkout, Harris waited, sweating in a suit and tie. The summers in D.C. could be brutal, but they were nothing compared to the summers on the Texas gulf.

Davison took his hand. "Thanks for showing up."

"Don't talk nonsense, Fletch." He ushered them past customs. "We got your stuff from Cancún. It's at the hotel."

Outside the building, Davison gestured to Masie. "This is Masie Wright."

"It's a pleasure to meet you, Masie."

Masie shook his hand. "Mr. Harris."

"And my brother, Hensley."

Harris extended a hand. "Hensley."

Hensley shook it warmly. "Salutations and gratitude, my good man."

Harris gestured them to the waiting SUV. Black, tinted windows. "The Mexicans have Torres in custody. No sign of Vera Crenshaw, I'm afraid. Or whoever she is. She completely disappeared in the middle of the gulf. Drowned, possibly."

Davison looked at Masie, then at Hensley. They returned his uneasy glance. He doubted that the skin-head master assassin would be daunted by anything as mundane as the ocean.

Harris looked at Davison. "What?"

Three Years Later

Chapter Fifty-Seven: Hensley

Hensley sat in the café across from *Iglesia de Cristo Ray*, a cup in his hand, a plate of buñuelos at his elbow. He sipped the coffee, set it down, and picked up the telegram, again.

COME AT ONCE. SAY NOTHING TO DAVISON. -R

Despite what he said on the ship years ago, he had not destroyed it. He looked at it now as he had done in Nepal, as if it held a deeper meaning he had not yet deciphered. Perhaps it could once again send him somewhere on a mission, give him a purpose, offer the possibility of changing his life.

He'd done his part to save Davison, but now Rex was gone. Mom was gone. Dad was gone. There was no one left who could send a note to beckon some coyote from the chaos of creation to save Hensley from himself.

A taxi pulled up to the curb. Hensley slipped the note back into the envelope, almost cloth-like in its worn fuzziness, and stowed it in his duffel bag.

Ernesto got out of the taxi. Hensley grabbed a buñuelo for the road, dragged his duffel bag to the curb and handed it to Ernesto. The taxi driver stowed it in the trunk, closed the lid, and glanced past Hensley down the sidewalk.

Hensley knew what he would see without turning. He should have known Ernesto would not keep this secret. He felt a hand on his shoulder.

"Going somewhere?" Davison asked.

Behind Davison, Masie waddled up, hugely pregnant under the freshly laundered lab coat.

"You don't have to go," she said.

That was where she was wrong. "Yes, I do." He glanced back at Ernesto, packing as much accusation into the expression as he could. "I was born restless. Ask Davison."

Davison shook his head. "I thought you were finally getting settled."

"It's my curse. I won't settle for anything but the best."

"Will you know it when you find it?"

Masie leaned against Davison, her arm clutched around his waist. It had taken a few years, but Hensley finally got it. It bothered him that Rex, and even Davison, had seen what he clearly had not.

But now that he knew, he couldn't stay. Not with such a powerful reminder of the past he had abandoned staring at him every day.

"I hope so."

He hugged Masie, then Davison, and got into the front seat of the taxi. Before they pulled away, Hensley looked back at Masie and the letters stitched on the lab coat. BRIDGET STONE FLETCHER CHILDREN'S CLINIC. He nodded to her.

"May your house be filled with joy and peace."

"May your house be free of sorrow," she replied.

Then the taxi pulled away and they drove through the streets of Cancún toward the airport. Ernesto kept his eyes on the mirror, but Hensley didn't look back. Instead, he turned to Ernesto.

"I think we have time for a quick one before my flight, *amigo*," he said, and wondered how Chrystal in Santa Fe was doing these days.

The Reluctant Saint

Chapter One: Quandary

There was something about narrowly escaping the deadly attentions of an international assassin that lent an air of luxury to the simplest of life's experiences. And so it was that when Hensley Fletcher set foot in Galveston fresh, off a cruise ship and into the waiting arms of the Secret Service, he did so with an unexpected sense of gratitude and bonhomie. Particularly since he had spent most of his life flying under the radar of the authorities, whether federal or local.

Even so, when Special Agent Harris breezed through customs and gestured to the open back door of the cliché black SUV, Hensley faltered, as perhaps even the most seasoned lion tamer might when placing his head between the massive jaws of a beast. It was the Secret Service, after all.

He glanced at Davison, who was making some remark to Harris, and then at Masie, who waited patiently, and the moment passed. He climbed in and made room for the others. Harris rode shotgun.

Despite it being the first week of June, the temperature was a balmy eighty. But after a few blocks, the SUV took on the dank atmosphere of a locker room just after the big game. Not surprising since the three of them hadn't had a chance to change clothes after they fled the resort five days ago.

Harris turned in his seat. "Relax and get plenty of rest. Tomorrow will be a full day." He targeted Davison with his next comment. "Since this whole Cancún fiasco went down after you officially retired from the service, it might get a little ticklish. And a lot of people want to talk to all three of you about the incident on the ship."

The SUV came to a stop in front of the Tremont House, a four-story Victorian hotel that took up an entire block. Given the state of federal budgets, Hensley had expected something more along the lines of the No Tell Motel. The warmth of human kindness swelled in his breast. This Harris fellow knew how to do them up proper.

As they piled out of the SUV, Hensley approached Harris, toying with the idea of thanking him with the two-cheek air-kiss he frequently employed in Europe. However, Davison shot a glare his way, and Hensley confined himself to the two-fisted handshake and a heartfelt, "Sir, I shall forever be in your debt. You have but to say the word . . ."

Harris extracted his hand from the grip. "Couldn't leave Davison's brother out in the cold." He smiled. "Company policy." He gestured to an agent standing under the entrance canopy and spoke to the group. "As a precaution, we've posted a protective detail."

Hensley inspected their protector. Since they were safely out of danger in the good old US of A, he suspected that this gatekeeper's primary goal was assuring that they made it to the debriefing tomorrow. And by *they* he meant *Hensley*.

If so, the joke was on them. Hensley intended to enjoy room service and whatever other amenities he could accrue at the largess of the state for as long as it lasted.

Approximately half an hour and exactly one shower later, Hensley wrapped himself in a towel, absorbed the life-affirming delight of a well-chosen beverage ordered via room service, and turned his thoughts to the puzzle that, despite all the chaos of the past few days, remained uppermost in his mind.

After a few minutes, Hensley recalled that speculation was the pastime of fools. He picked up the room phone and navigated the maze of button-pushing required to call Philadelphia.

"Ellis, my good man. Hensley Fletcher here, recently of Cancún, calling from Galveston, safe within the protective embrace of the Secret Service. Do you have time for a few questions regarding the matter of which we spoke last week?"

"Yes."

Hensley smiled. That was Ellis, ever the picture of efficiency. "How long have you been the Stone family legal adviser?"

"Fifty-seven years, three months, and eleven days."

"Since before Uncle Rex assumed control of the estate."

"Correct."

"Was he in the habit of making frequent alterations to his will?"

"I'm afraid that is privileged information."

Ellis was also ever the picture of rectitude. Hensley took a go at it from another angle. "In your office last week, you expressed surprise that Rex had changed his will to leave the entire estate to Masie Wright."

"You are correct."

"Was that due to the nature of the change or the timing?"

"Both."

Just as Hensley expected. Uncle Rex wasn't one of those eccentric millionaires who responded to every perceived slight with the threat of disenfranchisement. "The most recent intelligence is that Masie refused to accept the inheritance."

"Perhaps, but you should know that from a legal perspective her wishes are immaterial to the validity of the will, which I am bound to honor in my capacity as executor."

"But you also said there were grounds to contest."

"Yes, mental competence. But you may have some resistance in that regard."

"From whom? Masie doesn't want the money."

"A few minutes ago, Davison offered to submit a deposition affirming that Rex was of sound mind."

"Was Masie a party to this conversation?"

"Not that I am aware."

It appeared that devious forces might be at work. Clearly, Davison had done a one-eighty in the matter of one Masie Wright. Far from suspecting her of manipulating Uncle Rex into changing his will, he was now endorsing her as the rightful heir.

Not that Hensley suspected Davison of foul play. His brother had ever been the consummate Boy Scout, but they were both up against a dark horse, even if Davison didn't realize it.

Circumstantial evidence notwithstanding, Masie looked legit enough. That was the problem. More like too legit by half.

Hensley could think of only one reason why someone would turn down two hundred million dollars, and it wasn't to trade it for what was behind door number two. It was to dispel all suspicion before finally acquiescing to the will and walking away with the lot, free and clear.

Any woman worth her salt could fake sincere for a week. As far as Hensley could tell, most married women had learned to fake it for decades.

It came down to who was right, Hensley or Davison. Was she a sinner or a saint?

"This matter bears further investigation," Hensley said. "I shall be in touch with breaking news as required."

"In the event I need to contact you, may I reach you at this number?"

"At present I can't predict my future movements with any degree of certainty. I'll have to contact you."

Tomorrow they would be ferried to the Federal Building for a debriefing regarding their Endless Vacation experience. He would bask in this land of milk and honey as long as possible, but eventually he would have to find another landing spot from which to launch his next adventure.

He hung up the phone and turned a reluctant gaze upon the man-in-black outfit he had cast on the bed when he entered the room. It was long past its sell-by date, considering he'd donned it in Cancún five days ago.

Regretting the impossibility of ordering a fresh change of clothes via room service, he donned the now overfamiliar, aromatic ensemble and headed down to the in-house cafe for dinner, waving to the watchdog in the lobby on the way.

The menu offered a range of options, from sandwiches to entrées, each of which he examined carefully. While Hensley appreciated the singular focus that led John Montagu, the Earl of Sandwich, to instruct his servants to construct the eponymous collation so as not to be distracted from his work, in Hensley's world, a meal was not a distraction necessitated by the requirements of the body but an experience to be savored.

Whether ordering a full meal or simply a refreshing beverage, one did so only after careful consideration of a host of factors, the goal of which was to engineer optimum pleasure.

After perusing the menu at the counter, Hensley settled on jambalaya, paired it with a Turbo Dog Louisiana dark ale, and took a seat at the bar. He was about three bites in, and very good bites they were, when someone climbed onto the stool next to him.

"Didn't take you long to find the restaurant," Masie said.

Judging by the fresh outfit, Masie had spent her time shopping instead of discussing the terms of the will with the family retainer. "Greetings and felicitations, my dear lady. I can offer an unqualified recommendation in regard to the jambalaya."

"I ordered the tomato and mozzarella panini."

"Doubtless an equally excellent choice." Hensley scanned the room. "Will Davison be joining us?"

"Your brother is having dinner with Harris."

"Doing Secret Service stuff, no doubt."

"I think it's more of a reunion. Evidently they've known each other since prep school."

A server delivered Masie's sandwich, and conversation gave way to dining. Hensley took a reflective sip of the Turbo Dog and considered The Case of Masie and the Money.

It wasn't like he needed the whole nut, or even half. While he had, on many occasions, lived for weeks or months as the guest of the absurdly wealthy, in the course of his life he had learned to thrive on almost nothing.

In the nineties he had spent three years studying Wing Chun in the mountains of Guangxi, living off the equivalent of a thousand dollars a year. And just before this most recent interlude in Cancún, he had been living in a small Nepali village. A spartan existence by any measure.

At present he was relatively flush, thanks to the two thousand dollars Davison had thrown at him a few days ago, accompanied with the demand that Hensley make himself scarce in any location in which Davison found himself. Hensley had accepted the money but declined to vacate. Fortunately Davison hadn't demanded a refund.

It was a goodly sum, and Hensley knew how to make it last. It would serve to keep body and soul together for the nonce.

But as one approached the twilight of life—not that fifty-three was old, mind you—one began to give thought to the waning years, even a vagabond who lived by his wits. After all, it was a race to see which would fail first, the wits or the body, and Hensley didn't fancy dying in a gutter somewhere because he could no longer keep an audience spellbound with his charm.

Hensley finished off the jambalaya, downed the last of the ale, and dropped his napkin on the plate. He glanced at Masie. Considering how things had worked out, Hensley wasn't willing to take Davison's word on Masie's position about the estate. What sane person would turn their back on a fortune out of principle? Hensley would wager that he had as many principles as the next guy, but principles could take you only so far. At some point, one would always require a ready supply of solid currency.

He turned to Masie. "Could I interest you in a libation at the Rooftop Bar?"

Masie finished her sandwich at a leisurely pace and washed it down with the last of her ice water. Then she looked at him.

"I was looking forward to an early night. It's been four days since I slept in a proper bed."

"A nightcap then. It's still an hour until sunset."

She shrugged, and they took the elevator to the bar four floors above the street.

The temps were dropping into the seventies on the roof, but being on the gulf, the humidity was as close to one hundred percent as to make no difference. Hensley rolled up his sleeves as he smiled at the bartender.

"Remind me of your name," he said, although he'd never seen the man in his life.

"Julien." He swirled a cocktail napkin in front of Hensley and then another next to it as Masie stepped up. "What'll it be?" he asked without looking at either of them.

Hensley shook his head with a world-weary sigh. All business and no heart, this one, not realizing that as the man behind the bar, he was surfing the swirling maelstrom of mankind, the star-stuff of humanity, a million stories sitting on these stools every year, looking for a moment of connection, a moment of something real, something true.

The boy was a youngster, barely in his thirties, tanned and slender as a reed in his black short-sleeved shirt and black jeans, ponytail, tats. In five years, his metabolism would change. In ten he'd be a beefy bartender, as clueless as a boiled frog, wondering why the young girls no longer flirted with him. In twenty he'd be asking himself if this was all there was. And if he kept on this way, it would be.

"Yes," Hensley said. "Now I remember. Julien." He held out his hand and Julien automatically shook it. "Reginald Kite. I was in here a few months back on business, and I'll never forget what you said to me."

Julien froze and studied Hensley. "Really?"

Hensley caught his eyes and held them with an expression of intensity that had given princes pause and stopped knife-wielding thugs in their tracks. It didn't fail him now. Julien stood like a bird charmed by a snake.

"I went home and followed your advice, and I'm not exaggerating when I say it changed my life."

The sound of Masie's swift intake of breath echoed in Hensley's left ear, but he didn't break eye contact with Julien, who studied Hensley like he was a treasure map.

A waitress stepped up to the bar station and slapped an order on the counter, but Julien didn't even flinch.

"I could have missed out on the greatest love of my life," Hensley said. "I had to go to Paris to track her down, but because of you, we are now together and happier than we've ever been."

He swung out his arm and pulled Masie close. "Dovey, this is the man I told you about." He looked at her. She returned the gaze with a searching intensity that eclipsed Julien's confused stare.

"Selfless in his service, generous in his wisdom. If any man deserves the encouragement of seeing the fruits of his labors, it's my main man Julien."

Masie whispered between clenched teeth. "What are you talking about?"

"Just play along," Hensley breathed back.

Masie composed herself and turned to the bartender. "I don't know how to thank you."

"Uh . . . it was nothing, ma'am," Julien replied, still attempting to dial up a memory of the event.

"Let's celebrate," Hensley said, back to full volume. "What will you have, love?"

"Me?" Masie scanned the shelf behind the bar. "Do you have a pinot noir?"

"Absolutely," Julien said, springing into action.

Masie extracted herself from Hensley's embrace and whispered, "What are you—"

"Later, my love," Hensley replied softly. When Julien turned back to them with the glass of wine, Hensley said, "For me, a Hendrix martini, heavy on the vermouth with a slice of cucumber, and a bowl of olives. I'm sure you remember."

Julien looked him in the eye with a smile. "Of course, Mr. Kite."

"Please, call me Reggie," Hensley said. "It's not like we're strangers."

"Of course not," Julien said. "One classic martini coming up."

Hensley and Masie waited in silence as Julien did the needful and delivered it with a flourish. Hensley took a sip. "Excellent, as always." He charged it to the room with a generous tip that the Feds should be happy to pay, considering the circumstances, and led Masie to a set of armchairs bookending a coffee table in a corner away from the crowd.

"What was that?" Masie said as she sat down.

"The man was a drone. Didn't you see him?" Hensley settled into his chair and took a generous sip of the excellently prepared martini. He couldn't have done better himself.

"I'm not your long lost love."

"Of course you aren't." He munched serenely on an olive.

"Why?"

Hensley frowned. He didn't expect to have to connect the dots for someone clever enough to land a two hundred million dollar estate on the strength of two days of work.

"He's not at McDonald's. This is a high-end bar, and if he doesn't learn that he's not in the business of serving drinks but in the vocation of serving humanity, he's going to burn out a bitter old man." He took another sip of the martini. "Plus, it got me a level of service I could never have bought with something so crass as the promise of a good tip." He set the glass down. "And I bet every customer he serves tonight will benefit as well."

Masie slouched in the chair with her elbows on the armrests and her wine glass held in front of her face with both hands, regarding him as if he were a specimen under glass in a natural history museum.

Her confusion was not surprising. She had not yet experienced the full spectrum of the Hensley persona. Where she was concerned, to this point he had, of necessity, played the role of the antagonist. This was her first glimpse of Hensley, the philanthropist.

"What exactly are you up to?" Masie said.

"I'm just a man who worked the other side of a bar before Julien was born. Who learned that lesson in his teens from an old woman in Tunis who took in laundry. And strays."

Hensley snatched up his glass and took a long drink. He had orchestrated this moment to extract information, not divulge it, but this woman seemed to elicit the most reactionary side of his personality. Made him start arguments uninvited. He should have been on his guard. Or maybe more relaxed.

Whatever it was, he didn't like it. He set down his glass and went on the offensive. "It occurs to me that I have neglected to congratulate you on your windfall. What do you plan to do with the two hundred million?"

Masie continued to stare at him over her wine. From the level in the glass, it appeared that she hadn't taken a sip. He wished he had a cigar, some stage business to camouflage the fact that he was suddenly off balance. Instead he mirrored her posture and tented his fingers against his lips, waiting.

She broke first. "Seems that I'm suddenly unemployed. The first step is to find a job."

"A strange move for someone who just inherited a fortune. Or are you one of those types?"

"Which type is that?"

"The ones who win the lottery and say they're going to keep their job and continue with life as usual."

"I think we both know that—"

A chair landed next to them with a thud, and Davison dropped into it. "What the hell, Hensley?"

Chapter Two: Epiphany

Hensley was glad he wasn't holding the martini, which was housed in a glass admirable for its purpose but notoriously inadequate for containing liquid under the stress of sudden movements.

He took it up now, indulged in a sip, and turned to Davison. "Perhaps you could couch your question in a more explicit form."

"After the last few days, I was fool enough to think things would be different. But you'll never change, will you? "

Masie bristled. "Davison, don't you think—"

"I pick up the tab at dinner as thanks to Harris for bailing us out of this mess and discover the card is maxed out." Davison threw a stack of faxed pages on the table. "One-way plane tickets from Austin to Philadelphia and Philadelphia to Cancún. A room in the hotel in Cancún, clothes from the merchant shops in the resort, and a bar tab for close to a thousand dollars?"

Masie almost spilled her wine. She set it on the table and slid up to the edge of her chair, rifling through the pages.

Hensley popped an olive into his mouth. "The bar tab gained your freedom. And Masie's. A mere fraction of the two million you were willing to pay."

Davison stood. "Welcome to the future. I've cancelled the card and contested all the charges."

Masie pushed up from her chair and studied Hensley. "You stole his credit card?"

Hensley shrugged. "Merely an advance against expenses. To be paid out of the estate."

"How can you be so understanding with a stranger like Julien and so clueless about those closest to you?"

The fire that flashed in her eyes made Hensley envy Davison for the first time in his life. This was a woman to contend with, a woman worthy of the effort. "Have you considered that what you call clueless is actually an expectation that those closest to me, as you say, might display a similar level of understanding?"

"That ship sailed long ago," Davison said. "In a jungle in Angola." He held out his hand to Masie.

"Does this mean I don't need to attend the debriefing session?" Hensley called to their retreating forms.

In the blank space left by the lack of response, Hensley settled back into his chair, admired the sunset, and pondered these things in his heart. He had lived a full life and had many things to ponder, and pondering made a man thirsty.

He snatched Masie's untasted pinot noir from the table. Quite good. He finished it off by degrees.

Hensley considered himself to be of middle age, but the math worked out only if you did your calculations according to the lifespans recorded in the early parts of the Bible. If you calibrated your reckonings according to the Psalms or more recent mortality statistics, he had a couple of decades left to trod the boards. And given his recent experiences in Cancún, mortality was at the forefront of his considerations.

When it came right down to it, as it rarely did if Hensley could avoid it, while spreading light and salt among the far-flung masses, he had failed to establish any solid base from which to operate. That had been by design, and two weeks ago, he would have seen no reason to question the wisdom of that strategy. After all, when life was a con, only a sucker doubled down on a single number and kept playing it.

But that was before he had seen Davison's transformation. His own brother, the ultimate square peg versus the round hole of the world, too sensitive as a kid, too insensitive as an adult. Yet, if Davison's assessment of Masie was accurate, somehow this man of extremes, insensate to the nuances of the language of life as she is spoke across the expanse of humanity, had seemingly stumbled upon a connection to the holy grail of relationships. The real thing. The genuine article.

If such a thing was to be found, and if a man had the good fortune to stumble upon it, well, then all bets were off. You held onto the bronc-rigging for all you were worth, praying to go the eight seconds intact.

But in Hensley's experience, such things were not to be found in this world. They were like the mythical sure thing, oft dreamt of by suckers but as plentiful as unicorns on the front lawn grazing on four-leaf clover.

And yet he had seen it with his own eyes, if such things as eyes were to be believed. Well, to be more precise, he had seen Davison's transformation. If what Davison said about Masie was true, then Hensley had completely missed it.

He nodded and took another sip of wine. That was the problem, the grit of cognitive dissonance that had thrown him off balance all night. The subliminal bur in his saddle.

The unlikely possibility that Davison was right.

After all, if it came down to a contest of who had his finger on the throbbing pulse of the human condition, Hensley would stake Davison half the distance to the finish line with the confidence that he'd break the tape before Davison was out of the starting blocks. Which meant that Davison had to be wrong about Masie.

But what if he wasn't? More importantly, why this sudden bout of self-doubt?

Perhaps it was the fatigue of a week on the run. Or maybe the prospect of a comfortable situation for his twilight years suddenly snatched away.

Hensley shot up from the chair, walked to the edge of the deck, and gazed out across Galveston to the gulf. This was ridiculous. He was much too old for a midlife crisis. On the other hand, some might look upon Hensley's life and conclude that it resembled one long midlife crisis. Bouncing from one place to another. Always looking for the next thing.

An image flashed unbidden into his mind—tossing twigs into the fire pit outside the clinic in Angola, a three-year-old Davison dashing around on the fool's errand of rescuing moths from the flames. On the other side of the fire, his parents sitting in camp chairs, her hand seeking out his, finding sanctuary. Their shared expression of . . . something. Contentment? Confidence? Completion?

The expression Davison had directed toward Masie these last few days. The conviction of the true believer.

In Hensley's world, there was a word for the true believer.

Sucker.

When you lived by your wits on the streets, you couldn't afford the luxury of vulnerability. The consequences for misplaced trust were severe. Poverty. Hunger. Death.

Skepticism was the price of freedom. But now Hensley saw that he was as free as a stray cur in an alley scrapping for a bone. Maybe that latter-day poet and philosopher Kristofferson knew a thing or two about freedom when he said it was just another word for nothing left to lose.

Then another image intruded upon his morose ponderings. Chrystal. Santa Fe. The turn of the millennium. Strange that last month when he got the telegram that brought him back to the States, his first thought had been of her.

While Chrystal had her faults—and who didn't, Hensley would like to know—no one could deny that she went the distance to shore up the bruised reed. If the Father was the first to attend to the fallen sparrow, Chrystal was not far behind, lining a shoebox with cotton and laying in birdseed for the duration.

Of all the women in all the gin joints in all the towns in all the world that he had had the pleasure of knowing, and that number was considerable, she stood out from the crowd like the Statue of Liberty calling to the masses.

Bring me your tired, your poor, your huddled Hensleys yearning to breathe free.

The trick was that at the time, he was under the delusion that he was far from huddled and already breathing free. What if the universe had presented Hensley with the perfect match over a decade ago, and he hadn't possessed the wit to see it? Such opportunities didn't parade by in a never-ending queue, ripe for plucking as the mood struck. They came once and were gone.

He'd missed his one chance. Or had he? Was there actually a cosmic one-shot-in-a-lifetime rule? This was no time to retire the field based on nothing more than speculation and assumptions. Hensley had made a career of creating opportunities from slimmer materials than this.

As the world inched into darkness, Hensley settled on a course of action. He would miss out on a few free meals, and Special Agent Harris would have to manage his debriefing without benefit of the perspective of a citizen of the world, but it couldn't be helped.

Hensley would marshal his forces, march upon Chrystal's fortress in Santa Fe, and plant his flag. Perhaps she had moved on, and if so, he would do the same. But not before making his case for reinstatement to favored-nation status.

However, due to the cancelled credit card, he would have to make certain adjustments. The facts of life in twenty-first century America were that cash couldn't get you a rental car, but it could get you a ticket on a plane.

Hensley threaded through the crowd to the bar to see how Julien was getting along.

He climbed up on a stool and signaled for a refill. When the drink was in front of him, he said, "Julien, my main man, what are you doing in eight hours?"

Julien glanced at the bar clock. "Four a.m.?"

"I can see the years have not dimmed your powers of perspication or calculation." Hensley smiled. "If you have a car, I have a proposition that could tend toward your advantage."

After making arrangements over a final drink, Hensley took the elevator down to the lobby for a quick look around. The protection detail was in evidence, bright-eyed and bushy tailed. Hensley approached him with a broad smile and an open hand.

"My good man, I feel compelled to extend my utmost gratitude for your dedication and perseverance. You are a credit to your profession. Allow me to buy you a hearty breakfast on the morrow as a token of my appreciation."

The agent shook his hand with an air of confusion. Having planted the seed of an expectation, Hensley took the elevator up to his floor, located the service elevator, and returned to his room to hone the finer points of his exit strategy.

Chapter Three: Oasis

Because he had left Cancún with a certain sense of urgency, Hensley had no luggage, so when the alarm went off at four a.m., he was out the door within minutes. As he waited for the service elevator to arrive, he paused for a mental apology to the agent holding the fort in the lobby for leading him to believe a breakfast was coming to him gratis. Then he descended into the nether regions of the hotel, located the rear exit, and found Julien waiting in the alley as arranged.

The hundred dollars he had promised Julien in return for a forty-five minute ride to William P. Hobby airport in Houston was a bargain any way you looked at it, whether taxi or puddle jumper from the Galveston airport.

On the drive up, they compared notes on how they found the grand carnival some people called life, and Hensley offered a few tips from his four decades of wandering the mercurial climes of the planet as a sentient being.

In the departures lane at the airport in Houston, Hensley elicited a promise from Julien to reconsider the rudderless approach to life he had employed as of even date. Hensley himself had dealt with this milestone in his late teens, but not everyone had the advantage of the Fletcher family code.

Leave the planet better than you found it.

Hensley's own father, Reggie Fletcher, had tackled that goal on a grand scale, creating a clinic for the natives in Angola from whole cloth, and had paid for it with his life. Hensley chose to implement the philosophy on a more modest level, engaging individuals as he encountered them, like a Johnny Appleseed of the soul.

He liked to think that by now he had a grove, if not a small forest, of acolytes spread across the seven seas and nine continents. He could not hope to live to see the fruition of his efforts, but what man could?

Hensley proceeded into the airport and rustled up an agent to sell him a window seat to his destination, paying the exorbitant fee for the short leg from Albuquerque to Santa Fe to save the trouble of finding a taxi to drive the seventy miles.

As the plane banked westward, Hensley's thoughts veered to the first time he saw Chrystal. Just before the turn of the millennium, as a mere kid of forty, Hensley set out from Portland, Oregon, to hitchhike to Times Square. He wanted to be onsite to party like it was 1999 when the numbers rolled over and the ball dropped.

Just outside of Albuquerque, he ducked into a roadhouse to work out his options for the night over a happy hour pint. He walked straight to the jukebox, dropped in a handful of quarters, and punched random numbers. The first song was "Up on Cripple Creek." He took that as an omen. He parked his backpack in a dark corner where he could keep an eye on it, ambled over to the bar for a bottle of the local pale ale, and gravitated toward the pool tables.

Most of the tables featured either guys or couples playing with varying levels of intensity. At the table in the far corner, two women chatted while knocking the balls around in a haphazard fashion. Hensley approached them obliquely like a Weight Watchers devotee might address a bowl of nanner puddin'. He stopped about half a table away and parked an elbow on the foot-wide bar tacked up along the perimeter of the room.

The blonde, who played the game with the confidence and ineptitude of a former cheerleader, kept shooting sidelong glances at him. The brunette, after a single assessing look, studiously ignored him while lining up her shots, but doing no better than the blonde for all her effort.

Hensley nursed his beer, waiting for the psychological moment. When they had knocked in all the balls, in no particular order, the cheerleader faced him head on while the brunette racked them up for another go.

"You going to just stand there gawking, or you going to come over here and play?"

Hensley nodded slightly, picked up his Santa Fe Pale Ale, and approached the table. "I hesitate to intrude, but perhaps I could buy a round of whatever you lovely young women are having and interest you in a small tournament to determine the reigning champion of the back corner table."

The cheerleader snorted a little pig laugh. She had some meat on the bone, probably no more than ten pounds over her prime cheerleader days. Fifteen at the most, and how many could say that halfway between their ten- and twenty-year reunions? Certainly not Hensley, even if he had a reunion to attend. Which he didn't.

A waitress materialized, and Hensley made a small investment into his immediate future.

While Hensley could be as empathetic as the next guy, there were certain exigencies a guy had to take into consideration when sleeping rough from one end to the other of a continent three thousand miles wide. And as Albuquerque was over a mile high, nights could be chilly whatever the season.

What it came down to was sleeping arrangements. In ascending order of comfort and warmth—his tent, a motel room, or something more domestic. These were the parameters of existence for a boy with a dream, living by his wits for two decades and counting.

He was traveling light. A hiker's backpack and a Jackson in his wallet, and two thousand miles to go. Depending on how the game went, the worst-case scenario was an empty wallet and a night in the tent and who knew what would happen tomorrow morning. But no need to think of that now. Sufficient unto the day and all that. Right now there was a pool tournament to consider.

The first bracket featured Hensley versus the cheerleader.

"I defer to you for the break," he said.

She took the shot and missed entirely, the ball bouncing around the bumpers like a geometry problem. "Oops."

"Give it another try," he said.

"Why don't you do it?"

He did. He hit the side to avoid sinking a ball on the break, but the brunette had packed them tight and he sunk a solid and a stripe. He played another ball, aiming wide, and deferred to the cheerleader.

He tried to let her win. He really did. But he knocked in more balls on accident than she did on purpose.

So now it was down to the brunette. The worst thing he could do was to win again. Better to lose and then ask for the best out of three. That would give him more time to triangulate on the best strategy for the endgame.

He turned to the brunette.

She was racking up for the next game. "You want to put some money on it?"

It was the first time she had looked at him since his first reconnaissance. He looked back. She had the lean aspect of a woman who could go the distance. Razor-cut hair in the style of Joan Jett, boot-cut jeans, Tom Waits Rain Dogs t-shirt. This was no cheerleader. No woman who would be hanging with a cheerleader.

But here she was. And so was he. Life led you to places you could never predict, and Hensley had long since quit trying to figure it. He had learned that there was no percentage in questioning fate. Life dealt you a hand at any given moment, and you either played it or folded.

"What did you have in mind?"

"Ten dollars on the game," she said.

"Done." It was half his stake, not counting the drinks, but he was playing the long game. He could lose the game but double down on the rematch and sleep warm tonight. He hit the break head on, and the balls meandered about the table. A loose pack. She had sandbagged him. Or had she?

She took the next shot and scratched.

Hensley studied her hard. Half his cash and the rest of the night depended on what happened next. He set up a combination shot that would get close enough to sinking a ball to convince even the most suspicious player of his good intentions.

She sunk a solid and missed the next. She was ahead.

He tried to keep it that way, but no matter how he finessed his misses, she missed more. To be fair, she was playing at the same level as before he had engaged them. But he couldn't shake the thought that he was being played.

Despite his best efforts, he won the game. And then she said those fateful words.

"Best of three?"

He looked her in the eye and she looked back. And in that moment, he knew it was on.

"My dear lady, nothing would give me more pleasure."

This time he racked them up. Nice and tight. "Loser breaks."

She sunk three on the break. He played his best game, but he couldn't keep up with her. They were now one and one. The next game determined the winner.

She racked it and nailed him with a gleam in her eye. "Loser breaks."

Hensley had watched her closely and saw the loose pack. He had no chance on the break. It would be all mush and mashed potatoes. He gauged her but could get no solid reading. Should he go for the win or the sympathy play? He decided on the latter and scratched on the break.

Then she missed an easy shot in a corner pocket and avoided his narrowed eyes, chalking her cue. It looked like if he was going to lose, he was going to have to work for it.

It was a hard fought race to the bottom, each outdoing the other in missing shots.

Then the waitress showed up, and it became a question of who was buying the next round. Hensley had already forfeited half of the twenty for the first round. The ten in his pocket was on the game in progress, but it would never do to let this particular fact be known. He bought the round and changed his strategy. A win would give him enough for a night in a bed, which was more than he had experienced in the last month.

But as soon as he sank the first ball in his sights, a solid, with next to no effort, the game was on. The brunette set out to run the table. Even the cheerleader was reduced to silence in this battle of Titans.

Hensley was behind by one when she missed on the last ball before the eight, giving him a final chance to win it.

He had two balls left. He slammed one into a corner pocket and then intentionally fluffed the last one. Anyone within a half-mile could have seen that he could have made the shot. But he had a sudden hunch, and through the years, he had learned to pay attention to instinct.

The brunette raised an eyebrow, tapped in the last stripe, and then turned to the eight ball. It was a straight shot to a side pocket, but she walked to the other side of the table and made a double bank shot that sunk the eight, but also scratched.

"Dang," she said, laid her cue on the table, and pulled a wrinkled ten from her pocket. It hung limp in her fingers as she held it out toward him. When he reached for it, she said, "Winner buys."

The last round left him busted. Once the drinks were delivered, the cheerleader evaporated, and Hensley was left alone with the brunette.

She held up her bottle. "Congratulations."

Hensley returned her salute, not sure if she had intentionally handed him the Pyrrhic victory. On the one hand, she had at least saved him from the ignominy of revealing that he had no cash to cover the bet, but as he admired her impish smile, he got the impression it was more of a mocking grin, that she had guessed he was busted.

"As victor, I request a boon."

"The cash wasn't enough?"

"More than sufficient insofar as it served its purpose but sadly lacking in the most important element."

She cocked her head and waited.

"Something I long to have that you alone possess, and in the giving will make me immeasurably richer without diminishing you in the slightest."

A suspicious frown creased her forehead as the smile melted.

"It is the gift of learning your name."

A nervous laugh of relief escaped. "Chrystal."

"And I am Hensley." He bowed and then stepped aside to make way for a pack of cowboys with pool cues. Hensley stepped to a nearby table and pushed a bunch of empties to one side. "Shall we?"

Chrystal sat down. "You're not from around here, are you?"

Hensley sat and leaned forward. "Judging by your accent, neither are you."

"I think ten years qualifies me as a local."

"That should qualify you as a founding father, or mother, as the case may be."

"And what kind of father, or mother, are you?"

"The best kind." He smiled. "I am a citizen of the world, a denizen *du monde*, riding the tides of time and fortune."

"Riding the road on your thumb and by the seat of your pants, you mean." She took a sip of her Bud Light.

Hensley responded with a sip of his pale ale to buy time. He'd expected an habitué of a desert roadhouse to be a little more pliable and responsive to his charms, but she anticipated his every move, seeming to know what he would do before he did. He followed her glance to his pack and realized she'd had him pegged as soon as he walked in the door.

Chrystal set her beer on the table. "When was the last time you had a home-cooked meal?"

The question took him by surprise, and he became lost in the calculation. "I assume you mean cooked in an actual home."

"Or slept on clean sheets? Had a long shower with steaming hot water?"

The thought of all three luxuries at once overwhelmed Hensley. When he regained the power of speech, he blurted out, "Tempt not the gods with such excess, my lady! We are but mortals."

"Okay, here is the thing. I got two kids at home with the sitter, asleep. You will not wake them up. You will sleep on the couch. In case you get any ideas to the contrary, I sleep with a gun, and I could shoot the eye out of a lizard at thirty yards before I could write." Chrystal finished off her Bud Light and shoved the bottle next to the pre-existing empties. "But if you behave yourself, you can get all three—the meal, the clean sheets, the shower—before you go wherever it is that citizens of the world go."

This proposition was not one of any of the possible scenarios Hensley had played out in his mind. In fact, it was unique in his experience, and he was both delighted and disturbed. But he was in no position to engage in undue inspection of the oral cavity of any extant equines.

"Say no more. I am but your humble servant."

He had stayed the night, got the shower, the clean sheets, the meal. And then he had stayed for another two years.

Chapter Four: Mirage

After a short jaunt in Albuquerque to catch his connecting flight, Hensley landed in Santa Fe in a slight drizzle. Not the weather he was expecting, but the cool air was welcome as he stepped out of the airport.

He snagged a taxi to the Goodwill store on Cerrillos Road and had it wait while he bought a few changes of clothes, some other necessities, and a duffel bag. He scanned his change. A state quarter lurked among the nondescript coinage. Oklahoma. You didn't see those every day. He dropped it in his shirt pocket and shoved the rest in his pants pocket. Then he directed the driver to Chrystal's house on the northwest side of town.

The place looked much as it had twelve years ago, gravel drive that curved through southwest vegetation to the stucco house under the somber stare of the Sangre de Cristo mountains, but without the bikes and toys that had always seemed to be in the yard at the turn of the millennium.

Hensley paid the taxi and rang the doorbell. After a few more attempts, he gave the neighborhood a quick scan. Nothing on the street but a pest control van. He slipped through the wooden gate into the backyard and under the pecan tree to get out of the drizzle.

He found the key to the French doors right where he put it when he left over a decade ago, at the bottom of a planter of salvia hanging from the redwood pergola.

After knocking once more for good measure, Hensley unlocked the door, dropped the key in his pocket, and closed the door behind him. He set the duffel bag on the kitchen island and walked through the house.

A cat brushed against his ankles and threaded between his legs. He scratched it behind the ears. "Home alone, are you? Hello? Chrystal?" It was close to noon on a Thursday. Chrystal was probably at work.

Hensley tried to remember the kids' names. The boy was in junior high when he left, so he was in his twenties by now. Something connected with Dickens. Sidney? Oliver? No, Fagin. That was it. "Fagin? You home?" And the girl . . . something with a C. Or was it an S? Something of the sort. She was probably finished with school too. Possibly on her own.

In the living room, he found a sixty-gallon tank of tropical fish in one corner and a cage of finches in another, potted plants transforming the room into a tropical maze. The cat followed him in an uncharacteristic spirit of camaraderie and exploration, offering feline advice.

The master bedroom, on the end of the house by the driveway, was unoccupied. A cursory inspection of the closet revealed only women's clothes. So she was still single. As he passed the chest of drawers, he caught sight of a photo of himself, Chrystal, and the two kids. He picked it up, and the memory soon followed. A day filled with drama as any excursion involving tadpoles was likely to be. A hike up Picacho Peak with the girl on his back. Santa Fe stretched out behind them in the distance.

Hensley smiled and returned the picture to its place. It was a good omen for a warm welcome.

The two bedrooms on the other side of the house were messy but also unpopulated at the moment. Other than various flora and fauna, nobody was home.

Hensley's stomach reminded him it was coming on lunchtime, especially one time zone over from Texas. En route to the kitchen, he spied a pile of mail under the slot in the front door. He scooped it up and dropped it on the table on his way to the fridge. He'd lost the cat somewhere on the trail, but the species was known for its independence, so he gave it no further thought.

The Reluctant Saint

After trolling through various frozen and leftover options, he decided on a sandwich. While the bread toasted, he amassed slices of ham, roast beef, and chicken breast, supplemented with chipotle jack cheese, spicy mustard, and baby spinach. He sprinkled on a little balsamic vinaigrette and a dash of fresh ground black pepper, poured some sea salt chips in a bowl, and grabbed a Red Stripe from the fridge.

As he dined, he perused the envelopes he had gathered from the front hall. Mostly junk mail, a few bills, all addressed to Robin Bumstead, the name her parents gave her.

One of the envelopes was from a mobile service provider. As an old-school bohemian citizen of the world, Hensley had thus far avoided encumbering himself with a digital leash of any kind, but Chrystal was an American citizen with two kids. She could no more avoid a mobile phone than a social security number.

While the contents of the envelope would divulge to him a method of contacting her directly, patience would no doubt produce the woman in question in the flesh within a few hours without the inevitable drama that would ensue if he began reading her mail.

As he dropped it to the table, he heard the slide and click of a key in a deadbolt echo from the front hall. The sandwich dropped from his fingers and splayed out on the plate like a poker hand.

The hour had come. Hensley stepped to the kitchen island and prepared to confront Fagin, or the girl with the name starting with a C or an S, or the woman herself.

A teenaged girl walked into the kitchen, absorbed in rapid thumb play on a smartphone. She dropped her purse on the island, and then noticed the duffel bag. She froze, and her eyes drifted up to Hensley. She screamed and backed against the stove.

"Please, don't hurt me."

Hensley considered placing a comforting hand on her shoulder, but realized that for him to approach her would be far from comforting. After all, when Hensley left, Chrystal's daughter was only two or three years old. There was no way for her to connect that guy back then with the random stranger in her kitchen, a thick, scruffy guy with a healthy goatee, still dressed in Johnny-Cash black, because he had not yet taken time to shower and change into his Santa Fe clothes.

He wished he could remember her name, or had taken the time to scan her room for a clue, but that couldn't be helped now. "No need for concern, dovey. You don't remember me, but I am an old friend of your mother."

If Hensley thought this would calm her, he was severely mistaken. "How do you know my mother?" she squeaked.

"I used to dandle you on my knee in this very room when you could barely walk."

Her eyes grew as big as a super moon. "You did what?"

"You might remember me as Uncle Hensley. I arrived in this house not long after you were born and left just after your second birthday. Cake and candles at this very table." He slapped the table, then bowed his head in deferential regret. "Unfortunately world events prevented me from returning as I had promised. But I have returned at long last."

"Uncle Hensley? I don't have an Uncle Hensley."

"Of course not. Not an uncle of the family tree, but an uncle in spirit nonetheless." He brushed the crumbs from his shirt. "What time does your mother get home?"

"My mother is at home."

Hensley frowned. "In what sense is she at home?"

"She's been at home all day. I just came over to feed the animals."

The puzzle pieces rearranged themselves. He had unforgivably misread the situation. "Ah, dear creature. Please accept my deepest apologies for startling you. I was laboring under a misapprehension. And what might be your name?"

"Uh . . . Toni."

"And you are friends with . . ."

"Saff."

Yes, Sapphire. Started with an S, just like he thought. And a quite apt name, as he remembered commenting when they first met. "But why are you feeding the animals?"

"Ms. Bumstead has gone to visit Fagin."

"He doesn't live at home then?"

"Well, duh. He's twenty-five and a hotshot lawyer in the capital."

"We are in the capital, my dear."

"In DC."

"I'm not surprised. He used to torment me with syllogisms even in grammar school. I understand that his father was a pillar of rectitude and a credit to his race, God rest his soul. Do you know when they'll be back?"

Toni frowned. "They?"

"Chrystal and Sapphire."

"Oh, right. She didn't say."

"Well, then this is exceedingly bad timing for me. I was just passing through and thought I might look in and see how they are getting on."

Toni eyed him as she might an oyster with a pedigree that lacked a month with an R. "How did you get in?"

Hensley turned to reassemble his sandwich. "The door was unlocked." No need to alarm the skittish creature with the knowledge of a secret key.

"I locked it when I left yesterday."

"The back door."

Toni released a doubtful huff but proceeded to open a cabinet door and extract a can of cat food, all without turning her back on him. At the whir of the can opener, the feline materialized and became Toni's new best friend.

Toni gave Hensley a wide berth as she walked to the bowl by the French doors and scooped out the cat food in a most inefficient manner in Hensley's view, using a spoon instead of a butter knife. But experience was the best teacher for the young, who would have no other, so he refrained from casting his pearls in her direction. He had, after all, done his good deed for the week with Julien, who seemed more likely to profit from it.

Hensley finished his lunch while flipping through the mail as Toni distributed birdseed and fish food and closed the front door with what seemed to him unnecessary force. He waited until he heard the snick of the deadbolt and then watched from the living room window as she walked to her car parked at the curb, chatting on the phone all the while like the youngsters were wont to do these days.

If he wanted to connect with Chrystal, he would have to do so in the nation's capital, but that required an address for Fagin.

At the desk in a nook between the kitchen and living room, Hensley searched for an address book but quickly abandoned the project after digging through a few decades of memorabilia, minutiae, and detritus, the only item of interest being a new credit card that still had the activation sticker on it.

He powered up the computer, which thankfully offered no speed bumps in the way of passwords, and searched the web for Fagin Bumstead. It took him a quarter hour to remember that he bore the surname of Chrystal's first husband, Duff, another five minutes to discover that she had spelled it Fagan, and yet another fifteen minutes to find a site that didn't require payment by credit card to divulge that he had an apartment in Georgetown.

Then he searched for flights to Dulles or Reagan National. It turned out that he had already missed any flight that didn't require an overnight layover in DFW, so he recalibrated his timeline. Since the pets were fed and the residents were in DC, as long as he kept a low profile, he could spend the night here and catch an early flight tomorrow.

But it occurred to him that Chrystal's mobile number would come in handy, so he returned to the kitchen and opened the phone bill. Two numbers were listed, probably the first for Chrystal and the other for Sapphire. By now Fagan would be paying his own bills in DC.

He added them to the scrap of paper with Fagan's address and stuffed it in his wallet. He was digging through the freezer for something to thaw for dinner when the doorbell rang.

Hensley froze like a rat when the light is turned on. On the second ring, he dashed to the front bedroom and peered out the window that overlooked the front door.

A tall, muscled guy in a cowboy hat and a well-used cheap suit stood on the porch. He tried the door, but it was locked, thanks to Toni, unexpectedly wise beyond her years. Hensley vowed to put her in his will if he ever had anything worth bequeathing.

After a final shot at the doorbell, the man walked back down the sidewalk toward the street.

Hensley decided this was a good time to find other accommodations for the evening. He grabbed his duffel from the kitchen island, stepped out the back door, and locked it behind him. As he crossed the pergola, the man in the suit rounded the corner, spotted Hensley, and drew a gun from a shoulder holster.

Chapter Five: Apprehension

"Hold it right there," the man said.

Hensley froze. While he was as sanguine as the next guy, and maybe more so, he had great respect for the power of a .38 slug to settle an argument. Permanently.

"Drop the duffel, kick it away, keep your hands where I can see them."

"Is there a problem?"

"Damn straight there's a problem. I don't know you. Turn around. Hands on the door."

Hensley complied. "Forgive me for asking, sir, and I'm sure it's my loss, but how is that a problem?"

"Because I know the people who live here, and you aren't one of them. Plus, you match the description of an intruder that was called in half an hour ago."

Called in. The man must be some brand of law enforcement. He approached, placed a foot against the insole of Hensley's left foot, and began patting him down, confirming Hensley's assessment.

"I'm an old family friend visiting from France."

"How did you get in?"

"Toni let me in."

"That's funny, because she said you were already inside when she got here." The officer slapped a cuff on Hensley's right wrist and pulled it behind him.

Hensley craned his neck around. "It's understandable that you may not know me, Officer. I'm Hensley Fletcher. I used to live here."

The officer grabbed his left hand and pulled it down to his back, cinching it up with the other cuff. "I know who you are." He spun Hensley around. "You're that vagrant that shacked up here in the nineties."

Hensley caught his balance and regarded him coolly. It wasn't the first time he'd been cuffed, and in countries that made him much more nervous than the US. "You say you know me, but I don't know you."

"You didn't have cause to back then, but now you do."

Hensley searched his memory for the face in front of him, but he'd visited every continent in the past decade and met a lot of people. He thought he might be forgiven for forgetting a detective in Santa Fe. "You can look inside if you want to verify I didn't take anything. Other than the makings of a sandwich, for which I will gladly pay at the going rate."

The officer focused a smoldering stare on him for a long time. Long enough, and with sufficient hostility, that Hensley began to revise his earlier assessment of personal peril. The man obviously had some baggage. After all, there was a lot of desert out there, and a person who wouldn't be missed could go undiscovered for years. Decades. Centuries.

And to his dismay, Hensley realized that he was just that sort of person. If this cowboy were to put a slug in his skull, Hensley couldn't name a soul on the planet who would come looking for him.

To Hensley's immense relief, instead of shooting him in the head, the officer grabbed his arm, spun him around, and removed the cuffs.

"Chrystal gets off work at 4:30. You better not be here when she gets back. Or ever."

Hensley stopped himself from blurting out that Chrystal and Sapphire were in DC. Even though the cuffs had been on only a minute or so, he rubbed his wrists. "Current circumstances notwithstanding, I would say that's her choice."

"Oh, believe me, she wants to see you even less than I do." The officer shoved the cuffs back into his belt. "Either way, you're leaving now."

Hensley teased a memory from his ancient past. "Ah. I remember now. You're Deputy Powers."

"Sheriff Powell."

"Congratulations on your success. I'm sure your mother is very proud." Hensley picked up his bag. "Now, if you could recommend a decent coffee shop, I have some work to do."

Powell gave him a final contemptuous glance. "You seem like a clever guy. You can figure that out." He turned to leave but stopped at the edge of the pergola. "How did you get here?"

"Taxi. So it seems we have two options. No, three. You can radio for a cab. Or I can go back inside to call. Either way I'll have to wait around here for a while before it shows up. Or you can give me a ride."

Powell eyed Hensley and stepped past him to check the door. "Come on. The sooner you leave, the better."

They walked around the house. Hensley called shotgun. Powell didn't smile.

Powell pulled away from the curb past the pest control van in silence. The drive out of the neighborhood wasn't a picnic any way you sliced it. It was rare for Hensley to be at a loss for a conversational gambit, not that Powell had offered an opening.

If memory served, Powell had set his cap for Chrystal back in '96 when she became a widow, way before the moment Hensley rolled into town in '99, hitchhiking the US, west coast to east. Not that a cowboy like Powell ever had a chance with a nuanced chick like Chrystal. Hensley was just passing through until he met her and realized she was worth sticking around for.

She had a newborn on her hands at the time, Sapphire, and a ten-year-old, Fagan, and a new job as a court reporter, set up by some judge who had served in 'Nam with her father. Bonds forged in the military were hard to break, especially if they were tempered in combat, and the judge had taken her under his wing when her husband died in the Gulf War. The first one. Both the husband and the war.

Hensley's only regret was that he had never met Duffy, her first husband. Although if Duff had been in the picture in '99, Hensley would have been out and wouldn't be here now, wouldn't have been graced with the opportunity to get to know Chrystal to the degree that had transpired.

Sometimes life was an either/or thing, although it went against Hensley's philosophy to admit it. But that was not the point. The point was that Powell was still carrying the torch for Chrystal, so conversation with him was pointless, and Hensley only engaged in pointless pastimes when they were sufficiently amusing.

The only other reason to draw Powell into conversation was to extract information, but it appeared that Hensley already knew more than Powell about Chrystal's recent movements. So he kept his peace and spent the ride into town pondering where he might spend the night.

He could catch the 5:20 flight out of SAF and sleep in the terminal at DFW, or get a motel room and make the early flight for a quick trip. Since, like Masie, he hadn't spent a full night's sleep in a decent bed for close to a week, he was leaning toward the motel option, even if the establishment had a number in its name, when Powell swerved his Crown Victoria into the parking lot of a coffee shop and skidded to a stop.

"This is where you get off," Powell said. "Next stop, anywhere but here. And don't bother coming back."

Hensley grabbed his duffel and shoved the door open. "It has been a singular pleasure catching up with you, Sheriff Powers. I look forward to another opportunity in the near future."

"Powell," Powell said.

"Oh, yes. My mistake."

"And I'll see you in hell before I see you in Santa Fe, if I have anything to do with it."

Hensley scooted out of the car. "Well, my good sir, if we don't have the happy occasion of the latter, I have no doubt we shall have the opportunity of the former eventually."

He slammed the door. Powell shot out of the parking lot, barely missing the rear quarter panel of a passing Cadillac that honked as it sped past. Lucky he was in an unmarked car, because he might have T-boned a major donor to his reelection campaign.

As Hensley turned to the coffee shop, he heard the sound of wheels on gravel. He jumped to the side and turned to evade what he thought was the return of the sheriff when a white van with a pest control logo skidded to a stop in front of him.

The Reluctant Saint

A guy burst out of the shotgun door, slammed the sliding passenger door open, punched Hensley in the gut, grabbed the front of his shirt, and threw him into the van. Then the guy leapt in, directing a well-placed knee into the small of Hensley's back, and jerked the door shut. The van rocketed away from the coffee shop.

Acknowledgements

This book had a long and tortured journey from the moment of conception while brainstorming with Andy, through roughly fifteen drafts as a screenplay and fifteen drafts as a novel, to the final draft. At least five times I threw out what I had, as much as 80,000 words in some cases, and started over with a blank page. So much so that every critique group I worked with began to call it Endless Rewrites. It took longer to write this book than all four of my previous novels combined. If only it was four times as good. As if that wasn't enough, I'm hoping to release a screwball comedy version based on the same premise titled Strange Vacation. Check a website near you or sign up for the newsletter to get notified about new releases.

Thanks to Andy Combs for a year or more of brainstorming; Agnes for Irish expertise that unfortunately became irrelevant when I moved Masie from Belfast to Detroit; Tosh McIntosh for aviation expertise; Lanny Hall for law enforcement expertise; critique groups Austin Writers Workshop, NIP, and El Gee for invaluable feedback on matters great and small; first readers Mark Spyrison, Daniel Whittington, Paul Mooney, Jeremy Grigg, Sarah Combs, and Milly Whittington for refining the polish; Rebecca Leach for an eagle eye and a deft touch; Amanda Cobb for translating my incoherent ramblings into an excellent cover design.

Also, contrary to the instincts of every editor and advance reader, the term Texian on page 52 is not a typo. That is what Texans were called at the time of the battle of the Alamo.

— BRAD WHITTINGTON —

Sign up for the newsletter to get other sneak peeks and freebies.

BradWhittington.com

About the Author

Brad Whittington was born in Fort Worth, Texas, on James Taylor's eighth birthday and Jack Kerouac's thirty-fourth birthday and is old enough to know better. He lives in Austin, Texas with The Woman. Previously he has been known to inhabit Hawaii, Ohio, South Carolina, Arizona, and Colorado, annoying people as a janitor, math teacher, field hand, computer programmer, brickyard worker, editor, resident Gentile in a Conservative synagogue, IT director, weed-cutter, and in a number of influential positions in other less notable professions. He is greatly loved and admired by all right-thinking citizens and enjoys a complete absence of cats and dogs at home.

BradWhittington.com

www.ingramcontent.com/pod-product-compliance
Lightning Source LLC
Chambersburg PA
CBHW031506210626
46816CB00019B/1556